PRAISE FOR

New York Times Bestseller

Favorite Book Of The Year,
Goodreads Choice Awards

Amazon.Com Best Books Of The Year

Publishers Weekly Best Books Of The Year

"DIVERGENT is a captivating, fascinating book
that kept me in constant suspense and was never
short on surprises. It will be a long time before I quit
thinking about this haunting vision of the future."

—James Dashner,
New York Times Bestselling Author
of *The Maze Runner*

"A taut and shiveringly exciting read! Tris is exactly
the sort of unflinching and fierce heroine I love.
I couldn't turn the pages fast enough."

—Melissa Marr,
New York Times Bestselling Author
of *Wicked Lovely*

Also by Veronica Roth

DIVERGENT

Xmas 2014
Love Dad,

INSURGENT

VERONICA ROTH

HarperCollins *Children's Books*

First published in hardback in the USA by HarperCollins Publishers, Inc. in 2012
First published in paperback in Great Britain by HarperCollins *Children's Books* in 2012
HarperCollins Children's Books is a division of HarperCollins*Publishers* Ltd,
77-85 Fulham Palace Road, Hammersmith, London, W6 8JB.

www.harpercollins.co.uk

31

Insurgent

ISBN: 978-0-00-744292-8

Printed and bound in Australia by Griffin Press
Typography by Joel Tippie

To Nelson,
who was worth every risk

Like a wild animal, the truth is too powerful to remain caged.
—From the Candor faction manifesto

CHAPTER ONE

I WAKE WITH his name in my mouth.

Will.

Before I open my eyes, I watch him crumple to the pavement again. Dead.

My doing.

Tobias crouches in front of me, his hand on my left shoulder. The train car bumps over the rails, and Marcus, Peter, and Caleb stand by the doorway. I take a deep breath and hold it in an attempt to relieve some of the pressure that is building in my chest.

An hour ago, nothing that happened felt real to me. Now it does.

I breathe out, and the pressure is still there.

"Tris, come on," Tobias says, his eyes searching mine.

"We have to jump."

It is too dark to see where we are, but if we are getting off, we are probably close to the fence. Tobias helps me to my feet and guides me toward the doorway.

The others jump off one by one: Peter first, then Marcus, then Caleb. I take Tobias's hand. The wind picks up as we stand at the edge of the car opening, like a hand pushing me back, toward safety.

But we launch ourselves into darkness and land hard on the ground. The impact hurts the bullet wound in my shoulder. I bite my lip to keep from crying out, and search for my brother.

"Okay?" I say when I see him sitting in the grass a few feet away, rubbing his knee.

He nods. I hear him sniff like he's fending off tears, and I have to turn away.

We landed in the grass near the fence, several yards away from the worn path that the Amity trucks travel to deliver food to the city, and the gate that lets them out—the gate that is currently shut, locking us in. The fence towers over us, too high and flexible to climb over, too sturdy to knock down.

"There are supposed to be Dauntless guards here," says Marcus. "Where are they?"

"They were probably under the simulation," Tobias

says, "and are now . . ." He pauses. "Who knows where, doing who knows what."

We stopped the simulation—the weight of the hard drive in my back pocket reminds me—but we didn't pause to see the aftermath. What happened to our friends, our peers, our leaders, our factions? There is no way to know.

Tobias approaches a small metal box on the right side of the gate and opens it, revealing a keypad.

"Let's hope the Erudite didn't think to change this combination," he says as he types in a series of numbers. He stops at the eighth one, and the gate clicks open.

"How did you know that?" says Caleb. His voice sounds thick with emotion, so thick I am surprised it does not choke him on the way out.

"I worked in the Dauntless control room, monitoring the security system. We only change the codes twice a year," Tobias says.

"How lucky," says Caleb. He gives Tobias a wary look.

"Luck has nothing to do with it," Tobias says. "I only worked there because I wanted to make sure I could get out."

I shiver. The way he talks about getting out—it's like he thinks we're trapped. I never thought about it that way before, and now that seems foolish.

We walk in a small pack, Peter cradling his bloody

arm to his chest—the arm that I shot—and Marcus with his hand on Peter's shoulder, keeping him stable. Caleb wipes his cheeks every few seconds, and I know he's crying but I don't know how to comfort him, or why I am not crying myself.

Instead I take the lead, Tobias silent at my side, and though he does not touch me, he steadies me.

+ + +

Pinpricks of light are the first sign that we are nearing Amity headquarters. Then squares of light that turn into glowing windows. A cluster of wooden and glass buildings.

Before we can reach them, we have to walk through an orchard. My feet sink into the ground, and above me, the branches grow into one another, forming a kind of tunnel. Dark fruit hangs among the leaves, ready to drop. The sharp, sweet smell of rotting apples mixes with the scent of wet earth in my nose.

When we get close, Marcus leaves Peter's side and walks in front. "I know where to go," he says.

He leads us past the first building to the second one on the left. All the buildings except the greenhouses are made of the same dark wood, unpainted, rough. I hear laughter through an open window. The contrast between the laughter and the stone stillness within me is jarring.

Marcus opens one of the doors. I would be shocked by the lack of security if we were not at Amity headquarters. They often straddle the line between trust and stupidity.

In this building the only sound is of our squeaking shoes. I don't hear Caleb crying anymore, but then, he was quiet about it before.

Marcus stops before an open room, where Johanna Reyes, representative of Amity, sits, staring out the window. I recognize her because it is hard to forget Johanna's face, whether you've seen her once or a thousand times. A scar stretches in a thick line from just above her right eyebrow to her lip, rendering her blind in one eye and giving her a lisp when she talks. I have only heard her speak once, but I remember. She would have been a beautiful woman if not for that scar.

"Oh, thank God," she says when she sees Marcus. She walks toward him with her arms open. Instead of embracing him, she just touches his shoulders, like she remembers the Abnegation's distaste for casual physical contact.

"The other members of your party got here a few hours ago, but they weren't sure if you had made it," she says. She is referring to the group of Abnegation who were with my father and Marcus in the safe house. I didn't even think to worry about them.

She looks over Marcus's shoulder, first at Tobias and Caleb, then at me, then at Peter.

"Oh my," she says, her eyes lingering on the blood soaking Peter's shirt. "I'll send for a doctor. I can grant you all permission to stay the night, but tomorrow, our community must decide together. And"—she eyes Tobias and me—"they will likely not be enthusiastic about a Dauntless presence in our compound. I of course ask you to turn over any weapons you might have."

I wonder, suddenly, how she knows that I am Dauntless. I am still wearing a gray shirt. My father's shirt.

At that moment, his smell, which is an even mixture of soap and sweat, wafts upward, and it fills my nose, fills my entire head with him. I clench my hands so hard into fists that my fingernails cut into my skin. *Not here. Not here.*

Tobias hands over his gun, but when I reach behind me to take out my own concealed weapon, he grabs my hand, guiding it away from my back. Then he laces his fingers with mine to cover up what he just did.

I know it's smart to keep one of our guns. But it would have been a relief to hand it over.

"My name is Johanna Reyes," she says, extending her

hand to me, and then Tobias. A Dauntless greeting. I am impressed by her awareness of the customs of other factions. I always forget how considerate the Amity are until I see it for myself.

"This is T—" Marcus starts, but Tobias interrupts him.

"My name is Four," he says. "This is Tris, Caleb, and Peter."

A few days ago, "Tobias" was a name only I knew, among the Dauntless; it was the piece of himself that he gave me. Outside Dauntless headquarters, I remember why he hid that name from the world. It binds him to Marcus.

"Welcome to the Amity compound." Johanna's eyes fix on my face, and she smiles crookedly. "Let us take care of you."

+ + +

We do let them. An Amity nurse gives me a salve—developed by Erudite to speed healing—to put on my shoulder, and then escorts Peter to the hospital ward to mend his arm. Johanna takes us to the cafeteria, where we find some of the Abnegation who were in the safe house with Caleb and my father. Susan is there, and some of our old neighbors, and rows of wooden tables as long as the room itself. They greet us—especially Marcus—with held-in tears and suppressed smiles.

I cling to Tobias's arm. I sag under the weight of the members of my parents' faction, their lives, their tears.

One of the Abnegation puts a cup of steaming liquid under my nose and says, "Drink this. It will help you sleep as it helped some of the others sleep. No dreams."

The liquid is pink-red, like strawberries. I grab the cup and drink it fast. For a few seconds the heat from the liquid makes me feel like I am full of something again. And as I drain the last drops from the cup, I feel myself relaxing. Someone leads me down the hallway, to a room with a bed in it. That is all.

CHAPTER
TWO

I OPEN MY eyes, terrified, my hands clutching at the sheets. But I am not running through the streets of the city or the corridors of Dauntless headquarters. I am in a bed in Amity headquarters, and the smell of sawdust is in the air.

I shift, and wince as something digs into my back. I reach behind me, and my fingers wrap around the gun.

For a moment I see Will standing before me, both our guns between us—*his hand, I could have shot his hand, why didn't I, why?*—and I almost scream his name.

Then he's gone.

I get out of bed and lift the mattress with one hand, propping it up on my knee. Then I shove the gun beneath it and let the mattress bury it. Once it is out of sight and no longer pressed to my skin, my head feels clearer.

Now that the adrenaline rush of yesterday is gone, and whatever made me sleep has worn off, the deep ache and shooting pains of my shoulder are intense. I am wearing the same clothes I wore last night. The corner of the hard drive peeks out from under my pillow, where I shoved it right before I fell asleep. On it is the simulation data that controlled the Dauntless, and the record of what the Erudite did. It feels too important for me to even touch, but I can't leave it here, so I grab it and wedge it between the dresser and the wall. Part of me thinks it would be a good idea to destroy it, but I know it contains the only record of my parents' deaths, so I'll settle for keeping it hidden.

Someone knocks on my door. I sit on the edge of the bed and try to smooth my hair down.

"Come in," I say.

The door opens, and Tobias steps halfway in, the door dividing his body in half. He wears the same jeans as yesterday, but a dark red T-shirt instead of his black one, probably borrowed from one of the Amity. It's a strange color on him, too bright, but when he leans his head back against the doorframe, I see that it makes the blue in his eyes lighter.

"The Amity are meeting in a half hour." He quirks his eyebrows and adds, with a touch of melodrama, *"To decide our fate."*

I shake my head. "Never thought my fate would be in the hands of a bunch of Amity."

"Me either. Oh, I brought you something." He unscrews the cap of a small bottle and holds out a dropper filled with clear liquid. "Pain medicine. Take a dropperful every six hours."

"Thanks." I squeeze the dropper into the back of my throat. The medicine tastes like old lemon.

He hooks a thumb in one of his belt loops and says, "How are you, Beatrice?"

"Did you just call me *Beatrice*?"

"Thought I would give it a try." He smiles. "Not good?"

"Maybe on special occasions only. Initiation days, Choosing Days . . ." I pause. I was about to rattle off a few more holidays, but only the Abnegation celebrate them. The Dauntless have holidays of their own, I assume, but I don't know what they are. And anyway, the idea that we would celebrate anything right now is so ludicrous I don't continue.

"It's a deal." His smile fades. "How are you, Tris?"

It's not a strange question, after what we've been through, but I tense up when he asks it, worried that he'll somehow see into my mind. I haven't told him about Will yet. I want to, but I don't know how. Just the thought of saying the words out loud makes me feel so heavy I could break through the floorboards.

"I'm . . ." I shake my head a few times. "I don't know, Four. I'm awake. I . . ." I am still shaking my head. He slides his hand over my cheek, one finger anchored behind my ear. Then he tilts his head down and kisses me, sending a warm ache through my body. I wrap my hands around his arm, holding him there as long as I can. When he touches me, the hollowed-out feeling in my chest and stomach is not as noticeable.

I don't have to tell him. I can just try to forget—he can help me forget.

"I know," he says. "Sorry. I shouldn't have asked."

For a moment all I can think is, *How could you* possibly *know?* But something about his expression reminds me that he does know something about loss. He lost his mother when he was young. I don't remember how she died, just that we attended her funeral.

Suddenly I remember him clutching the curtains in his living room, about nine years old, wearing gray, his dark eyes shut. The image is fleeting, and it could be my imagination, not a memory.

He releases me. "I'll let you get ready."

+++

The women's bathroom is two doors down. The floor is dark brown tile, and each shower stall has wooden walls and a plastic curtain separating it from the central aisle. A sign on the back wall says REMEMBER: TO CONSERVE RESOURCES, SHOWERS RUN FOR ONLY FIVE MINUTES.

The stream of water is cold, so I wouldn't want the extra minutes even if I could have them. I wash quickly with my left hand, leaving my right hand hanging at my side. The pain medicine Tobias gave me worked fast—the pain in my shoulder has already faded to a dull throb.

When I get out of the shower, a stack of clothes waits on my bed. It contains some yellow and red, from the Amity, and some gray, from the Abnegation, colors I rarely see side by side. If I had to guess, I would say that one of the Abnegation put the stack there for me. It's something they would think to do.

I pull on a pair of dark red pants made of denim—so long I have to roll them up three times—and a gray Abnegation shirt that is too big for me. The sleeves come down to my fingertips, and I roll them up too. It hurts to move my right hand, so I keep the movements small and slow.

Someone knocks on the door. "Beatrice?" The soft voice is Susan's.

I open the door for her. She carries a tray of food, which she sets down on the bed. I search her face for a sign of what she has lost—her father, an Abnegation leader, didn't survive the attack—but I see only the placid determination characteristic of my old faction.

"I'm sorry the clothes don't fit," she says. "I'm sure we can find some better ones for you if the Amity allow us to stay."

"They're fine," I say. "Thank you."

"I heard you were shot. Do you need my help with your hair? Or your shoes?"

I am about to refuse, but I really do need help.

"Yes, thank you."

I sit down on a stool in front of the mirror, and she stands behind me, her eyes dutifully trained on the task at hand rather than her reflection. They do not lift, not even for an instant, as she runs a comb through my hair. And she doesn't ask about my shoulder, how I was shot, what happened when I left the Abnegation safe house to stop the simulation. I get the sense that if I were to whittle her down to her core, she would be Abnegation all the way through.

"Have you seen Robert yet?" I say. Her brother, Robert, chose Amity when I chose Dauntless, so he is somewhere in this compound. I wonder if their reunion will be anything like Caleb's and mine.

"Briefly, last night," she says. "I left him to grieve with his faction as I grieve with mine. It is nice to see him again, though."

I hear a finality in her tone that tells me the subject is closed.

"It's a shame this happened when it did," Susan says. "Our leaders were about to do something wonderful."

"Really? What?"

"I don't know." Susan blushes. "I just knew that something was happening. I didn't mean to be curious; I just noticed things."

"I wouldn't blame you for being curious even if you had been."

She nods and keeps combing. I wonder what the Abnegation leaders—including my father—were doing. And I can't help but marvel at Susan's assumption that whatever they were doing was wonderful. I wish I could believe that of people again.

If I ever did.

"The Dauntless wear their hair down, right?" she says.

"Sometimes," I say. "Do you know how to braid?"

So her deft fingers tuck pieces of my hair into one braid that tickles the middle of my spine. I stare hard at my reflection until she finishes. I thank her when she's done, and she leaves with a small smile, closing the door behind her.

I keep staring, but I don't see myself. I can still feel her fingers brushing the back of my neck, so much like my mother's fingers, the last morning I spent with her. My eyes wet with tears, I rock back and forth on the stool, trying to push the memory from my mind. I am afraid that if I start to sob, I will never stop until I shrivel up like a raisin.

I see a sewing kit on the dresser. In it are two colors of thread, red and yellow, and a pair of scissors.

I feel calm as I undo the braid in my hair and comb it again. I part my hair down the middle and make sure that it is straight and flat. I close the scissors over the hair by my chin.

How can I look the same, when she's gone and everything is different? I can't.

I cut in as straight a line as I can, using my jaw as a guide. The tricky part is the back, which I can't see very well, so I do the best I can by touch instead of sight. Locks of blond hair surround me on the floor in a semicircle.

I leave the room without looking at my reflection again.

+ + +

When Tobias and Caleb come to get me later, they stare at me like I am not the person they knew yesterday.

"You cut your hair," says Caleb, his eyebrows high. Grabbing hold of facts in the midst of shock is very Erudite of him. His hair sticks up on one side from where he slept on it, and his eyes are bloodshot.

"Yeah," I say. "It's . . . too hot for long hair."

"Fair enough."

We walk down the hallway together. The floorboards creak beneath our feet. I miss the way my footsteps echoed in the Dauntless compound; I miss the cool underground air. But mostly I miss the fears of the past few weeks, rendered small by my fears now.

We exit the building. The outside air presses around me like a pillow meant to suffocate me. It smells green, the way a leaf does when you tear it in half.

"Does everyone know you're Marcus's son?" Caleb says. "The Abnegation, I mean?"

"Not to my knowledge," says Tobias, glancing at Caleb. "And I would appreciate it if you didn't mention it."

"I don't need to mention it. Anyone with eyes can see it for themselves." Caleb frowns at him. "How old are you, anyway?"

"Eighteen."

"And you don't think you're too old to be with my little sister?"

Tobias lets out a short laugh. "She isn't *your little* anything."

"Stop it. Both of you," I say. A crowd of people in yellow walks ahead of us, toward a wide, squat building made entirely of glass. The sunlight reflecting off the panes feels like a pinch to my eyes. I shield my face with my hand and keep walking.

The doors to the building are wide open. Around the edge of the circular greenhouse, plants and trees grow in troughs of water or small pools. Dozens of fans positioned around the room serve only to blow the hot air around, so I am already sweating. But that fades from my mind when the crowd before me thins and I see the rest of the room.

In its center grows a huge tree. Its branches are spread over most of the greenhouse, and its roots bubble up from the ground, forming a dense web of bark. In the spaces between the roots, I see not dirt but water, and metal rods holding the roots in place. I should not be surprised—the Amity spend their lives accomplishing feats of agriculture like this one, with the help of Erudite technology.

Standing on a cluster of roots is Johanna Reyes, her hair falling over the scarred half of her face. I learned in Faction History that the Amity recognize no official leader—they vote on everything, and the result is usually close to unanimous. They are like many parts of a single mind, and Johanna is their mouthpiece.

The Amity sit on the floor, most with their legs crossed, in knots and clusters that vaguely resemble the tree roots to me. The Abnegation sit in tight rows a few yards to my left. My eyes search the crowd for a few seconds before I realize what I'm looking for: my parents.

I swallow hard, and try to forget. Tobias touches the small of my back, guiding me to the edge of the meeting space, behind the Abnegation. Before we sit down, he puts his mouth next to my ear and says, "I like your hair that way."

I find a small smile to give him, and lean into him when I sit down, my arm against his.

Johanna lifts her hands and bows her head. All conversation in the room ceases before I can draw my next breath. All around me the Amity sit in silence, some with their eyes closed, some with their lips mouthing words I can't hear, some staring at a point far away.

Every second chafes. By the time Johanna lifts her head I am worn to the bone.

"We have before us today an urgent question," she says, "which is: How will we conduct ourselves in this time of conflict as people who pursue peace?"

Every Amity in the room turns to the person next to him or her and starts talking.

"How do they get anything done?" I say, as the minutes of chatter wear on.

"They don't care about efficiency," Tobias says. "They care about agreement. Watch."

Two women in yellow dresses a few feet away rise and join a trio of men. A young man shifts so that his small circle becomes a large one with the group next to him. All around the room, the smaller crowds grow and expand, and fewer and fewer voices fill the room, until there are only three or four. I can only hear pieces of what they say: "Peace—Dauntless—Erudite—safe house—involvement—"

"This is bizarre," I say.

"I think it's beautiful," he says.

I give him a look.

"What?" He laughs a little. "They each have an equal role in government; they each feel equally responsible. And it makes them care; it makes them kind. I think that's beautiful."

"I think it's unsustainable," I say. "Sure, it works for the Amity. But what happens when not everyone wants to strum banjos and grow crops? What happens when someone does something terrible and talking about it can't solve the problem?"

He shrugs. "I guess we'll find out."

Eventually someone from each of the big groups stands and approaches Johanna, picking their way carefully over the roots of the big tree. I expect them to address the rest of us, but instead they stand in a circle with Johanna and the other spokespeople and talk quietly. I begin to get the feeling that I will never know what they're saying.

"They're not going to let us argue with them, are they," I say.

"I doubt it," he says.

We are done for.

When everyone has said his or her piece, they sit down again, leaving Johanna alone in the center of the room. She angles her body toward us and folds her hands in front of her. Where will we go when they tell us to leave? Back into the city, where nothing is safe?

"Our faction has had a close relationship with Erudite for as long as any of us can remember. We need each other to survive, and we have always cooperated with each other," says Johanna. "But we have also had a strong relationship with Abnegation in the past, and we do not think it is right to revoke the hand of friendship when it has for so long been extended."

Her voice is honey-sweet, and moves like honey too, slow and careful. I wipe the sweat from my hairline with the back of my hand.

"We feel that the only way to preserve our relationships with both factions is to remain impartial and uninvolved," she continues. "Your presence here, though welcome, complicates that."

Here it comes, I think.

"We have arrived at the conclusion that we will establish our faction headquarters as a safe house for members of all factions," she says, "under a set of conditions. The first is that no weaponry of any kind is allowed on the compound. The second is that if any serious conflict arises, whether verbal or physical, all involved parties will be asked to leave. The third is that the conflict may not be discussed, even privately, within the confines of this compound. And the fourth is that everyone who stays here must contribute to the welfare of this environment by working. We will report this to Erudite, Candor, and Dauntless as soon as we can."

Her stare drifts to Tobias and me, and stays there.

"You are welcome to stay here if and only if you can abide by our rules," she says. "That is our decision."

I think of the gun I hid under my mattress, and the tension between me and Peter, and Tobias and Marcus, and my mouth feels dry. I am not good at avoiding conflict.

"We won't be able to stay long," I say to Tobias under my breath.

A moment ago, he was still faintly smiling. Now the corners of his mouth have disappeared into a frown. "No, we won't."

CHAPTER
THREE

THAT EVENING I return to my room and slide my hand beneath my mattress to make sure the gun is still there. My fingers brush over the trigger, and my throat tightens like I am having an allergic reaction. I withdraw my hand and kneel on the edge of the bed, taking hard swallows of air until the feeling subsides.

What is wrong with you? I shake my head. *Pull it together.*

And that is what it feels like: pulling the different parts of me up and in like a shoelace. I feel suffocated, but at least I feel strong.

I see a flicker of movement in my periphery, and look out the window that faces the apple orchard. Johanna Reyes and Marcus Eaton walk side by side, pausing at the herb garden to pluck mint leaves from their stems. I am out of my room before I can evaluate why I want to follow them.

I sprint through the building so that I don't lose them. Once I am outside, I have to be more careful. I walk around the far side of the greenhouse and, after I see Johanna and Marcus disappear into one row of trees, I creep down the next row, hoping the branches will hide me if either of them looks back.

". . . been confused about is the timing of the attack," says Johanna. "Is it just that Jeanine finally finished planning it, and acted, or was there an inciting incident of some kind?"

I see Marcus's face through a divided tree trunk. He presses his lips together and says, "Hmm."

"I suppose we'll never know." Johanna raises her good eyebrow. "Will we?"

"No, perhaps not."

Johanna places her hand on his arm and turns toward him. I stiffen, afraid for a moment that she will see me, but she looks only at Marcus. I sink into a crouch and crawl toward one of the trees so that the trunk will hide me. The bark itches my spine, but I don't move.

"But you *do* know," she says. "You know why she attacked when she did. I may not be Candor anymore, but I can still tell when someone is keeping the truth from me."

"Inquisitiveness is self-serving, Johanna."

If I were Johanna, I would snap at him for a comment like that, but she says kindly, "My faction depends on me to advise them, and if you know information this crucial, it is important that I know it also so that I can share it with them. I'm sure you can understand that, Marcus."

"There is a reason you don't know all the things I know. A long time ago, the Abnegation were entrusted with some sensitive information," says Marcus. "Jeanine attacked us to steal it. And if I am not careful, she will destroy it, so that is all I can tell you."

"But surely—"

"No," Marcus cuts her off. "This information is far more important than you can imagine. Most of the leaders of this city risked their lives to protect it from Jeanine and died, and I will not jeopardize it now for the sake of sating your selfish curiosity."

Johanna is quiet for a few seconds. It's so dark now I can barely see my own hands. The air smells like dirt and apples, and I try not to breathe it too loudly.

"I'm sorry," says Johanna. "I must have done something to make you believe I am not trustworthy."

"The last time I trusted a faction representative with this information, all my friends were murdered," he replies. "I don't trust anyone anymore."

I can't help it—I lean forward so that I can see around the trunk of the tree. Both Marcus and Johanna are too preoccupied to notice the movement. They are close together, but not touching, and I've never seen Marcus look so tired or Johanna so angry. But her face softens, and she touches Marcus's arm again, this time with a light caress.

"In order to have peace, we must first have trust," says Johanna. "So I hope you change your mind. Remember that I have always been your friend, Marcus, even when you did not have many to speak of."

She leans in and kisses his cheek, then walks to the end of the orchard. Marcus stands for a few seconds, apparently stunned, and starts toward the compound.

The revelations of the past half hour buzz in my mind. I thought Jeanine attacked the Abnegation to seize power, but she attacked them to steal information—information only they knew.

Then the buzzing stops as I remember something else Marcus said: *Most of the leaders of this city risked their lives for it.* Was one of those leaders my father?

I have to know. I have to find out what could possibly be important enough for the Abnegation to die for—and the Erudite to kill for.

+ + +

I pause before knocking on Tobias's door, and listen to what's going on inside.

"No, not like *that*," Tobias says through laughter.

"What do you mean, 'not like that'? I imitated you perfectly." The second voice belongs to Caleb.

"You did not."

"Well, do it again, then."

I push open the door just as Tobias, who is sitting on the floor with one leg stretched out, hurls a butter knife at the opposite wall. It sticks, handle out, from a large hunk of cheese they positioned on top of the dresser. Caleb, standing beside him, stares in disbelief, first at the cheese and then at me.

"Tell me he's some kind of Dauntless prodigy," says Caleb. "Can you do this too?"

He looks better than he did earlier—his eyes aren't red anymore and some of the old spark of curiosity is in them, like he is interested in the world again. His brown hair is tousled, his shirt buttons in the wrong buttonholes. He is handsome in a careless way, my brother, like he has no idea what he looks like most of the time.

"With my right hand, maybe," I say. "But yes, *Four* is some kind of Dauntless prodigy. Can I ask *why* you're throwing knives at cheese?"

Tobias's eyes catch mine on the word "Four." Caleb

doesn't know that Tobias wears his excellence all the time in his own nickname.

"Caleb came by to discuss something," Tobias says, leaning his head against the wall as he looks at me. "And knife-throwing just came up somehow."

"As it so often does," I say, a small smile inching its way across my face.

He looks so relaxed, his head back, his arm slung over his knee. We stare at each other for a few more seconds than is socially acceptable. Caleb clears his throat.

"Anyway, I should be getting back to my room," Caleb says, looking from Tobias to me and back again. "I'm reading this book about the water-filtration systems. The kid who gave it to me looked at me like I was crazy for wanting to read it. I think it's supposed to be a repair manual, but it's fascinating." He pauses. "Sorry. You probably think I'm crazy too."

"Not at all," Tobias says with mock sincerity. "Maybe *you* should read that repair manual too, Tris. It sounds like something you might like."

"I can loan it to you," Caleb says.

"Maybe later," I say. When Caleb closes the door behind him, I give Tobias a dirty look.

"Thanks for that," I say. "Now he's going to talk my ear off about water filtration and how it works. Though I guess

I might prefer that to what he wants to talk to me about."

"Oh? And what's that?" Tobias quirks his eyebrows. "Aquaponics?"

"Aqua-what?"

"It's one of the ways they grow food here. You don't want to know."

"You're right, I don't," I say. "What did he come to talk to you about?"

"You," he says. "I think it was the big-brother talk. 'Don't mess around with my sister' and all that."

He gets up.

"What did you tell him?"

He comes toward me.

"I told him how we got together—that's how knife-throwing came up," he says, "and I told him I wasn't messing around."

I feel warm everywhere. He wraps his hands around my hips and presses me gently against the door. His lips find mine.

I don't remember why I came here in the first place.

And I don't care.

I wrap my uninjured arm around him, pulling him against me. My fingers find the hem of his T-shirt, and slide beneath it, spreading wide over the small of his back. He feels so strong.

He kisses me again, more insistent this time, his hands squeezing my waist. His breaths, my breaths, his body, my body, we are so close there is no difference.

He pulls back, just a few centimeters. I almost don't let him get that far.

"This isn't what you came here for," he says.

"No."

"What did you come for, then?"

"Who cares?"

I push my fingers through his hair, and draw his mouth to mine again. He doesn't resist, but after a few seconds, he mumbles, "Tris," against my cheek.

"Okay, okay." I close my eyes. I did come here for something important: to tell him the conversation I overheard.

We sit side by side on Tobias's bed, and I start from the beginning. I tell him how I followed Marcus and Johanna into the orchard. I tell him Johanna's question about the timing of the simulation attack, and Marcus's response, and the argument that followed. As I do, I watch his expression. He does not look shocked or curious. Instead, his mouth works its way into the bitter pucker that accompanies any mention of Marcus.

"Well, what do you think?" I say once I finish.

"I think," he says carefully, "that it's Marcus trying to feel more important than he is."

That was not the response I was expecting.

"So . . . what? You think he's just talking nonsense?"

"I think there probably is some information the Abnegation knew that Jeanine wanted to know, but I think he's exaggerating its importance. Trying to build up his own ego by making Johanna think he's got something she wants and he won't give it to her."

"I don't . . ." I frown. "I don't think you're right. He didn't sound like he was lying."

"You don't know him like I do. He is an excellent liar."

He is right—I don't know Marcus, and certainly not as well as he does. But my instinct was to believe Marcus, and I usually trust my instincts.

"Maybe you're right," I say, "but shouldn't we find out what's going on? Just to be sure?"

"I think it's more important that we deal with the situation at hand," says Tobias. "Go back to the city. Find out what's going on there. Find a way to take Erudite down. Then maybe we can find out what Marcus was talking about, after this is all resolved. Okay?"

I nod. It sounds like a good plan—a smart plan. But I don't believe him—I don't believe it's more important to move forward than to find out the truth. When I found out that I was Divergent . . . when I found out that Erudite would attack Abnegation . . . those revelations changed everything. The truth has a way of changing a person's plans.

But it is difficult to persuade Tobias to do something he doesn't want to do, and even more difficult to justify my feelings with no evidence except my intuition.

So I agree. But I do not change my mind.

CHAPTER
FOUR

"BIOTECHNOLOGY HAS BEEN around for a long time, but it wasn't always very effective," Caleb says. He starts on the crust of his toast—he ate the middle first, just like he used to when we were little.

He sits across from me in the cafeteria, at the table closest to the windows. Carved into the wood along the table's edge are the letters "D" and "T" linked together by a heart, so small I almost didn't see them. I run my fingers over the carving as Caleb speaks.

"But Erudite scientists developed this highly effective mineral solution a while back. It was better for the plants than dirt," he says. "It's an earlier version of that salve they put on your shoulder—it accelerates the growth of new cells."

His eyes are wild with new information. Not all the Erudite are power hungry and devoid of conscience, like their leader, Jeanine Matthews. Some of them are like Caleb: fascinated by everything, dissatisfied until they find out how it works.

I rest my chin on my hand and smile a little at him. He seems upbeat this morning. I am glad he has found something to distract him from his grief.

"So Erudite and Amity work together, then?" I say.

"More closely than Erudite and any other faction," he says. "Don't you remember from our Faction History book? It called them the 'essential factions'—without them, we would be incapable of survival. Some of the Erudite texts called them the 'enriching factions.' And one of Erudite's missions as a faction was to become both—essential and enriching."

It doesn't sit well with me, how much our society needs Erudite to function. But they *are* essential—without them, there would be inefficient farming, insufficient medical treatments, and no technological advance.

I bite my apple.

"You aren't going to eat your toast?" he says.

"The bread tastes strange," I say. "You can have it if you want."

"I'm amazed by how they live here," he says as he

takes the toast from my plate. "They're completely self-sustaining. They have their own source of power, their own water pumps, their own water filtration, their own food sources. . . . They're independent."

"Independent," I say, "and uninvolved. Must be nice."

It *is* nice, from what I can tell. The large windows beside our table let in so much sunlight I feel like I'm sitting outside. Clusters of Amity sit at the other tables, their clothes bright against their tanned skin. On me the yellow looks dull.

"So I take it Amity wasn't one of the factions you had an aptitude for," he says, grinning.

"No." The group of Amity a few seats away from us bursts into laughter. They haven't even glanced in our direction since we sat down to eat. "Keep it down, all right? It's not something I want to broadcast."

"Sorry," he says, leaning over the table so that he can talk quieter. "So what were they?"

I feel myself tensing, straightening. "Why do you want to know?"

"Tris," he says, "I'm your brother. You can tell me anything."

His green eyes never waver. He's abandoned the useless spectacles he wore as a member of Erudite in favor of an Abnegation gray shirt and their trademark short haircut.

He looks just as he did a few months ago, when we were living across the hall from each other, both of us considering switching factions but not brave enough to tell one another. Not trusting him enough to tell him was a mistake I do not want to make again.

"Abnegation, Dauntless," I say, "and Erudite."

"*Three* factions?" His eyebrows lift.

"Yes. Why?"

"It just seems like a lot," he says. "We each had to choose a research focus in Erudite initiation, and mine was the aptitude test simulation, so I know a lot about the way it's designed. It's really difficult for a person to get two results—the program actually doesn't allow it. But to get *three* . . . I'm not even sure how that's possible."

"Well, the test administrator had to alter the test," I say. "She forced it to go to that situation on the bus so that she could rule out Erudite—except Erudite wasn't ruled out."

Caleb props his chin on a fist. "A program override," he says. "I wonder how your test administrator knew how to do that. It's not something they're taught."

I frown. Tori was a tattoo artist and an aptitude test volunteer—how *did* she know how to alter the aptitude test program? If she was good with computers, it was only as a hobby, and I doubt that a computer hobby would enable someone to fiddle with an Erudite simulation.

Then something from one of my conversations with her surfaces. *My brother and I both transferred from Erudite.*

"She was Erudite," I say. "A faction transfer. Maybe that's how."

"Maybe," he says, tapping his fingers—from left to right—against his cheek. Our breakfasts sit, almost forgotten, between us. "What does this mean about your brain chemistry? Or anatomy?"

I laugh a little. "I don't know. All I know is that I'm always aware during simulations, and sometimes I can wake myself up from them. Sometimes they don't even work. Like the attack simulation."

"How do you wake yourself up from them? What do you do?"

"I . . ." I try to remember. I feel like it has been a long time since I was in one, though it was only a few weeks. "It's hard to say, because the Dauntless simulations were supposed to end when we had calmed down. But in one of mine . . . the one where Tobias figured out what I was . . . I just did something impossible. I broke glass just by putting my hand on it."

Caleb's expression becomes distant, like he is looking into faraway places. Nothing like what I just described ever happened to him in the aptitude test simulation, I know. So maybe he is wondering what it felt like, or how it's possible. My cheeks grow warmer—he is analyzing my brain like he would analyze a computer or a machine.

"Hey," I say. "Come back."

"Sorry," he says, focusing on me again. "It's just . . ."

"Fascinating. Yeah, I know. You always look like someone's sucked the life right out of you when something fascinates you."

He laughs.

"Can we talk about something else, though?" I say. "There may not be any Erudite or Dauntless traitors around, but it still feels weird, talking about it in public like this."

"All right."

Before he can go on, the cafeteria doors open, and a group of Abnegation come in. They wear Amity clothes, like me, but also like me, it's obvious what faction they are really in. They are silent, but not somber—they smile at the Amity they pass, inclining their heads, a few of them stopping to exchange pleasantries.

Susan sits down next to Caleb with a small smile. Her hair is pulled back in its usual knot, but her blond hair shines like gold. She and Caleb sit just slightly closer than friends would, though they do not touch. She bobs her head to greet me.

"I'm sorry," she says. "Did I interrupt?"

"No," says Caleb. "How are you?"

"I'm well. How are you?"

I am just about to flee the dining hall rather than participate in careful, polite Abnegation conversation when Tobias comes in, looking harassed. He must have been working in the kitchen this morning, as part of our agreement with the Amity. I have to work in the laundry rooms tomorrow.

"What happened?" I say as he sits down next to me.

"In their enthusiasm for conflict resolution, the Amity have apparently forgotten that meddling creates *more* conflict," says Tobias. "If we stay here much longer, I am going to punch someone, and it's not going to be pretty."

Caleb and Susan both raise their eyebrows at him. A few of the Amity at the table next to ours stop talking to stare.

"You heard me," Tobias says to them. They all look away.

"As I said," I say, covering my mouth to hide my smile, "what happened?"

"I'll tell you later."

It must have to do with Marcus. Tobias doesn't like the dubious looks the Abnegation give him when he refers to Marcus's cruelty, and Susan is sitting right across from him. I clasp my hands in my lap.

The Abnegation sit at our table, but not right next to

us—a respectful distance of two seats away, though most of them still nod at us. They were my family's friends and neighbors and coworkers, and before, their presence would have encouraged me to be quiet and self-effacing. Now it makes me want to talk louder, to be as far from that old identity and the pain that accompanies it as possible.

Tobias goes completely still when a hand falls on my right shoulder, sending prickles of pain down my right arm. I clench my teeth to keep from groaning.

"She got shot in that shoulder," Tobias says without looking at the man behind me.

"My apologies." Marcus lifts his hand and sits down on my left. "Hello."

"What do *you* want?" I say.

"Beatrice," Susan says quietly. "There's no need to—"

"Susan, please," says Caleb quietly. She presses her lips into a line and looks away.

I frown at Marcus. "I asked you a question."

"I would like to discuss something with you," says Marcus. His expression is calm, but he's angry—the terseness in his voice betrays him. "The other Abnegation and myself have discussed it and decided that we should not stay here. We believe that, given the inevitability of further conflict in our city, it would be selfish of us to stay here while what remains of our faction is inside that fence. We would like to request that you escort us."

I did not expect that. Why does Marcus want to return to the city? Is it really just an Abnegation decision, or does he intend to do something there—something that has to do with whatever information the Abnegation have?

I stare at him for a few seconds and then look at Tobias. He has relaxed a little, but he keeps his eyes focused on the table. I don't know why he acts this way around his father. No one, not even Jeanine, makes Tobias cower.

"What do you think?" I say.

"I think we should leave the day after tomorrow," Tobias says.

"Okay. Thank you," says Marcus. He gets up and sits at the other end of the table with the rest of the Abnegation.

I inch closer to Tobias, not sure how to comfort him without making things worse. I pick up my apple with my left hand, and grab his hand under the table with my right.

But I can't keep my eyes away from Marcus. I want to know more about what he said to Johanna. And sometimes, if you want the truth, you have to demand it.

CHAPTER
FIVE

AFTER BREAKFAST, I tell Tobias I'm going for a walk, but instead I follow Marcus. I expect him to walk to the guests' dormitory, but he crosses the field behind the dining hall and walks into the water-filtration building. I hesitate on the bottom step. Do I really want to do this?

I walk up the steps and through the door that Marcus just closed behind him.

The filtration building is small, just one room with a few huge machines in it. As far as I can tell, some of the machines take in dirty water from the rest of the compound, a few of them purify it, others test it, and the last set pumps clean water back out to the compound. The piping systems are all buried except one, which runs along the ground to send water to the power plant, near the fence. The plant provides power to the entire city, using a combination of wind, water, and solar energy.

Marcus stands near the machines that filter the water. There the pipes are transparent. I can see brown-tinged water rushing through one pipe, disappearing into the machine, and emerging clear. Both of us watch the purification happen, and I wonder if he is thinking what I am: that it would be nice if life worked this way, stripping the dirt from our lives and sending us out into the world clean. But some dirt is destined to linger.

I stare at the back of Marcus's head. I have to do this now.

Now.

"I heard you, the other day," I blurt out.

Marcus whips his head around. "What are you doing, Beatrice?"

"I followed you here." I fold my arms over my chest. "I heard you talking to Johanna about what motivated Jeanine's attack on Abnegation."

"Did the Dauntless teach you that it's all right to invade another person's privacy, or did you teach yourself?"

"I'm a naturally curious person. Don't change the subject."

Marcus's forehead is creased, especially between the eyebrows, and there are deep lines next to his mouth. He looks like a man who has spent most of his life frowning. He might have been handsome when he was younger—perhaps he still is, to women his age, like Johanna—but all I see when I look at him are the black-pit eyes from Tobias's fear landscape.

"If you heard me talking to Johanna, then you know that I didn't even tell *her* about this. So what makes you think that I would share the information with *you*?"

I don't have an answer at first. But then it comes to me.

"My father," I say. "My father is dead." It's the first time I've said it since I told Tobias, on the train ride over, that my parents died for me. "Died" was just a fact to me then, detached from emotion. But "dead," mingling with the churning and bubbling noises in this room, strikes a blow like a hammer to my chest, and the monster of grief awakens, clawing at my eyes and throat.

I force myself to continue.

"He may not have actually died for whatever information you were referring to," I say. "But I want to know if it was something he risked his life for."

Marcus's mouth twitches.

"Yes," he says. "It was."

My eyes fill with tears. I blink them away.

"Well," I say, almost choking, "then what on earth was

it? Was it something you were trying to protect? Or steal? Or what?"

"It was . . ." Marcus shakes his head. "I'm not going to tell you that."

I step toward him. "But you want it back. And Jeanine has it."

Marcus *is* a good liar—or at least, someone who is skilled at hiding secrets. He does not react. I wish I could see like Johanna sees, like the Candor see—I wish I could read his expression. He could be close to telling me the truth. If I press just hard enough, maybe he'll crack.

"I could help you," I say.

Marcus's upper lip curls. "You have no idea how ridiculous that sounds." He spits the words at me. "You may have succeeded in shutting down the attack simulation, girl, but it was by luck alone, not skill. I would die of shock if you managed to do anything useful again for a long time."

This is the Marcus that Tobias knows. The one who knows right where to hit to cause the most damage.

My body shudders with anger. "Tobias is right about you," I say. "You're nothing but an arrogant, lying piece of garbage."

"He said that, did he?" Marcus raises his eyebrows.

"No," I say. "He doesn't mention you enough to say anything like that. I figured it out all on my own." I clench my teeth. "You're almost nothing to him, you know. And as time goes on, you become less and less."

Marcus doesn't answer me. He turns back to the water purifier. I stand for a moment in my triumph, the sound of rushing water combining with the heartbeat in my ears. Then I leave the building, and it isn't until I'm halfway across the field that I realize I didn't win. Marcus did.

Whatever the truth is, I'll have to get it from somewhere else, because I won't be asking him again.

+ + +

That night I dream that I am in a field, and I encounter a flock of crows clustered on the ground. When I swat a few of them away, I realize that they are perched on top of a man, pecking at his clothes, which are Abnegation gray. Without warning, they take flight, and I realize that the man is Will.

Then I wake up.

I turn my face into the pillow and release, instead of his name, a sob that throws my body against the mattress. I feel the monster of grief again, writhing in the empty space where my heart and stomach used to be.

I gasp, pressing both palms to my chest. Now the monstrous thing has its claws around my throat, squeezing my airway. I twist and put my head between my knees, breathing until the strangled feeling leaves me.

Even though the air is warm, I shiver. I get out of bed and creep down the hallway toward Tobias's room. My bare legs almost glow in the dark. His door creaks when I pull it open, loud enough to wake him. He stares at me for a second.

"C'mere," he says, sluggish from sleep. He shifts back on the bed to leave space for me.

I should have thought this through. I sleep in a long T-shirt one of the Amity lent me. It comes down just past my butt, and I didn't think to put on a pair of shorts before I came here. Tobias's eyes skim my bare legs, making my face warm. I lie down, facing him.

"Bad dream?" he says.

I nod.

"What happened?"

I shake my head. I can't tell him that I'm having nightmares about Will, or I would have to explain why. What would he think of me, if he knew what I had done? How would he look at me?

He keeps his hand on my cheek, moving his thumb over my cheekbone idly.

"We're all right, you know," he says. "You and me. Okay?"

My chest aches, and I nod.

"Nothing else is all right." His whisper tickles my cheek. "But we are."

"Tobias," I say. But whatever I was about to say gets lost in my head, and I press my mouth to his, because I know that kissing him will distract me from everything.

He kisses me back. His hand starts on my cheek, and then brushes over my side, fitting to the bend in my waist, curving over my hip, sliding to my bare leg, making me shiver. I press closer to him and wrap my leg around him. My head buzzes with nervousness, but the rest of me seems to know exactly what it's doing, because it all pulses to the same rhythm, all wants the same thing: to escape itself and become a part of him instead.

His mouth moves against mine, and his hand slips under the hem of the T-shirt, and I don't stop him, though I know I should. Instead a faint sigh escapes me, and heat rushes into my cheeks, embarrassment. Either he didn't hear me or he didn't care, because he presses his palm to my lower back, presses me closer. His fingers move slowly up my back, tracing my spine. My shirt creeps up my body, and I don't pull it down, even when I feel cool air on my stomach.

He kisses my neck, and I grab his shoulder to steady myself, gathering his shirt into my fist. His hand reaches the top of my back and curls around my neck. My shirt is twisted around his arm, and our kisses become desperate. I know my hands are shaking from all the nervous energy inside me, so I tighten my grip on his shoulder so he won't notice.

Then his fingers brush the bandage on my shoulder, and a dart of pain goes through me. It didn't hurt much, but it brings me back to reality. I can't be with him in *that* way if one of my reasons for wanting it is to distract myself from grief.

I lean back and carefully pull the hem of my shirt down so it covers me again. For a second we just lie there, our heavy breaths mixing. I don't mean to cry—now is not a good time to cry; no, it has to stop—but I can't get the tears out of my eyes, no matter how many times I blink.

"Sorry," I say.

He says almost sternly, "Don't apologize." He brushes the tears from my cheeks.

I know that I am birdlike, made narrow and small as if for taking flight, built straight-waisted and fragile. But when he touches me like he can't bear to take his hand away, I don't wish I was any different.

"I don't mean to be such a mess," I say, my voice

cracking. "I just feel so . . ." I shake my head.

"It's wrong," he says. "It doesn't matter if your parents are in a better place—they aren't here with you, and that's *wrong*, Tris. It shouldn't have happened. It shouldn't have happened to you. And anyone who tells you it's okay is a liar."

A sob racks my body again, and he wraps his arms around me so tightly I find it difficult to breathe, but it doesn't matter. My dignified weeping gives way to full-on ugliness, my mouth open and my face contorted and sounds like a dying animal coming from my throat. If this continues I will break apart, and maybe that would be better, maybe it would be better to shatter and bear nothing.

He doesn't speak for a long time, until I am quiet again.

"Sleep," he says. "I'll fight the bad dreams off if they come to get you."

"With what?"

"My bare hands, obviously."

I wrap my arm around his waist and take a deep breath of his shoulder. He smells like sweat and fresh air and mint, from the salve he sometimes uses to relax his sore muscles. He smells safe, too, like sunlit walks in the orchard and silent breakfasts in the dining hall. And in the moments before I drift off to sleep, I almost forget about our war-torn city and all the conflict that will come to find us soon, if we don't find it first.

In the moments before I drift off to sleep, I hear him whisper, "I love you, Tris."

And maybe I would say it back, but I am too far gone.

CHAPTER
SIX

THAT MORNING I wake up to the buzz of an electric razor. Tobias stands in front of the mirror, his head tilted so he can see the corner of his jaw.

I hug my knees, covered by the sheet, and watch him.

"Good morning," he says. "How did you sleep?"

"Okay." I get up, and as he tilts his head back to address his chin with the razor, I wrap my arms around him, pressing my forehead to his back where the Dauntless tattoo peeks out from beneath his shirt.

He sets the razor down and folds his hands over mine. Neither of us breaks the silence. I listen to him breathe, and he strokes my fingers idly, the task at hand forgotten.

"I should go get ready," I say after a while. I am reluctant to leave, but I am supposed to work in the laundry rooms, and I don't want the Amity to say I'm not fulfilling my part of the deal they offered us.

"I'll get you something to wear," he says.

I walk barefoot down the hallway a few minutes later, wearing the shirt I slept in and a pair of shorts Tobias borrowed from the Amity. When I get back to my bedroom, Peter is standing next to my bed.

Instinct makes me straighten up and search the room for a blunt object.

"Get out," I say as steadily as I can. But it's hard to keep my voice from shaking. I can't help but remember the look in his eyes as he held me over the chasm by my throat or slammed me against the wall in the Dauntless compound.

He turns to look at me. Lately when he looks at me it's without his usual malice—instead he just seems exhausted, his posture slouched, his wounded arm in a sling. But I am not fooled.

"What are you doing in my room?"

He walks closer to me. "What are you doing stalking Marcus? I saw you after breakfast yesterday."

I match his stare with my own. "That's none of your business. Get out."

"I'm here because I don't know why *you* get to keep track of that hard drive," he says. "It's not like you're particularly stable these days."

"*I'm* unstable?" I laugh. "I find that a little funny, coming from you."

Peter pinches his lips together and says nothing.

I narrow my eyes. "Why are you so interested in the hard drive anyway?"

"I'm not stupid," he says. "I know it contains more than the simulation data."

"No, you aren't stupid, are you?" I say. "You think if you deliver it to the Erudite, they'll forgive your indiscretion and let you back in their good graces."

"I don't want to be back in their good graces," he says, stepping forward again. "If I had, I wouldn't have helped you in the Dauntless compound."

I jab his sternum with my index finger, digging in my fingernail. "You helped me because you didn't want me to shoot you again."

"I may not be an Abnegation-loving faction traitor." He seizes my finger. "But no one gets to control me, especially not the Erudite."

I yank my hand back, twisting so that he won't be able to hold on. My hands are sweaty.

"I don't expect you to understand." I wipe my hands on the hem of my shirt as I inch toward the dresser. "I'm sure if it had been Candor and not Abnegation that got attacked, you would have just let your family get shot between the eyes without protest. But I'm not like that."

"Careful what you say about my family, Stiff." He moves with me, toward the dresser, but I carefully shift so that I stand between him and the drawers. I'm not going to reveal the hard drive's location by getting it out while he's in here, but I don't want to leave the path to it clear, either.

His eyes shift to the dresser behind me, to the left side, where the hard drive is hidden. I frown at him, and then notice something I didn't before: a rectangular bulge in one of his pockets.

"Give it to me," I say. "Now."

"No."

"Give it to me, or so help me, I will kill you in your sleep."

He smirks. "If only you could see how ridiculous you look when you threaten people. Like a little girl telling me she's going to strangle me with her jump rope."

I start toward him, and he shifts back, into the hallway.

"Don't call me 'little girl.'"

"I'll call you whatever I want."

I jerk into action, aiming my left fist where I know it will hurt the worst: at the bullet wound in his arm. He dodges the punch, but instead of trying again, I seize his arm as hard as I can and wrench it to the side. Peter screams at the top of his lungs, and while he's distracted by the pain, I kick him hard in the knee, and he falls to the ground.

People rush into the hallway, wearing gray and black and yellow and red. Peter surges toward me in a half crouch, and punches me in the stomach. I hunch over, but the pain doesn't stop me—I let out something between a groan and a scream, and launch myself at him, my left elbow pulled back near my mouth so that I can slam it into his face.

One of the Amity grabs me by the arms and half lifts, half pulls me away from Peter. The wound in my shoulder throbs, but I hardly feel it through the pulse of adrenaline. I strain toward him and try to ignore the stunned faces of the Amity and the Abnegation—and Tobias—around me, and the woman kneels next to Peter, whispering words in a soothing tone of voice. I try to ignore his groans of pain and the guilt stabbing at my stomach. I hate him. I don't care. I hate him.

"Tris, calm down!" Tobias says.

"He has the hard drive!" I yell. "He stole it from me! He has it!"

Tobias walks over to Peter, ignoring the woman crouched beside him, and presses his foot into Peter's rib cage to keep him in place. He then reaches into Peter's pocket and takes out the hard drive.

Tobias says to him—very quietly—"We won't be in a safe house forever, and this wasn't very smart of you." Then he turns toward me and adds, "Not very smart of you, either. Do you want to get us kicked out?"

I scowl. The Amity man with his hand on my arm starts to pull me down the hallway. I try to wrench my body out of his grasp.

"What do you think you're doing? Let go of me!"

"You violated the terms of our peace agreement," he says gently. "We must follow protocol."

"Just go," says Tobias. "You need to cool down."

I search the faces of the crowd that has gathered. No one argues with Tobias. Their eyes skirt mine. So I allow two Amity men to escort me down the hallway.

"Watch your step," one of them says. "The floorboards are uneven here."

My head pounds, a sign that I am calming down. The graying Amity man opens a door on the left. A label on the door says CONFLICT ROOM.

"Are you putting me in time-out or something?" I scowl. That is something the Amity would do: put me in time-out, and then teach me to do cleansing breaths or think positive thoughts.

The room is so bright I have to squint to see. The opposite wall has large windows that look out over the orchard.

Despite this, the room feels small, probably because the ceiling, like the walls and floor, is also covered with wooden boards.

"Please sit," the older man says, gesturing toward the stool in the middle of the room. It, like all other furniture in the Amity compound, is made of unpolished wood, and looks sturdy, like it is still attached to the earth. I do not sit.

"The fight is over," I say. "I won't do it again. Not here."

"We have to follow protocol," the younger man says. "Please sit, and we'll discuss what happened, and then we'll let you go."

All their voices are so soft. Not hushed, like the Abnegation speak, always treading holy ground and trying not to disturb. Soft, soothing, low—I wonder, then, if that is something they teach their initiates here. How best to speak, move, smile, to encourage peace.

I don't want to sit down, but I do, perched on the edge of the chair so I can get up fast, if necessary. The younger man stands in front of me. Hinges creak behind me. I look over my shoulder—the older man is fumbling with something on a counter behind me.

"What are you doing?"

"I am making tea," he says.

"I don't think tea is really the solution to this."

"Then tell us," the younger man says, drawing my

attention back to the windows. He smiles at me. "What do you believe is the solution?"

"Throwing Peter out of this compound."

"It seems to me," the man says gently, "that you are the one who attacked him—indeed, that you are the one who shot him in the arm."

"You have no idea what he did to deserve those things." My cheeks get hot again and mimic my heartbeat. "He tried to kill me. And someone else—he stabbed someone else in the eye . . . with a *butter* knife. He is evil. I had every *right* to—"

I feel a sharp pain in my neck. Dark spots cover the man in front of me, obscuring my view of his face.

"I'm sorry, dear," he says. "We are just following protocol."

The older man is holding a syringe. A few drops of whatever he injected me with are still in it. They are bright green, the color of grass. I blink rapidly, and the dark spots disappear, but the world still swims before me, like I am tilting forward and back in a rocking chair.

"How do you feel?" the younger man says.

"I feel . . ." *Angry,* I was about to say. Angry with Peter, angry with the Amity. *But that's not true, is it?* I smile. "I feel good. I feel a little like . . . like I'm floating. Or swaying. How do *you* feel?"

"Dizziness is a side effect of the serum. You may want to rest this afternoon. And I'm feeling well. Thank you for asking," he says. "You may leave now, if you would like."

"Can you tell me where to find Tobias?" I say. When I imagine his face, affection for him bubbles up inside me, and all I want to do is kiss him. "Four, I mean. He's handsome, isn't he? I don't really know why he likes me so much. I'm not very nice, am I?"

"Not most of the time, no," the man says. "But I think you could be, if you tried."

"Thank you," I say. "That's nice of you to say."

"I think you'll find him in the orchard," he says. "I saw him go outside after the fight."

I laugh a little. "The fight. What a silly thing . . ."

And it does seem like a silly thing, slamming your fist into someone else's body. Like a caress, but too hard. A caress is much nicer. Maybe I should have run my hand along Peter's arm instead. That would have felt better to both of us. My knuckles wouldn't ache right now.

I get up and steer myself toward the door. I have to lean against the wall for balance, but it's sturdy, so I don't mind. I stumble down the hallway, giggling at my inability to balance. I'm clumsy again, just like I was when I was younger. My mother used to smile at me and say, "Be careful where you put your feet, Beatrice. I don't want you to hurt yourself."

I walk outside and the green on the trees seems greener, so potent I can almost taste it. Maybe I *can* taste it, and it is like the grass I decided to chew when I was a child just to see what it was like. I almost fall down the stairs because of the swaying and burst into laughter when the grass tickles my bare feet. I wander toward the orchard.

"Four!" I call out. Why am I calling out a number? Oh yes. Because that's his name. I call out again, "Four! Where are you?"

"Tris?" says a voice from the trees on my right. It almost sounds like the tree is talking to me. I giggle, but of course it's just Tobias, ducking under a branch.

I run toward him, and the ground lurches to the side, so I almost fall. His hand touches my waist, steadies me. The touch sends a shock through my body, and all my insides burn like his fingers ignited them. I pull closer to him, pressing my body against his, and lift my head to kiss him.

"What did they—" he starts, but I stop him with my lips. He kisses me back, but too quickly, so I sigh heavily.

"That was lame," I say. "Okay, no it wasn't, but . . ."

I stand on my tiptoes to kiss him again, and he presses his finger to my lips to stop me.

"Tris," he says. "What did they do to you? You're acting like a lunatic."

"That's not very nice of you to say," I say. "They put me in a good mood, that's all. And now I really want to kiss you, so if you could just *relax*—"

"I'm not going to kiss you. I'm going to figure out what's going on," he says.

I pout my lower lip for a second, but then I grin as the pieces come together in my mind.

"*That's* why you like me!" I exclaim. "Because you're not very nice either! It makes so much more sense now."

"Come on," he says. "We're going to see Johanna."

"I like you, too."

"That's encouraging," he replies flatly. "Come *on*. Oh, for God's sake. I'll just carry you."

He swings me into his arms, one arm under my knees and the other around my back. I wrap my arms around his neck and plant a kiss on his cheek. Then I discover that the air feels nice on my feet when I kick them, so I move my feet up and down as he walks us toward the building where Johanna works.

When we reach her office, she is sitting behind a desk with a stack of paper in front of her, chewing on a pencil eraser. She looks up at us, and her mouth drifts open slightly. A hunk of dark hair covers the left side of her face.

"You really shouldn't cover up your scar," I say. "You look prettier with your hair out of your face."

Tobias sets me down too heavily. The impact is jarring and hurts my shoulder a little, but I like the sound my feet made when they hit the floor. I laugh, but neither Johanna nor Tobias laughs with me. Strange.

"What did you do to her?" Tobias says, terse. "What in God's name did you do?"

"I . . ." Johanna frowns at me. "They must have given her too much. She's very small; they probably didn't take her height and weight into account."

"They must have given her too much of *what*?" he says.

"You have a nice voice," I say.

"Tris," he says, "please be quiet."

"The peace serum," Johanna says. "In small doses, it has a mild, calming effect and improves the mood. The only side effect is some slight dizziness. We administer it to members of our community who have trouble keeping the peace."

Tobias snorts. "I'm not an idiot. *Every* member of your community has trouble keeping the peace, because they're all human. You probably dump it into the water supply."

Johanna does not respond for a few seconds. She folds her hands in front of her.

"Clearly you know that is not the case, or this conflict

would not have occurred," she says. "But whatever we agree to do here, we do together, as a faction. If I could give the serum to everyone in this city, I would. You would certainly not be in the situation you are in now if I had."

"Oh, definitely," he says. "Drugging the entire population is the best solution to our problem. Great plan."

"Sarcasm is not kind, Four," she says gently. "Now, I am sorry about the mistake in giving too much to Tris, I really am. But she violated the terms of our agreement, and I'm afraid that you might not be able to stay here much longer as a result. The conflict between her and the boy—Peter— is not something we can forget."

"Don't worry," says Tobias. "We intend to leave as soon as humanly possible."

"Good," she says with a small smile. "Peace between Amity and Dauntless can only happen when we maintain our distance from each other."

"That explains a lot."

"Excuse me?" she says. "What are you insinuating?"

"It explains," he says, gritting his teeth, "why, under a pretense of *neutrality*—as if such a thing is possible!—you have left us to die at the hands of the Erudite."

Johanna sighs quietly and looks out the window. Beyond it is a small courtyard with vines growing in it. The vines creep onto the window's corners, like they are trying to come in and join the conversation.

"The Amity wouldn't do something like that," I say. "That's *mean*."

"It is for the sake of peace that we remain uninvolved—" Johanna begins.

"Peace." Tobias almost spits the word. "Yes, I'm sure it will be very peaceful when we are all either dead or cowering in submission under the threat of mind control or stuck in an endless simulation."

Johanna's face contorts, and I mimic her, to see what it feels like to have my face that way. It doesn't feel very good. I'm not sure why she did it to begin with.

She says slowly, "The decision was not mine to make. If it was, perhaps we would be having a different conversation right now."

"Are you saying you disagree with them?"

"I am saying," she says, "that it isn't my place to disagree with my faction publicly, but I might, in the privacy of my own heart."

"Tris and I will be gone in two days," says Tobias. "I hope your faction doesn't change their decision to make this compound a safe house."

"Our decisions are not easily unmade. What about Peter?"

"You'll have to deal with him separately," he says.

"Because he won't be coming with us."

Tobias takes my hand, and his skin feels nice against mine, though it's not smooth or soft. I smile apologetically at Johanna, and her expression remains unchanged.

"Four," she says. "If you and your friends would like to remain . . . untouched by our serum, you may want to avoid the bread."

Tobias says thank you over his shoulder as we make our way down the hallway together, me skipping every other step.

CHAPTER
SEVEN

THE SERUM WEARS off five hours later, when the sun is just beginning to set. Tobias shut me in my room for the rest of the day, checking on me every hour. This time when he comes in, I am sitting on the bed, glaring at the wall.

"Thank God," he says, pressing his forehead to the door. "I was beginning to think it would never wear off and I would have to leave you here to . . . smell flowers, or whatever you wanted to do while you were on that stuff."

"I'll kill them," I say. "I will *kill* them."

"Don't bother. We're leaving soon anyway," he says, closing the door behind him. He takes the hard drive from his back pocket. "I thought we could hide this behind your dresser."

"That's where it was before."

"Yeah, and that's why Peter won't look for it here again." Tobias pulls the dresser away from the wall with one hand and wedges the hard drive behind it with the other.

"Why couldn't I fight the peace serum?" I say. "If my brain is weird enough to resist the simulation serum, why not this one?"

"I don't know, really," he says. He drops down next to me on the bed, jostling the mattress. "Maybe in order to fight off a serum, you have to *want* to."

"Well, obviously I *wanted* to," I say, frustrated, but without conviction. Did I want to? Or was it nice to forget about anger, forget about pain, forget about everything for a few hours?

"Sometimes," he says, sliding his arm across my shoulders, "people just want to be happy, even if it's not real."

He's right. Even now, this peace between us comes from not talking about things—about Will, or my parents, or me almost shooting him in the head, or Marcus. But I do not dare to disturb it with the truth, because I am too busy clinging to it for support.

"You might be right," I say quietly.

"Are you *conceding*?" he says, his mouth falling open with mock surprise. "Seems like that serum did you some good after all. . . ."

I shove him as hard as I can. "Take that back. Take it back *now*."

"Okay, okay!" He puts up his hands. "It's just . . . I'm not very nice either, you know. That's why I like you so—"

"Out!" I shout, pointing at the door.

Laughing to himself, Tobias kisses my cheek and leaves the room.

+ + +

That evening, I am too embarrassed by what happened to go to dinner, so I spend the time in the branches of an apple tree at the far end of the orchard, picking ripe apples. I climb as high as I dare to get them, muscles burning. I have discovered that sitting still leaves little spaces for the grief to get in, so I stay busy.

I am wiping my forehead with the hem of my shirt, standing on a branch, when I hear the sound. It is faint, at first, joining the buzz of cicadas. I stand still to listen, and after a moment, I realize what it is: cars.

The Amity own about a dozen trucks that they use for transporting goods, but they only do that on weekends. The back of my neck tingles. If it isn't the Amity, it's probably the Erudite. But I have to be sure.

I grab the branch above me with both hands, but pull myself up with only my left arm. I'm surprised I'm still able to do that. I stand hunched, twigs and leaves tangled in my hair. A few apples fall to the ground when I shift my weight. Apple trees aren't very tall; I may not be able to see far enough.

I use the nearby branches as steps, with my hands to steady me, twisting and leaning around the tree's maze. I remember climbing the Ferris wheel on the pier, my muscles shaking, my hands throbbing. I am wounded now, but stronger, and the climbing feels easier.

The branches get thinner, weaker. I lick my lips and look at the next one. I need to climb as high as possible, but the branch I'm aiming for is short and looks pliable. I put my foot on it, testing its strength. It bends, but holds. I start to lift myself up, to put the other foot down, and the branch snaps.

I gasp as I fall back, seizing the tree trunk at the last second. This will have to be high enough. I stand on my tiptoes and squint in the direction of the sound.

At first I see nothing but a stretch of farmland, a strip of empty ground, the fence, and the fields and beginnings of buildings that lie beyond it. But approaching the gate are a few moving specks—silver, when the light catches them. Cars with black roofs—solar panels, which means only one thing. Erudite.

A breath hisses between my teeth. I don't allow myself

to think; I just put one foot down, then the other, so fast that bark peels off the branches and drifts toward the ground. As soon as my feet touch the earth, I run.

I count the rows of trees as I pass them. *Seven, eight.* The branches dip low, and I pass just beneath them. *Nine, ten.* I hold my right arm against my chest as I sprint faster, the bullet wound in my shoulder throbbing with each footstep. *Eleven, twelve.*

When I reach the thirteenth row, I throw my body to the right, down one of the aisles. The trees are close together in the thirteenth row. Their branches grow into one another, creating a maze of leaves and twigs and apples.

My lungs sting from a lack of oxygen, but I am not far from the end of the orchard. Sweat runs into my eyebrows. I reach the dining hall and throw open the door, shoving my way through a group of Amity men, and he is there; Tobias sits at one end of the cafeteria with Peter and Caleb and Susan. I can barely see them between the spots on my vision, but Tobias touches my shoulder.

"Erudite," is all I manage to say.

"Coming here?" he says.

I nod.

"Do we have time to run?"

I am not sure about that.

By now, the Abnegation at the other end of the table are

paying attention. They gather around us.

"Why do we need to run?" says Susan. "The Amity established this place as a safe house. No conflict allowed."

"The Amity will have trouble enforcing that policy," says Marcus. "How do you stop conflict without conflict?"

Susan nods.

"But we can't leave," Peter says. "We don't have time. They'll see us."

"Tris has a gun," Tobias says. "We can try to fight our way out."

He starts toward the dormitory.

"Wait," I say. "I have an idea." I scan the crowd of Abnegation. "Disguises. The Erudite don't know for sure that we're still here. We can pretend to be Amity."

"Those of us who aren't dressed like the Amity should go to the dormitories, then," Marcus says. "The rest of you, put your hair down; try to mimic their behavior."

The Abnegation who are dressed in gray leave the dining hall in a pack and cross the courtyard to the guests' dormitory. Once inside, I run to my bedroom, get on my hands and knees, and reach under the mattress for the gun.

I feel around for a few seconds before I find it, and when I do, my throat pinches, and I can't swallow. I don't want to touch the gun. I don't want to touch it again.

Come on, Tris. I shove the gun under the waistband of

my red pants. It is lucky they are so baggy. I notice the vials of healing salve and pain medicine on the bedside table and shove them in my pocket, just in case we do manage to escape.

Then I reach behind the dresser for the hard drive.

If the Erudite catch us—which is likely—they will search us, and I don't want to just hand over the attack simulation again. But this hard drive also contains the surveillance footage from the attack. The record of our losses. Of my parents' deaths. The only piece of them I have left. And because the Abnegation don't take photographs, the only documentation I have of how they looked.

Years from now, when my memories begin to fade, what will I have to remind me of what they looked like? Their faces will change in my mind. I will never see them again.

Don't be stupid. It's not important.

I squeeze the hard drive so tightly it hurts.

Then why does it feel *so important?*

"Don't be stupid," I say aloud. I grit my teeth and grab the lamp from my bedside table. I yank the plug from the socket, throw the lampshade onto the bed, and crouch over the hard drive. Blinking tears from my eyes, I slam the base of the lamp into it, creating a dent.

I bring the lamp down again, and again, and again, until the hard drive cracks and pieces of it spread across the floor. Then I kick the shards under the dresser, put the lamp back, and walk into the hallway, wiping my eyes with the back of my hand.

A few minutes later, a small crowd of gray-clad men and women—and Peter—stand in the hallway, sorting through stacks of clothes.

"Tris," says Caleb. "You're still wearing gray."

I pinch my father's shirt, and hesitate.

"It's Dad's," I say. If I change out of it, I will have to leave it behind. I bite my lip so that the pain will steady me. I have to get rid of it. It's just a shirt. That's all it is.

"I'll put it on under mine," Caleb says. "They'll never see it."

I nod and grab a red shirt from the dwindling pile of clothes. It is large enough to conceal the bulge of the gun. I duck into a nearby room to change, and hand off the gray shirt to Caleb when I get to the hallway. The door is open, and through it I see Tobias stuffing Abnegation clothes into the trash bin.

"Do you think the Amity will lie for us?" I ask him, leaning out the open doorway.

"To prevent conflict?" Tobias nods. "Absolutely."

He wears a red collared shirt and a pair of jeans that are fraying at the knee. The combination looks ridiculous on him.

"Nice shirt," I say.

He wrinkles his nose at me. "It was the only thing that covered up the neck tattoo, okay?"

I smile nervously. I forgot about my tattoos, but the shirt hides them well enough.

The Erudite cars pull up to the compound. There are five of them, all silver with black roofs. Their engines seem to purr as the wheels bump over uneven ground. I slip just inside the building, leaving the door open behind me, and Tobias busies himself with the latch on the trash bin.

The cars all pull to a stop, and the doors pop open, revealing at least five men and women in Erudite blue.

And about fifteen in Dauntless black.

When the Dauntless come closer, I see strips of blue fabric wrapped around their arms that can only signify their allegiance to Erudite. The faction that enslaved their minds.

Tobias takes my hand and leads me into the dormitory.

"I didn't think our faction would be that stupid," he says. "You have the gun, right?"

"Yes," I say. "But there's no guarantee I can fire it with any accuracy with my left hand."

"You should work on that," he says. Always an instructor.

"I will," I say. I shake a little as I add, "If we live."

His hands skim my bare arms. "Just bounce a little when you walk," he says, kissing my forehead, "and pretend you're afraid of their guns"—another kiss between my eyebrows—"and act like the shrinking violet you could never be"—a kiss on my cheek—"and you'll be fine."

"Okay," I say. My hands tremble as I grip his shirt collar. I pull his mouth down to mine.

A bell sounds, once, twice, three times. It is a summons to the dining hall, where the Amity gather for less formal occasions than the meeting we attended. We join the crowd of Abnegation-turned-Amity.

I pull pins from Susan's hair—the hairstyle is too severe for Amity. She gives me a small, grateful smile as her hair falls on her shoulders, the first time I have ever seen it that way. It softens her square jaw.

I am supposed to be braver than the Abnegation, but they don't seem as worried as I am. They offer each other smiles and walk in silence—in too much silence. I wedge my way between them and jab one of the older women in the shoulder.

"Tell the kids to play tag," I say to her.

"Tag?" she says.

"They're acting respectful and . . . Stiff," I say, cringing as I say the word that was my nickname in Dauntless.

"And Amity kids would be causing a ruckus. Just do it, okay?"

The woman touches one Abnegation child on the shoulder and whispers something to him, and a few seconds later a small group of children run down the hallway, dodging Amity feet and yelling, "I touched you! You're *it*!" "No, that was my sleeve!"

Caleb catches on, jabbing Susan in the ribs so she shrieks with laughter. I try to relax, injecting a bounce into my step as Tobias suggested, letting my arms swing as I turn corners. It is amazing how pretending to be in a different faction changes everything—even the way I walk. That must be why it's so strange that I could easily belong in three of them.

We catch up to the Amity in front of us as we cross the courtyard to the dining hall and disperse among them. I keep Tobias in my peripheral vision, not wanting to stray too far from him. The Amity don't ask questions; they just let us dissolve into their faction.

A pair of Dauntless traitors stand by the door to the dining hall, their guns in hand, and I stiffen. It feels real to me, suddenly, that I am unarmed and being herded into a building surrounded by Erudite and Dauntless, and if they discover me, there will be nowhere to run. They will shoot me on the spot.

I consider making a break for it. But where would I go that they could not catch me? I try to breathe normally. I am almost past them—*don't look, don't look.* A few steps away—*eyes away, away.*

Susan loops her arm through mine.

"I'm telling you a joke," she says, "that you find very funny."

I cover my hand with my mouth and force a giggle that sounds high-pitched and foreign, but judging by the smile she gives me, it was believable. We hang on each other the way Amity girls do, glancing at the Dauntless and then giggling again. I am amazed by how I manage to do it, with the leaden feeling inside me.

"Thank you," I mutter once we're inside.

"You're welcome," she replies.

Tobias sits across from me at one of the long tables, and Susan sits next to me. The rest of the Abnegation spread throughout the room, and Caleb and Peter are a few seats down from me.

I tap my fingers on my knees as we wait for something to happen. For a long time we just sit there, and I pretend to be listening to an Amity girl telling a story on my left. But every so often I look at Tobias, and he looks back at me, like we're passing fear back and forth between us.

Finally Johanna walks in with an Erudite woman. Her

bright blue shirt seems to glow against her skin, which is dark brown. She searches the room as she speaks to Johanna. I hold my breath as her eyes find me—and then let it out when she moves on without a moment's hesitation. She did not recognize me.

At least, not yet.

Someone bangs on a tabletop, and the room goes quiet. This is it. This is the moment she either hands us over, or doesn't.

"Our Erudite and Dauntless friends are looking for some people," Johanna says. "Several members of Abnegation, three members of Dauntless, and a former Erudite initiate." She smiles. "In the interest of full cooperation, I told them that the people they were looking for were, in fact, here, but have since moved on. They would like permission to search the premises, which means we have to vote. Does anyone object to a search?"

The tension in her voice suggests that if anyone does object, they should keep their mouth shut. I don't know if the Amity pick up on that kind of thing, but no one says anything. Johanna nods to the Erudite woman.

"Three of you stick around," the woman says to the Dauntless guards clustered by the entrance. "The rest of you, search all the buildings and report back if you find anything. Go."

There is so much they could find. The pieces of the hard drive. Clothes I forgot to throw out. A suspicious lack of trinkets and decorations in our living spaces. I feel my pulse behind my eyes as the three Dauntless soldiers who stayed behind pace up and down the rows of tables.

The back of my neck tingles as one of them walks behind me, his footsteps loud and heavy. Not for the first time in my life, I'm glad that I'm small and plain. I don't draw people's eyes to me.

But Tobias does. He wears his pride in his posture, in the way his eyes claim everything they land on. That is not an Amity trait. It can only be a Dauntless one.

The Dauntless woman walking toward him looks at him right away. Her eyes narrow as she walks closer, and then stops directly behind him.

I wish the collar of his shirt were higher. I wish he didn't have so many tattoos. I wish . . .

"Your hair is pretty short for an Amity," she says.

. . . he did not cut his hair like the Abnegation.

"It's hot," he says.

The excuse might work if he knew how to deliver it, but he says it with a snap.

She stretches out her hand and, with her index finger, pulls back the collar of his shirt to see his tattoo.

And Tobias moves.

He grabs the woman's wrist, yanking her forward so she loses her balance. She hits her head against the edge of the table and falls. Across the room, a gun goes off, someone screams, and everyone dives under the tables or crouches next to the benches.

Everyone except me. I sit where I was before the gunshot sounded, clutching the edge of the table. I know that's where I am, but I don't see the cafeteria anymore. I see the alley I escaped down after my mother died. I stare at the gun in my hands, at the smooth skin between Will's eyebrows.

A small sound gurgles in my throat. It would have been a scream if my teeth had not been clamped shut. The flash of memory fades, but I still can't move.

Tobias grabs the Dauntless woman by the back of her neck and wrenches her to her feet. He has her gun in his hand. He uses her to shield him as he fires over her right shoulder at the Dauntless soldier across the room.

"Tris!" he shouts. "A little help here?"

I pull my shirt up just far enough to reach the handle of the gun, and my fingers meet metal. It feels so cold that it hurts my fingertips, but that can't be; it's so hot in here. A Dauntless man at the end of the aisle aims his own revolver at me. The black spot at the end of the barrel grows around me, and I can hear my heart but nothing else.

Caleb lunges forward and grabs my gun. He holds it in both hands and fires at the knees of the Dauntless man who stands just feet away from him.

The Dauntless man screams and collapses, his hands clutching his leg, which gives Tobias the opportunity to shoot him in the head. His pain is momentary.

My entire body is trembling and I can't stop it. Tobias still has the Dauntless woman by the throat, but this time, he aims his gun at the Erudite woman.

"Say another word," says Tobias, "and I'll shoot."

The Erudite woman's mouth is open, but she doesn't speak.

"Whoever's with us should start running," Tobias says, his voice filling the room.

All at once, the Abnegation rise from their places under tables and benches, and start toward the door. Caleb pulls me up from the bench. I start toward the door.

Then I see something. A twitch, a flicker of movement. The Erudite woman lifts a small gun, points it at a man in a yellow shirt in front of me. Instinct, not presence of mind, pushes me into a dive. My hands collide with the man, and the bullet hits the wall instead of him, instead of me.

"Put the gun down," says Tobias, pointing his revolver at the Erudite woman. "I have *very* good aim, and I'm betting that you don't."

I blink a few times to get the blurriness out of my eyes. Peter stares back at me. I just saved his life. He does not thank me, and I don't acknowledge him.

The Erudite woman drops her gun. Together Peter and I walk toward the door. Tobias follows us, walking backward so he can keep his gun on the Erudite woman. At the last second before he passes through the threshold, he slams the door between him and her.

And we all run.

We sprint down the center aisle of the orchard in a breathless pack. The night air is heavy as a blanket and smells like rain. Shouts follow us. Car doors slam. I run faster than I can possibly run, like I'm breathing adrenaline instead of air. The purr of engines chases me into the trees. Tobias's hand closes around mine.

We run through a cornfield in a long line. By then, the cars have caught up to us. The headlights creep through the tall stalks, illuminating a leaf here, an ear of corn there.

"Split up!" someone yells, and it sounds like Marcus.

We divide and spread through the field like spilling water. I grab Caleb's arm. I hear Susan gasping behind Caleb.

We crash over cornstalks. The heavy leaves cut my

cheeks and arms. I stare between Tobias's shoulder blades as we run. I hear a heavy thump and a scream. There are screams everywhere, to my left, to my right. Gunshots. The Abnegation are dying again, dying like they were when I pretended to be under the simulation. And all I'm doing is running.

Finally we reach the fence. Tobias runs along it, pushing it until he finds a hole. He holds the chain links back so Caleb, Susan, and I can crawl through. Before we start running again, I stop and look back at the cornfield we just left. I see headlights distantly glowing. But I don't hear anything.

"Where are the others?" whispers Susan.

I say, "Gone."

Susan sobs. Tobias pulls me to his side roughly, and starts forward. My face burns with shallow cuts from the corn leaves, but my eyes are dry. The Abnegation deaths are just another weight I am unable to set down.

We stay away from the dirt road the Erudite and Dauntless took to get to the Amity compound, following the train tracks toward the city. There is nowhere to hide out here, no trees or buildings that can shield us, but it doesn't matter. The Erudite can't drive through the fence anyway, and it will take them a while to reach the gate.

"I have to . . . stop . . ." says Susan from somewhere in

the darkness behind me.

We stop. Susan collapses to the ground, crying, and Caleb crouches next to her. Tobias and I look toward the city, which is still illuminated, because it's not midnight yet. I want to feel something. Fear, anger, grief. But I don't. All I feel is the need to keep moving.

Tobias turns toward me.

"What was that, Tris?" he says.

"What?" I say, and I am ashamed of how weak my voice sounds. I don't know whether he's talking about Peter or what came before or something else.

"You froze! Someone was about to kill you and you just *sat* there!" He is yelling now. "I thought I could rely on you at least to save your own life!"

"Hey!" says Caleb. "Give her a break, all right?"

"No," says Tobias, staring at me. "She doesn't need a break." His voice softens. "What happened?"

He still believes that I am strong. Strong enough that I don't need his sympathy. I used to think he was right, but now I am not sure. I clear my throat.

"I panicked," I say. "It won't happen again."

He raises an eyebrow.

"It won't," I say again, louder this time.

"Okay." He looks unconvinced. "We have to get somewhere safe. They'll regroup and start looking for us."

"You think they care that much about us?" I say.

"Us, yes," he says. "We were probably the only ones they were really after, apart from Marcus, who is most likely dead."

I don't know how I expected him to say it—with relief, maybe, because Marcus, his father and the menace of his life, is finally gone. Or with pain and sadness, because his father might have been killed, and sometimes grief doesn't make much sense. But he says it like it's just a fact, like the direction we're moving or the time of day.

"Tobias . . ." I start to say, but then I realize I don't know what comes after it.

"Time to go," Tobias says over his shoulder.

Caleb coaxes Susan to her feet. She moves only with the help of his arm across her back, pressing her forward.

I didn't realize until that moment that Dauntless initiation had taught me an important lesson: how to keep going.

CHAPTER
EIGHT

WE DECIDE TO follow the railroad tracks to the city, because none of us is good at navigation. I walk from tie to tie, Tobias balances on the rail, wobbling only occasionally, and Caleb and Susan shuffle behind us. I twitch at every unidentified noise, tensing until I realize it is just the wind, or the squeak of Tobias's shoes on the rail. I wish we could keep running, but it's a feat that my legs are even moving at this point.

Then I hear a low groan from the rails.

I bend down and press my palms to the rail, closing my eyes to focus on the feeling of the metal beneath my hands. The vibration feels like a sigh going through my body. I stare between Susan's knees down the tracks and see no train light, but that doesn't mean anything. The train could be running with no horns and no lamps to announce its arrival.

I see the gleam of a small train car, far away now but approaching fast.

"It's coming," I say. It is an effort to get to my feet when all I want to do is sit down, but I do, brushing my hands on my jeans. "I think we should get on."

"Even if it's run by the Erudite?" says Caleb.

"If the Erudite were running the train, they would have taken it to the Amity compound to look for us," Tobias says. "I think it's worth the risk. We'll be able to hide in the city. Here we're just waiting for them to find us."

We all get off the tracks. Caleb gives Susan step-by-step instructions for getting on a moving train, the way only a former Erudite can. I watch the first car approach; listen to the rhythmic bump of the car over the ties, the whisper of metal wheel against metal rail.

As the first car passes me, I start to run. I ignore the burning in my legs. Caleb helps Susan into a middle car first, then jumps in himself. I take a quick breath and throw my body to the right, slamming into the floor of the car with my legs dangling over the edge. Caleb grabs my left arm and pulls me in the rest of the way. Tobias uses the handle to swing himself in after me.

I look up, and stop breathing.

Eyes glitter in the darkness. Dark shapes sit in the car, more numerous than we are.

The factionless.

+ + +

The wind whistles through the car. Everyone is on their feet and armed—except Susan and me, who have no weapons. A factionless man with an eye patch has a gun pointed at Tobias. I wonder how he got it.

Next to him, an older factionless woman holds a knife— the kind I used to cut bread with. Behind him, someone else holds a large plank of wood with a nail sticking out of it.

"I've never seen the Amity armed before," the factionless woman with the knife says.

The factionless man with the gun looks familiar. He wears tattered clothes in different colors—a black T-shirt with a torn Abnegation jacket over it, blue jeans mended with red thread, brown boots. All faction clothing is represented in the group before me: black Candor pants paired with black Dauntless shirts, yellow dresses with blue sweatshirts over them. Most items are torn or smudged in some way, but some are not. Freshly stolen, I imagine.

"They aren't Amity," the man with the gun says. "They're Dauntless."

Then I recognize him: he is Edward, a fellow initiate who left Dauntless after Peter attacked him with a butter knife. That is why he wears an eye patch.

I remember steadying his head as he lay screaming on the floor, and cleaning the blood he left behind.

"Hello, Edward," I say.

He inclines his head to me, but doesn't lower his gun. "Tris."

"Whatever you are," the woman says, "you'll have to get off this train if you want to stay alive."

"Please," says Susan, her lip wobbling. Her eyes fill with tears. "We've been running . . . and the rest of them are dead and I don't . . ." She starts to sob again. "I don't think I can keep going, I . . ."

I get the strange urge to hit my head against the wall. Other people's sobs make me uncomfortable. It's selfish of me, maybe.

"We're running from the Erudite," says Caleb. "If we get off, it will be easier for them to find us. So we would appreciate it if you let us ride into the city with you."

"Yeah?" Edward tilts his head. "What have you ever done for us?"

"I helped you when no one else would," I say. "Remember?"

"You, maybe. But the others?" says Edward. "Not so much."

Tobias steps forward, so Edward's gun is almost against his throat.

"My name is Tobias Eaton," Tobias says. "I don't think you want to push me off this train."

The effect of the name on the people in the car is immediate and bewildering: they lower their weapons. They exchange meaningful looks.

"Eaton? Really?" Edward says, eyebrows raised. "I have to admit, I did not see that coming." He clears his throat. "Fine, you can come. But when we get to the city, you've got to come with us."

Then he smiles a little. "We know someone who's been looking for you, Tobias Eaton."

+++

Tobias and I sit on the edge of the car with our legs dangling over the edge.

"Do you know who it is?"

Tobias nods.

"Who, then?"

"It's hard to explain," he says. "I have a lot to tell you."

I lean against him.

"Yeah," I say. "So do I."

+ + +

I don't know how much time passes before they tell us to get off. But when they do, we are in the part of the city where the factionless live, about a mile from where I grew up. I recognize each building we pass as one I walked by every time I missed the bus home from school. The one with the broken bricks. The one with a fallen streetlight leaning against it.

We stand in the doorway of the train car, all four of us in a line. Susan whimpers.

"What if we get hurt?" she says.

I grab her hand. "We'll jump together. You and me. I've done this a dozen times and never got hurt."

She nods and squeezes my fingers so hard they hurt.

"On three. One," I say, "Two. *Three*."

I jump, and pull her with me. My feet slam into the ground and continue forward, but Susan just falls to the pavement and rolls onto her side. Aside from a scraped knee, though, she seems to be all right. The others jump off without difficulty—even Caleb, who has only jumped from a train once before, as far as I know.

I'm not sure who could know Tobias among the factionless. It could be Drew or Molly, who failed Dauntless initiation—but they didn't even know Tobias's real name, and besides, Edward probably would have killed them by now, judging by how ready he was to shoot us. It must be someone from Abnegation, or from school.

Susan seems to have calmed down. She walks on her own now, next to Caleb, and her cheeks are drying with no new tears to wet them.

Tobias walks beside me, touching my shoulder lightly.

"It's been a while since I checked that shoulder," he says. "How is it?"

"Okay. I brought the pain medicine, luckily," I say. I'm glad to talk about something light—as light as a wound can be, anyway. "I don't think I'm letting it heal very well. I keep using my arm or landing on it."

"There will be plenty of time for healing once all this is over."

"Yeah." *Or it won't matter if I heal,* I add silently, *because I'll be dead.*

"Here," he says, taking a small knife from his back pocket and handing it to me. "Just in case."

I put it in my own pocket. I feel even more nervous now.

The factionless lead us down the street and left into a grimy alleyway that stinks of garbage. Rats scatter in front of us with squeaks of terror, and I see only their tails, slipping between mounds of waste, empty trash cans, soggy cardboard boxes. I breathe through my mouth so I don't throw up.

Edward stops next to one of the crumbling brick buildings and forces a steel door open. I wince, half expecting the entire building to fall down if he pulls too hard. The windows are so thick with grime that almost no light penetrates them. We follow Edward into a dank room. In the flickering glow of a lantern, I see . . . people.

People sitting next to rolls of bedding. People prying open cans of food. People sipping bottles of water. And children, weaving between the groups of adults, not confined to a particular color of clothing—factionless children.

We are in a factionless storehouse, and the factionless, who are supposed to be scattered, isolated, and without community . . . are together inside it. Are together, like a *faction*.

I don't know what I expected of them, but I am surprised by how normal they seem. They don't fight one another or avoid one another. Some of them tell jokes, others speak to each other quietly. Gradually, though, they all seem to realize that we aren't supposed to be there.

"Come on," Edward says, bending his finger to beckon

us toward him. "She's back here."

Stares and silence greet us as we follow Edward deeper into the building that is supposed to be abandoned. Finally I can't contain my questions any longer.

"What's going on here? Why are you all together like this?"

"You thought they—we—were all split up," Edward says over his shoulder. "Well, they were, for a while. Too hungry to do much of anything except look for food. But then the Stiffs started giving them food, clothes, tools, everything. And they got stronger, and waited. They were like that when I found them, and they welcomed me."

We walk into a dark hallway. I feel at home, in the dark and the quiet that are like the tunnels in Dauntless headquarters. Tobias, however, winds a loose thread from his shirt around his finger, backward and forward, over and over. He knows who we're meeting, but I still have no idea. How is it I know this little about the boy who says he loves me—the boy whose real name is powerful enough to keep us alive in a train car full of enemies?

Edward stops at a metal door and pounds on it with his fist.

"Wait, you said they were waiting?" says Caleb. "What were they waiting *for*, exactly?"

"For the world to fall apart," Edward says. "And now it has."

The door opens, and a severe-looking woman with a lazy eye stands in the doorway. Her steady eye scans the four of us.

"Strays?" she says.

"Not hardly, Therese." He jabs his thumb over his shoulder, at Tobias. "This one's Tobias Eaton."

Therese stares at Tobias for a few seconds, then nods. "He certainly is. Hold on."

She shuts the door again. Tobias swallows hard, his Adam's apple bobbing.

"You know who she's going to get, don't you," says Caleb to Tobias.

"Caleb," Tobias says. "Please shut up."

To my surprise, my brother suppresses his Erudite curiosity.

The door opens again, and Therese steps back to let us in. We walk into an old boiler room with machinery that emerges from the darkness so suddenly I hit it with my knees and elbows. Therese leads us through the maze of metal to the back of the room, where several bulbs dangle from the ceiling over a table.

A middle-aged woman stands behind the table. She has curly black hair and olive skin. Her features are stern, so angular they almost make her unattractive, but not quite.

Tobias clutches my hand. At that moment I realize that he and the woman have the same nose—hooked, a little too big on her face but the right size on his. They also have the same strong jaw, distinct chin, spare upper lip, stick-out ears. Only her eyes are different—instead of blue, they are so dark they look black.

"Evelyn," he says, his voice shaking a little.

Evelyn was the name of Marcus's wife and Tobias's mother. My grip on Tobias's hand loosens. Just days ago I was remembering her funeral. Her *funeral*. And now she stands in front of me, her eyes colder than the eyes of any Abnegation woman I've ever seen.

"Hello." She walks around the table, surveying him. "You look older."

"Yes, well. The passage of time tends to do that to a person."

He already knew she was alive. How long ago did he find out?

She smiles. "So you've finally come—"

"Not for the reason you think," he interrupts her. "We were running from Erudite, and the only chance of escape we had required me to tell your poorly armed lackeys my name."

She must have made him angry somehow. But I can't

help but think that if I discovered my mother was alive after thinking she was dead for so long, I would never speak to her the way Tobias speaks to his mother now, no matter what she had done.

The truth of that thought makes me ache. I push it aside and focus instead on what's in front of me. On the table behind Evelyn is a large map with markers all over it. A map of the city, obviously, but I'm not sure what the markers mean. On the wall behind her is a chalkboard with a chart on it. I can't decipher the information in the chart; it's written in shorthand I don't know.

"I see." Evelyn's smile remains, but without its former touch of amusement. "Introduce me to your fellow refugees, then."

Her eyes drift down to our joined hands. Tobias's fingers spring apart. He gestures to me first. "This is Tris Prior. Her brother, Caleb. And their friend Susan Black."

"Prior," she says. "I know of several Priors, but none of them are named Tris. Beatrice, however . . ."

"Well," I say, "I know of several living Eatons, but none of them are named Evelyn."

"Evelyn Johnson is the name I prefer. Particularly among a pack of Abnegation."

"Tris is the name *I* prefer," I reply. "And we're not Abnegation. Not all of us, anyway."

Evelyn gives Tobias a look. "Interesting friends you've made."

"Those are population counts?" says Caleb from behind me. He walks forward, his mouth open. "And . . . what? Factionless safe houses?" He points to the first line on the chart, which reads 7 . . . . *Grn Hse.* "I mean, these places, on the map? They're safe houses, like this one, right?"

"That's a lot of questions," says Evelyn, arching an eyebrow. I recognize the expression. It belongs to Tobias—as does her distaste for questions. "For security purposes, I will not answer any of them. Anyway, it is time for dinner."

She gestures toward the door. Susan and Caleb start toward it, followed by me, and Tobias and his mother are last. We work our way through the maze of machinery again.

"I'm not stupid," she says in a low voice. "I know you want nothing to do with me—though I still don't quite understand why—"

Tobias snorts.

"But," she says, "I will extend my invitation again. We could use your help here, and I know you are like-minded about the faction system—"

"Evelyn," Tobias says. "I chose Dauntless."

"Choices can be made again."

"What makes you think I'm interested in spending time anywhere *near* you?" he demands. I hear his footsteps stop, and slow down so I can hear how she responds.

"Because I'm your mother," she says, and her voice almost breaks over the words, uncharacteristically vulnerable. "Because you're my son."

"You really don't get it," he says. "You don't have the vaguest conception of what you've done to me." He sounds breathless. "I don't want to join up with your little band of factionless. I want to get out of here as quickly as possible."

"My *little* band of factionless is twice the size of Dauntless," says Evelyn. "You would do well to take it seriously. Its actions may determine the future of this city."

With that, she walks ahead of him, and ahead of me. Her words echo in my mind: *Twice the size of Dauntless.* When did they become so large?

Tobias looks at me, eyebrows lowered.

"How long have you known?" I say.

"About a year." He slumps against the wall and closes his eyes. "She sent a coded message to me in Dauntless, telling me to meet her at the train yard. I did, because I was curious, and there she was. Alive. It wasn't a happy reunion, as you can probably guess."

"Why did she leave Abnegation?"

"She had an affair." He shakes his head. "And no

wonder, since my father . . ." He shakes his head again. "Well, let's just say Marcus wasn't any nicer to her than he was to me."

"Is . . . that why you're angry with her? Because she was unfaithful to him?"

"No," he says too sternly, his eyes opening. "No, that's not why I'm angry."

I walk toward him as if approaching a wild animal, each footstep careful on the cement floor. "Then why?"

"She had to leave my father, I get that," he says. "But did she think of taking me with her?"

I purse my lips. "Oh. She left you with *him.*"

She left him alone with his worst nightmare. No wonder he hates her.

"Yeah." He kicks at the floor. "She did."

My fingers find his, fumbling, and he guides them into the spaces between his own. I know that's enough questions, for now, so I let the silence linger between us until he decides to break it.

"It seems to me," he says, "that the factionless are better friends than enemies."

"Maybe. But what would the cost of that friendship be?" I say.

He shakes his head. "I don't know. But we may not have any other option."

CHAPTER NINE

ONE OF THE factionless started a fire so we could heat up our food. Those who want to eat sit in a circle around the large metal bowl that contains the fire, first heating the cans, then passing out spoons and forks, then passing cans around so everyone can have a bite of everything. I try not to think about how many diseases could spread this way as I dip my spoon into a can of soup.

Edward drops to the ground next to me and takes the can of soup from my hands.

"So you were all Abnegation, huh?" He shovels several noodles and a piece of carrot into his mouth, and passes the can to the woman on his left.

"We were," I say. "But obviously Tobias and I transferred, and . . ." Suddenly it occurs to me that I shouldn't tell anyone Caleb joined Erudite. "Caleb and Susan are still Abnegation."

"And he's your brother. Caleb," he says. "You ditched your family to become Dauntless?"

"You sound like the Candor," I say irritably. "Mind keeping your judgments to yourself?"

Therese leans over. "He was Erudite first, actually. Not Candor."

"Yeah, I know," I say, "I—"

She interrupts me. "So was I. Had to leave, though."

"What happened?"

"I wasn't smart enough." She shrugs and takes a can of beans from Edward, plunging her spoon into it. "I didn't get a high enough score on my initiation intelligence test. So they said, 'Spend your entire life cleaning up the research labs, or leave.' And I left."

She looks down and licks her spoon clean. I take the beans from her and pass them along to Tobias, who is staring at the fire.

"Are many of you from Erudite?" I say.

Therese shakes her head. "Most are from Dauntless, actually." She jerks her head toward Edward, who scowls. "Then Erudite, then Candor, then a handful of Amity. No one fails Abnegation initiation, though, so we have very few of those, except for a bunch who survived the simulation attack and came to us for refuge."

"I guess I shouldn't be surprised about Dauntless," I say.

"Well, yeah. You've got one of the worst initiations, and there's that whole old-age thing."

"Old-age thing?" I say. I glance at Tobias. He is listening now, and he looks almost normal again, his eyes thoughtful and dark in the firelight.

"Once the Dauntless reach a certain level of physical deterioration," he says, "they are asked to leave. In one way or another."

"What's the other way?" My heart pounds, like it already knows an answer I can't face without prompting.

"Let's just say," says Tobias, "that for some, death is preferable to factionlessness."

"Those people are idiots," says Edward. "I'd rather be factionless than Dauntless."

"How fortunate that you ended up where you did, then," says Tobias coldly.

"Fortunate?" Edward snorts. "Yeah. I'm so fortunate, with my one eye and all."

"I seem to recall hearing rumors that you provoked that attack," says Tobias.

"What are you talking about?" I say. "He was winning, that's all, and Peter was jealous, so he just . . ."

I see the smirk on Edward's face and stop talking. Maybe I don't know everything about what happened during initiation.

"There was an inciting incident," says Edward. "In which Peter did not come out the victor. But it certainly didn't warrant a butter knife to the eye."

"No arguments here," says Tobias. "If it makes you feel any better, he got shot in the arm from a foot away during the simulation attack."

And it does seem to make Edward feel better, because his smirk carves a deeper line into his face.

"Who did that?" he says. "You?"

Tobias shakes his head. "Tris did."

"Well done," Edward says.

I nod, but I feel a little sick to be congratulated for that. Well, not *that* sick. It was Peter, after all.

I stare at the flames wrapping around the fragments of wood that fuel them. They move and shift, like my thoughts. I remember the first time I realized I had never seen an elderly Dauntless. And when I realized my father was too old to climb the paths of the Pit. Now I understand more about that than I'd like to.

"Do you know much about how things are right now?"

Tobias asks Edward. "Did all the Dauntless side with Erudite? Has Candor done anything?"

"Dauntless is split in half," Edward says, talking around the food in his mouth. "Half at Erudite headquarters, half at Candor headquarters. What's left of Abnegation is with us. Nothing much has happened yet. Except for whatever happened to you, I guess."

Tobias nods. I feel a little relieved to know that half of the Dauntless, at least, are not traitors.

I eat spoonful after spoonful until my stomach is full. Then Tobias gets us sleeping pallets and blankets, and I find an empty corner for us to lie down in. When he bends over to untie his shoes, I see the symbol of Amity on the small of his back, the branches curling over his spine. When he straightens, I step across the blankets and put my arms around him, brushing the tattoo with my fingers.

Tobias closes his eyes. I trust the dwindling fire to disguise us as I run my hand up his back, touching each tattoo without seeing it. I imagine Erudite's staring eye, Candor's unbalanced scales, Abnegation's clasped hands, and the Dauntless flames. With my other hand I find the patch of fire tattooed over his rib cage. I feel his heavy breaths against my cheek.

"I wish we were alone," he says.

"I almost always wish that," I say.

I drift off to sleep, carried by the sound of distant conversations. These days it's easier for me to fall asleep when there is noise around me. I can focus on the sound instead of whatever thoughts would crawl into my head in silence. Noise and activity are the refuges of the bereaved and the guilty.

I wake when the fire is just a glow, and only a few of the factionless are still up. It takes me a few seconds to figure out why I woke up: I heard Evelyn's and Tobias's voices, a few feet away from me. I stay still and hope they don't discover that I'm awake.

"You'll have to tell me what's going on here if you expect me to consider helping you," he says. "Though I'm still not sure why you need me at all."

I see Evelyn's shadow on the wall, flickering with the fire. She is lean and strong, just like Tobias. Her fingers twist into her hair as she speaks.

"What would you like to know, exactly?"

"Tell me about the chart. And the map."

"Your friend was correct in thinking that the map and the chart listed all of our safe houses," she says. "He was wrong about the population counts . . . sort of. The numbers don't document all the factionless—only certain ones. And I'll bet you can guess which ones those are."

"I'm not in the mood for guessing."

She sighs. "The Divergent. We're documenting the Divergent."

"How do you know who they are?"

"Before the simulation attack, part of the Abnegation aid effort involved testing the factionless for a certain genetic anomaly," she says. "Sometimes that testing involved re-administering the aptitude test. Sometimes it was more complicated than that. But they explained to us that they suspected we might have the highest Divergent population of any group in the city."

"I don't understand. Why—"

"Why would the factionless have a high Divergent population?" It sounds like she's smirking. "Obviously those who can't confine themselves to a particular way of thinking would be most likely to leave a faction or fail its initiation, right?"

"That's not what I was going to ask," he says. "I want to know why *you* care how many Divergent there are."

"The Erudite are looking for manpower. They found it temporarily in Dauntless. Now they'll be looking for more, and we're the obvious place, unless they figure out that we've got more Divergent than any other group. Just in case they don't, I want to know how many people we've got who are resistant to simulations."

"Fair enough," he says, "but why were the Abnegation so concerned with finding the Divergent? It wasn't to help Jeanine, was it?"

"Of course not," she says. "But I'm afraid I don't know. The Abnegation were reluctant to provide information that only serves to relieve curiosity. They told us as much as they believed we should know."

"Strange," he mumbles.

"Perhaps you should ask your father about it," she says. "He was the one who told me about you."

"About me," says Tobias. "What about me?"

"That he suspected you were Divergent," she says. "He was always watching you. Noting your behavior. He was very attentive to you. That's why . . . that's why I thought you would be safe with him. Safer with him than with me."

Tobias says nothing.

"I see now that I must have been wrong."

He still says nothing.

"I wish—" she starts.

"Don't you dare try to apologize." His voice shakes. "This is not something you can bandage with a word or two and some hugging, or something."

"Okay," she says. "Okay. I won't."

"For what purpose are the factionless uniting?" he says. "What do you intend to do?"

"We want to usurp Erudite," she says. "Once we get rid of them, there's not much stopping us from controlling the government ourselves."

"That's what you expect me to help you with. Overthrowing one corrupt government and instating some kind of factionless tyranny." He snorts. "Not a chance."

"We don't want to be tyrants," she says. "We want to establish a new society. One without factions."

My mouth goes dry. No factions? A world in which no one knows who they are or where they fit? I can't even fathom it. I imagine only chaos and isolation.

Tobias lets out a laugh. "Right. So how are you going to usurp Erudite?"

"Sometimes drastic change requires drastic measures." Evelyn's shadow lifts a shoulder. "I imagine it will involve a high level of destruction."

I shiver at the word "destruction." Somewhere in the darker parts of me, I crave destruction, as long as it is Erudite being destroyed. But the word carries new meaning for me, now that I have seen what it can look like: gray-clothed bodies slung across curbs and over sidewalks, Abnegation leaders shot on their front lawns, next to their mailboxes. I press my face into the pallet I'm sleeping on, so hard it hurts my forehead, just to force the memory out, out, *out*.

"As for why we need you," Evelyn says. "In order to do this, we will need Dauntless's help. They have the weapons and the combat experience. You could bridge the gap between us and them."

"Do you think I'm important to the Dauntless? Because I'm not. I'm just someone who isn't afraid of much."

"What I am suggesting," she says, "is that you *become* important." She stands, her shadow stretching from ceiling to floor. "I am sure you can find a way, if you want to. Think about it."

She pulls back her curly hair and ties it in a knot. "The door is always open."

A few minutes later he lies next to me again. I don't want to admit that I was eavesdropping, but I want to tell him I don't trust Evelyn, or the factionless, or anyone who speaks so casually about demolishing an entire faction.

Before I can muster the courage to speak, his breaths become even, and he falls asleep.

CHAPTER
TEN

I RUN MY hand over the back of my neck to lift the hair that sticks there. My entire body aches, especially my legs, which burn with lactic acid even when I am not moving. And I don't smell very good. I need to shower.

I wander down the hall and into the bathroom. I am not the only person with bathing in mind—a group of women stand at the sinks, half of them naked, the other half completely unfazed by it. I find a free sink in the corner and stick my head under the faucet, letting cold water spill over my ears.

"Hello," Susan says. I turn my head to the side. Water courses down my cheek and into my nose. She is carrying two towels: one white, one gray, both frayed at the edges.

"Hi," I say.

"I have an idea," she says. She turns her back to me and holds up a towel, blocking my view of the rest of the bathroom. I sigh with relief. Privacy. Or as much of it as possible.

I strip quickly and grab the bar of soap next to the sink.

"How are you?" she says.

"I'm fine." I know she's only asking because faction rules dictate that she does. I wish she would just speak to me freely. "How are you, Susan?"

"Better. Therese told me there is a large group of Abnegation refugees in one of the factionless safe houses," says Susan as I lather soap into my hair.

"Oh?" I say. I shove my head under the faucet again, this time massaging my scalp with my left hand to get the soap out. "Are you going to go?"

"Yes," says Susan. "Unless you need my help."

"Thanks for the offer, but I think your faction needs you more," I say, turning off the faucet. I wish I didn't have to get dressed. It's too hot for denim pants. But I grab the other towel from the floor and dry myself in a hurry.

I put on the red shirt I was wearing before. I don't want to put on something that dirty again, but I have no other choice.

"I suspect some of the factionless women have spare clothes," says Susan.

"You're probably right. Okay, your turn."

I stand with the towel as Susan washes up. My arms start to ache after a while, but she ignored the pain for me, so I'll do the same for her. Water splashes on my ankles when she washes her hair.

"This is a situation I never thought we would be in together," I say after a while. "Bathing from the sink of an abandoned building, on the run from the Erudite."

"I thought we would live near each other," says Susan. "Go to social events together. Have our kids walk to the bus stop together."

I bite my lip at that. It is my fault, of course, that that was never a possibility, because I chose another faction.

"I'm sorry, I didn't mean to bring it up," she says. "I just regret that I didn't pay more attention. If I had, maybe I would have known what you were going through. I acted selfishly."

I laugh a little. "Susan, there's nothing wrong with the way you acted."

"I'm done," she says. "Can you hand me that towel?"

I close my eyes and turn so she can grab the towel from my hands. When Therese walks into the bathroom, smoothing her hair into a braid, Susan asks her for spare clothes.

By the time we leave the bathroom, I wear jeans and a black shirt that is so loose up top that it slips off my shoulders, and Susan wears baggy jeans and a white Candor shirt with a collar. She buttons it up to her throat. The Abnegation are modest to the point of discomfort.

When I enter the large room again, some of the factionless are walking out with buckets of paint and paintbrushes. I watch them until the door closes behind them.

"They're going to write a message to the other safe houses," says Evelyn from behind me. "On one of the billboards. Codes formed out of personal information—so-and-so's favorite color, someone else's childhood pet."

I am not sure why she would choose to tell me something about the factionless codes until I turn around. I see a familiar look in her eyes—it is the same as the one Jeanine wore when she told Tobias she had developed a serum that could control him: pride.

"Clever," I say. "Your idea?"

"It was, actually." She shrugs, but I am not fooled. She is anything but nonchalant. "I was Erudite before I was Abnegation."

"Oh," I say. "Guess you couldn't keep up with a life of academia, then?"

She doesn't take the bait. "Something like that, yes." She pauses. "I imagine your father left for the same reason."

I almost turn away to end the conversation, but her words create a kind of pressure inside my mind, like she is squeezing my brain between her hands. I stare.

"You didn't know?" She frowns. "I'm sorry; I forgot that faction members rarely discuss their old factions."

"What?" I say, my voice cracking.

"Your father was born in Erudite," she says. "His parents were friends with Jeanine Matthews's parents, before they died. Your father and Jeanine used to play together as children. I used to watch them pass books back and forth at school."

I imagine my father, a grown man, sitting next to Jeanine, a grown woman, at a lunch table in my old cafeteria, a book between them. The idea is so ridiculous to me that I half snort, half laugh. It can't be true.

Except.

Except: He never talked about his family or his childhood.

Except: He did not have the quiet demeanor of someone who grew up in Abnegation.

Except: His hatred of Erudite was so vehement it must have been *personal*.

"I'm sorry, Beatrice," Evelyn says. "I didn't mean to reopen closing wounds."

I frown. "Yes, you did."

"What do you mean—"

"Listen carefully," I say, lowering my voice. I check over her shoulder for Tobias, to make sure he isn't listening in. All I see is Caleb and Susan on the ground in the corner, passing a jar of peanut butter back and forth. No Tobias.

"I'm not stupid," I say. "I can see that you're trying to use him. And I'll tell him so, if he hasn't figured it out already."

"My dear girl," she says. "I am his family. I am permanent. You are only temporary."

"Yeah," I say. "His mom abandoned him, and his dad beat him up. How could his loyalty *not* be with his blood, with a family like that?"

I walk away, my hands shaking, and sit down next to Caleb on the floor. Susan is now across the room, helping one of the factionless clean up. He passes me the jar of peanut butter. I remember the rows of peanut plants in the Amity greenhouses. They grow peanuts because they are high in protein and fat, which is important for the factionless in particular. I scoop some of the peanut butter out with my fingers and eat it.

Should I tell him what Evelyn just told me? I don't want

to make him think that he has Erudite in his blood. I don't want to give him any reason to return to them.

I decide to keep it to myself for now.

"I wanted to talk to you about something," says Caleb.

I nod, still working the peanut butter off the roof of my mouth.

"Susan wants to go see the Abnegation," he says. "And so do I. I also want to make sure she's all right. But I don't want to leave you."

"It's okay," I say.

"Why don't you come with us?" he asks. "Abnegation would welcome you back; I'm sure of it."

So am I—the Abnegation don't hold grudges. But I am teetering on the edge of grief's mouth, and if I returned to my parents' old faction, it would swallow me.

I shake my head. "I have to go to Candor headquarters and find out what's going on," I say. "I'm going crazy, not knowing." I force a smile. "But you should go. Susan needs you. She seems better, but she still needs you."

"Okay." Caleb nods. "Well, I'll try to join you soon. Be careful, though."

"Aren't I always?"

"No, I think the word for how you usually are is 'reckless.'"

Caleb squeezes my good shoulder lightly. I eat another

fingertip's worth of peanut butter.

Tobias emerges from the men's bathroom a few minutes later, his red Amity shirt replaced by a black T-shirt, and his short hair glistening with water. Our eyes meet across the room, and I know it's time to leave.

+++

Candor headquarters is large enough to contain an entire world. Or so it seems to me.

It is a wide cement building that overlooks what was once the river. The sign says MERC   IS MART—it used to read "Merchandise Mart," but most people refer to it as the Merciless Mart, because the Candor are merciless, but honest. They seem to have embraced the nickname.

I don't know what to expect, because I have never been inside. Tobias and I pause outside the doors and look at each other.

"Here we go," he says.

I can't see anything beyond my reflection in the glass doors. I look tired and dirty. For the first time, it occurs to me that we don't have to do anything. We could hole up with the factionless and let the rest of them sort through this mess. We could be nobodies, safe, together.

He still hasn't told me about the conversation he had with his mother last night, and I don't think he's going to. He seemed so determined to get to Candor headquarters that I wonder if he's planning something without me.

I don't know why I walk through the doors. Maybe I decide that we've come this far, we might as well see what's going on. But I suspect it's more that I know what's true and what's not. I am Divergent, so I am not nobody, there's no such thing as "safe," and I have other things on my mind than playing house with Tobias. And so, apparently, does he.

The lobby is large and well-lit, with black marble floors that stretch back to an elevator bank. A ring of white marble tiles in the center of the room form the symbol of Candor: a set of unbalanced scales, meant to symbolize the weighing of truth against lies. The room is crawling with armed Dauntless.

A Dauntless soldier with an arm in a sling approaches us, gun held ready, barrel fixed on Tobias.

"Identify yourselves," she says. She is young, but not young enough to know Tobias.

The others gather behind her. Some of them eye us with suspicion, the rest with curiosity, but far stranger than both is the light I see in some of their eyes. Recognition. They might know Tobias, but how could they possibly recognize me?

"Four," he says. He nods toward me. "And this is Tris. Both Dauntless."

The Dauntless soldier's eyes widen, but she does not lower her gun.

"Some help here?" she asks. Some of the Dauntless step forward, but they do it cautiously, like we're dangerous.

"Is there a problem?" Tobias says.

"Are you armed?"

"Of course I'm armed. I'm Dauntless, aren't I?"

"Stand with your hands behind your head." She says it wildly, like she expects us to refuse. I glance at Tobias. Why is everyone acting like we're about to attack them?

"We walked through the front door," I say slowly. "You think we would have done that if we were here to hurt you?"

Tobias doesn't look back at me. He just touches his fingertips to the back of his head. After a moment, I do the same. Dauntless soldiers crowd around us. One of them pats down Tobias's legs while the other takes the gun tucked under his waistband. Another one, a round-faced boy with pink cheeks, looks at me apologetically.

"I have a knife in my back pocket." I say. "Put your hands on me, and I will make you regret it."

He mumbles some kind of apology. His fingers pinch the knife handle, careful not to touch me.

"What's going on?" asks Tobias.

The first soldier exchanges looks with some of the others.

"I'm sorry," she says. "But we were instructed to arrest you upon your arrival."

CHAPTER
ELEVEN

THEY SURROUND US, but don't handcuff us, and walk us to the elevator bank. No matter how many times I ask why we are under arrest, no one says anything or even looks in my direction. Eventually I give up and stay silent, like Tobias.

We go to the third level, where they take us to a small room with a white marble floor instead of a black one. There's no furniture except for a bench along the back wall. Every faction is supposed to have holding rooms for those who make trouble, but I've never been in one before.

The door closes behind us, and locks, and we're alone again.

Tobias sits down on the bench, his brow furrowed. I pace back and forth in front of him. If he had any idea why we were in here, he would tell me, so I don't ask. I walk five steps forward and five steps back, five steps forward and five steps back, at the same rhythm, hoping it will help me figure something out.

If Erudite didn't take over Candor—and Edward told us they didn't—why would the Candor arrest us? What could we have done to them?

If Erudite *didn't* take over, the only real crime left is siding with them. Did I do anything that could have been interpreted as siding with Erudite? My teeth dig into my lower lip so hard I wince. Yes, I did. I shot Will. I shot a number of other Dauntless. They were under the simulation, but maybe Candor doesn't know that or doesn't think it's a good enough reason.

"Can you please calm down?" Tobias says. "You're making me nervous."

"This is me calming down."

He leans forward, resting his elbows on his knees, and stares between his sneakers. "The wound in your lip begs to differ."

I sit next to him and hug my knees to my chest with one arm, my right arm hanging at my side. For a long time, he says nothing, and my arm wraps tighter and tighter around my legs. I feel like, the smaller I become, the safer I am.

"Sometimes," he says, "I worry that you don't trust me."

"I trust you," I say. "Of course I trust you. Why would you think otherwise?"

"Just seems like there's something you're not telling me. I told *you* things. . . ." He shakes his head. "I would never have told anyone else. Something's been going on with you, though, and you haven't told me yet."

"There's been a lot going on. You know that," I say. "And anyway, what about you? I could say the same thing to you."

He touches my cheek, his fingers pushing into my hair. Ignoring my question just like I ignored his.

"If it's just about your parents," he says softly, "tell me and I'll believe you."

His eyes should be wild with apprehension, given where we are, but they are still and dark. They transport me to familiar places. Safe places, where confessing that I shot one of my best friends would be easy, where I would not be afraid of the way that Tobias will look at me when he finds out what I did.

I cover his hand with mine. "That's all it is," I say weakly.

"Okay," he says. He touches his mouth to mine. Guilt clutches at my stomach.

The door opens. A few people file in—two Candor with guns; a dark-skinned, older Candor man; a Dauntless woman I don't recognize. And then: Jack Kang, representative of Candor.

By most faction standards, he is a young leader—only thirty-nine years old. But by Dauntless standards, that's nothing. Eric became a Dauntless leader at seventeen. But that's probably one of the reasons the other factions don't take our opinions or decisions seriously.

Jack is handsome, too, with short black hair and warm, slanted eyes, like Tori's, and high cheekbones. Despite his good looks, he isn't known for being charming, probably because he's Candor, and they see charm as deceptive. I do trust him to tell us what's going on without wasting time on pleasantries. That is something.

"They told me you seemed confused about why you were arrested," he says. His voice is deep, but strangely flat, like it could not create an echo even at the bottom of an empty cavern. "To me that means either you're falsely accused or good at pretending. The only—"

"What are we accused of?" I interrupt him.

"*He* is accused of crimes against humanity. *You* are accused of being his accomplice."

"Crimes against humanity?" Tobias finally sounds angry. He gives Jack a disgusted look. "What?"

"We saw video footage of the attack. You were *running* the attack simulation," says Jack.

"How could you have seen footage? We took the data," says Tobias.

"You took one copy of the data. All the footage of the Dauntless compound recorded during the attack was also sent to other computers throughout the city," says Jack. "All we saw was you running the simulation and *her* nearly getting punched to death before she gave up. Then you stopped, had a rather abrupt lovers' reconciliation, and stole the hard drive together. One possible reason is because the simulation was over and you didn't want us to get our hands on it."

I almost laugh. My great act of heroism, the only important thing I have ever done, and they think I was working for the Erudite when I did it.

"The simulation didn't end," I say. "We *stopped* it, you—"

Jack holds up his hand. "I am not interested in what you have to say right now. The truth will come out when you are both interrogated under the influence of truth serum."

Christina told me about truth serum once. She said the most difficult part of Candor initiation was being given truth serum and answering personal questions in front of everyone in the faction. I don't need to search myself for my deepest, darkest secrets to know that truth serum is the last thing I want in my body.

"Truth serum?" I shake my head. "No. No way."

"There's something you have to hide?" Jack says, lifting both eyebrows.

I want to tell him that anyone with an ounce of dignity wants to keep some things to herself, but I don't want to arouse his suspicions. So I shake my head.

"All right, then." He checks his watch. "It is now noon. The interrogation will be at seven. Don't bother preparing for it. You can't withhold information while under the influence of truth serum."

He turns on his heel and walks out of the room.

"What a pleasant man," says Tobias.

+ + +

A group of armed Dauntless escort me to the bathroom in the early afternoon. I take my time, letting my hands turn red in the hot-faucet water and staring at my reflection. When I was in Abnegation and wasn't allowed to look into mirrors, I used to think that a lot could change in a person's appearance in three months. But it only took a few days to change me this time.

I look older. Maybe it's the short hair or maybe it's just that I wear all that has happened like a mask. Either way, I always thought I would be happy when I stopped looking like a child. But all I feel is a lump in my throat. I am no longer the daughter my parents knew. They will never know me as I am now.

I turn away from the mirror and shove the door to the hallway open with the heels of my hands.

When the Dauntless drop me off at the holding room, I linger by the door. Tobias looks like he did when I first met him—black T-shirt, short hair, stern expression. The sight of him used to fill me with nervous excitement. I remember when I grabbed his hand outside the training room, just for a few seconds, and when we sat together on the rocks next to the chasm, and I feel a pang of longing for how things used to be.

"Hungry?" he says. He offers me a sandwich from the plate next to him.

I take it and sit down, leaning my head on his shoulder. All that's left for us to do is wait, so that's what we do. We eat until the food is gone. We sit until we get uncomfortable. Then we lie down next to each other on the floor, shoulders touching, staring at the same patch of white ceiling.

"What are you afraid of saying?" he says.

"Any of it. All of it. I don't want to relive anything."

He nods. I close my eyes and pretend to sleep. There's no clock in the room, so I can't count down the minutes until the interrogation. Time might as well not exist in this place, except I feel it pressing against me as seven o'clock inevitably draws closer, pushing me into the floor tiles.

Maybe time would not feel as heavy if I didn't have this guilt—the guilt of knowing the truth and stuffing it down where no one can see it, not even Tobias. Maybe I should not be so afraid of saying anything, because honesty will make me feel lighter.

I must fall asleep eventually, because I jerk awake at the sound of the door opening. A few Dauntless walk in as we get to our feet, and one of them says my name. Christina shoves her way past the others and throws her arms around me. Her fingers dig into the wound in my shoulder, and I cry out.

"Got shot," I say. "Shoulder. Ow."

"Oh God!" She releases me. "Sorry, Tris."

She doesn't look like the Christina I remember. Her hair is shorter, like a boy's, and her skin is grayish instead of a warm brown. She smiles at me, but the smile doesn't travel to her eyes, which still look tired. I try to smile back, but I'm too nervous. Christina will be there at my interrogation. She will hear what I did to Will. She will never forgive me.

Unless I fight the serum, swallow the truth—if I can.

But is that really what I want? To let it fester inside me forever?

"You okay? I heard you were here so I asked to escort you," she says as we leave the holding room. "I know you didn't do it. You're not a traitor."

"I'm fine," I say. "And thank you. How are you?"

"Oh, I'm . . ." Her voice trails off, and she bites her lip. "Did anyone tell you . . . I mean, maybe now isn't the time, but . . ."

"What? What is it?"

"Um . . . Will died in the attack," she says.

She gives me a worried look, and an expectant one. Expecting what?

Oh. I am not supposed to know that Will is dead. I could pretend to be emotional, but I probably wouldn't do it convincingly. It's best to admit that I already knew. But I don't know how to explain that without telling her everything.

I feel suddenly sick. Am I really evaluating how best to deceive my friend?

"I know," I say. "I saw him on the monitors when I was in the control room. I'm sorry, Christina."

"Oh." She nods. "Well, I'm . . . glad you already knew. I really didn't want to break the news to you in a hallway."

A short laugh. A flash of a smile. Neither of them like they used to be.

We file into an elevator. I can feel Tobias staring at me— he knows I didn't see Will in the monitors, and he didn't know that Will was dead. I stare straight ahead and pretend his eyes aren't setting me on fire.

"Don't worry about the truth serum," she says. "It's easy. You barely know what's happening when you're under. It's only when you resurface that you even know what you said. I went under when I was a kid. It's pretty commonplace in Candor."

The other Dauntless in the elevator give each other looks. In normal circumstances, someone would probably reprimand her for discussing her old faction, but these are not normal circumstances. At no other time in Christina's life will she escort her best friend, now a suspected traitor, to a public interrogation.

"Is everyone else all right?" I say. "Uriah, Lynn, Marlene?"

"All here," she says. "Except Uriah's brother, Zeke, who is with the other Dauntless."

"What?" Zeke, who secured my straps on the zip line, a traitor?

The elevator stops on the top floor, and the others file out.

"I know," she says. "No one saw it coming."

She takes my arm and tugs me toward the doors. We walk down a black-marble hallway—it must be easy to get lost in Candor headquarters, since everything looks the same. We walk down another hallway and through a set of double doors.

From the outside, the Merciless Mart is a squat block with a narrow raised portion in its center. From the inside, that raised portion is a hollow three-story room with empty spaces in the walls instead of windows. I see the darkening sky above me, starless.

Here the marble floors are white, with a black Candor symbol in the center of the room, and the walls are lit with rows of dim yellow lights, so the whole room glows. Every voice echoes.

Most of Candor and the remnants of Dauntless are already gathered. Some of them sit on the tiered benches that wrap around the edge of the room, but there isn't enough space for everyone, so the rest are crowded around the Candor symbol. In the center of the symbol, between the unbalanced scales, are two empty chairs.

Tobias reaches for my hand. I lace my fingers in his.

Our Dauntless guards lead us to the center of the room, where we are greeted with, at best, murmurs, and at worst, jeers. I spot Jack Kang in the front row of the tiered benches.

An old, dark-skinned man steps forward, a black box in his hands.

"My name is Niles," he says. "I will be your questioner. You—" He points at Tobias. "You will be going first. So if you will please step forward . . ."

Tobias squeezes my hand, and then releases it, and I stand with Christina at the edge of the Candor symbol. The air in the room is warm—moist, summer air, sunset air—but I feel cold.

Niles opens the black box. It contains two needles, one for Tobias and one for me. He also takes an antiseptic wipe from his pocket and offers it to Tobias. We didn't bother with that kind of thing in Dauntless.

"The injection site is in your neck," Niles says.

All I hear, as Tobias applies antiseptic to his skin, is the wind. Niles steps forward and plunges the needle into Tobias's neck, squeezing the cloudy, bluish liquid into his veins. The last time I saw someone inject Tobias with something, it was Jeanine, putting him under a new simulation, one that was effective even on the Divergent— or so she believed. I thought, then, that he was lost to me forever.

I shudder.

CHAPTER
TWELVE

"I WILL ASK you a series of simple questions so that you can grow accustomed to the serum as it takes full effect," says Niles. "Now. What is your name?"

Tobias sits with slouched shoulders and a lowered head, like his body is too heavy for him. He scowls and squirms in the chair, and through gritted teeth says, "Four."

Maybe it isn't possible to lie under the truth serum, but to select which version of the truth to tell: Four is his name, but it is not his name.

"That is a nickname," Niles says. "What is your real name?"

"Tobias," he says.

Christina elbows me. "Did you know that?"

I nod.

"What are the names of your parents, Tobias?"

Tobias opens his mouth to answer, and then clenches his jaw as if to stop the words from spilling out.

"Why is this relevant?" Tobias asks.

The Candor around me mutter to each other, some of them scowling. I raise my eyebrow at Christina.

"It's extremely difficult not to immediately answer questions while under the truth serum," she says. "It means he has a seriously strong will. And something to hide."

"Maybe it wasn't relevant before, Tobias," Niles says, "but it is now that you've resisted answering the question. The names of your parents, please."

Tobias closes his eyes. "Evelyn and Marcus Eaton."

Surnames are just an additional means of identification, useful only to prevent confusion in official records. When we marry, one spouse has to take the other's surname, or both have to take a new one. Still, while we may carry our names from family to faction, we rarely mention them.

But everyone recognizes Marcus's surname. I can tell by the clamor that rises in the room after Tobias speaks. The Candor all know Marcus is the most influential government official, and some of them must have read the article Jeanine released about his cruelty toward his son.

It was one of the only things she said that was true. And now everyone knows that Tobias is that son.

Tobias Eaton is a powerful name.

Niles waits for silence, then continues. "So you are a faction transfer, are you not?"

"Yes."

"You transferred from Abnegation to Dauntless?"

"Yes," snaps Tobias. "Isn't that obvious?"

I bite my lip. He should calm down; he is giving away too much. The more reluctant he is to answer a question, the more determined Niles will be to hear the answer.

"One of the purposes of this interrogation is to determine your loyalties," says Niles, "so I must ask: Why did you transfer?"

Tobias glares at Niles, and keeps his mouth shut. Seconds pass in complete silence. The longer he tries to resist the serum, the harder it seems to be for him: color fills his cheeks, and he breathes faster, heavier. My chest aches for him. The details of his childhood should stay inside him, if that's where he wants them to be. Candor is cruel for forcing them from him, for taking away his freedom.

"This is horrible," I say hotly to Christina. "Wrong."

"What?" she says. "It's a simple question."

I shake my head. "You don't understand."

Christina smiles a little at me. "You really care about him."

I am too busy watching Tobias to respond.

Niles says, "I'll ask again. It is important that we understand the extent of your loyalty to your chosen faction. So why did you transfer to Dauntless, Tobias?"

"To protect myself," says Tobias. "I transferred to protect myself."

"Protect yourself from what?"

"From my father."

All the conversations in the room stop, and the silence they leave in their wake is worse than the muttering was. I expect Niles to keep probing, but he doesn't.

"Thank you for your honesty," Niles says. The Candor repeat the phrase under their breath. All around me are the words "Thank you for your honesty" at different volumes and pitches, and my anger begins to dissolve. The whispered words seem to welcome Tobias, to embrace and then discard his darkest secret.

It's not cruelty, maybe, but a desire to understand, that motivates them. That doesn't make me any less afraid of going under truth serum.

"Is your allegiance with your current faction, Tobias?" Niles says.

"My allegiance lies with anyone who does not support

the attack on Abnegation," he says.

"Speaking of which," Niles says, "I think we should focus on what happened that day. What do you remember about being under the simulation?"

"I was not under the simulation, at first," says Tobias. "It didn't work."

Niles laughs a little. "What do you mean, it didn't *work*?"

"One of the defining characteristics of the Divergent is that their minds are resistant to simulations," says Tobias. "And I am Divergent. So no, it didn't work."

More mutters. Christina nudges me with her elbow.

"Are you too?" she says, close to my ear so she can stay quiet. "Is that why you were awake?"

I look at her. I have spent the past few months afraid of the word "Divergent," terrified that anyone would discover what I am. But I won't be able to hide it anymore. I nod.

It's like her eyes swell to fill their sockets; that's how big they get. I have trouble identifying her expression. Is it shock? Fear?

Awe?

"Do you know what it means?" I say.

"I heard about it when I was young," she says in a reverent whisper.

Definitely awe.

"Like it was a fantasy story," she says. "'There are people with special powers among us!' Like that."

"Well, it's not a fantasy, and it's not that big a deal," I say. "It's like the fear landscape simulation—you were aware while you were in it, and you could manipulate it. Except for me, it's like that in every simulation."

"But Tris," she says, setting her hand on my elbow. "That's *impossible*."

In the center of the room, Niles has his hands up and is trying to silence the crowd, but there are too many whispers—some hostile, some terrified, and some awed, like Christina's. Finally Niles stands and yells, "If you don't quiet down, you will be asked to leave!"

At last everyone quiets down. Niles sits.

"Now," he says. "When you say 'resistant to simulations,' what do you mean?"

"Usually, it means we're aware during simulations," says Tobias. He seems to have an easier time with the truth serum when he answers factual questions instead of emotional ones. He doesn't sound like he's under the truth serum at all now, though his slumped posture and wandering eyes indicate otherwise. "But the attack simulation was different, using a different kind of simulation serum, one with long-range transmitters. Evidently the long-range transmitters didn't work on the Divergent at all, because I awoke in my own mind that morning."

"You say you weren't under the simulation *at first*. Can you explain what you mean by that?"

"I mean that I was discovered and brought to Jeanine, and she injected a version of the simulation serum that specifically targeted the Divergent. I was aware during *that* simulation, but it didn't do much good."

"The video footage from the Dauntless headquarters shows you *running* the simulation," Niles says darkly. "How, exactly, do you explain that?"

"When a simulation is running, your eyes still see and process the actual world, but your brain no longer comprehends them. On some level, though, your brain still knows what you're seeing and where you are. The nature of this new simulation was that it recorded my emotional responses to outside stimuli," Tobias says, closing his eyes for a few seconds, "and responded by altering the appearance of that stimuli. The simulation made my enemies into friends, my friends into enemies. I thought I was shutting the simulation down. Really I was receiving instructions about how to keep it running."

Christina nods along to his words. I feel calmer when I see that most of the crowd is doing the same thing. This is the benefit of the truth serum, I realize. Tobias's testimony is irrefutable this way.

"We have seen footage of what ultimately happened to you in the control room," says Niles, "but it is confusing. Please describe it to us."

"Someone entered the room, and I thought it was a Dauntless soldier, trying to stop me from destroying the simulation. I was fighting her, and . . ." Tobias scowls, struggling. ". . . and then she stopped, and I got confused. Even if I had been awake, I would have been confused. Why would she surrender? Why didn't she just kill me?"

His eyes search the crowd until they find my face. My heartbeat lives in my throat; lives in my cheeks.

"I still don't understand," he says softly, "how she knew that it would work."

Lives in my fingertips.

"I think my conflicted emotions confused the simulation," he says. "And then I heard her voice. Somehow, that enabled me to fight the simulation."

My eyes burn. I have tried not to think of that moment, when I thought he was lost to me and that I would soon be dead, when all I wanted was to feel his heartbeat. I try not to think of it now; I blink the tears from my eyes.

"I recognized her, finally," he says. "We went back into the control room and stopped the simulation."

"What is the name of this person?"

"Tris," he says. "Beatrice Prior, I mean."

"Did you know her before this happened?"

"Yes."

"How did you know her?"

"I was her instructor," he says. "Now we're together."

"I have a final question," Niles says. "Among the Candor, before a person is accepted into our community, they have to completely expose themselves. Given the dire circumstances we are in, we require the same of you. So, Tobias Eaton: what are your deepest regrets?"

I look him over, from his beat-up sneakers to his long fingers to his straight eyebrows.

"I regret . . ." Tobias tilts his head, and sighs. "I regret my choice."

"What choice?"

"Dauntless," he says. "I was born for Abnegation. I was planning on leaving Dauntless, and becoming faction-less. But then I met *her*, and . . . I felt like maybe I could make something more of my decision."

Her.

For a moment, it's like I'm looking at a different person, sitting in Tobias's skin, one whose life is not as simple as I thought. He wanted to leave Dauntless, but he stayed because of me. He never told me that.

"Choosing Dauntless in order to escape my father was an act of cowardice," he says. "I regret that cowardice.

It means I am not worthy of my faction. I will always regret it."

I expect the Dauntless to let out indignant shouts, maybe to charge the chair and beat him to a pulp. They are capable of far more erratic things than that. But they don't. They stand in stony silence, with stony faces, staring at the young man who did not betray them, but never truly felt that he belonged to them.

For a moment we are all silent. I don't know who starts the whisper; it seems to originate from nothing, to come from no one. But someone whispers, "Thank you for your honesty," and the rest of the room repeats it.

"Thank you for your honesty," they whisper.

I don't join in.

I am the only thing that kept him in the faction he wanted to leave. I am not worth that.

Maybe he deserves to know.

+++

Niles stands in the center of the room with a needle in hand. The lights above him make it shine. All around me, the Dauntless and the Candor wait for me to step forward and spill my entire life before them.

The thought occurs to me again: *Maybe I can fight the serum.* But I don't know if I should try. It might be better for the people I love if I come clean.

I walk stiffly to the center of the room as Tobias leaves it. As we pass each other, he takes my hand and squeezes my fingers. Then he's gone, and it's just me and Niles and the needle. I wipe the side of my neck with the antiseptic, but when he reaches out with the needle, I pull back.

"I would rather do it myself," I say, holding out my hand. I will never let someone else inject me again, not after letting Eric inject me with attack simulation serum after my final test. I can't change the contents of the syringe just by doing it myself, but at least this way, I am the instrument of my own destruction.

"Do you know how?" he says, raising a bushy eyebrow.

"Yes."

Niles offers me the syringe. I position it over the vein in my neck, insert the needle, and press the plunger. I barely feel the pinch. I am too charged with adrenaline.

Someone comes forward with a trash can, and I toss the needle in. I feel the effects of the serum immediately afterward. It makes my blood feel like lead in my veins. I almost collapse on my way to the chair—Niles has to grab my arm and guide me toward it.

Seconds later my brain goes silent. *What was I thinking about?* It doesn't seem to matter. Nothing matters except the chair beneath me and the man sitting across from me.

"What is your name?" he says.

The second he asks the question, the answer pops out of my mouth. "Beatrice Prior."

"But you go by Tris?"

"I do."

"What are the names of your parents, Tris?"

"Andrew and Natalie Prior."

"You are also a faction transfer, are you not?"

"Yes," I say, but a new thought whispers at the back of my mind. *Also?* Also refers to someone else, and in this case, someone else is Tobias. I frown as I try to picture Tobias, but it is difficult to force the image of him into my mind. Not so difficult that I can't do it, though. I see him, and then I see a flash of him sitting in the same chair I'm sitting in.

"You came from Abnegation? And chose Dauntless?"

"Yes," I say again, but this time, the word sounds terse. I don't know why, exactly.

"Why did you transfer?"

That question is more complicated, but I still know the answer. *I was not good enough for Abnegation* is on the tip of my tongue, but another phrase replaces it: *I wanted to be free.* They are both true. I want to say them both. I squeeze the armrests as I try to remember where I am, what I'm doing. I see people all around me, but I don't know why they're there.

I strain, the way I used to strain when I could almost remember the answer to a test question but couldn't call it to mind. I used to close my eyes and picture the textbook page the answer was on. I struggle for a few seconds, but I can't do it; I can't remember.

"I wasn't good enough for Abnegation," I say, "and I wanted to be free. So I chose Dauntless."

"Why weren't you good enough?"

"Because I was selfish," I say.

"You *were* selfish? You aren't anymore?"

"Of course I am. My mother said that everyone is selfish," I say, "but I became less selfish in Dauntless. I discovered there were people I would fight for. Die for, even."

The answer surprises me—but why? I pinch my lips together for a moment. Because it's true. If I say it here, it must be true.

That thought gives me the missing link in the chain of thought I was trying to find. I am here for a lie-detector test. Everything I say is true. I feel a bead of sweat roll down the back of my neck.

Lie-detector test. Truth serum. I have to remind myself. It is too easy to get lost in honesty.

"Tris, would you please tell us what happened the day of the attack?"

"I woke up," I say, "and everyone was under the simulation. So I played along until I found Tobias."

"What happened after you and Tobias were separated?"

"Jeanine tried to have me killed, but my mother saved me. She used to be Dauntless, so she knew how to use a gun." My body feels even heavier now, but no longer cold. I feel something stir in my chest, something worse than sadness, worse than regret.

I know what comes next. My mother died and then I killed Will; I shot him; I killed him.

"She distracted the Dauntless soldiers so I could get away, and they killed her," I say.

Some of them ran after me, and I killed them. But there are Dauntless in the crowd around me, Dauntless, I killed some of the Dauntless, I shouldn't talk about it here.

"I kept running," I say, "And . . ." *And Will ran after me. And I killed him.* No, no. I feel sweat near my hairline.

"And I found my brother and father," I say, my voice strained. "We formed a plan to destroy the simulation."

The edge of the armrest digs into my palm. I withheld some of the truth. Surely that counts as deception.

I fought the serum. And in that short moment, I won.

I should feel triumphant. Instead I feel the weight of

what I did crush me again.

"We infiltrated the Dauntless compound, and my father and I went up to the control room. He fought off Dauntless soldiers at the expense of his life," I say. "I made it to the control room, and Tobias was there."

"Tobias said you fought him, but then stopped. Why did you do that?"

"Because I realized that one of us would have to kill the other," I say, "and I didn't want to kill him."

"You gave up?"

"No!" I snap. I shake my head. "No, not exactly. I remembered something I had done in my fear landscape in Dauntless initiation . . . in a simulation, a woman demanded that I kill my family, and I let her shoot me instead. It worked then. I thought . . ." I pinch the bridge of my nose. My head is starting to ache and my control is gone and my thoughts run into words. "I was so frantic, but all I could think was that there was something to it; there was a strength in it. And I couldn't kill him, so I had to try."

I blink tears from my eyes.

"So you were never under the simulation?"

"No." I press the heel of my hands to my eyes, pushing the tears out of them so they don't fall on my cheeks where everyone can see them.

"No," I say again. "No, I am Divergent."

"Just to clarify," says Niles. "Are you telling me that you were almost murdered by the Erudite . . . and then fought your way into the Dauntless compound . . . and destroyed the simulation?"

"Yes," I say.

"I think I speak for everyone," he says, "when I say that you have earned the title of Dauntless."

Shouts rise up from the left side of the room, and I see blurs of fists pressing into the dark air. My faction, calling to me.

But no, they're wrong, I'm not brave, I'm not brave, I shot Will and I can't admit it, I can't even admit it. . . .

"Beatrice Prior," says Niles, "what are your deepest regrets?"

What do I regret? I do not regret choosing Dauntless or leaving Abnegation. I do not even regret shooting the guards outside the control room, because it was so important that I get past them.

"I regret . . ."

My eyes leave Niles's face and drift over the room, and land on Tobias. He is expressionless, his mouth in a firm line, his stare blank. His hands, crossed over his chest, clasp his arms so hard his knuckles are white. Next to him stands Christina. My chest squeezes, and I can't breathe.

I have to tell them. I have to tell the truth.

"Will," I say. It sounds like a gasp, like it was pulled straight from my stomach. Now there is no turning back.

"I shot Will," I say, "while he was under the simulation. I killed him. He was going to kill me, but I killed him. My friend."

Will, with the crease between his eyebrows, with green eyes like celery and the ability to quote the Dauntless manifesto from memory. I feel pain in my stomach so intense that I almost groan. It hurts to remember him. It hurts every part of me.

And there is something else, something worse that I didn't realize before. I was willing to die rather than kill Tobias, but the thought never occurred to me when it came to Will. I decided to kill Will in a fraction of a second.

I feel bare. I didn't realize that I wore my secrets as armor until they were gone, and now everyone sees me as I really am.

"Thank you for your honesty," they say.

But Christina and Tobias say nothing.

CHAPTER
THIRTEEN

I RISE FROM the chair. I don't feel as dizzy as I did a moment ago; the serum is already wearing off. The crowd tilts, and I search for a door. I don't usually run away from things, but I would run from this.

Everyone starts to file out of the room except for Christina. She stands where I left her, her hands in fists that are in the process of uncurling. Her eyes meet mine and yet they do not. Tears swim in her eyes and yet she is not crying.

"Christina," I say, but the only words I can think of—*I'm sorry*—sound more like an insult than an apology. Sorry is what you are when you bump someone with your elbow, what you are when you interrupt someone. I am more than sorry.

"He had a gun," I say. "He was about to shoot me. He was under the simulation."

"You killed him," she says. Her words sound bigger than words usually do, like they expanded in her mouth before she spoke them. She looks at me as if she doesn't recognize me for a few seconds, then turns away.

A younger girl with the same skin color and the same height takes her hand—Christina's younger sister. I saw her on Visiting Day, a thousand years ago. The truth serum makes the sight of them swim before me, or that could be the tears gathering in my eyes.

"You okay?" says Uriah, emerging from the crowd to touch my shoulder. I haven't seen him since before the simulation attack, but I can't find it in me to greet him.

"Yeah."

"Hey." He squeezes my shoulder. "You did what you had to do, right? To save us from being Erudite slaves. She'll see that eventually. When the grief fades."

I can't even find it in me to nod. Uriah smiles at me and walks away. Some Dauntless brush against me and they murmur words that sound like gratitude, or compliments, or reassurance. Others give me a wide berth, look at me with narrowed, suspicious eyes.

The black-clothed bodies smear together in front of me. I am empty. Everything has spilled out of me.

Tobias stands next to me. I brace myself for his reaction.

"I got our weapons back," he says, offering me my knife.

I shove it in my back pocket without meeting his eyes.

"We can talk about it tomorrow," he says. Quietly. Quiet is dangerous, with Tobias.

"Okay."

He slides his arm across my shoulders. My hand finds his hip, and I pull him against me.

I hold on tight as we walk toward the elevators together.

+ + +

He finds us two cots at the end of a hallway somewhere. We lie with our heads inches apart, not speaking.

When I'm sure he's asleep, I slip out from beneath the blankets and walk down the hallway, past a dozen sleeping Dauntless. I find the door that leads to the stairs.

As I climb step after step, and my muscles begin to burn, and my lungs fight for air, I feel the first moments of relief I've experienced in days.

I may be good at running on flat ground, but walking up stairs is another matter. I massage a spasm from my hamstring as I march past the twelfth floor, and try to recover some of my lost air. I grin at the fierce burn in my legs, in my chest. Using pain to relieve pain. It doesn't make much sense.

By the time I reach the eighteenth floor, my legs feel like they have turned to liquid. I shuffle toward the room where I was interrogated. It's empty now, but the amphitheater benches are still there, as is the chair I sat in. The moon glows behind a haze of clouds.

I set my hands on the back of the chair. It's plain: wooden, a little creaky. How strange that something so simple could have been instrumental in my decision to ruin one of my most important relationships, and damage another.

It's bad enough that I killed Will, that I didn't think fast enough to come up with another solution. Now I have to live with everyone else's judgment as well as my own, and the fact that nothing—not even me—will ever be the same again.

The Candor sing the praises of the truth, but they never tell you how much it costs.

The edge of the chair bites into my palms. I was squeezing it harder than I thought. I stare down at it for a second and then lift it, balancing it legs-up on my good shoulder. I search the edge of the room for a ladder or a staircase that will help me climb. All I see are the amphitheater benches, rising high above the floor.

I walk up to the highest bench, and lift the chair above my head. It just barely touches the ledge beneath one of the window spaces. I jump, shoving the chair for-ward, and it slides onto the ledge. My shoulder aches—I shouldn't really be using my arm—but I have other things on my mind.

I jump, grab the ledge, and pull myself up, my arms shaking. I swing my leg up and drag the rest of my body onto the ledge. When I'm up, I lie there for a moment, sucking in air and heaving it back out again.

I stand on the ledge, under the arch of what used to be a window, and stare out at the city. The dead river curls around the building and disappears. The bridge, its red paint peeling, stretches over the muck. Across it are buildings, most of them empty. It is hard to believe there were ever enough people in the city to fill them.

For a second, I allow myself to reenter the memory of the interrogation. Tobias's lack of expression; his anger afterward, suppressed for the sake of my sanity. Christina's empty look. The whispers, "Thank you for your honesty." Easy to say that when what I did doesn't affect them.

I grab the chair and hurl it over the ledge. A faint cry escapes me. It grows into a yell, which transforms into a scream, and then I'm standing on the ledge of the Merciless Mart, screaming as the chair sails toward the ground, screaming until my throat burns. Then the chair hits the ground, shattering like a brittle skeleton. I sit down on the ledge, leaning into the side of the window frame, and close my eyes.

And then I think of Al.

I wonder how long Al stood at the ledge before he pitched himself over it, into the Dauntless Pit.

He must have stood there for a long time, making a list of all the terrible things he had done—almost killing me was one of those things—and another list of all the good, heroic, brave things he had not done, and then decided that he was tired. Tired, not just of living, but of existing. Tired of being Al.

I open my eyes, and stare at the pieces of chair I can faintly see on the pavement below. For the first time I feel like I understand Al. I am tired of being Tris. I have done bad things. I can't take them back, and they are part of who I am. Most of the time, they seem like the only thing I am.

I lean forward, into the air, holding on to the side of the window with one hand. Another few inches and my weight would pull me to the ground. I would not be able to stop it.

But I can't do it. My parents lost their lives out of love for me. Losing mine for no good reason would be a terrible way to repay them for that sacrifice, no matter what I've done.

"Let the guilt teach you how to behave next time," my father would say.

"I love you. No matter what," my mother would say.

Part of me wishes I could burn them from my mind, so I would never have to mourn for them. But the rest of me is afraid of who I would be without them.

My eyes blurry with tears, I lower myself back into the interrogation room.

+++

I return to my cot early that morning, and Tobias is already awake. He turns and walks toward the elevators, and I follow him, because I know that's what he wants. We stand in the elevator, side by side. I hear ringing in my ears.

The elevator sinks to the second floor, and I start to shake. It starts with my hands, but travels to my arms and my chest, until little shudders go through my entire body and I have no way to stop them. We stand between the elevators, right above another Candor symbol, the uneven scales. The symbol that is also drawn on the middle of his spine.

He doesn't look at me for a long time. He stands with his arms crossed and his head down until I can't stand it anymore, until I feel like I might scream. I should say something, but I don't know what to say. I can't apologize, because I only told the truth, and I can't change the truth into a lie. I can't give excuses.

"You didn't tell me," he says. "Why not?"

"Because I didn't . . ." I shake my head. "I didn't know how to."

He scowls. "It's pretty *easy*, Tris—"

"Oh yeah," I say, nodding. "It's *so* easy. All I have to do is go up to you and say, 'By the way, I shot Will, and now guilt is ripping me to shreds, but what's for breakfast?' Right? *Right?*" Suddenly it is too much, too much to contain. Tears fill my eyes, and I yell, "Why don't *you* try killing one of your best friends and then dealing with the consequences?"

I cover my face with my hands. I don't want him to see me sobbing again. He touches my shoulder.

"Tris," he says, gently this time. "I'm sorry. I shouldn't pretend that I understand. I just meant that . . ." He struggles for a moment. "I wish you trusted me enough to tell me things like that."

I do trust you, is what I want to say. But it isn't true—I didn't trust him to love me despite the terrible things I had done. I don't trust anyone to do that, but that isn't his problem; it's mine.

"I mean," he says, "I had to find out that you almost drowned in a water tank from *Caleb.* Doesn't that seem a little strange to you?"

Just when I was about to apologize.

I wipe my cheeks hard with my fingertips and stare at him.

"Other things seem stranger," I say, trying to make my voice light. "Like finding out that your boyfriend's supposedly dead mother is still alive by *seeing her in person*. Or overhearing his plans to ally with the factionless, but he never tells you about it. That seems a little strange to me."

He takes his hand from my shoulder.

"Don't pretend this is only my problem," I say. "If I don't trust you, you don't trust me either."

"I thought we would get to those things eventually," he says. "Do I have to tell you everything right away?"

I feel so frustrated I can't even speak for a few seconds. Heat fills my cheeks.

"God, *Four!*" I snap. "You don't want to have to tell me everything right away, but I have to tell *you* everything right away? Can't you see how stupid that is?"

"First of all, don't use that name like a weapon against me," he says, pointing at me. "Second, I was not making plans to ally with the factionless; I was just thinking it over. If I had made a decision, I would have said something to you. And third, it would be different if you had actually intended to tell me about Will at some point, but it's obvious that you didn't."

"I *did* tell you about Will!" I say. "That wasn't truth serum; it was me. *I* said it because I chose to."

"What are you talking about?"

"I was aware. Under the serum. I could have lied; I could have kept it from you. But I didn't, because I thought you deserved to know the truth."

"What a way to tell me!" he says, scowling. "In front of over a hundred people! How intimate!"

"Oh, so it's not enough that I told you; it has to be in the right setting?" I raise my eyebrows. "Next time should I brew some tea and make sure the lighting is right, too?"

Tobias lets out a frustrated sound and turns away from me, pacing a few steps. When he turns back, his cheeks are splotchy. I can't remember ever seeing his face change color before.

"Sometimes," he says quietly, "it isn't easy to be with you, Tris." He looks away.

I want to tell him that I know it's not easy, but I wouldn't have made it through the past week without him. But I just stare at him, my heart pounding in my ears.

I can't tell him I need him. I can't need him, period—or really, we can't need each other, because who knows how long either of us will last in this war?

"I'm sorry," I say, all my anger gone. "I should have been honest with you."

"That's it? That's all you have to say?" He frowns.

"What else do you want me to say?"

He just shakes his head. "Nothing, Tris. Nothing."

I watch him walk away. I feel like a space has opened up within me, expanding so rapidly it will break me apart.

CHAPTER
FOURTEEN

"OKAY, WHAT THE hell are you doing here?" a voice demands.

I sit on a mattress in one of the hallways. I came here to do something, but I lost my train of thought when I arrived, so I just sat down instead. I look up. Lynn—who I first met when she stomped on my toes in a Hancock building elevator—stands over me with raised eyebrows. Her hair is growing out—it's still short, but I can't see her skull anymore.

"I'm sitting," I say. "Why?"

"You're ridiculous, is what you are." She sighs. "Get your stuff together. You're Dauntless, and it's time you acted like it. You're giving us a bad reputation among the Candor."

"How exactly am I doing that?"

"By acting like you don't know us."

"I'm just doing Christina a favor."

"Christina." Lynn snorts. "She's a lovesick puppy. People die. That's what happens in war. She'll figure it out eventually."

"Yeah, people die, but it's not always your good friend who kills them."

"Whatever." Lynn sighs impatiently. "Come on."

I don't see a reason to refuse. I get up and follow her down a series of hallways. She moves at a brisk pace, and it's difficult to keep up with her.

"Where's your scary boyfriend?" she says.

My lips pucker like I just tasted something sour. "He's not scary."

"Sure he's not." She smirks.

"I don't know where he is."

She shrugs. "Well, you can grab him a bunk, too. We're trying to forget those Dauntless-Erudite bastard children. Pull together again."

I laugh. "Dauntless-Erudite bastard children, huh."

She pushes a door open, and we stand in a large, open room that reminds me of the building's lobby. Unsurprisingly, the floors are black with a huge white symbol in the center of the room, but most of it has been covered up with bunk beds. Dauntless men, women, and children are everywhere, and there isn't a single Candor in sight.

Lynn leads me to the left side of the room and between the rows of bunks. She looks at the boy sitting on one of the bottom bunks—he is a few years younger than we are, and he's trying to undo a knot in his shoelaces.

"Hec," she says, "you're going to have to find another bunk."

"What? No way," he says without looking up. "I'm not relocating *again* just because you want to have late-night pillow chats with one of your stupid friends."

"She is not my friend," snaps Lynn. I almost laugh. She's right—the first thing she did when she met me was stomp on my toes. "Hec, this is Tris. Tris, this is my little brother, Hector."

At the sound of my name, his head jerks up, and he stares at me, openmouthed.

"Nice to meet you," I say.

"You're *Divergent*," he says. "My mom said to stay away from you because you might be dangerous."

"Yeah. She's a big scary Divergent, and she's going to make your head explode with only the power of her brain," says Lynn, jabbing him between the eyes with her index finger. "Don't tell me you actually *believe* all that kid stuff about the Divergent."

He turns bright red and snatches some of his things from a pile next to the bed. I feel bad for making him move until I see him toss his things down a few bunks over. He doesn't have to go far.

"I could have done that," I say. "Slept over there, I mean."

"Yeah, I know." Lynn grins. "He deserves it. He called Zeke a traitor right to Uriah's face. It's not like it's not true, but that's no reason to be a jerk about it. I think Candor is rubbing off on him. He feels like he can just say whatever he wants. Hey, Mar!"

Marlene pokes her head around one of the bunks and smiles toothily at me.

"Hey, Tris!" says Marlene. "Welcome. What's up, Lynn?"

"Can you get some of the smaller girls to give up a few pieces of clothing each?" Lynn says, "Not all shirts, though. Jeans, underwear, maybe a spare pair of shoes?"

"Sure," says Marlene.

I put my knife down next to the bottom bunk.

"What 'kid stuff' were you referring to?" I say.

"*The Divergent.* People with special brainpowers? Come on." She shrugs. "I know you believe in it, but I don't."

"So how do you explain me being awake during simulations?" I say. "Or resisting one entirely?"

"I think the leaders choose people at random and change the simulations for them."

"Why would they do that?"

She waves her hand in my face. "Distraction. You're so busy worrying about the Divergent—like my mom—that you forget to worry about what the leaders are doing. It's just a different kind of mind control."

Her eyes skirt mine, and she kicks at the marble floor with the toe of her shoe. I wonder if she's remembering the last time she was on mind control. During the attack simulation.

I have been so focused on what happened to Abnegation that I almost forgot what happened to Dauntless. Hundreds of Dauntless woke to discover the black mark of murder on them, and they didn't even choose it for themselves.

I decide not to argue with her. If she wants to believe in a government conspiracy, I don't think I can dissuade her. She would have to experience it for herself.

"I come bearing clothes," says Marlene, stepping in front of our bunk. She holds a stack of black clothes the size of her torso, which she offers to me with a proud look on her face. "I even guilt-tripped your sister into handing over a dress, Lynn. She brought three."

"You have a sister?" I ask Lynn.

"Yeah," she says, "she's eighteen. She was in Four's initiate class."

"What's her name?"

"Shauna," she says. She looks at Marlene. "I *told* her none of us would need dresses anytime soon, but she didn't listen, as usual."

I remember Shauna. She was one of the people who caught me after zip lining.

"I think it would be easier to fight in a dress," says Marlene, tapping her chin. "It would give your legs freer movement. And who really cares if you flash people your underwear, as long as you're kicking the crap out of them?"

Lynn goes silent, like she recognizes that as a spark of brilliance but can't bring herself to admit it.

"What's this about flashing underwear?" says Uriah, sidestepping a bunk. "Whatever it is, I'm in."

Marlene punches him in the arm.

"Some of us are going to the Hancock building tonight," says Uriah. "You should all come. We're leaving at ten."

"Zip lining?" says Lynn.

"No. Surveillance. We've heard the Erudite keep their lights on all night, which will make it easier to look through their windows. See what they're doing."

"I'll go," I say.

"Me too," says Lynn.

"What? Oh. Me too," Marlene says, smiling at Uriah. "I'm going to get food. Want to come?"

"Sure," he says.

Marlene waves as they walk away. She used to walk with a lift in her step, like she was skipping. Now her steps are smoother—more elegant, maybe, but lacking the childish joy I associate with her. I wonder what she did when she was under the simulation.

Lynn's mouth puckers.

"What?" I say.

"Nothing," she snaps. She shakes her head. "They've just been hanging out alone all the time lately."

"He needs all the friends he can get, it sounds like," I say. "What with Zeke and all."

"Yeah. What a nightmare that was. One day he was here, and the next . . ." She sighs. "No matter how long you train someone to be brave, you never know if they are or not until something real happens."

Her eyes fix on mine. I never noticed before how strange they are, a golden brown. And now that her hair has grown in somewhat, and her baldness isn't the first thing I see, I also notice her delicate nose, her full lips— she is striking without trying to be. I am envious of her for a moment, and then I think she must hate it, and that's why she shaved her head.

"*You* are brave," she says. "You don't need me to say it, because you already know it. But I want you to know that I know."

She is complimenting me, but I still feel like she smacked me with something.

Then she adds, "Don't mess it up."

+ + +

A few hours later, after I've eaten lunch and taken a nap, I sit down on the edge of my bed to change the bandage on my shoulder. I take off my T-shirt, leaving my tank top on—there are a lot of Dauntless around, gathering between the bunks, laughing at one another's jokes. I have just finished applying more healing salve when I hear a shriek of laughter. Uriah charges down the aisle between the bunks with Marlene thrown over his shoulder. She waves at me as they pass, her face red.

Lynn, who is sitting on the next bunk, snorts. "I don't see how he can be *flirty*, with everything that's going on."

"He's supposed to shuffle around, scowling all the time?" I say, reaching over my shoulder to press the bandage to my skin. "Maybe you can learn something from him."

"You're one to talk," she says. "You're always moping. We should start calling you Beatrice Prior, Queen of Tragedy."

I stand and punch her arm, harder than if I was kidding, softer than if I was serious. "Shut up."

Without looking at me, she shoves my shoulder into the bunk. "I don't take orders from Stiffs."

I notice a slight curl in her lip and suppress a grin myself.

"Ready to go?" Lynn says.

"Where are you going?" Tobias says, slipping between his bunk and mine to stand in the aisle with us. My mouth feels dry. I haven't spoken to him all day, and I'm not sure what to expect. Will it be awkward, or will we go back to normal?

"Top of the Hancock building to spy on Erudite," Lynn says. "Want to come?"

Tobias gives me a look. "No, I've got a few things to take care of here. But be careful."

I nod. I know why he doesn't want to come—Tobias tries to avoid heights, if at all possible. He touches my arm, holding me back for just a moment. I tense up—he hasn't touched me since before our fight—and he releases me.

"I'll see you later," he mutters. "Don't do anything stupid."

"Thanks for that vote of confidence," I say, frowning.

"I didn't mean that," he says. "I meant don't let anyone else do anything stupid. They'll listen to you."

He leans toward me like he's going to kiss me, then seems to think better of it and leans back, biting his lip. It's a small act, but it still feels like rejection. I avoid his eyes and run after Lynn.

Lynn and I walk down the hallway toward the elevator bank. Some of the Dauntless have started to mark the walls with colored squares. Candor headquarters is like a maze to them, and they want to learn to navigate it. I know only how to get to the most basic places: the sleeping area, the cafeteria, the lobby, the interrogation room.

"Why did everyone leave Dauntless headquarters?" I say. "The traitors aren't there, are they?"

"No, they're at Erudite headquarters. We left because Dauntless headquarters has the most surveillance cameras of any area in the city," Lynn says. "We knew the Erudite could probably access all the footage, and that it would take forever to find all the cameras, so we thought it was best to just leave."

"Smart."

"We have our moments."

Lynn jabs her finger into the button for the first floor. I stare at our reflections in the doors. She's taller than I am by just a few inches, and though her baggy shirt and pants try to obscure it, I can tell that her body bends and curves like it's supposed to.

"What?" she says, scowling at me.

"Why did you shave your head?"

"Initiation," she says. "I love Dauntless, but Dauntless guys don't see Dauntless girls as a threat during initiation. I got sick of it. So I figured, if I don't look so much like a girl, maybe they won't look at me that way."

"I think you could have used being underestimated to your advantage."

"Yeah, and what? Acted all faint every time something scary came around?" Lynn rolls her eyes. "Do you think I have zero dignity or something?"

"I think a mistake the Dauntless make is refusing to be cunning," I say. "You don't always have to smack people in the face with how strong you are."

"Maybe you should dress in blue from now on," she says, "if you're going to act like such an Erudite. Plus, you do the same thing, but without the head shaving."

I slip out of the elevator before I say something I'll regret. Lynn is quick to forgive, but quick to ignite, like most Dauntless. Like me, except for the "quick to forgive" part.

As usual, a few Dauntless with large guns cross back and forth in front of the doors, watching for intruders. Just in front of them stands a small group of younger Dauntless, including Uriah; Marlene; Lynn's sister,

Shauna; and Lauren, who taught the Dauntless-born initiates as Four taught the faction transfers during initiation. Her ear gleams when she moves her head—it is pierced from top to bottom.

Lynn stops short, and I step on her heel. She swears.

"What a charmer you are," says Shauna, smiling at Lynn. They don't look much alike, except for their hair color, which is a medium brown, but Shauna's is chin length, like mine.

"Yes, that's my goal. To be charming," Lynn replies.

Shauna drapes an arm across Lynn's shoulders. It's strange to see Lynn with a sister—to see Lynn with a connection to someone at all. Shauna glances at me, her smile disappearing. She looks wary.

"Hi," I say, because there's nothing else to say.

"Hello," she says.

"Oh God, Mom's gotten to you, too, hasn't she." Lynn covers her face with one hand. "Shauna—"

"Lynn. Keep your mouth shut for once," says Shauna, her eyes still on me. She seems tense, like she thinks I might attack her at any moment. With my special brainpowers.

"Oh!" says Uriah, rescuing me. "Tris, do you know Lauren?"

"Yeah," Lauren says, before I can answer. Her voice is

sharp and clear, like she's scolding him, except it seems to be the way she naturally sounds. "She went through my fear landscape for practice during initiation. So she knows me better than she should, probably."

"Really? I thought the transfers would go through Four's landscape," says Uriah.

"Like he would let anyone do that," she says, snorting.

Something inside me gets warm and soft. He let *me* go through it.

I see a flicker of blue over Lauren's shoulder, and peer around her to get a better look.

Then the guns go off.

The glass doors explode into fragments. Dauntless soldiers with blue armbands stand on the sidewalk outside, carrying guns I've never seen before, guns with narrow, blue beams of light streaming from above their barrels.

"Traitors!" someone screams.

The Dauntless draw their guns, almost in unison. I do not have one to draw, so I duck behind the wall of loyal Dauntless in front of me, my shoes crunching pieces of glass beneath their soles, and pull my knife out of my back pocket.

All around me, people drop to the ground. My fellow faction members. My closest friends. All of them falling—they must be dead, or dying—as the earsplitting bang of bullets filling my ears.

Then I freeze. One of the blue beams is fixed on my chest. I dive sideways to get out of the line of fire, but I don't move fast enough.

The gun goes off. I fall.

CHAPTER
FIFTEEN

THE PAIN SUBSIDES to a dull ache. I slide my hand under my jacket and feel for the wound.

I'm not bleeding. But the force of the gunshot knocked me down, so I had to have been hit with something. I run my fingers over my shoulder, and feel a hard bump where the skin used to be smooth.

I hear a crack against the floor next to my face, and a metal cylinder about the size of my hand rolls to a stop against my head. Before I can move it, white smoke sprays out of both ends. I cough, and throw it away from me, deeper into the lobby. It isn't the only cylinder, though— they are everywhere, filling the room with smoke that does not burn or sting. In fact, it only obscures my view for a few seconds before evaporating completely.

What was the point of that?

Lying on the floor all around me are Dauntless soldiers with their eyes closed. I frown as I look Uriah up and down—he doesn't seem to be bleeding. I see no wound near his vital organs, which means he isn't dead. So what knocked him unconscious? I look over my left shoulder, where Lynn fell in a strange, half-curled position. She's also unconscious.

The Dauntless traitors walk into the lobby, their guns held up. I decide to do what I always do when I'm not sure what's going on: I act like everyone else. I let my head drop and close my eyes. My heart pounds as the Dauntless's footsteps come closer, and closer, squeaking on the marble floors. I bite my tongue to suppress a cry of pain as one of them steps on my hand.

"Not sure why we can't just shoot them all in the head," one of them says. "If there's no army, we win."

"Now, Bob, we can't just kill *everyone*," a cold voice says.

The hair on the back of my neck stands up. I would know that voice anywhere. It belongs to Eric, leader of the Dauntless.

"No people means no one left to create prosperous conditions," Eric continues. "Anyway, it's not your job to ask questions." He raises his voice. "Half in the elevators, half in the stairwells, left and right! Go!"

There's a gun a few feet to my left. If I opened my eyes, I could grab it and fire at him before he knew what hit him. But there's no guarantee I would be able to touch it without panicking again.

I wait until I hear the last footstep disappear behind an elevator door or into a stairwell before opening my eyes. Everyone in the lobby appears to be unconscious. Whatever they gassed us with, it had to be simulation-inducing or I wouldn't be the only one awake. It doesn't make any sense—it doesn't follow the simulation rules I'm familiar with—but I don't have time to think it through.

I grab my knife and get up, trying to ignore the ache in my shoulder. I run over to one of the dead Dauntless traitors near the doorway. She was middle-aged; there are hints of gray in her dark hair. I try not to look at the bullet wound in her head, but the dim light glows on what looks like bone, and I gag.

Think. I don't care who she was, or what her name was, or how old she was. I care only about the blue armband she wears. I have to focus on that. I try to hook my finger around the fabric, but it doesn't come loose. It appears to be attached to her black jacket. I will have to take that, too.

I unzip my jacket and toss it over her face so I don't have to look at her. Then I unzip her jacket and pull it, first from her left arm, and then from her right arm, gritting my teeth as I slide it from beneath her heavy body.

"Tris!" someone says. I turn around, jacket in one hand, knife in the other. I put the knife away—the invading Dauntless weren't carrying them, and I don't want to be conspicuous.

Uriah stands behind me.

"Divergent?" I ask him. There is no time to be shocked.

"Yeah," he says.

"Get a jacket," I say.

He crouches next to one of the other Dauntless traitors, this one young, not even old enough to be a Dauntless member. I flinch at the sight of his death-pale face. Someone so young shouldn't be dead; shouldn't even have been here in the first place.

My face hot with anger, I shrug the woman's jacket on. Uriah pulls his own jacket on, his mouth pinched.

"*They're* the only ones who are dead," he says quietly. "Something about that seem wrong to you?"

"They must have known we would shoot at them, but they came anyway," I say. "Questions later. We have to get up there."

"Up there? Why?" he says. "We should get out of here."

"You want to run away before you know what's going on?" I scowl at him. "Before the Dauntless upstairs know what hit them?"

"What if someone recognizes us?"

I shrug. "We just have to hope they won't."

I sprint toward the stairwell, and he follows me. As soon as my foot touches the first stair, I wonder what on earth I intend to do. There are bound to be more of the Divergent in this building, but will they know what they are? Will they know to hide? And what do I expect to gain from submerging myself in an army of Dauntless traitors?

Deep inside me I know the answer: I am being reckless. I will probably gain nothing. I will probably die.

And more disturbing still: I don't really care.

"They'll work their way upward," I say between breaths. "So you should . . . go to the third floor. Tell them to . . . evacuate. Quietly."

"Where are *you* going, then?"

"Floor two," I say. I shove my shoulder into the second-floor door. I know what to do on the second floor: look for the Divergent.

+ + +

As I walk down the hallway, stepping over unconscious people dressed in black and white, I think of a verse of the song Candor children used to sing when they thought no one could hear them:

Dauntless is the cruelest of the five
They tear each other to pieces. . . .

It has never seemed truer to me than now, watching Dauntless traitors induce a sleeping simulation that is not so different from the one that forced them to kill members of Abnegation not a month ago.

We are the only faction that could divide like this. Amity would not allow a schism; no one in Abnegation would be so selfish; Candor would argue until they found a common solution; and even Erudite would never do something so illogical. We really are the cruelest faction.

I step over a draped arm and a woman with her mouth hanging open, and hum the beginning of the next verse of the song under my breath.

Erudite is the coldest of the five
Knowledge is a costly thing. . . .

I wonder when Jeanine realized that Erudite and Dauntless would make a deadly combination. Ruthlessness and cold logic, it seems, can accomplish almost anything, including putting one and a half factions to sleep.

I scan faces and bodies as I walk, searching for irregular breaths, flickering eyelids, anything to suggest that the people lying on the ground are just pretending to be unconscious. So far, all the breathing is even and all the eyelids are still. Maybe none of the Candor are Divergent.

"Eric!" I hear someone shout from down the hall. I hold my breath as he walks right toward me. I try not to move. If I move, he'll look at me, and he'll recognize me, I know it. I look down, and tense so hard I tremble. *Don't look at me don't look at me don't look at me . . .*

Eric strides past me and down the hallway to my left. I should continue my search as quickly as possible, but curiosity urges me forward, toward whoever called for Eric. The shout sounded urgent.

When I lift my eyes, I see a Dauntless soldier standing over a kneeling woman. She wears a white blouse and a black skirt, and has her hands behind her head. Eric's smile looks greedy even in profile.

"Divergent," he says. "Well done. Bring her to the elevator bank. We'll decide which ones to kill and which ones to bring back later."

The Dauntless soldier grabs the woman by the ponytail and starts toward the elevator bank, dragging her behind him. She shrieks, and then scrambles to her feet, bent over. I try to swallow but it feels like I have a wad of cotton balls in my throat.

Eric continues down the hallway, away from me, and I try not to stare as the Candor woman stumbles past me, her hair still trapped in the fist of the Dauntless soldier. By now I know how terror works: I let it control me for a few seconds, and then force myself to act.

One . . . two . . . three . . .

I start forward with a new sense of purpose. Watching each person to see if they're awake is taking too much time. The next unconscious person I come across, I step hard on their pinkie finger. No response, not even a twitch. I step over them and find the next person's finger, pressing hard with the toe of my shoe. No response there either.

I hear someone else shout, "Got one!" from a distant hallway and start to feel frantic. I hop over fallen man after fallen woman, over children and teenagers and the elderly, stepping on fingers or stomachs or ankles, searching for signs of pain. I barely see their faces after a while, but still I get no response. I am playing hide-and-seek with the Divergent, but I'm not the only person who's "it."

And then it happens. I step on a Candor girl's pinkie, and her face twitches. Just a little—an impressive attempt at concealing the pain—but enough to catch my attention.

I look over my shoulder to see if anyone is near me, but they've all moved on from this central hallway. I check for the nearest stairwell—there's one just ten feet away, down a side hallway to my right. I crouch next to the girl's head.

"Hey, kid," I say as quietly as I can. "It's okay. I'm not one of them."

Her eyes open, just a little.

"There's a staircase about three yards away," I say. "I'll tell you when no one is watching, and then you have to run, understand?"

She nods.

I stand and turn in a slow circle. A Dauntless traitor to my left is looking away, nudging a limp Dauntless with her foot. Two Dauntless traitors behind me are laughing about something. One in front of me is spacing out in my direction, but then he lifts his head and starts down the hallway again, away from me.

"Now," I say.

The girl gets up and sprints toward the door to the stairwell. I watch her until the door clicks shut, and see my reflection in one of the windows. But I'm not standing alone in a hallway of sleeping people, like I thought. Eric is standing right behind me.

+ + +

I look at his reflection, and he looks back at me. I could make a break for it. If I move fast enough, he might not have the presence of mind to grab me. But I know, even as the idea occurs to me, that I won't be able to outrun him. And I won't be able to shoot him, because I didn't take a gun.

I spin around, bringing my elbow up as I do, and thrust it toward Eric's face. It catches the end of his chin, but not hard enough to do any damage. He grabs my left arm with one hand and presses a gun barrel to my forehead with the other, smiling down at me.

"I don't understand," he says, "how you could possibly be stupid enough to come up here with no gun."

"Well, I'm smart enough to do this," I say. I stomp hard on his foot, which I fired a bullet into less than a month ago. He screams, his face contorting, and drives the heel of the gun into my jaw. I clench my teeth to suppress a groan. Blood trickles down my neck—he broke the skin.

Through all that, his grip on my arm does not loosen once. But the fact that he didn't just shoot me in the head tells me something: He's not allowed to kill me yet.

"I was surprised to discover you were still alive," he says. "Considering I'm the one who told Jeanine to construct that water tank just for you."

I try to figure out what I can do that will be painful enough for him to release me. I've just decided on a hard kick to the groin when he slips behind me and grabs me by both arms, pressing against me so I can barely move my feet. His fingernails dig into my skin, and I grit my teeth, both from the pain and from the sickening feeling of his chest on my back.

"She thought studying one of the Divergent's reaction to a real-life version of a simulation would be fascinating," he says, and he presses me forward so I have to walk. His breath tickles my hair. "And I agreed. You see, ingenuity—one of the qualities we most value in Erudite—requires creativity."

He twists his hands so the calluses scrape against my arms. I shift my body slightly to the left as I walk, trying to position one of my feet between his advancing feet. I notice with fierce pleasure that he's limping.

"Sometimes creativity seems wasteful, illogical . . . unless it's done for a greater purpose. In this case, the accumulation of knowledge."

I stop walking just long enough to bring my heel up, hard, between his legs. A high-pitched cry hitches in his throat, stopped before it really began, and his hands go limp for just a moment. In that moment, I twist my body as hard as I can and break free. I don't know where I will run, but I have to run, I have to—

He grabs my elbow, yanking me back, and pushes his thumb into the wound in my shoulder, twisting until pain makes my vision go black at the edges, and I scream at the top of my lungs.

"I *thought* I recalled from the footage of you in that water tank that you got shot in that shoulder," he says. "It seems I was right."

My knees crumple beneath me, and he grabs my collar almost carelessly, dragging me toward the elevator bank. The fabric digs into my throat, choking me, and I stumble after him. My body throbs with lingering pain.

When we reach the elevator bank, he forces me to my knees next to the Candor woman I saw earlier. She and four others sit between the two rows of elevators, kept in place by Dauntless with guns.

"I want one gun on her at all times," says Eric. "Not just aimed at her. *On* her."

A Dauntless man pushes a gun barrel into the back of my neck. It forms a cold circle on my skin. I lift my eyes to Eric. His face is red, his eyes watering.

"What's the matter, Eric?" I say, raising my eyebrows. "Afraid of a little girl?"

"I'm not stupid," he says, pushing his hands through his hair. "That little-girl act may have worked on me before, but it won't work again. You're the best attack dog they've got." He leans closer to me. "Which is why I'm sure you'll be put down soon enough."

One of the elevator doors opens, and a Dauntless soldier shoves Uriah—whose lips are stained with blood—toward the short row of the Divergent. Uriah glances at me, but I can't read his expression well enough to know if he succeeded or failed. If he's here, he probably failed. Now they'll find all the Divergent in the building, and most of us will die.

I should probably be afraid. But instead a hysterical laugh bubbles inside me, because I just remembered something:

Maybe I can't hold a gun. But I have a knife in my back pocket.

CHAPTER
SIXTEEN

I SHIFT MY hand back, centimeter by centimeter, so the soldier pointing a gun at me doesn't notice. The elevator doors open again, bringing more of the Divergent with more Dauntless traitors. The Candor woman on my right whimpers. Strands of her hair are stuck to her lips, which are wet with spit, or tears, I can't tell.

My hand reaches the corner of my back pocket. I keep it steady, my fingers shaking with anticipation. I have to wait for the right moment, when Eric is close.

I focus on the mechanics of my breathing, imagining air filling every part of my lungs as I inhale, then remembering as I exhale how all my blood, oxygenated and unoxygenated, travels to and from the same heart.

It's easier to think of biology than the line of the

Divergent sitting between the elevators. A Candor boy who can't be older than eleven sits to my left. He's braver than the woman to my right—he stares at the Dauntless soldier in front of him, unflinching.

Air in, air out. Blood pushed all the way to my extremities—the heart is a powerful muscle, the strongest muscle in the body in terms of longevity. More Dauntless arrive, reporting successful sweeps of specific floors of the Merciless Mart. Hundreds of people unconscious on the floor, shot with something other than bullets, and I have no idea why.

But I am thinking of the heart. Not of my heart anymore, but of Eric's, and how empty his chest will sound when his heart is no longer beating. Despite how much I hate him, I don't really want to kill him, at least not with a knife, up close where I can see the life leave him. But I have one chance left to do something useful, and if I want to hit the Erudite where it hurts, I have to take one of their leaders from them.

I notice that no one ever brought the Candor girl I warned to the elevator bank, which means she must have gotten away. Good.

Eric clasps his hands behind his back and begins to pace, back and forth, before the line of Divergent.

"My orders are to take only two of you back to Erudite

headquarters for testing," says Eric. "The rest of you are to be executed. There are several ways to determine who among you will be least useful to us."

His footsteps slow when he approaches me. I tense my fingers, about to grab the knife handle, but he doesn't come close enough. He keeps walking and stops in front of the boy to my left.

"The brain finishes developing at age twenty-five," says Eric. "Therefore your Divergence is not completely developed."

He lifts his gun and fires.

A strangled scream leaps out of my body as the boy slumps to the ground, and I squeeze my eyes shut. Every muscle in my body strains toward him, but I hold myself back. *Wait, wait, wait.* I can't think of the boy. *Wait.* I force my eyes open and blink tears from them.

My scream accomplished one thing: now Eric stands in front of me, smiling. I caught his attention.

"You are also rather young," he says. "Nowhere near finished developing."

He steps toward me. My fingertips inch closer to the knife handle.

"Most of the Divergent get two results in the aptitude test. Some only get one. No one has ever gotten three, not because of aptitude, but simply because in order to get that result, you have to refuse to choose something," he says, moving closer still. I tilt my head back to look at him, at all the metal gleaming in his face, at his empty eyes.

"My superiors suspect that you got two, Tris," he says. "They don't think you're that complex—just an even blend of Abnegation and Dauntless—selfless to the point of idiocy. Or is that brave to the point of idiocy?"

I close my hand around the knife handle and squeeze. He leans closer.

"Just between you and me . . . *I* think you might have gotten three, because you're the kind of bullheaded person who would refuse to make a simple choice just because she was told to," he says. "Care to enlighten me?"

I lurch forward, pulling my hand out of my pocket. I close my eyes as I thrust the blade up and toward him. I don't want to see his blood.

I feel the knife go in and then pull it out again. My entire body throbs to the rhythm of my heart. The back of my neck is sticky with sweat. I open my eyes as Eric slumps to the ground, and then—chaos.

The Dauntless traitors aren't holding lethal guns, only ones that shoot whatever it is they shot at us before, so they all scramble for their real guns. As they do, Uriah launches himself at one of them and punches him hard in the jaw. The life goes out of the soldier's eyes and he falls, knocked out. Uriah takes the soldier's gun and starts shooting at the Dauntless closest to us.

I reach for Eric's gun, so panicked I can barely see, and when I look up, I swear the amount of Dauntless in the room has doubled. Gunshots fill my ears, and I drop to the ground as everyone starts running. My fingers brush the gun barrel, and I shudder. My hands are too weak to grasp it.

A heavy arm wraps around my shoulders and shoves me toward the wall. My right shoulder burns, and I see the Dauntless symbol tattooed on the back of a neck. Tobias turns, crouched around me to shield me from the gunfire, and shoots.

"Tell me if anyone's behind me!" he says.

I peer over his shoulder, curling my hands into fists around his shirt.

There *are* more Dauntless in the room, Dauntless without blue armbands—loyal Dauntless. My faction. My faction has come to save us. How are they awake?

The Dauntless traitors sprint away from the elevator bank. They were not prepared for an attack, not from all sides. Some of them fight back, but most run for the stairs. Tobias fires over and over again, until his gun runs out of bullets, and the trigger makes a clicking sound instead. My vision is too blurry with tears and my hands too useless to fire a gun. I scream into gritted teeth, frustrated. I can't help. I am worthless.

On the floor, Eric moans. Still alive, for now.

The gunshots gradually stop. My hand is wet. One glimpse of red tells me it's covered in blood—Eric's. I wipe it off on my pants and try to blink the tears away. My ears ring.

"Tris," Tobias says. "You can put the knife down now."

CHAPTER
SEVENTEEN

TOBIAS TELLS ME this story:

When the Erudite reached the lobby stairwell, one of them didn't go up to the second floor. Instead, she ran up to one of the highest levels of the building. There she evacuated a group of loyal Dauntless—including Tobias—to a fire escape the Dauntless traitors had not sealed off. Those loyal Dauntless gathered in the lobby and split into four groups that stormed the stairwells simultaneously, surrounding the Dauntless traitors, who had clustered around the elevator banks.

The Dauntless traitors were not prepared for that much resistance. They thought everyone but the Divergent was unconscious, so they ran.

The Erudite woman was Cara. Will's older sister.

+ + +

Heaving a sigh, I let the jacket slide from my arms and examine my shoulder. A metal disc about the size of my pinkie fingernail is pressed against my skin. Surrounding it is a patch of blue strands, like someone injected blue dye into the tiny veins just beneath the surface of my skin. Frowning, I try to peel the metal disc away from my arm, and feel a sharp pain.

Gritting my teeth, I wedge the flat of my knife blade under the disc and force it up. I scream into my teeth as the pain races through me, making everything go black for a moment. But I keep pushing, as hard as I can, until the disc lifts from my skin enough for me to get my fingers around it. Attached to the bottom of the disc is a needle.

I gag, grasp the disc in my fingertips, and pull one last time. This time, the needle comes free. It's as long as my littlest finger and smeared with my blood. I ignore the blood running down my arm and hold the disc and the needle up to the light above the sink.

Judging by the blue dye in my arm and the needle, they must have injected us with something. But what? Poison? An explosive?

I shake my head. If they had wanted to kill us, most of us were unconscious already, so they could have just shot us all. Whatever they injected us with isn't meant to kill us.

Someone knocks on the door. I don't know why—I'm in a public restroom, after all.

"Tris, you in there?" Uriah's muffled voice asks.

"Yeah," I call back.

Uriah looks better than he did an hour ago—he washed the blood from his mouth, and some of the color has returned to his face. I'm struck, suddenly, by how handsome he is—all his features are proportionate, his eyes dark and lively, his skin bronze-brown. And he has probably always been that handsome. Only boys who have been handsome from a young age have that arrogance in their smile.

Not like Tobias, who is almost shy when he smiles, like he is surprised you bothered to look at him in the first place.

My throat aches. I put the needle and disc on the edge of the sink.

Uriah looks from me to the needle in my hand to the line of blood running from my shoulder to my wrist.

"Gross," he says.

"Wasn't paying attention," I say. I set the needle down and grab a paper towel, mopping up the blood on my arm. "How are the others?"

"Marlene's cracking jokes, as usual." Uriah's smile grows, putting a dimple in his cheek. "Lynn's grumbling.

Wait, you yanked that out of your own arm?" He points to the needle. "God, Tris. Do you have no nerve endings or something?"

"I think I need a bandage."

"You think?" Uriah shakes his head. "You should get some ice for your face, too. So, everyone's waking up now. It's a madhouse out there."

I touch my jaw. It is tender where Eric's gun struck me— I will have to put healing salve on it so it doesn't bruise.

"Is Eric dead?" I don't know which answer I'm hoping for, yes or no.

"No. Some of the Candor decided to give him medical treatment." Uriah scowls at the sink. "Something about honorable treatment of prisoners. Kang's interrogating him in private right now. Doesn't want us there, disturbing the peace or whatever."

I snort.

"Yeah. Anyway, no one gets it," he says, perching on the edge of the sink next to mine. "Why storm in here and fire those things at us and then knock us all out? Why not just kill us?"

"No idea," I say. "The only use I see for it is that it helped them figure out who's Divergent and who's not. But that can't be the only reason they did it."

"I don't get why they have it out for us. I mean, when

they were trying to mind control themselves an army, sure, but now? Seems useless."

I frown as I press a clean paper towel to my shoulder, to stop the bleeding. He's right. Jeanine already has an army. So why kill the Divergent now?

"Jeanine doesn't want to kill everyone," I say slowly. "She knows that would be illogical. Without each faction, society doesn't function, because each faction trains its members for particular jobs. What she wants is *control*."

I glance up at my reflection. My jaw is swollen, and fingernail marks are still on my arms. Disgusting.

"She must be planning another simulation," I say. "Same thing as before, but this time, she wants to make sure that everyone is either under its influence or dead."

"But the simulation only lasts for a certain period of time," he says. "It's not useful unless you're trying to accomplish something specific."

"Right." I sigh. "I don't know. I don't get it." I pick up the needle. "I don't get what this thing is either. If it was like the other simulation-inducing injections, it was just meant for one use. So why shoot these things at us just to put us unconscious? It doesn't make any sense."

"I dunno, Tris, but right now we've got a huge building full of panicked people to deal with. Let's go get you a bandage." He pauses and then says, "Can you do me a favor?"

"What is it?"

"Don't tell anyone I'm Divergent." He bites his lip. "Shauna's my friend, and I don't want her to suddenly become afraid of me."

"Sure," I say, forcing a smile. "I'll keep it to myself."

+ + +

I am awake all night removing needles from people's arms. After a few hours I stop trying to be gentle. I just pull as hard as I can.

I find out that the Candor boy Eric shot in the head was named Bobby, and that Eric is in stable condition, and that of the hundreds of people in the Merciless Mart, only eighty don't have needles buried in their flesh, seventy of whom are Dauntless, one of whom is Christina. All night I puzzle over needles and serums and simulations, trying to inhabit the minds of my enemies.

In the morning, I run out of needles to remove and go to the cafeteria, rubbing my eyes. Jack Kang announced that we would have a meeting at noon, so maybe I can fit in a long nap after I eat.

When I walk into the cafeteria, though, I see Caleb.

Caleb runs up to me and folds me carefully into his arms. I breathe a sigh of relief. I thought I had gotten to the point where I didn't need my brother anymore, but I don't think such a point actually exists. I relax against him for a moment, and catch Tobias's eye over Caleb's shoulder.

"Are you all right?" Caleb says, pulling back. "Your jaw . . ."

"It's nothing," I say. "Just swollen."

"I heard they got a bunch of the Divergent and started shooting them. Thank God they didn't find you."

"Actually, they did. But they only killed one," I say. I pinch the bridge of my nose to relieve some of the pressure in my head. "But I'm all right. When did you get here?"

"About ten minutes ago. I came with Marcus," he says. "As our only legal political leader, he felt it was his duty to be here—we didn't hear about the attack until an hour ago. One of the factionless saw the Dauntless storming into the building, and news takes a while to travel among the factionless."

"Marcus is *alive*?" I say. We never actually saw him die when we escaped the Amity compound, but I just assumed he had—I'm not sure how I feel. Disappointed, maybe, because I hate him for how he treated Tobias? Or relieved, because the last Abnegation leader is still alive? Is it possible to feel both?

"He and Peter escaped, and walked back to the city," says Caleb.

I am not at all relieved to find out that Peter is still alive. "Where's Peter, then?"

"He is where you would expect him to be," Caleb replies.

"Erudite," I say. I shake my head. "What a—"

I can't even think of a word strong enough to describe him. Apparently I need to expand my vocabulary.

Caleb's face twists for a moment, then he nods and touches my shoulder. "Are you hungry? Want me to get you something?"

"Yes, please," I say. "I'll be back in a little while, okay? I have to talk to Tobias."

"All right." Caleb squeezes my arm and walks off, probably to get in the miles-long cafeteria line. Tobias and I stand yards away from each other for a few seconds.

He approaches me slowly.

"You okay?" he says.

"I might throw up if I have to answer that one more time," I say. "I don't have a bullet in my head, do I? So I'm good."

"Your jaw is so swollen you look like you have a wad of food in your cheek, and you just stabbed Eric," he says, frowning. "I'm not allowed to ask if you're okay?"

I sigh. I should tell him about Marcus, but I don't want to do it here, with so many people around. "Yeah. I'm okay."

His arm jerks like he was thinking of touching me but

decided against it. Then he reconsiders and slides his arm around me, pulling me to him.

Suddenly I think maybe I'll let someone else take all the risks, maybe I'll just start acting selfishly so that I can stay close to Tobias without hurting him. All I want is to bury my face in his neck and forget anything else exists.

"I'm sorry it took me so long to come get you," he whispers into my hair.

I sigh and touch his back with just my fingertips. I could stand here until I go unconscious from exhaustion, but I shouldn't; I can't. I pull back and say, "I need to talk to you. Can we go somewhere quiet?"

He nods, and we leave the cafeteria. One of the Dauntless we pass yells, "Oh, look! It's *Tobias Eaton!*"

I had almost forgotten about the interrogation, and the name it revealed to all of Dauntless.

Another one yells, "I saw your daddy here earlier, Eaton! Are you gonna go hide?"

Tobias straightens and stiffens, like someone is training a gun at his chest instead of jeering at him.

"Yeah, are you gonna hide, coward?"

A few people around us laugh. I grab Tobias's arm and steer him toward the elevators before he can react. He looked like he was about to punch someone. Or worse.

"I was going to tell you—he came with Caleb," I say. "He and Peter escaped Amity—"

"What were you waiting for, then?" he says, but not harshly. His voice sounds somehow detached from him, like it is floating between us.

"It's not the kind of news you deliver in a cafeteria," I say.

"Fair enough," he says.

We wait in silence for the elevator, Tobias chewing on his lip and staring into space. He does that all the way to the eighteenth floor, which is empty. There, the silence wraps around me like Caleb's embrace did, calming me. I sit down on one of the benches on the edge of the interrogation room, and Tobias pulls Niles's chair over to sit in front of me.

"Didn't there used to be two of these?" he says, frowning at the chair.

"Yeah," I say. "I, uh . . . it got thrown out the window."

"Strange," he says. He sits. "So what did you want to talk about? Or was that about Marcus?"

"No, that wasn't it. Are you . . . all right?" I say cautiously.

"I don't have a bullet in my head, do I?" he says, staring at his hands. "So I'm fine. I'd like to talk about something else."

"I want to talk about simulations," I say. "But first,

something else—your mother thought Jeanine would go after the factionless next. Obviously she was wrong—and I'm not sure why. It's not like the Candor are battle ready or anything—"

"Well, think about it," he says. "Think it through, like the Erudite."

I give him a look.

"What?" he says. "If you can't, the rest of us have no hope."

"Fine," I say. "Um . . . it had to be because Dauntless and Candor were the most logical targets. Because . . . the factionless are in multiple places, whereas we're all in the same place."

"Right," he says. "Also, when Jeanine attacked Abnegation, she got all the Abnegation data. My mother told me that the Abnegation had documented the factionless Divergent populations, which means that after the attack, Jeanine must have found out that the proportion of Divergent among the factionless is higher than among the Candor. That makes them an illogical target."

"All right. Then tell me about the serum again," I say. "It has a few parts, right?"

"Two," he says, nodding. "The transmitter and the liquid that induces the simulation. The transmitter communicates information to the brain from the computer, and vice versa, and the liquid alters the brain to put it in a simulation state."

I nod. "And the transmitter only works for one simulation, right? What happens to it after that?"

"It dissolves," he says. "As far as I know, the Erudite haven't been able to develop a transmitter that lasts for more than one simulation, although the attack simulation lasted far longer than any simulation I've seen before."

The words "as far as I know" stick in my mind. Jeanine has spent most of her adult life developing the serums. If she's still hunting down the Divergent, she's probably still obsessed with creating more advanced versions of the technology.

"What's this about, Tris?" he says.

"Have you seen this yet?" I say, pointing at the bandage covering my shoulder.

"Not up close," he says. "Zeke and I were hauling wounded Erudite up to the fourth floor all morning."

I peel away the edge of the bandage, revealing the puncture wound—no longer bleeding, thankfully—and the patch of blue dye that doesn't seem to be fading. Then I reach into my pocket and take out the needle that was buried in my arm.

"When they attacked, they weren't trying to kill us. They were shooting us with these," I say.

His hand touches the dyed skin around the puncture wound. I didn't notice it before because it was happening right in front of me, but he looks different than he used to, during initiation. He's let his facial hair grow in a little, and his hair is longer than I've ever seen it—dense enough to show me that it is brown, not black.

He takes the needle from me and taps the metal disc at the end of it. "This is probably hollow. It must have contained whatever that blue stuff in your arm is. What happened after you were shot?"

"They tossed these gas-spewing cylinders into the room, and everyone went unconscious. That is, everyone but Uriah and me and the other Divergent."

Tobias doesn't seem surprised. I narrow my eyes.

"Did you know that Uriah was Divergent?"

He shrugs. "Of course. I ran his simulations, too."

"And you never told me?"

"Privileged information," he says. "Dangerous information."

I feel a flare of anger—how many things is he going to keep from me?—and try to stifle it. Of course he couldn't tell me Uriah was Divergent. He was just respecting Uriah's privacy. It makes sense.

I clear my throat. "You saved our lives, you know," I say. "Eric was trying to hunt us down."

"I think we're past keeping track of who has saved whose life." He looks at me for a few long seconds.

"Anyway," I say to break the silence. "After we figured out that everyone was asleep, Uriah ran upstairs to warn the people who were up there, and I went to the second floor to figure out what was going on. Eric had all the Divergent by the elevators, and he was trying to figure out which of us he was going to take back with him. He said he was allowed to take two. I don't know why he was going to take any."

"Odd," he says.

"Any ideas?"

"My guess is that the needle injected you with a transmitter," he says, "and the gas was an aerosol version of the liquid that alters the brain. But why . . ." A crease appears between his eyebrows. "Oh. She put everyone to sleep to find out who the Divergent were."

"You think that's the only reason for shooting us with transmitters?"

He shakes his head, and his eyes lock on mine. Their blue is so dark and familiar that I feel like it could swallow me whole. For a moment I wish it would, so that I could escape this place and all that has happened.

"I think you've already figured it out," he says, "but you want me to contradict you. And I'm not going to."

"They've developed a long-lasting transmitter," I say. He nods.

"So now we're all wired for multiple simulations," I add. "As many as Jeanine wants, maybe."

He nods again.

My next breath shakes on the way out of my mouth. "This is really bad, Tobias."

+ + +

In the hallway outside the interrogation room, he stops, leaning against the wall.

"So you attacked Eric," he says. "Was that during the invasion? Or when you were by the elevators?"

"By the elevators," I say.

"One thing I don't understand," he says. "You were downstairs. You could have just run away. But instead, you decided to dive into a crowd of armed Dauntless all by yourself. And I'm willing to bet you weren't carrying a gun."

I press my lips together.

"Is that true?" he demands.

"What makes you think I didn't have a gun?" I scowl.

"You haven't been able to touch a gun since the attack," he says. "I understand why, with the whole Will thing, but—"

"That has nothing to do with it."

"No?" He lifts his eyebrows.

"I did what I had to do."

"Yeah. But now you should be done," he says, pulling away from the wall to face me. Candor hallways are wide, wide enough for all the space I want to keep between us. "You should have stayed with the Amity. You should have stayed far away from all of this."

"No, I shouldn't have," I say. "You think you know what's best for me? You have no idea. I was going crazy with the Amity. Here I finally feel . . . sane again."

"Which is odd, considering you are acting like a psychopath," he says. "It's not brave, choosing the position you were in yesterday. It's beyond stupid—it's suicidal. Don't you have any regard for your own life?"

"Of course I do!" I retort. "I was trying to do something useful!"

For a few seconds he just stares at me.

"You're more than Dauntless," he says in a low voice. "But if you want to be just like them, hurling yourself into ridiculous situations for no reason and retaliating against your enemies without any regard for what's ethical, go right ahead. I thought you were better than that, but maybe I was wrong!"

I clench my hands, my jaw.

"You shouldn't insult the Dauntless," I say. "They took

you in when you had nowhere else to go. Trusted you with a good job. Gave you all your friends."

I lean against the wall, my eyes on the floor. The tiles in the Merciless Mart are always black and white, and here they are in a checkered pattern. If I unfocus my eyes, I see exactly what the Candor don't believe in—gray. Maybe Tobias and I don't believe in it either. Not really.

I weigh too much, more than my frame can support, so much I should fall right through the floor.

"Tris."

I keep staring.

"Tris."

I finally look at him.

"I just don't want to lose you."

We stand there for a few minutes. I don't say what I'm thinking, which is that he might be right. There is a part of me that wants to be lost, that struggles to join my parents and Will so that I don't have to ache for them anymore. A part of me that wants to see whatever comes next.

+ + +

"So you're her brother?" says Lynn. "I guess we know who got the good genes."

I laugh at the expression on Caleb's face, his mouth

drawn into a slight pucker and his eyes wide.

"When do you have to get back?" I say, nudging him with my elbow.

I bite into the sandwich Caleb got me from the cafeteria line. I am nervous to have him here, mixing the sad remains of my family life with the sad remains of my Dauntless life. What will he think of my friends, my faction? What will my faction think of him?

"Soon," he says. "I don't want anyone to worry."

"I didn't realize Susan had changed her name to 'Anyone,'" I say, raising an eyebrow.

"Ha-ha," he says, making a face at me.

Teasing between siblings should feel familiar, but it doesn't for us. Abnegation discouraged anything that might make someone feel uncomfortable, and teasing was included.

I can feel how cautious we are with each other, now that we're discovering a different way to relate in light of our new factions and our parents' deaths. Every time I look at him, I realize that he's the only family I have left and I feel desperate, desperate to keep him around, desperate to narrow the gap between us.

"Is Susan another Erudite defector?" says Lynn, stabbing a string bean with her fork. Uriah and Tobias are still in the lunch line, waiting behind two dozen Candor who are too busy bickering to get their food.

"No, she was our neighbor when we were kids. She's Abnegation," I say.

"And you're involved with her?" she asks Caleb. "Don't you think that's kind of a stupid move? I mean, when all this is over, you'll be in different factions, living in completely different places. . . ."

"Lynn," Marlene says, touching her shoulder, "shut up, will you?"

Across the room, something blue catches my attention. Cara just walked in. I put down my sandwich, my appetite gone, and look up at her with my head lowered. She walks to the far corner of the cafeteria, where a few tables of Erudite refugees sit. Most of them have abandoned their blue clothes in favor of black-and-white ones, but they still wear their glasses. I try to focus on Caleb instead— but Caleb is watching the Erudite, too.

"I can't go back to Erudite any more than *they* can," says Caleb. "When this is over, I won't have a faction."

For the first time I notice how sad he looks when he talks about the Erudite. I didn't realize how difficult the decision to leave them must have been for him.

"You could go sit with them," I say, nodding toward the Erudite refugees.

"I don't know them." He shrugs. "I was only there for a month, remember?"

Uriah drops his tray on the table, scowling. "I overheard someone talking about Eric's interrogation in the lunch line. Apparently he knew almost *nothing* about Jeanine's plan."

"What?" Lynn slaps her fork on the table. "How is that even possible?"

Uriah shrugs, and sits.

"I'm not surprised," Caleb says.

Everyone stares at him.

"What?" He flushes. "It would be stupid to confide your entire plan to one person. It's infinitely smarter to give little pieces of it to each person working with you. That way, if someone betrays you, the loss isn't too great."

"Oh," says Uriah.

Lynn picks up her fork and starts eating again.

"I heard the Candor made ice cream," says Marlene, twisting her head around to see the lunch line. "You know, as a kind of 'it sucks we got attacked, but at least there are desserts' thing."

"I feel better already," says Lynn dryly.

"It probably won't be as good as Dauntless cake," says Marlene mournfully. She sighs, and a strand of mousy brown hair falls in her eyes.

"We had good cake," I tell Caleb.

"We had fizzy drinks," he says.

"Ah, but did you have a ledge overlooking an underground river?" says Marlene, waggling her eyebrows. "Or a room where you faced all your nightmares at once?"

"No," says Caleb, "and to be honest, I'm kind of okay with that."

"*Si-ssy,*" sings Marlene.

"*All* your nightmares?" says Caleb, his eyes lighting up. "How does that work? I mean, are the nightmares produced by the computer or by your brain?"

"Oh God." Lynn drops her head into her hands. "Here we go."

Marlene launches into a description of the simulations, and I let her voice, and Caleb's voice, wash over me as I finish my sandwich. Then, despite the clatter of forks and the roar of hundreds of conversations all around me, I rest my head on the table and fall asleep.

CHAPTER EIGHTEEN

"QUIET DOWN, EVERYONE!"

Jack Kang lifts his hands, and the crowd goes silent. That is a talent.

I stand among the crowd of Dauntless who got here late, when there were no seats left. A flash of light catches my eye—lightning. It's not the best time to be meeting in a room with holes in the walls instead of windows, but this is the biggest room they have.

"I know many of you are confused and shaken by what happened yesterday," Jack says. "I have heard many reports from a variety of perspectives, and have gotten a sense for what is straightforward and what requires more investigation."

I tuck my wet hair behind my ears. I woke up ten

minutes before the meeting was supposed to start and ran to the showers. Though I'm still exhausted, I feel more alert now.

"What seems to me to require more investigation," Jack says, "is the Divergent."

He looks tired—he has dark circles under his eyes, and his short hair sticks out at random, like he's been pulling it all night. Despite the stifling heat of the room, he wears a long-sleeved shirt that buttons at the wrists—he must have been distracted when he dressed this morning.

"If you are one of the Divergent, please step forward so that we can hear from you."

I look sideways at Uriah. This feels dangerous. My Divergence is something I am supposed to hide. Admitting it is supposed to mean death. But there is no sense in hiding it now—they already know about me.

Tobias is the first to move. He starts into the crowd, at first turning his body to wedge his way between people, and then, when they step back for him, moving straight toward Jack Kang with his shoulders back.

I move, too, muttering "Excuse me" to the people in front of me. They draw back like I just threatened to spit poison at them. A few others step forward, in Candor black and white, but not many. One of them is the girl I helped.

Despite the notoriety Tobias now has among the

Dauntless, and my new title as That Girl Who Stabbed Eric, we are not the real focus of everyone's attention. Marcus is.

"You, Marcus?" says Jack when Marcus reaches the middle of the room and stands on top of the lower scale in the floor.

"Yes," Marcus says. "I understand that you are concerned—that you all are concerned. You had never heard of the Divergent a week ago, and now all that you know is that they are immune to something to which you arc susceptible, and that is a frightening thing. But I can assure you that there is nothing to be afraid of, as far as we are concerned."

As he speaks, his head tilts and his eyebrows lift in sympathy, and I understand at once why some people like him. He makes you feel that if you just placed everything in his hands, he would take care of it.

"It seems clear to me," says Jack, "that we were attacked so that the Erudite could find the Divergent. Do you know why that is?"

"No, I do not," says Marcus. "Perhaps their intention was merely to identify us. It seems like useful information to have, if they intend to use their simulations again."

"That was *not* their intention." The words are past my lips before I decide to speak them. My voice sounds high and weak compared to Marcus's and Jack's, but it's too late to stop. "They wanted to kill us. They've been killing us since before any of this happened."

Jack's eyebrows draw together. I hear hundreds of tiny sounds, raindrops hitting the roof. The room darkens, as if under the gloom of what I just said.

"That sounds very much like a conspiracy theory," Jack says. "What reason would the Erudite have to kill you?"

My mother said people feared the Divergent because we couldn't be controlled. That may be true, but fear of the uncontrollable is not a concrete enough reason to give Jack Kang for the Erudite wanting us dead. My heart races as I realize that I can't answer his question.

"I . . ." I start. Tobias interrupts me.

"Obviously we don't know," he says, "but there are nearly a dozen mysterious deaths recorded among the Dauntless from the past six years, and there is a correlation between those people and irregular aptitude test results or initiation simulation results."

Lightning strikes, making the room glow. Jack shakes his head. "While that is intriguing, correlation does not constitute evidence."

"A Dauntless leader shot a Candor child in the *head*," I snap. "Did you get a report of *that*? Did it seem 'worthy of investigation'?"

"In fact I did," he says. "And shooting a child in cold blood is a terrible crime that cannot go unpunished. Fortunately, we have the perpetrator in custody and will be able to put him on trial. *However*, we must keep in mind that the Dauntless soldiers did not give any evidence of wanting to harm the majority of us, or they would have killed us while we were unconscious."

I hear irritated murmurs all around me.

"Their peaceful invasion suggests to me that it may be possible to negotiate a peace treaty with the Erudite and the other Dauntless," he continues. "So I will arrange a meeting with Jeanine Matthews to discuss that possibility as soon as possible."

"Their invasion wasn't *peaceful*," I say. I can see the corner of Tobias's mouth from where I stand, and he is smiling. I take a deep breath and begin again. "Just because they didn't shoot you all in the head doesn't mean their intentions were somehow honorable. Why do you think they came here? Just to run through your hallways, knock you unconscious, and leave?"

"I assume they came here for people like you," says Jack. "And while I am concerned for your safety, I don't think we can attack them just because they wanted to kill a fraction of our population."

"Killing you is not the worst thing they can do to

you," I say. "Controlling you is."

Jack's lips curl with amusement. *Amusement.* "Oh? And how will they manage that?"

"They shot you with needles," Tobias says. "Needles full of simulation transmitters. Simulations control you. That's how."

"We know how simulations work," says Jack. "The transmitter is not a permanent implant. If they intended to control us, they would have done it right away."

"But—" I begin.

He interrupts me. "I know you have been under a lot of stress, Tris," he says quietly, "and that you have done a great service to your faction and to Abnegation. But I think your traumatic experience may have compromised your ability to be completely objective. I can't launch an attack based on a little girl's speculations."

I stand statue-still, unable to believe that he could be so stupid. My face burning. *Little girl,* he called me. A little girl who is stressed out to the point of paranoia. That is not me, but now, it's who the Candor think I am.

"*You* don't make our decisions for us, Kang," says Tobias.

All around me, the Dauntless shout their assent. Someone else yells, "You are not the leader of our faction!"

Jack waits for their shouts to die down and then says,

"That is true. If you want to, you can feel free to storm the Erudite compound by yourselves. But you will do so without our support, and may I remind you, you are greatly outnumbered and unprepared."

He's right. We can't attack Dauntless traitors and Erudite without Candor's numbers. It would be a bloodbath if we tried. Jack Kang has all the power. And now we all know it.

"I thought so," he says smugly. "Very well. I will contact Jeanine Matthews, and see if we can negotiate a peace. Any objections?"

We can't attack without Candor, I think, *unless we have the factionless.*

CHAPTER
NINETEEN

THAT AFTERNOON I join a group of Candor and Dauntless
cleaning up the broken windows in the lobby. I focus on
the path of the broom, keeping my eyes on the dust that
collects between glass fragments. My muscles remember
the movement before the rest of me does, but when I look
down, instead of dark marble I see plain white tile and the
bottom of a light gray wall; I see strands of blond hair that
my mother trimmed, and the mirror safely tucked behind
its wall panel.

My body goes weak, and I lean into the broom handle
for support.

A hand touches my shoulder, and I twitch away from
it. But it's just a Candor girl—a child. She looks up at me,
wide-eyed.

"Are you all right?" she says, her voice high and indistinct.

"I'm fine," I say. Too sharply. I hurry to amend it. "Just tired. Thank you."

"I think you're lying," she says.

I notice a bandage peeking out from the end of her sleeve, probably covering the needle puncture. The idea of this little girl under a simulation nauseates me. I can't even look at her. I turn away.

And I see them: outside, a traitor Dauntless man, propping up a woman with a bleeding leg. I see the gray streaks in the woman's hair and the end of the man's hooked nose and the blue armband of a Dauntless traitor just beneath their shoulders, and recognize them both. Tori and Zeke.

Tori is trying to walk, but one of her legs drags behind her, useless. A wet, dark patch covers most of her thigh.

The Candor stop sweeping and stare at them. The Dauntless guards standing near the elevators rush toward the entrance with their guns lifted. My fellow sweepers back up to get out of the way, but I stay where I am, heat rushing through me as Zeke and Tori approach.

"Are they even armed?" someone says.

Tori and Zeke reach what used to be the doors, and he puts up one of his hands when he sees the row of Dauntless with guns. The other he keeps wrapped around Tori's waist.

"She needs medical attention," says Zeke. "Right now."

"Why should we give a traitor medical attention?" a Dauntless man with wispy blond hair and a double-pierced lip asks over his gun. A patch of blue dye marks his forearm.

Tori moans, and I slip between two Dauntless to reach for her. She puts her hand, which is sticky with blood, in mine. Zeke lowers her to the ground with a grunt.

"Tris," she says, sounding dazed.

"Better step back, girl," the blond Dauntless man says.

"No," I say. "Put your gun down."

"Told you the Divergent were crazy," one of the other armed Dauntless mutters to the woman next to him.

"I don't care if you bring her upstairs and tie her to a bed to keep her from going on a shooting spree!" says Zeke, scowling. "Don't let her bleed to death in the lobby of Candor headquarters!"

Finally, a few Dauntless come forward and lift Tori up.

"Where should we . . . take her?" one of them asks.

"Find Helena," Zeke says. "Dauntless nurse."

The men nod and carry her toward the elevators. Zeke and I meet eyes.

"What happened?" I ask him.

"The traitor Dauntless found out we were collecting information from them," he says. "Tori tried to get away, but they shot her as she was running. I helped her get here."

"That's a nice story," says the blond Dauntless man. "Want to tell it again under truth serum?"

Zeke shrugs. "All right." He puts his wrists together in front of him dramatically. "Haul me away, if you're so desperate to."

Then his eyes focus on something over my shoulder, and he starts walking. I turn to see Uriah jogging from the elevator bank. He is grinning.

"Heard a rumor you were a dirty traitor," Uriah says.

"Yeah, whatever," says Zeke.

They collide in an embrace that looks almost painful to me, slapping each other's backs and laughing with their fists clasped between them.

+ + +

"I can't believe you didn't tell us," says Lynn, shaking her head. She sits across from me at the table, her arms crossed and one of her legs propped up.

"Oh, don't get all huffy about it," says Zeke. "I wasn't even supposed to tell Shauna and Uriah. And it sort of defeats the purpose of being a spy if you tell everyone that's what you are."

We sit in a room in Candor headquarters called the Gathering Place, which the Dauntless have taken to saying in a mocking way whenever they can. It is large and open, with black-and-white cloth draped on every wall, and a circle of podiums in the center of the room. Large round tables surround the podiums. Lynn told me they host monthly debates here, for entertainment, and also hold religious services here once a week. But even when no events are scheduled, the room is usually full.

Zeke was cleared by the Candor an hour ago, in a short interrogation on the eighteenth floor. It was not as somber an occasion as Tobias's and my interrogation, partly because there was no suspicious video footage implicating Zeke, and partly because Zeke is funny even when under truth serum. Maybe especially so. In any case, we came to the Gathering Place "for a 'Hey, you're not a dirty traitor!' celebration," as Uriah put it.

"Yeah, but we've been insulting you since the simulation attack," Lynn says. "And now I feel like a jerk about it."

Zeke puts his arm around Shauna. "You *are* a jerk, Lynn. It's part of your charm."

Lynn launches a plastic cup at him, which he deflects. Water sprays over the table, hitting him in the eye.

"Anyway, as I was saying," says Zeke, rubbing his eye, "I was mostly working on getting Erudite defectors out safely. That's why there's a big group of them here, and a small group at Amity headquarters. But Tori . . . I have no idea what she was doing. She kept sneaking away for hours at a time, and whenever she was around, it was like she was about to explode. It's no wonder she gave us away."

"How'd *you* get the job?" says Lynn. "You're not that special."

"It was more because of where I was after the simulation attack. Smack-dab in a pack of Dauntless traitors. I decided to go with it," he says. "Not sure about Tori, though."

"She transferred from Erudite," I say.

What I don't say, because I'm sure she wouldn't want everyone to know, is that Tori probably seemed explosive in Erudite headquarters because they murdered her brother for being Divergent.

She told me once that she was waiting for an opportunity to get revenge.

"Oh," says Zeke. "How do you know that?"

"Well, all the faction transfers have a secret club," I say, leaning back in my chair. "We meet every third Thursday."

Zeke snorts.

"Where's Four?" says Uriah, checking his watch. "Should we start without him?"

"We can't," says Zeke. "He's getting The Info."

Uriah nods like that means something. Then he pauses and says, "What info, again?"

"The info about Kang's little peacemaking meeting with Jeanine," says Zeke. "Obviously."

Across the room, I see Christina sitting at a table with her sister. They are both reading something.

My entire body tenses. Cara, Will's older sister, is walking across the room toward Christina's table. I duck my head.

"What?" Uriah says, looking over his shoulder. I want to punch him.

"Stop it!" I say. "Could you be any more obvious?" I lean forward, folding my arms on the table. "Will's sister is over there."

"Yeah, I talked to her about getting out of Erudite once, while I was there," says Zeke. "Said she saw an Abnegation woman get killed while she was on a mission for Jeanine and couldn't stomach it anymore."

"Are we sure she's not just an Erudite spy?" Lynn says.

"Lynn, she saved half our faction from *this* stuff," says Marlene, tapping the bandage on her arm from where the Dauntless traitors shot her. "Well, half of half of our faction."

"In some circles they call that a quarter, Mar," Lynn says.

"Anyway, who cares if she is a traitor?" Zeke says. "We're not planning anything that she can inform them about. And we certainly wouldn't include her if we were."

"There is plenty of information for her to gather here," Lynn says. "How many of us there are, for example, or how many of us aren't wired for simulations."

"You didn't see her when she was telling me why she left," says Zeke. "I believe her."

Cara and Christina have gotten up, and are walking out of the room.

"I'll be right back," I say. "I have to go to the bathroom."

I wait until Cara and Christina have gone through the doors, then half walk, half jog in that direction. I open one of the doors slowly, so it doesn't make any noise, and then close it slowly behind me. I am in a dim hallway that smells like garbage—this must be where the Candor trash chute is.

I hear two female voices around the corner and creep toward the end of the hallway to hear better.

". . . just can't handle her being here," one of them sobs. Christina. "I can't stop picturing it . . . what she did. . . . I don't understand how she could have done that!"

Christina's sobs make me feel like I am about to crack open.

Cara takes her time responding.

"Well, I do," she says.

"What?" Christina says with a hiccup.

"You have to understand; we're trained to see things as logically as possible," says Cara. "So don't think that I'm callous. But that girl was probably scared out of her mind, certainly not capable of assessing situations cleverly at the time, if she was ever able to do so."

My eyes fly open. *What a—* I run through a short list of insults in my mind before listening to her continue.

"And the simulation made her incapable of reasoning with him, so when he threatened her life, she reacted as she had been trained by the Dauntless to react: Shoot to kill."

"So what are you saying?" says Christina bitterly. "We should just forget about it, because it makes perfect sense?"

"Of course not," says Cara. Her voice wobbles, just a little, and she repeats herself, quietly this time. "Of *course* not."

She clears her throat. "It's just that you have to be around her, and I want to make it easier for you. You don't have to forgive her. Actually, I'm not sure why you were friends with her in the first place; she always seemed a bit erratic to me."

I tense up as I wait for Christina to agree with her, but

to my surprise—and relief—she doesn't.

Cara continues. "Anyway. You don't have to forgive her, but you should try to understand that what she did was not out of malice; it was out of panic. That way, you can look at her without wanting to punch her in her exceptionally long nose."

My hand moves automatically to my nose. Christina laughs a little, which feels like a hard poke to the stomach. I back up through the door to the Gathering Place.

Even though Cara was rude—and the nose comment was a low blow—I am grateful for what she said.

+ + +

Tobias emerges from a door hidden behind a length of white cloth. He flicks the cloth out of the way irritably before coming toward us and sitting beside me at the table in the Gathering Place.

"Kang is going to meet with a representative of Jeanine Matthews at seven in the morning," he says.

"A representative?" Zeke says. "She's not going herself?"

"Yeah, and stand out in the open where a bunch of angry people with guns can take aim?" Uriah smirks a little. "I'd like to see her try. No, really, I would."

"Is Kang the Brilliant taking a Dauntless escort, at least?" Lynn says.

"Yes," Tobias says. "Some of the older members volunteered. Bud said he would keep his ears open and report back."

I frown at him. How does he know all this information? And why, after two years of avoiding becoming a Dauntless leader at all costs, is he suddenly acting like one?

"So I guess the real question is," says Zeke, folding his hands on the table, "if you were Erudite, what would *you* say at this meeting?"

They all look at me. Expectantly.

"What?" I say.

"You're Divergent," Zeke replies.

"So is Tobias."

"Yeah, but he doesn't have aptitude for Erudite."

"And how do you know I do?"

Zeke lifts his shoulder. "Seems likely. Doesn't it seem likely?"

Uriah and Lynn nod. Tobias's mouth twitches, as if in a smile, but if that's what it was, he suppresses it. I feel like a stone just dropped into my stomach.

"You all have functional brains, last time I checked," I say. "You can think like the Erudite, too."

"But we don't have special *Divergent* brains!" says Marlene. She touches her fingertips to my scalp and squeezes lightly. "Come on, do your magic."

"There's no such thing as Divergent magic, Mar," says Lynn.

"And if there is, we shouldn't be consulting it," says Shauna. It's the first thing she's said since we sat down. She doesn't even look at me when she says it; she just scowls at her younger sister.

"Shauna—" Zeke starts.

"Don't 'Shauna' me!" she says, focusing her scowl on him instead. "Don't you think someone with the aptitude for multiple factions might have a loyalty problem? If she's got aptitude for Erudite, how can we be sure she's not *working* for Erudite?"

"Don't be ridiculous," says Tobias, his voice low.

"I am not being ridiculous." She smacks the table. "I know I belong in Dauntless because everything I did in that aptitude test told me so. I'm loyal to my faction for that reason—because there's nowhere else I could possibly be. But her? And you?" She shakes her head. "I have no idea who you're loyal to. And I'm not going to pretend like everything's okay."

She gets up, and when Zeke reaches for her, she throws his hand aside, marching toward one of the doors. I watch her until the door closes behind her and the black fabric that hangs in front of it settles.

I feel wound up, like I might scream, only Shauna isn't

here for me to scream at.

"It's not *magic*," I say hotly. "You just have to ask yourself what the most logical response to a particular situation is."

I am greeted with blank stares.

"Seriously," I say. "If I were in this situation, staring at a group of Dauntless guards and Jack Kang, I probably wouldn't resort to violence, right?"

"Well, you might, if you had your own Dauntless guards. And then all it takes is one shot—bam, he's dead, and Erudite's better off," says Zeke.

"Whoever they send to talk to Jack Kang isn't going to be some random Erudite kid; it's going to be someone important," I say. "It would be a stupid move to fire on Jack Kang and risk losing whoever they send as Jeanine's representative."

"See? This is why we need you to analyze the situation," Zeke says. "If it was me, I would kill him; it would be worth the risk."

I pinch the bridge of my nose. I already have a headache. "Fine."

I try to put myself in Jeanine Matthews's place. I already know she won't negotiate with Jack Kang. Why would she need to? He has nothing to offer her. She will use the situation to her advantage.

"I think," I say, "that Jeanine Matthews will manipulate

him. And that he will do anything to protect his faction, even if it means sacrificing the Divergent." I pause
for a moment, remembering how he held his faction's
influence over our heads at the meeting. "Or sacrificing
the Dauntless. So we *need* to hear what they say in that
meeting."

Uriah and Zeke exchange a look. Lynn smiles, but it
isn't her usual smile. It doesn't spread to her eyes, which
look more like gold than ever, with that coldness in them.

"So let's listen in," she says.

CHAPTER
TWENTY

I CHECK MY watch. It is seven o'clock in the evening. Just twelve hours until we can hear what Jeanine has to say to Jack Kang. I have checked my watch at least a dozen times in the past hour, as if that will make the time go faster. I am itching to do something—*anything* except sit in the cafeteria with Lynn, Tobias, and Lauren, picking at my dinner and sneaking looks at Christina, who sits with her Candor family at one of the other tables.

"I wonder if we'll be able to return to the old way after all this is over," says Lauren. She and Tobias have been talking about Dauntless initiate training methods for at least five minutes already. It's probably the only thing they have in common.

"If there's a faction *left* after all this is over," Lynn says, piling her mashed potatoes onto a roll.

"Don't tell me you're going to eat a mashed-potato sandwich," I say to her.

"So what if I am?"

A group of Dauntless walk between our table and the one next to us. They are older than Tobias, but not by much. One of the girls has five different colors in her hair, and her arms are covered with tattoos so that I can't see even an inch of bare skin. One of the boys leans close to Tobias, whose back is to them, and whispers, "Coward," as he passes.

A few of the others do the same thing, hissing "coward" into Tobias's ears and then continuing on their way. He pauses with his knife against a piece of bread, a glob of butter waiting to be spread, and stares at the table.

I wait, tense, for him to explode.

"What idiots," says Lauren. "And the Candor, for making you spill your life story for everyone to see . . . they're idiots too."

Tobias doesn't answer. He puts down his knife and the piece of bread, and pushes back from the table. His eyes lift and focus on something across the room.

"This needs to stop," he says distantly, and starts toward whatever it is he's looking at before I figure out what it is. This can't be good.

He slips between the tables and the people like he's more liquid than solid, and I stumble after him, muttering apologies as I push people aside.

And then I see exactly who Tobias is headed toward. Marcus. He is sitting with a few of the older Candor.

Tobias reaches him and grabs him by the back of the neck, wrestling him from his seat. Marcus opens his mouth to say something, and that is a mistake, because Tobias punches him hard in the teeth. Someone shouts, but no one rushes to Marcus's aid. We are in a room full of Dauntless, after all.

Tobias shoves Marcus toward the middle of the room, where there is a space between the tables to reveal the symbol of Candor. Marcus stumbles over one of the scales, his hands covering his face so I can't see the damage Tobias did.

Tobias shoves Marcus to the ground and presses the heel of his shoe to his father's throat. Marcus smacks at Tobias's leg, blood streaming past his lips, but even if he was at his strongest, he still wouldn't be as strong as his son. Tobias undoes his belt buckle and slides it from its loops.

He lifts his foot from Marcus's throat and draws the belt back.

"This is for your own good," he says.

That, I remember, is what Marcus, and his many manifestations, always says to Tobias in his fear landscape.

Then the belt flies through the air and hits Marcus in the arm. Marcus's face is bright red, and he covers his head as the next blow falls, this one hitting his back. All around me is laughter, coming from the Dauntless tables, but I am not laughing, I cannot possibly laugh at this.

Finally I come to my senses. I run forward and grab Tobias's shoulder.

"Stop!" I say. "Tobias, stop *right now!*"

I expect to see a wild look in his eyes, but when he looks at me, I do not. His face is not flushed and his breaths are steady. This was not an act performed in the heat of passion.

It was a calculated act.

He drops the belt and reaches into his pocket. From it he takes a silver chain with a ring dangling from it. Marcus is on his side, gasping. Tobias drops the ring onto the ground next to his father's face. It is made of tarnished, dull metal, an Abnegation wedding band.

"My mother," says Tobias, "says hello."

Tobias walks away, and it takes a few seconds for me to breathe again. When I do, I leave Marcus cringing on the floor and run after him. It takes me until I reach the hallway to catch up to him.

"What *was* that?" I demand.

Tobias presses the DOWN button for the elevator and doesn't look at me.

"It was necessary," he says.

"Necessary for what?" I say.

"What, you're feeling sorry for *him* now?" Tobias says, turning toward me with a scowl. "Do you know how many times he did that to me? How do you think I learned the moves?"

I feel brittle, like I might break. It did seem rehearsed, like Tobias had gone over the steps in his mind, recited the words in front of a mirror. He knew it by heart; he was just playing the other part this time.

"No," I say quietly. "No, I don't feel sorry for him, not at all."

"Then *what*, Tris?" His voice is rough; it could be the thing that breaks me. "You haven't cared about what I do or say for the past week; what's so different about this?"

I am almost afraid of him. I don't know what to say or do around the erratic part of him, and it is here, bubbling just beneath the surface of what he does, just like the cruel part of me. We both have war inside of us. Sometimes it keeps us alive. Sometimes it threatens to destroy us.

"Nothing," I say.

The elevator beeps as it arrives. He gets on, and presses

the CLOSE button so the doors shut between us. I stare at the brushed metal and try to think through the last ten minutes.

"This needs to stop," he said. "This" was the ridicule, which was a result of the interrogation, where he admitted that he joined Dauntless to escape his father. And then he beat up Marcus—publicly, where all the Dauntless could see it.

Why? To salvage his pride? It can't be. It was far too intentional for that.

+ + +

On my way back to the cafeteria, I see a Candor man walk Marcus toward the bathroom. He walks slowly, but he isn't hunched over, which makes me think Tobias didn't do him any serious damage. I watch the door close behind him.

I had all but forgotten about what I heard in the Amity compound, about the information my father risked his life for. *Supposedly,* I remind myself. It may not be wise to trust Marcus. And I promised myself I wouldn't ask him about this again.

I dawdle outside the bathroom until the Candor man walks out, and then walk in before the door has a chance to shut properly. Marcus is sitting on the floor by the sink with a wad of paper towel pressed to his mouth. He doesn't look happy to see me.

"What, here to gloat?" he says. "Get out."

"No," I say.

Why am I here, exactly?

He looks at me expectantly. "Well?"

"I thought you could use a reminder," I say. "Whatever it is you want to get from Jeanine, you won't be able to do it alone, and you won't be able to do it with only the Abnegation to help you."

"I thought we went over this." His voice is muffled by the paper towels. "The idea that *you* could help—"

"I don't know where you get this delusion that I'm useless, but that's what it is," I snap. "And I'm not interested in hearing about it. All I want to say is that when you stop being delusional and start feeling desperate because you're too inept to figure this out on your own, you know who to come to."

I leave the bathroom just as the Candor man comes back with an ice pack.

CHAPTER
TWENTY-ONE

I STAND BEFORE the sinks in the women's bathroom on the newly claimed Dauntless floor, a gun resting on my palm. Lynn put it there a few minutes ago; she seemed confused that I did not wrap my hand around it and put it somewhere, in a holster or under the waistband of my jeans. I just let it stay there, and walked to the bathroom before I started to panic.

Don't be an idiot. I can't set out to do what I'm doing without a gun. It would be crazy. So I will have to solve this problem I've been having in the next five minutes.

I curl my pinkie around the handle first, then my second finger, then the others. The weight is familiar. My index finger slips around the trigger. I release a breath.

I start to lift it, bringing my left hand to meet my right

to steady it. I hold the gun out from my body, my arms straight, just as Four taught me, when that was his only name. I used a gun like this to defend my father and brother from simulation-bound Dauntless. I used it to stop Eric from shooting Tobias in the head. It is not inherently evil. It is just a tool.

I see a flicker of movement in the mirror, and before I can stop myself, I stare at my reflection. *This is how I looked to him,* I think. *This is how I looked when I shot him.*

Moaning like a wounded animal, I let the gun fall from my hands and wrap my arms around my stomach. I want to sob because I know it will make me feel better, but I can't force the tears to come. I just crouch in the bathroom, staring at the white tiles. I can't do it. I can't take the gun with me.

I shouldn't even go; I am still going to.

"Tris?" Someone knocks. I stand and uncross my arms as the door squeaks open a few inches. Tobias steps into the room.

"Zeke and Uriah told me you were going to eavesdrop on Jack," he says.

"Oh."

"Are you?"

"Why should I tell you? You don't tell me about *your* plans."

His straight eyebrows furrow. "What are you talking about?"

"I'm talking about beating Marcus to a pulp in front of all the Dauntless for no apparent reason." I step toward him. "But there is a reason, isn't there? Because it's not like you lost control; it's not like he did something to provoke you, so there has to be a reason!"

"I needed to prove to the Dauntless that I am not a coward," he says. "That's all. That's all it was."

"Why would you need to . . ." I start.

Why would Tobias need to prove himself to the Dauntless? Only if he wanted them to hold him in high regard. Only if he wants to become a Dauntless leader. I remember Evelyn's voice, speaking in the shadows in the factionless safe house: "What I am suggesting is that you *become* important."

He wants the Dauntless to ally with the factionless, and he knows the only way he can make that happen is to do it himself.

Why he didn't feel the need to share this plan with me is another mystery entirely. Before I can ask, he says, "So are you going to eavesdrop or not?"

"What does it matter?"

"You're throwing yourself into danger for no reason again," he says. "Just like when you stormed up to fight the

Erudite with only a . . . a *pocket knife* to protect yourself."

"There is a reason. A good one. We won't know what's going on unless we eavesdrop, and we need to know what's going on."

He crosses his arms. He is not bulky, the way some Dauntless boys are. And some girls might focus on the way his ears stick out, or the way his nose hooks at the end, but to me . . .

I swallow the rest of that thought. He's here to yell at me. He's been keeping things from me. Whatever we are now, I can't indulge thoughts about how attractive he is. It will just make it harder for me to do what needs to be done. And right now, that is going to listen to what Jack Kang has to say to the Erudite.

"You're not cutting your hair like the Abnegation anymore," I say. "That because you want to look more Dauntless?"

"Don't change the subject," he says. "There are four people going to eavesdrop already. You don't need to be there."

"Why are you so insistent on me staying home?" My voice gets louder. "I am not the kind of person who just sits back and lets other people take all the risks!"

"As long as you are someone who doesn't seem to value her own life . . . someone who can't even pick up and fire a *gun* . . ." He leans toward me. "You should sit back and let other people take the risks."

His quiet voice pulses around me like a second heartbeat. I hear the words "doesn't seem to value her own life" again and again.

"What are you going to do?" I say. "Lock me in the bathroom? Because that's the only way you'll be able to keep me from going."

He touches his forehead and lets his hand drag down the side of his face. I have never seen his face sag that way before.

"I don't want to stop you. I want you to stop yourself," he says. "But if you're going to be reckless, you can't prevent me from coming along."

+ + +

It is still dark, but just barely, when we reach the bridge, which is two-tiered, with stone pillars at each corner. We descend the stairs next to one of the stone pillars and creep with silent feet at river level. Large puddles of standing water gleam as the light of day hits them. The sun is rising; we have to get into position.

Uriah and Zeke are in the buildings on either side of the bridge so they can get a better view and cover us from a distance. They have better aim than Lynn or Shauna, who came because Lynn asked her to, despite her outburst in the Gathering Place.

Lynn goes first, her back pressed to the stone as she inches along the lower lip of the bridge supports. I follow her, with Shauna and Tobias behind me. The bridge is supported by four curved metal structures that secure it to the stone wall, and by a maze of narrow girders beneath its lower tier. Lynn wedges herself under one of the metal structures and climbs quickly, keeping the narrow girders beneath her as she works her way to the middle of the bridge.

I let Shauna go in front of me because I can't climb as well. My left arm shakes as I try to balance on top of the metal structure. I feel Tobias's cool hand on my waist, steadying me.

I crouch low to fit in the space between the bottom of the bridge and the girders beneath me. I don't make it very far before I have to stop, my feet on one girder and my left arm on another. And I will have to stay that way for a long time.

Tobias slides along one of the girders and puts his leg under me. It is long enough to stretch beneath me and onto a second girder. I breathe out and smile at him as a kind of thank-you. It's the first time we have acknowledged each other since we left the Merciless Mart.

He smiles back, but grimly.

We bide our time in silence. I breathe through my mouth and try to control the shaking of my arms and legs. Shauna and Lynn seem to communicate without speaking. They make faces at each other that I can't read, and nod and smile at each other when they reach an understanding. I have never thought about what it would be like to have a sister. Would Caleb and I be closer if he were a girl?

The city is so quiet in the morning that the footsteps echo as they approach the bridge. The sound comes from behind me, which must mean it's Jack and his Dauntless escort, not the Erudite, who have arrived. The Dauntless know that we are here, though Jack Kang himself does not. If he stares down for more than a few seconds, he might see us through the metal mesh beneath his feet. I try to breathe as quietly as possible.

Tobias checks his watch, and then holds his arm out to me to show me the time. Seven o'clock exactly.

I glance up and peer through the steel web above me. Feet pass over my head. And then I hear him.

"Hello, Jack," he says.

It's Max, who appointed Eric to Dauntless leadership

at Jeanine's demand, who implemented policies of cruelty and brutality in Dauntless initiation. I have never spoken to him directly, but the sound of his voice makes me shiver.

"Max," Jack says. "Where's Jeanine? I thought she would at least have the courtesy to show up herself."

"Jeanine and I divide our responsibilities according to our strengths," he says. "That means I make all military decisions. I believe that includes what we are doing today."

I frown. I haven't heard Max speak much, but something about the words he's using, and their rhythm, sounds . . . *off*.

"Fine," says Jack. "I came to—"

"I should inform you that this will not be a negotiation," Max says. "In order to negotiate, you have to be on even footing, and you, Jack, are not."

"What do you mean?"

"I mean that you are the only disposable faction. Candor does not provide us with protection, sustenance, or technological innovation. Therefore you are expendable to us. And you have not done much to win the favor of your Dauntless guests," says Max, "so you are completely vulnerable and completely useless. I recommend, therefore, that you do exactly as I say."

"You piece of scum," says Jack through gritted teeth. "How *dare*—"

"Now let's not get testy," Max says.

I chew on my lip. I should trust my instincts, and my instincts tell me that something is wrong here. No self-respecting Dauntless man would say the word "testy." Nor would he react so calmly to an insult. He's speaking like someone else. He's speaking like Jeanine.

The back of my neck prickles. It makes perfect sense. Jeanine would not trust anyone, particularly not a volatile Dauntless, to speak on her behalf. The best solution to that problem is to give Max an earpiece. And the signal from an earpiece can stretch only a quarter of a mile at most.

I catch Tobias's eye, and slowly move my hand to point at my ear. Then I point above me, at my best approximation of where Max stands.

Tobias frowns for a moment, then nods, but I'm not sure he understands me.

"I have three requirements," says Max. "First, that you return the Dauntless leader you currently hold in captivity unharmed. Second, that you allow your compound to be searched by our soldiers so that we can extract the Divergent; and third, that you provide us with the names of those who were not injected with the simulation serum."

"Why?" Jack says bitterly. "What are you searching for? And why do you need those names? What do you intend to do with them?"

"The purpose of our search would be to locate and remove any of the Divergent from the premises. And as for the names, that is none of your concern."

"None of my concern!" I hear footsteps squeak above me and stare up through the mesh. From what I can see, Jack has the collar of Max's shirt wrapped around his fist.

"Release me," says Max. "Or I will order my guards to fire."

I frown. If Jeanine is speaking through Max, she had to be able to see him in order to know that he was grabbed. I lean forward to look at the buildings on the other side of the bridge. On my left, the river bends, and a squat glass building stands at the edge. That must be where she is.

I start to climb backward, toward the metal structure that supports the bridge, toward the staircase that will lead me to Wacker Drive. Tobias follows me immediately, and Shauna taps Lynn on the shoulder. But Lynn is doing something else.

I was too busy thinking about Jeanine. I failed to notice that Lynn took out her gun and started to climb toward the edge of the bridge. Shauna's mouth opens and her eyes go wide as Lynn swings herself forward, grabbing the lip of the bridge, and shoves her arm over it. Her finger squeezes the trigger.

Max gasps, his hand clapping over his chest, and stumbles back. When he pulls his hand away, it is dark with blood.

I don't bother to climb anymore. I drop into the mud, closely followed by Tobias, Lynn, and Shauna. My legs sink into the mire, and my feet make sucking noises as I pull them free. My shoes slip off but I keep going until I reach the concrete. Guns fire and bullets stick in the mud next to me. I throw myself against the wall under the bridge so they can't aim at me.

Tobias presses into the wall behind me, so close to me that his chin floats over my head and I can feel his chest against my shoulders. Shielding me.

I can run back to Candor headquarters, and to temporary safety. Or I can find Jeanine in what is probably the most vulnerable state she will ever be in.

It's not even a choice.

"Come on!" I say. I sprint up the stairs, the others on my heels. On the lower tier of the bridge, our Dauntless shoot at the Dauntless traitors. Jack is safe, bent over with a Dauntless arm slung across his back. I run faster. I run across the bridge and don't look behind me. I can already hear Tobias's footsteps. He is the only one who can keep up with me.

The glass building is in my sights. And then I hear more footsteps, more gunshots. I weave as I run, to make it more difficult for the Dauntless traitors to hit me.

I am close to the glass building. I am yards away. I grit my teeth and push myself harder. My legs are numb; I barely feel the ground beneath me. But before I reach the doors, I see movement in the alley to my right. I swerve and follow it with my feet.

Three figures run down the alley. One is blond. One is tall. And one is Peter.

I stumble, and almost fall.

"Peter!" I shout. He lifts his gun, and behind me, Tobias lifts his own, and we stand just yards away from each other, at a standstill. Behind him, the blond woman—Jeanine, probably—and the tall Dauntless traitor turn the corner. Though I don't have a weapon, and I don't have a plan, I want to run after them, and maybe I would if Tobias did not clamp his hand over my shoulder and hold me in place.

"You traitor," I say to Peter. "I knew it. I *knew* it."

A scream pierces the air. It is anguished and female.

"Sounds like your friends need you," Peter says with

the flash of a smile—or bared teeth, I can't tell. He keeps his gun steady. "So you have a choice. You can let us go, and help them, or you can die trying to follow us."

I almost scream. We both know what I'm going to do.

"I hope you die," I say.

I back up into Tobias, who backs up with me, until we reach the end of the alley, and then turn and run.

CHAPTER
TWENTY-TWO

SHAUNA LIES ON the ground, facedown, blood pooling on her shirt. Lynn crouches at her side. Staring. Doing nothing.

"It's my fault," Lynn mumbles. "I shouldn't have shot him. I shouldn't have . . ."

I stare at the patch of blood. A bullet hit her in the back. I can't tell if she's breathing or not. Tobias places two fingers on the side of her neck, and nods.

"We've got to get out of here," he says. "Lynn. Look at me. I'm going to carry her, and it's going to hurt her a lot, but it's our only option."

Lynn nods. Tobias crouches next to Shauna and puts his hands under her arms. He lifts her, and she moans. I rush forward to help him pull her limp body over his shoulder. My throat tightens, and I cough to relieve the pressure.

Tobias stands with a grunt of effort, and together we walk toward the Merciless Mart—Lynn in front, with her gun, and me in the back. I walk backward to watch behind us, but I don't see anyone. I think the Dauntless traitors retreated. But I have to make sure.

"Hey!" someone shouts. It's Uriah, jogging toward us. "Zeke had to help them get Jack . . . oh no." He stops. "Oh no. Shauna?"

"Now's not the time," says Tobias sharply. "Run back to the Merciless Mart and get a doctor."

But Uriah just stares.

"Uriah! Go, *now!*" The shout rings with nothing on the street to soften the sound of it. Uriah finally turns and sprints in the direction of the Merciless Mart.

It's only half a mile back, but with Tobias's grunts and Lynn's uneven breathing and the knowledge that Shauna is bleeding to death, it feels endless. I watch the muscles in Tobias's back expanding and contracting with each labored breath, and I don't hear our footsteps; I hear only my heartbeat. When we finally reach the doors, I feel like I might throw up, or faint, or scream at the top of my lungs.

Uriah, an Erudite man with a comb-over, and Cara meet us just inside the entrance. They set up a sheet for

Shauna to lie on. Tobias lowers her onto it, and the doctor gets to work immediately, cutting the shirt away from Shauna's back. I turn away. I don't want to see the bullet wound.

Tobias stands in front of me, his face red with exertion. I want him to fold me into his arms again, like he did after the last attack, but he doesn't, and I know better than to initiate it.

"I'm not going to pretend to know what's going on with you," he says. "But if you senselessly risk your life again—"

"I am not senselessly risking my life. I am trying to make *sacrifices*, like my parents would have, like—"

"You are *not* your parents. You are a sixteen-year-old girl—"

I grit my teeth. "How *dare* you—"

"—who doesn't understand that the value of a sacrifice lies in its *necessity*, not in throwing your life away! And if you do that again, you and I are done."

I wasn't expecting him to say that.

"You're giving me an ultimatum?" I try to keep my voice down so the others can't hear.

He shakes his head. "No, I'm telling you a fact." His lips are just a line. "If you throw yourself into danger for no reason again, you will have become nothing more than a Dauntless adrenaline junkie looking for a hit, and I'm not going to help you do it." He spits the words out bitterly. "I love Tris the Divergent, who makes decisions apart from faction loyalty, who isn't some faction archetype. But the Tris who's trying as hard as she can to destroy herself . . . I can't love her."

I want to scream. But not because I'm angry, because I'm afraid he's right. My hands shake and I grab the hem of my shirt to steady them.

He touches his forehead to mine and closes his eyes. "I believe you're still in there," he says against my mouth. "Come back."

He kisses me lightly, and I am too shocked to stop him.

He walks back to Shauna's side, and I stand over one of the Candor scales in the lobby, at a loss.

+ + +

"It's been a while."

I sink down on the bed across from Tori. She is sitting up, her leg propped on a stack of pillows.

"Yes, it has," I say. "How are you feeling?"

"Like I got shot." A smile plays over her lips. "I hear you're familiar with the feeling."

"Yeah. It's great, right?" All I can think of is the bullet in Shauna's back. At least Tori and I will recover from our wounds.

"Did you discover anything interesting at Jack's meeting?" she says.

"A few things. Do you know how we might go about calling a Dauntless meeting?"

"I can make it happen. One thing about being a tattoo artist in Dauntless is . . . you know pretty much everyone."

"Right," I say. "You also have the prestige of being a former spy."

Tori's mouth twists. "I had almost forgotten."

"Did *you* discover anything interesting? As a spy, I mean."

"My mission was primarily focused on Jeanine Matthews." She glares at her hands. "How she spends her days. And, more importantly, *where* she spends them."

"Not in her office, then?"

Tori doesn't answer at first.

"I guess I can trust you, Divergent." She looks at me from the corner of her eye. "She has a private laboratory on the top level. Insane security measures protecting it. I was trying to get up there when they figured out what I was."

"You were trying to get up there," I say. Her eyes flit away from mine. "Not to spy, I take it."

"I thought it would be more . . . *expedient* if Jeanine Matthews didn't survive much longer."

I see a kind of thirst in her expression, the same one I saw when she told me about her brother in the back room of the tattoo parlor. Before the attack simulation I might have called it a thirst for justice, or even revenge, but now I am able to identify it as a thirst for blood. And even as it frightens me, I understand it.

Which should probably frighten me even more.

Tori says, "I'll work on calling that meeting."

+ + +

The Dauntless are gathered in the space between the rows of bunk beds and the doors, which are held shut by a tightly wrapped bedsheet, the best lock the Dauntless could muster. I have no doubt that Jack Kang will agree to Jeanine's demands. We aren't safe here anymore.

"What were the terms?" Tori says. She sits in a chair between a few of the bunks, her wounded leg stuck out in front of her. She asks Tobias, but he doesn't seem to be paying attention. He is leaning against one of the bunks, his arms crossed, staring at the floor.

I clear my throat. "There were three. Return Eric to the Erudite. Report the names of all people who did not get shot with needles last time. And deliver the Divergent to Erudite headquarters."

I look at Marlene. She smiles back at me a little sadly. She is probably worried about Shauna, who is still with the Erudite doctor. Lynn, Hector, their parents, and Zeke are with her.

"If Jack Kang is making deals with the Erudite, we can't stay here," says Tori. "So where can we go?"

I think of the blood on Shauna's shirt, and long for the Amity orchards, the sound of the wind in the leaves, the feeling of bark beneath my hands. I never thought I would crave that place. I didn't think it was in me.

I close my eyes briefly, and when I open them I am in reality, and Amity is a dream.

"Home," Tobias says, lifting his head at last. Everyone is listening. "We should take back what's ours. We can break the security cameras in Dauntless headquarters so the Erudite can't see us. We should go home."

Someone assents with a shout, and someone else joins in. That is how things in Dauntless are decided: with nods and yells. In these moments we don't seem like individuals anymore. We are all a part of the same mind.

"But before we do that," says Bud, who once worked with Tori in the tattoo parlor and who now stands with his hand on the back of Tori's chair, "we need to decide what to do about Eric. To let him stay here with the Erudite, or to execute him."

"Eric is Dauntless," Lauren says, turning the ring in her lip with her fingertips. "That means *we* decide what happens to him. Not Candor."

This time a yell tears from my body of its own volition, joining with the others in agreement.

"According to Dauntless law, only Dauntless leaders can perform an execution. All five of our former leaders are Dauntless traitors," says Tori. "So I think it's time we pick new ones. The law says we need more than one, and we need an odd number. If you've got suggestions, you should shout them out now, and we'll vote if we need to."

"You!" someone calls out.

"Okay," says Tori. "Anyone else?"

Marlene cups her hands around her mouth and calls out, "Tris!"

My heart pounds. But to my surprise, no one mutters in dissent and no one laughs. Instead, a few people nod, just like they did when Tori's name was mentioned. I scan the crowd and find Christina. She stands with her arms crossed, and does not seem to react at all to my nomination.

I wonder how I seem to them. They must see someone I don't see. Someone capable and strong. Someone I can't be; someone I can be.

Tori acknowledges Marlene with a nod and scans the

crowd for another recommendation.

"Harrison," someone says. I don't know who Harrison is until someone slaps a middle-aged man with a blond ponytail on the shoulder, and he grins. I recognize him— he's the Dauntless man who called me "girl" when Zeke and Tori came back from Erudite headquarters.

The Dauntless are quiet for a moment.

"I'm going to nominate Four," says Tori.

Apart from a few angry murmurs in the back of the room, no one disagrees. No one is calling him a coward anymore, not after he beat up Marcus in the cafeteria. I wonder how they would react if they knew how calculated that move was.

Now he could get exactly what he intended to get. Unless I stand in his way.

"We only need three leaders," Tori says. "We'll have to vote."

They would never have considered me if I had not stopped the attack simulation. And maybe they wouldn't have considered me if I hadn't stabbed Eric by those elevators, or put myself under that bridge. The more reckless I get, the more popular I am with the Dauntless.

Tobias looks at me. I can't be popular with the Dauntless, because Tobias is right—I'm not Dauntless; I'm Divergent. I am whatever I choose to be. And I can't choose to be *this*.

I have to stay separate from them.

"No," I say. I clear my throat and say it louder. "No, you don't have to vote. I refuse my nomination."

Tori raises her eyebrows at me. "Are you sure, Tris?"

"Yes," I say. "I don't want it. I'm sure."

And then, without argument and without ceremony, Tobias is elected to be a leader of Dauntless. And I am not.

CHAPTER
TWENTY-THREE

NOT TEN SECONDS after we choose our new leaders, something rings—one long pulse, two short ones. I move toward the sound, my right ear toward the wall, and find a speaker suspended from the ceiling. There is another one across the room.

Then Jack Kang's voice speaks all around us.

"Attention all occupants of Candor headquarters. A few hours ago I met with a representative of Jeanine Matthews. He reminded me that we Candor are in a weak position, dependent on Erudite for our survival, and told me that if I intend to keep my faction free, I will have to meet a few demands."

I stare up at the speaker, stunned. I shouldn't be surprised that the leader of Candor is this forthright, but I wasn't expecting a public announcement.

"In order to comply with these demands, I ask that everyone make their way to the Gathering Place to report whether you have an implant or not," he says. "The Erudite have also ordered all Divergent to be turned over to Erudite. I do not know for what purpose."

He sounds listless. Defeated. *Well, he is defeated,* I think. *Because he was too weak to fight back.*

One thing Dauntless knows that Candor does not is how to fight even when fighting seems useless.

Sometimes I feel like I am collecting the lessons each faction has to teach me, and storing them in my mind like a guidebook for moving through the world. There is always something to learn, always something that is important to understand.

Jack Kang's announcement ends with the same three rings it started with. The Dauntless rush through the room, throwing their things into bags. A few young Dauntless men cut the sheet away from the door, screaming something about Eric. Someone's elbow presses me to a wall, and I just stand and watch the pandemonium intensify.

On the other hand, one thing Candor knows that Dauntless does not is how not to get carried away.

+++

The Dauntless stand in a semicircle around the interrogation chair, where Eric now sits. He looks more dead
than alive. He is slumped in the chair, sweat shining on
his pale forehead. He stares at Tobias with his head tilted
down, so his eyelashes blend into his eyebrows. I try to
keep my eyes on him, but his smile—how the piercings
pull wide when his lips spread—is almost too awful to
take.

"Would you like me to tell you your crimes?" says Tori.
"Or would you like to list them yourself?"

Rain sprays against the side of the building and streams
down the walls. We stand in the interrogation room, on
the top floor of the Merciless Mart. The afternoon storm
is louder here. Every crack of thunder and flash of lightning makes the back of my neck prickle, as if electricity is
dancing over my skin.

I like the smell of wet pavement. It is faint here, but
once this is done, all the Dauntless will storm down the
stairs and leave the Merciless Mart behind, and wet pavement will be the only thing I smell.

We have our bags with us. Mine is a sack made of a sheet
and some rope. It contains my clothes and a spare pair of
shoes. I wear the jacket I stole from the Dauntless traitor—
I want Eric to see it if he looks at me.

Eric scans the crowd for a few seconds, and then his

eyes settle on me. He laces his fingers and sets them—gingerly—on his stomach. "I'd like *her* to list them. Since she's the one who stabbed me, clearly she is familiar with them."

I don't know what game he's playing, or what the point of rattling me is, especially now, before his execution. He seems arrogant, but I notice that his fingers tremble when he moves them. Even Eric must be afraid of death.

"Leave her out of this," says Tobias.

"Why? Because you're doing her?" Eric smirks. "Oh wait, I forgot. Stiffs don't *do* that sort of thing. They just tie each other's shoes and cut each other's hair."

Tobias's expression does not change. I think I understand: Eric doesn't really care about me. But he knows exactly where to hit Tobias, and how hard. And one of the places to hit Tobias the hardest is to hit me.

This is what I wanted most to avoid: for my rises and falls to become Tobias's rises and falls. That's why I can't let him step in to defend me now.

"I want her to list them," repeats Eric.

I say, as evenly as possible:

"You conspired with Erudite. You are responsible for the deaths of hundreds of Abnegation." As I go on, I can't keep my voice steady anymore; I start to spit out the words like venom. "You betrayed Dauntless. You shot a child in the head. You are a ridiculous plaything of Jeanine Matthews."

His smile fades.

"Do I deserve to die?" he says.

Tobias opens his mouth to interrupt. But I respond before he can.

"Yes."

"Fair enough." His dark eyes are empty, like pits, like starless nights. "But do you have the right to decide that, Beatrice Prior? Like you decided the fate of that other boy—what was his name? Will?"

I don't answer. I hear my father asking me, "What makes you think you have the right to shoot someone?" as we fought our way to the control room in Dauntless headquarters. He told me there is a right way to do something, and I needed to figure it out. I feel something in my throat, like a ball of wax, so thick I can barely swallow, barely breathe.

"You have committed every crime that warrants execution among the Dauntless," says Tobias. "*We* have the right to execute you, under the laws of Dauntless."

He crouches by the three guns on the floor near Eric's feet. One by one, he empties the chambers of bullets. They almost jingle as they hit the floor, and then roll, coming to rest against the toes of Tobias's shoes. He picks up the middle gun and puts a bullet into the first slot.

Then he moves the three guns on the floor, around and around, until my eyes can't follow the middle gun anymore. I lose track of which one holds the bullet. He picks up the guns and offers one to Tori, and another one to Harrison.

I try to think of the attack simulation, and what it did to the Abnegation. All the gray-clothed innocents lying dead on the street. There weren't even enough Abnegation left to take care of the bodies, so most of them are probably still there. And that would not have been possible without Eric.

I think of the Candor boy, shot without a second's hesitation, how stiff he was as he hit the ground next to me.

Maybe we are not the ones deciding if Eric lives or dies. Maybe he is the one who decided that, when he did all those terrible things.

But it's still hard to breathe.

I look at him without malice, without hatred, and without fear. The rings in his face shine, and a lock of dirty hair falls into his eyes.

"Wait," he says. "I have a request."

"We don't take requests from criminals," says Tori. She's standing on one leg, and has been for the past few minutes. She sounds tired—she probably wants to get this over with so she can sit down again. To her this execution is just an inconvenience.

"I am a leader of Dauntless," he says. "And all I want is for Four to be the one who fires that bullet."

"*Why?*" Tobias says.

"So you can live with the guilt," Eric replies. "Of knowing that you usurped me and then shot me in the head."

I think I understand. He wants to see people break—has always wanted to, ever since he set up the camera in my execution room when I nearly drowned, and probably long before then. And he believes that if Tobias has to kill him, he will see that before he dies.

Sick.

"There won't be any guilt," says Tobias.

"Then you'll have no problem doing it." Eric smiles again.

Tobias picks up one of the bullets.

"Tell me," says Eric quietly, "because I've always wondered. Is it your daddy who shows up in every fear landscape you've ever gone through?"

Tobias puts the bullet into an empty chamber without looking up.

"You didn't like that question?" Eric says. "What, afraid the Dauntless are going to change their minds about you?

Realize that even though you've only got four fears, you're still a coward?"

He straightens in the chair and puts his hands on the armrests.

Tobias holds his gun out from his left shoulder.

"Eric," he says, "be brave."

He squeezes the trigger.

I shut my eyes.

CHAPTER
TWENTY-FOUR

BLOOD IS A strange color. It's darker than you expect it to be.

I stare down at Marlene's hand, which is wrapped around my arm. Her fingernails are short and jagged—she bites them. She pushes me forward, and I must be walking, because I can feel myself moving, but in my mind I stand before Eric and he is still alive.

He died just like Will did. Slumped just like Will did.

I thought the swollen feeling in my throat would go away once he was dead, but it didn't. I have to take deep, hard breaths to get enough air. Good thing the crowd around me is so loud that no one can hear me. We march toward the doors. At the front of the pack is Harrison, carrying Tori on his back like a child. She laughs, her arms wrapped around his neck.

Tobias sets his hand on my back. I know because I see him come up behind me and do it, not because I feel it. I don't feel anything at all.

The doors open from the outside. We stop short of stampeding Jack Kang and the group of Candor that followed him here.

"What have you done?" he says. "I was just told that Eric is missing from his holding cell."

"He was under our jurisdiction," says Tori. "We gave him a trial and executed him. You should be thanking us."

"Why . . ." Jack's face turns red. Blood is darker than blush, even though one consists of the other. "Why should I be thanking you?"

"Because you wanted him to be executed, too, right? Since he murdered one of your children?" Tori tilts her head, her eyes wide, innocent. "Well, we took care of it for you. And now, if you'll excuse us, we're leaving."

"Wha—*Leaving?*" Jack splutters.

If we leave, he will be incapable of fulfilling two of the three demands Max had of him. The thought terrifies him, and it is all over his face.

"I can't let you do that," he says.

"You don't *let* us do anything," says Tobias. "If you don't step aside, we will be forced to walk over you instead of past you."

"Didn't you come here to find allies?" Jack scowls. "If you do this, we will side with Erudite, I promise you, and you will never find an ally in us again, you—"

"We don't need you as an ally," says Tori. "We're Dauntless."

Everyone shouts, and somehow their screams pierce the haze in my mind. The entire crowd presses forward at once. The Candor in the corridor yelp and dive out of the way as we spill into the hallway like a burst pipe, Dauntless water spreading to fill the empty space.

Marlene's grip on my arm breaks. I run down the stairs, chasing the heels of the Dauntless in front of me, ignoring the jostle of elbows and all the shouts around me. I feel like I am an initiate again, storming the stairs of the Hub right after the Choosing Ceremony. My legs burn, but that is all right.

We reach the lobby. A group of Candor and Erudite are waiting there, including the blond Divergent woman who got dragged to the elevators by her hair, the girl I helped escape, and Cara. They watch the Dauntless stream past them with helpless looks on their faces.

Cara spots me and grabs my arm, wrenching me back. "Where are you all going?"

"Dauntless headquarters." I try to pull my arm free, but she won't let go. I don't look at her face. I can't look at her right now.

"Go to Amity," I say. "They promised safety to anyone who wants it. You won't be safe here."

She releases me, almost pushing me away from her in the process.

Outside, the ground feels slick beneath my sneakers, and my sack of clothes thumps against my back as I slow to a jog. Rain sprinkles my head and my back. My feet splash through puddles, soaking my pant legs.

I smell wet pavement, and pretend that this is all there is.

+ + +

I stand at the railing overlooking the chasm. Water hits the wall beneath me, but it doesn't come high enough to splash my shoes.

A hundred yards away, Bud passes out paintball guns. Someone else passes out paintballs. Soon the hidden corners of Dauntless headquarters will be coated in multicolored paint, blocking the lenses of the surveillance cameras.

"Hey, Tris," Zeke says, joining me at the railing. His eyes are red and swollen, but his mouth is curled into a small smile.

"Hey. You made it."

"Yeah. We waited until Shauna was stable and then

took her here." He rubs one of his eyes with his thumb. "I didn't want to move her, but . . . wasn't safe with Candor anymore. Obviously."

"How is she?"

"Dunno. She's gonna survive it, but the nurse thinks she might be paralyzed from the waist down. And that wouldn't bother me, but . . ." He lifts a shoulder. "How can she be Dauntless if she can't walk?"

I stare across the Pit, where some Dauntless children chase each other up the path, hurling paintballs at the walls. One of them breaks and splatters the stone with yellow.

I think of what Tobias told me when we spent the night with the factionless, about the older Dauntless leaving the faction because they were no longer physically capable of staying in it. I think of Candor's rhyming song, which calls us the cruelest faction.

"She can," I say.

"Tris. She won't even be able to move around."

"Sure she will." I look up at him. "She can get a wheelchair, and someone can push her up the paths in the Pit, and there's an elevator in the building up *there*." I point above our heads. "She doesn't need to be able to walk to slide down the zip line or fire a gun."

"She won't want me to push her." His voice cracks a

little. "She won't want me to lift her, or carry her."

"She'll have to get over it, then. Are you going to let her drop out of Dauntless for a stupid reason like not being able to walk?"

Zeke is quiet for a few seconds. His eyes shift over my face, and he squints, as if weighing and measuring me.

Then he turns and bends and wraps his arms around me. It's been so long since someone hugged me that I stiffen. Then I relax, and let the gesture force warmth into my body, which is chilled by damp clothing.

"I'm gonna go shoot things," he says as he pulls away. "Want to come?"

I shrug and chase him across the Pit floor. Bud hands each of us a paintball gun, and I load mine. Its weight, shape, and material are so different from a revolver that I have no trouble holding it.

"We've mostly got the Pit and the underground covered," Bud says. "But you should tackle the Pire."

"The Pire?"

Bud points up at the glass building above us. The sight pierces me like a needle. The last time I stood in this spot and stared up at this ceiling, I was on a mission to destroy the simulation. I was with my father.

Zeke is already on his way up the path. I force myself to follow him, one foot and then the other. It's difficult to walk because it's difficult to breathe, but somehow I manage. By the time I reach the stairs, the pressure on my chest is almost gone.

Once we're in the Pire, Zeke lifts up his gun and aims at one of the cameras near the ceiling. He fires, and green paint sprays across one of the windows, missing the camera lens.

"Ooh," I say, wincing. "Ouch."

"Yeah? I'd like to see you do it perfectly the first time."

"Would you?" I lift my own gun, propping it up on my left shoulder instead of my right. The gun feels unfamiliar in my left hand, but I can't bear its weight with my right yet. Through the scope I find the camera, and then squint to stare at the lens. A voice whispers in my head. *Inhale. Aim. Exhale. Fire.* It takes me a few seconds to realize it's Tobias's voice, because he's the one who taught me to shoot. I squeeze the trigger and the paintball hits the camera, spraying blue paint across the lens. "There. Now you have. With the wrong hand, too."

Zeke mutters something under his breath that doesn't sound pleasant.

"Hey!" shouts a cheerful voice. Marlene pokes her head above the glass floor. Paint is smeared across her forehead, giving her a purple eyebrow. With a wicked smile, she aims at Zeke, hitting his leg, and then at me. The paintball hits my arm, stinging.

Marlene laughs and ducks under the glass. Zeke and I look at each other, and then run after Marlene. She laughs as she sprints down the path, weaving through a crowd of kids. I shoot at her, and hit the wall instead. Marlene fires at a boy near the railing—Hector, Lynn's little brother. He looks shocked at first, but then fires back, hitting the person next to Marlene.

Popping sounds fill the air as everyone in the Pit starts to fire at one another, young and old, the cameras momentarily forgotten. I charge down the path, surrounded by laughter and shouting. We cluster together to form teams, and then turn against one another.

By the time the fight dies down, my clothes are more paint-colored than black. I decide to keep the shirt to remind me why I chose Dauntless in the first place: not because they are perfect, but because they are alive. Because they are free.

CHAPTER
TWENTY-FIVE

SOMEONE RAIDS THE Dauntless kitchens and heats up the imperishables kept there, so we have a warm dinner that night. I sit at the same table I used to claim with Christina, Al, and Will. From the moment I sit down, I feel a lump in my throat. How is it that only half of us are left?

I feel responsible for that. My forgiveness could have saved Al, but I withheld it. My clearheadedness could have spared Will, but I could not summon it.

Before I can sink too far into my guilt, Uriah drops his tray next to me. It is loaded with beef stew and chocolate cake. I stare at the cake pile.

"There was cake?" I say, looking at my own plate, which is more sensibly stocked than Uriah's.

"Yeah, someone just brought it out. Found a couple

boxes of the mix in the back and baked it," he says. "You can have a few bites of mine."

"A *few* bites? So you're planning on eating that mountain of cake by yourself?"

"Yes." He looks confused. "Why?"

"Never mind."

Christina sits across the table, as far away from me as she can get. Zeke puts his tray down next to her. We are soon joined by Lynn, Hector, and Marlene. I see a flash of movement under the table, and see Marlene's hand meet Uriah's over his knee. Their fingers twist together. They are both clearly trying to look casual, but they sneak looks at each other.

To Marlene's left, Lynn looks like she just tasted something sour. She shovels food into her mouth.

"Where's the fire?" Uriah asks her. "You're going to hurl if you keep eating that fast."

Lynn scowls at him. "I'm going to hurl anyway, with you two making eyes at each other all the time."

Uriah's ears turn red. "What are you talking about?"

"I am not an idiot, and neither is anyone else. So why don't you just make out with her and get it over with?"

Uriah looks stunned. Marlene, however, glares at Lynn, leans over, and kisses Uriah firmly on the mouth, her fingers sliding around his neck, under the collar of his shirt.

I notice that all the peas have fallen off my fork, which was on its way to my mouth.

Lynn grabs her tray and storms away from the table.

"What was that all about?" says Zeke.

"Don't ask me," says Hector. "She's always angry about something. I've stopped trying to keep track."

Uriah's and Marlene's faces are still close together. And they are still smiling.

I force myself to stare at my plate. It is so strange to see two people you have known separately join together, though I have watched it happen before. I hear a squeak as Christina scratches her plate with her fork idly.

"Four!" Zeke calls out, beckoning. He looks relieved. "C'mere, there's room."

Tobias rests his hand on my good shoulder. A few of his knuckles are split, and the blood looks fresh. "Sorry, I can't stay."

He leans down and says, "Can I borrow you for a while?"

I get up, waving a good-bye to everyone at the table who is paying attention—which is just Zeke, really, because Christina and Hector are staring at their plates, and Uriah and Marlene are talking quietly. Tobias and I walk out of the cafeteria.

"Where are we going?"

"The train," he says. "I have a meeting, and I want you

there to help me read the situation."

We walk up one of the paths that lines the Pit walls, toward the stairs that lead us to the Pire.

"Why do you need *me* to—"

"Because you're better at it than I am."

I don't have a response to that. We ascend the stairs and cross the glass floor. On our way out, we walk through the dank room in which I faced my fear landscape. Judging by the syringe on the floor, someone has been there recently.

"Did you go through your fear landscape today?" I say.

"What makes you say that?" His dark eyes skirt mine. He pushes the front door open, and the summer air swims around me. There is no wind.

"Your knuckles are cut up and someone's been using that room."

"This is exactly what I mean. You're far more perceptive than most." He checks his watch. "They told me to catch the one leaving at 8:05. Come on."

I feel a surge of hope. Maybe we won't argue this time. Maybe things will finally get better between us.

We walk to the tracks. The last time we did this, he wanted to show me that the lights were on in the Erudite compound, wanted to tell me that Erudite was planning an attack on Abnegation. Now I get the sense we are about to meet with the factionless.

"Perceptive enough to know you're evading the question," I say.

He sighs. "Yes, I went through my fear landscape. I wanted to see if it had changed."

"And it has. Hasn't it?"

He brushes a stray hair away from his face and avoids my eyes. I didn't know his hair was so thick—it was hard to tell when it was buzzed short, Abnegation hair, but now it's two inches long and almost hangs over his forehead. It makes him look less threatening, more like the person I've come to know in private.

"Yes," he says. "But the number is still the same."

I hear the train horn blasting to my left, but the light fixed to the first car is not on. Instead it slides over the rails like some hidden, creeping thing.

"Fifth car back!" he shouts.

We both break into a sprint. I find the fifth car and grab the handle on the side with my left hand, pulling as hard as I can. I try to swing my legs inside, but they don't quite make it; they are dangerously close to the wheels— I shriek, and scrape my knee against the floor as I yank myself inside.

Tobias gets in after me and crouches by my side. I clutch my knee and grit my teeth.

"Here, let me see," he says. He pushes my jeans up my

leg and over my knee. His fingers leave streaks of cold on my skin, invisible to the eye, and I think about wrapping his shirt around my fist and pulling him in to kiss me; I think about pressing myself against him, but I can't, because all our secrets would keep a space between us.

My knee is red with blood. "It's shallow. It'll heal quickly," he says.

I nod. The pain is already subsiding. He rolls my jeans so they will stay up. I lie back, staring at the ceiling.

"So is *he* still in your fear landscape?" I say.

It looks like someone lit a match behind his eyes. "Yes. But not in the same way."

He told me, once, that his fear landscape hadn't changed since he first went through it, during his initiation. So if it has, even in a small way, that's something.

"You're in it, though." He frowns at his hands. "Instead of having to shoot that woman, like I used to, I have to watch you die. And there's nothing I can do to stop it."

His hands shake. I try to think of something helpful to say. *I'm not going to die*—but I don't know that. We live in a dangerous world, and I am not so attached to life that I will do anything to survive. I can't reassure him.

He checks his watch. "They'll be here any minute."

I get up, and see Evelyn and Edward standing next to the tracks. They run before the train passes them, and jump in with almost as little trouble as Tobias. They must have been practicing.

Edward smirks at me. Today his eye patch has a big blue "X" stitched over it.

"Hello," Evelyn says. She looks only at Tobias as she says it, like I'm not even there.

"Nice meeting location," says Tobias. It is almost dark now, so I see only shadows of buildings against a dark blue sky, and a few glowing lights near the lake that must belong to Erudite headquarters.

The train takes a turn it doesn't usually take—left, away from the glow of Erudite and into the abandoned part of the city. I can tell by the growing quiet in the car that it is slowing down.

"It seemed safest," says Evelyn. "So you wanted to meet."

"Yes. I'd like to discuss an alliance."

"An alliance," repeats Edward. "And who gave you the authority to do that?"

"He's a Dauntless leader," I say. "He has the authority."

Edward raises his eyebrows, looking impressed. Evelyn's eyes finally shift to me, but only for a second before she smiles at Tobias again.

"Interesting," she says. "And is *she* also a Dauntless leader?"

"No," he says. "She's here to help me decide whether or not to trust you."

Evelyn purses her lips. Part of me wants to thumb my nose at her and say, "Ha!" But I settle for a small smile.

"We will, of course, agree to an alliance . . . under a certain set of conditions," Evelyn says. "A guaranteed—and equal—place in whatever government forms after Erudite is destroyed, and full control over Erudite data after the attack. Clearly—"

"What are you going to do with the Erudite data?" I interrupt her.

"Obviously we will destroy it. The only way to deprive the Erudite of power is to deprive them of knowledge."

My first instinct is to tell her she's a fool. But something stops me. Without the simulation technology, without the data they had about all the other factions, without their focus on technological advancement, the attack on Abnegation would not have happened. My parents would be alive.

Even if we manage to kill Jeanine, could the Erudite be trusted not to attack and control us again? I am not sure.

"What would we receive in return, under those terms?" Tobias says.

"Our much-needed manpower, in order to take Erudite headquarters, and an equal place in government, with us."

"I am sure that Tori would also request the right to rid the world of Jeanine Matthews," he says in a low voice.

I raise my eyebrows. I didn't know that Tori's hatred of Jeanine was common knowledge—or maybe it isn't. He must know things about her that others don't, now that he and Tori are leaders.

"I'm sure that could be arranged," Evelyn replies. "I don't care who kills her; I just want her dead."

Tobias glances at me. I wish I could tell him why I feel so conflicted . . . explain to him why I, of all people, have reservations about burning Erudite to the ground, so to speak. But I would not know how to say it even if I had the time to. He turns toward Evelyn.

"Then we are agreed," he says.

He extends his hand, and she shakes it.

"We should convene in a week's time," she says. "In neutral territory. Most of the Abnegation have graciously agreed to let us stay in their sector of the city to plan as they clean up the aftermath of the attack."

"Most of them," he says.

Evelyn's expression turns flat. "I'm afraid your father still commands the loyalty of many of them, and he advised them to avoid us when he came to visit a few days ago." She smiles bitterly. "And they agreed, just as they did when he persuaded them to exile me."

"They exiled you?" says Tobias. "I thought you *left*."

"No, the Abnegation were inclined toward forgiveness and reconciliation, as you might expect. But your father has a lot of influence over the Abnegation, and he always has. I decided to leave rather than face the indignity of public exile."

Tobias looks stunned.

Edward, who has been leaning out the side of the car for a few seconds, says, "It's time!"

"See you in a week," Evelyn says.

As the train dips down to street level, Edward leaps. A few seconds later, Evelyn follows. Tobias and I remain on the train, listening to it hiss against the rails, without speaking.

"Why did you even bring me along, if you were just going to make an alliance anyway?" I say flatly.

"You didn't stop me."

"What was I supposed to do, wave my hands in the air?" I scowl at him. "I don't like it."

"It has to be done."

"I don't think it does," I say. "There has to be another way—"

"What other way?" he says, folding his arms. "You just

don't like her. You haven't since you first met her."

"Obviously I don't like her! She abandoned you!"

"They *exiled* her. And if I decide to forgive her, you had better try to do it too! I'm the one who got left behind, not you."

"This is about more than that. I don't trust her. I think she's trying to use you."

"Well, it isn't for you to decide."

"Why did you bring me, again?" I say, mirroring him by folding my arms. "Oh yeah—so that I could read the situation for you. Well, I read it, and just because you don't like what I decided doesn't mean—"

"I forgot about how your biases cloud your judgment. If I had remembered, I might not have brought you."

"*My* biases. What about *your* biases? What about thinking everyone who hates your father as much as you do is an ally?"

"This is not about him!"

"Of course it is! He knows things, Tobias. And we should be trying to find out what they are."

"This again? I thought we resolved this. He is a *liar*, Tris."

"Yeah?" I raise my eyebrows. "Well, so is your mother. You think the Abnegation would really exile someone? Because I don't."

"Don't talk about my mother that way."

I see light up ahead. It belongs to the Pire.

"Fine." I walk to the edge of the car door. "I won't."

I jump out, running a few steps to keep my balance. Tobias jumps out after me, but I don't give him a chance to catch up—I walk straight into the building, down the stairs, and back into the Pit to find a place to sleep.

CHAPTER
TWENTY-SIX

SOMETHING SHAKES ME awake.

"Tris! Get up!"

A shout. I don't question it. I throw my legs over the edge of the bed and let a hand pull me toward the door. My feet are bare, and the ground is uneven here. It scrapes at my toes and the edges of my heels. I squint ahead of me to figure out who's dragging me. Christina. She's almost pulling my left arm from its socket.

"What happened?" I say. "What's going on?"

"Shut up and run!"

We run to the Pit, and the roar of the river follows me up the paths. The last time Christina pulled me out of bed, it was to see Al's body lifted out of the chasm. I grit my teeth and try not to think about that. It can't have happened again. It can't.

I gasp—she runs faster than I do—as we sprint across the glass floor of the Pire. Christina slams her palm into an elevator button and slips inside before the doors are fully open, dragging me behind her. She jabs the DOOR CLOSE button, and then the button for the top floor.

"Simulation," she says. "There's a simulation. It's not everyone, it's just . . . just a few."

She puts her hands on her knees and takes deep breaths.

"One of them said something about the Divergent," she says.

"Said that?" I say. "While under a simulation?"

She nods. "Marlene. Didn't sound like her, though. Too . . . monotone."

The doors open, and I follow her down the hallway to the door marked ROOF ACCESS.

"Christina," I say, "why are we going to the roof?"

She doesn't answer me. The stairs to the roof smell like old paint. Dauntless graffiti is scrawled on the cement-block walls in black paint. The symbol of Dauntless. Initials paired together with plus signs: RG + NT, BR + FH. Couples who are probably old now, maybe broken up. I touch my chest to feel my heartbeat. It's so fast, it's a wonder I'm still breathing at all.

The night air is cool; it gives me goose bumps on my

arms. My eyes have adjusted to the darkness by now, and across the roof I see three figures standing on the ledge, facing me. One is Marlene. One is Hector. One is someone I don't recognize—a young Dauntless, barely eight years old, with a green streak in her hair.

They stand still on the ledge, though the wind is blowing hard, tossing their hair over their foreheads, into their eyes, into their mouths. Their clothes snap in the wind, but still they stand motionless.

"Just come down off the ledge now," Christina says. "Don't do anything stupid. Come on, now . . ."

"They can't hear you," I say quietly as I walk toward them. "Or see you."

"We should all jump at them at once. I'll take Hec, you—"

"We'll risk shoving them off the roof if we do that. Stand by the girl, just in case."

She is too young for this, I think, but I don't have the heart to say it, because it means Marlene is old enough.

I stare at Marlene, whose eyes are blank like painted stones, like spheres of glass. I feel as if those stones are slipping down my throat and settling in my stomach, pulling me toward the ground. There is no way to get her off that ledge.

Finally she opens her mouth and speaks.

"I have a message for the Divergent." Her voice sounds flat. The simulation is using her vocal cords, but robs them of the natural fluctuations of human emotion.

I look from Marlene to Hector. Hector, who was so afraid of what I am because his mother told him to be. Lynn is probably still at Shauna's bedside, hoping Shauna can move her legs when she wakes up again. Lynn can't lose Hector.

I step forward to receive the message.

"This is not a negotiation. It is a warning," says the simulation through Marlene, moving her lips and vibrating in her throat. "Every two days until one of you delivers yourself to Erudite headquarters, this will happen again."

This.

Marlene steps back, and I throw myself forward, but not at her. Not at Marlene, who once let Uriah shoot a muffin off her head on a dare. Who gathered a stack of clothing for me to wear. Who always, always greeted me with a smile. No, not at Marlene.

As Marlene and the other Dauntless girl step off the edge of the roof, I dive at Hector.

I grab whatever my hands can find. An arm. A fistful of shirt. The rough rooftop scrapes my knees as his weight drags me forward. I am not strong enough to lift him. I whisper, "Help," because I can't speak any louder than that.

Christina is already at my shoulder. She helps me haul Hector's limp body onto the roof. His arm flops to the side, lifeless. A few feet away, the little girl lies on her back on the rooftop.

Then the simulation ends. Hector opens his eyes, and they are no longer empty.

"Ow," he says. "What's going on?"

The little girl whimpers, and Christina walks over to her, mumbling something in a reassuring voice.

I stand, my entire body shaking. I inch toward the edge of the roof and stare at the ground. The street below isn't lit very well, but I can see Marlene's faint outline on the pavement.

Breathing—who cares about breathing?

I turn from the sight, listening to my heart beat in my ears. Christina's mouth moves. I ignore her, and walk to the door and down the stairs and down the hallway and into the elevator.

The doors close and as I drop to the earth, just as Marlene did after I decided not to save her, I scream, my hands tearing at my clothes. My throat is raw after just a few seconds, and there are scratches on my arms where I missed the fabric, but I keep screaming.

The elevator stops with a *ding*. The doors open.

I straighten my shirt, smooth my hair down, and walk out.

+ + +

I have a message for the Divergent.

I am Divergent.

This is not a negotiation.

No, it is not.

It is a warning.

I understand.

Every two days until one of you delivers yourself to Erudite headquarters . . .

I will.

. . . this will happen again.

It will never happen again.

CHAPTER
TWENTY-SEVEN

I WEAVE THROUGH the crowd next to the chasm. It's loud in the Pit, and not just because of the river's roar. I want to find some silence, so I escape into the hallway that leads to the dormitories. I don't want to hear the speech Tori will make on Marlene's behalf or be around for the toasting and the shouting as the Dauntless celebrate her life and her bravery.

This morning Lauren reported that we missed some of the cameras in the initiate dormitories, where Christina, Zeke, Lauren, Marlene, Hector, and Kee, the girl with the green hair, were sleeping. That's how Jeanine figured out who the simulation was controlling. I do not doubt that Jeanine chose young Dauntless because she knew their deaths would affect us more.

I stop in an unfamiliar hallway and press my forehead to the wall. The stone feels rough and cool on my skin. I can hear the Dauntless shouting behind me, their voices muffled by layers of rock.

I hear someone approaching, and look to the side. Christina, still wearing the same clothes she wore last night, stands a few feet away.

"Hey," she says.

"I'm not really in the mood to feel more guilt right now. So go away, please."

"I just want to say one thing, and then I will."

Her eyes are puffy and her voice sounds a little sleepy, which is either due to exhaustion or a little alcohol, or both. But her stare is direct enough that she must know what she's saying. I pull away from the wall.

"I'd never seen that kind of simulation before. You know, from the outside. But yesterday . . ." She shakes her head. "You were right. They couldn't hear you, couldn't see you. Just like Will . . ."

She chokes on his name. Stops, takes a breath, swallows hard. Blinks a few times. Then looks at me again.

"You told me you had to do it, or he would have shot you, and I didn't believe you. I believe you now, and . . . I'm going to try to forgive you. That's . . . all I wanted to say."

There's a part of me that feels relief. She believes me,

she's trying to forgive me, even though it won't be easy.

But a larger part of me feels anger. What did she think, before now? That I *wanted* to shoot Will, one of my best friends? She should have trusted me from the beginning, should have *known* that I wouldn't have done it if I had been able to see another option at the time.

"How fortunate for me that you finally got *proof* that I'm not a cold-blooded murderer. You know, other than my word. I mean, what reason would you have to trust that?" I force a laugh, trying to stay nonchalant. She opens her mouth, but I keep talking, unable to stop myself. "You'd better hurry on that forgiving-me thing, because there isn't much time—"

My voice cracks, and I can't hold myself together anymore. I start sobbing. I lean against the wall for support and feel myself sliding down as my legs get weak.

My eyes are too blurry to see her, but I feel her when she wraps her arms around me and squeezes so hard it hurts. She smells like coconut oil and she feels strong, exactly like she was during initiation into Dauntless, when she hung over the chasm by her fingertips. Back then—which was not so long ago—she made me feel weak, but now her strength makes me feel like I could be stronger too.

We kneel together on the stone floor, and I clutch her as tightly as she clutches me.

"It's already done," she says. "That's what I meant to say. That the forgiving was already done."

+++

All the Dauntless go quiet when I walk into the cafeteria that night. I don't blame them. As one of the Divergent, I have the power to let Jeanine kill one of them. Most of them probably want me to sacrifice myself. Or they are terrified that I won't.

If this were Abnegation, no Divergent would be sitting here right now.

For a moment I don't know where to go or how to get there. But then Zeke waves me over to his table, looking grim, and I guide my feet in that direction. But before I make it there, Lynn approaches me.

She is a different Lynn from the one I have always known. She doesn't have a fierce look in her eyes. Instead she is pale and biting her lip to hide its wobble.

"Um . . ." she says. She looks to the left, to the right, anywhere but at my face. "I really . . . I miss Marlene. I've known her for a long time, and I . . ." She shakes her head. "The point is, don't think that my saying this means *any-thing* about Marlene," she says, like she's scolding me, "but . . . thank you for saving Hec."

Lynn shifts her weight from one foot to the other, her

eyes flicking around the room. Then she hugs me with one arm, her hand gripping my shirt. Pain shoots through my shoulder. I don't say anything about it.

She lets go, sniffs, and walks back to her table like nothing happened. I stare at her retreating back for a few seconds, and then sit down.

Zeke and Uriah sit side by side at the otherwise empty table. Uriah's face is slack, like he's not completely awake. He has a dark brown bottle in front of him that he sips from every few seconds.

I feel cautious around him. I saved Hec—which means I failed to save Marlene. But Uriah doesn't look at me. I pull out the chair across from him and sit on the edge of it.

"Where's Shauna?" I say. "Still in the hospital?"

"No, she's over there," says Zeke, nodding to the table Lynn walked back to. I see her there, so pale she might as well be translucent, sitting in a wheelchair. "Shauna shouldn't be up, but Lynn's pretty messed up, so she's keeping her company."

"But if you're wondering why they're all the way over there . . . Shauna found out I'm Divergent," says Uriah sluggishly. "And she doesn't want to catch it."

"Oh."

"She got all weird with me, too," says Zeke, sighing. "'How do you know your brother isn't working against us?

Have you been watching him?' What I wouldn't give to punch whoever poisoned her mind."

"You don't have to give anything," says Uriah. "Her mother's sitting right there. Go ahead and hit her."

I follow his gaze to a middle-aged woman with blue streaks in her hair and earrings all the way down her earlobe. She is pretty, just like Lynn.

Tobias enters the room a moment later, followed by Tori and Harrison. I have been avoiding him. I haven't spoken to him since that fight we had, before Marlene . . .

"Hello, Tris," Tobias says when I'm close enough to hear him. His voice is low, rough. It transports me to quiet places.

"Hi," I say in a tight little voice that does not belong to me.

He sits next to me and puts his arm on the back of my chair, leaning close. I don't stare back—I *refuse* to stare back.

I stare back.

Dark eyes—a peculiar shade of blue, somehow capable of shutting the rest of the cafeteria out, of comforting me and also of reminding me that we are farther away from each other than I want us to be.

"Aren't you going to ask me if I'm all right?" I say.

"No, I'm pretty sure you're not all right." He shakes his

head. "I'm going to ask you not to make any decisions until we've talked about it."

It's too late, I think. *The decision's made.*

"Until we've all talked about it, you mean, since it involves all of us," says Uriah. "I don't think anyone should turn themselves in."

"No one?" I say.

"No!" Uriah scowls. "I think we should attack back."

"Yeah," I say hollowly, "let's provoke the woman who can force half of this compound to kill themselves. That sounds like a great idea."

I was too harsh. Uriah tips the contents of his bottle down his throat. He brings the bottle down on the table so hard I'm afraid it will shatter.

"Don't talk about it like that," he says in a growl.

"I'm sorry," I say. "But you know I'm right. The best way to ensure that half our faction doesn't die is to sacrifice one life."

I don't know what I expected. Maybe that Uriah, who knows too well what will happen if one of us does not go, would volunteer himself. But he looks down. Unwilling.

"Tori and Harrison and I decided to increase security. Hopefully if everyone is more aware of these attacks, we will be able to stop them," Tobias says. "If it doesn't work, then we will think of another solution. End of discussion.

But no one is going to do anything yet. Okay?"

He looks at me when he asks and raises his eyebrows.

"Okay," I say, not quite meeting his eyes.

+ + +

After dinner, I try to go back to the dormitory where I've been sleeping, but I can't quite walk through the door. Instead I walk through the corridors, brushing the stone walls with my fingers, listening to the echoes of my footsteps.

Without meaning to, I pass the water fountain where Peter, Drew, and Al attacked me. I knew it was Al by the way he smelled—I can still call the scent of lemongrass to mind. Now I associate it not with my friend but with the powerlessness I felt as they dragged me to the chasm.

I walk faster, keeping my eyes wide open so it will be harder to picture the attack in my mind. I have to get away from here, far from the places where my friend attacked me, where Peter stabbed Edward, where a sightless army of my friends began its march toward the Abnegation sector and all this insanity began.

I go straight toward the last place where I felt safe: Tobias's small apartment. The second I reach the door, I feel calmer.

The door is not completely closed. I nudge it open with

my foot. He isn't there, but I don't leave. I sit on his bed
and gather the quilt in my arms, burying my face in the
fabric and taking deep breaths of it through my nose. The
smell it used to have is almost gone, it's been so long since
he slept on it.

The door opens and Tobias slips in. My arms go limp,
and the quilt falls into my lap. How will I explain my presence here? I'm supposed to be angry with him.

He doesn't scowl, but his mouth is so tense that I know
he's angry with *me*.

"Don't be an idiot," he says.

"An idiot?"

"You were lying. You said you wouldn't go to Erudite,
and you were lying, and going to Erudite would make you
an idiot. So don't."

I set the blanket down and get up.

"Don't try to make this simple," I say. "It's not. You
know as well as I do that this is the right thing to do."

"You choose *this* moment to act like the Abnegation?"
His voice fills the room and makes fear prickle in my
chest. His anger seems too sudden. Too strange. "All
that time you spent insisting that you were too selfish for
them, and now, when your *life* is on the line, you've got to
be a hero? What's wrong with you?"

"What's wrong with *you*? People died. They walked

right off the edge of a building! And I can stop it from happening again!"

"You're too important to just . . . die." He shakes his head. He won't even look at me—his eyes keep shifting across my face, to the wall behind me or the ceiling above me, to everything but me. I am too stunned to be angry.

"I'm not important. Everyone will do just fine without me," I say.

"Who cares about everyone? What about *me*?"

He lowers his head into his hand, covering his eyes. His fingers are trembling.

Then he crosses the room in two long strides and touches his lips to mine. Their gentle pressure erases the past few months, and I am the girl who sat on the rocks next to the chasm, with river spray on her ankles, and kissed him for the first time. I am the girl who grabbed his hand in the hallway just because I wanted to.

I pull back, my hand on his chest to keep him away. The problem is, I am also the girl who shot Will and lied about it, and chose between Hector and Marlene, and now a thousand other things besides. And I can't erase those things.

"You *would* be fine." I don't look at him. I stare at his T-shirt between my fingers and the black ink curling around his neck, but I don't look at his face. "Not at first.

But you would move on, and do what you have to."

He wraps an arm around my waist and pulls me against him. "That's a *lie*," he says, before he kisses me again.

This is wrong. It's wrong to forget who I have become, and to let him kiss me when I know what I'm about to do.

But I want to. Oh, I want to.

I stand on my tiptoes and wrap my arms around him. I press one hand between his shoulder blades and curl the other one around the back of his neck. I can feel his breaths against my palm, his body expanding and contracting, and I know he's strong, steady, unstoppable. All things I need to be, but I am not, I am not.

He walks backward, pulling me with him so I stumble. I stumble right out of my shoes. He sits on the edge of the bed and I stand in front of him, and we're finally eye to eye.

He touches my face, covering my cheeks with his hands, sliding his fingertips down my neck, fitting his fingers to the slight curve of my hips.

I can't stop.

I fit my mouth to his, and he tastes like water and smells like fresh air. I drag my hand from his neck to the small of his back, and put it under his shirt. He kisses me harder.

I knew he was strong; I didn't know how strong until I

felt it myself, the muscles in his back tightening beneath my fingers.

Stop, I tell myself.

Suddenly it's as if we're in a hurry, his fingertips brushing my side under my shirt, my hands clutching at him, struggling closer but there is no closer. I have never longed for someone this way, or this much.

He pulls back just enough to look into my eyes, his eyelids lowered.

"Promise me," he whispers, "that you won't go. For me. Do this one thing for me."

Could I do that? Could I stay here, fix things with him, let someone else die in my place? Looking up at him, I believe for a moment that I could. And then I see Will. The crease between his eyebrows. The empty, simulation-bound eyes. The slumped body.

Do this one thing for me. Tobias's dark eyes plead with me.

But if I don't go to Erudite, who will? Tobias? It's the kind of thing he would do.

I feel a stab of pain in my chest as I lie to him. "Okay."

"Promise," he says, frowning.

The pain becomes an ache, spreads everywhere—all mixed together, guilt and terror and longing. "I promise."

CHAPTER
TWENTY-EIGHT

WHEN HE STARTS to fall asleep, he keeps his arms around me fiercely, a life-preserving prison. But I wait, kept awake by the thought of bodies hitting pavement, until his grip loosens and his breathing steadies.

I will not let Tobias go to Erudite when it happens again, when someone else dies. I will not.

I slip out of his arms. I shrug on one of his sweatshirts so I can carry the smell of him with me. I slip my feet into my shoes. I don't take any weapons or keepsakes.

I pause by the doorway and look at him, half buried under the quilt, peaceful and strong.

"I love you," I say quietly, trying out the words. I let the door close behind me.

It's time to put everything in order.

I walk to the dormitory where the Dauntless-born initiates once slept. The room looks just like the one I slept in when I was an initiate: it is long and narrow, with bunk beds on either side and a chalkboard on one wall. I see by a blue light in the corner that no one bothered to erase the rankings that are written there—Uriah's name is still at the top.

Christina sleeps in the bottom bunk, beneath Lynn. I don't want to startle her, but there's no way to wake her otherwise, so I cover her mouth with my hand. She wakes with a start, her eyes wide until they find me. I touch my finger to my lips and beckon for her to follow me.

I walk to the end of the hallway and turn a corner. The corridor is lit by a paint-spattered emergency lamp that hangs over one of the exits. Christina isn't wearing shoes; she curls her toes under to protect them from the cold.

"What is it?" she says. "Are you going somewhere?"

"Yeah, I'm . . ." I have to lie, or she'll try to stop me. "I'm going to see my brother. He's with the Abnegation, remember?"

She narrows her eyes.

"I'm sorry to wake you," I say. "But there's something I need you to do. It's really important."

"Okay. Tris, you're acting really strange. Are you sure you're not—"

"I'm not. Listen to me. The timing of the simulation attack wasn't random. The reason it happened when it did is because the Abnegation were about to do something—I don't know what it was, but it had to do with some important information, and now Jeanine *has* that information. . . ."

"What?" She frowns. "You don't know what they were about to do? Do you know what the information is?"

"No." I must sound crazy. "The thing is, I haven't been able to find out very much about this, because Marcus Eaton is the only person who knows everything, and he won't tell me. I just . . . it's the reason for the attack. It's the *reason*. And we need to know it."

I don't know what else to say. But Christina is already nodding.

"The reason Jeanine forced us to attack innocent people," she says bitterly. "Yeah. We need to know it."

I had almost forgotten—*she* was under the simulation. How many Abnegation did she kill, guided by the simulation? How did she feel when she awoke from that dream a murderer? I have never asked, and I never will.

"I want your help, and soon. I need someone to persuade Marcus to cooperate, and I think you can do it."

She tilts her head and stares at me for a few seconds.

"Tris. Don't do anything stupid."

I force a smile. "Why do people keep saying that to me?"

She grabs my arm. "I'm not kidding around."

"I told you, I'm going to visit Caleb. I'll be back in a few days, and we can make a strategy then. I just thought it would be better if someone else knew about all this before I left. Just in case. Okay?"

She holds my arm for a few seconds, and then releases me. "Okay," she says.

I walk toward the exit. I hold myself together until I'm through the door, and then I feel the tears come.

The last conversation I'll ever have with her, and it was full of lies.

+++

Once I'm outside, I put up the hood of Tobias's sweatshirt. When I reach the end of the street, I glance up and down, searching for signs of life. There is nothing.

The cool air prickles in my lungs on the way in, and on the way out unfurls in a cloud of vapor. Winter will be here soon. I wonder if Erudite and Dauntless will still be at a standstill then, waiting for one group to obliterate the other. I'm glad I won't have to see it.

Before I chose Dauntless, thoughts like that never

occurred to me. I felt assured of my long lifespan, if nothing else. Now there are no reassurances, except that where I go, I go because I choose to.

I walk in the shadows of buildings, hoping my footsteps won't attract any attention. None of the city lights are on in this area, but the moon is bright enough that I can walk by it without too much trouble.

I walk beneath the elevated tracks. They shudder with the movement of an oncoming train. I have to walk fast if I want to get there before anyone notices that I'm gone. I sidestep a large crack in the street, and jump over a fallen streetlight.

I didn't think about how far I would have to walk when I set out. It isn't long before my body warms with the exertion of walking and checking over my shoulder and dodging hazards in the road. I pick up the pace, half walking and half jogging.

Soon I reach a part of the city that I recognize. The streets are better kept here, swept clean, with few holes. Far away I see the glow of Erudite headquarters, their lights violating our energy conservation laws. I don't know what I will do when I get there. Demand to see Jeanine? Or just stand there until someone notices me?

My fingertips skim a window in the building beside

me. Not long now. Tremors go through my body now that I am close, making it difficult to walk. Breathing is tricky too; I stop trying to be quiet, and let air wheeze in and out of my lungs. What will they do with me when I get there? What plans do they have for me before I outlive my usefulness, and they kill me? I don't doubt that they will kill me eventually. I concentrate on forward motion, on moving my legs even though they seem to be unwilling to support my weight.

And then I'm standing in front of Erudite headquarters.

Inside, crowds of blue-shirted people sit around tables, typing on computers or bent over books or passing sheets of paper back and forth. Some of them are decent people who do not understand what their faction has done, but if their entire building collapsed in on them before my eyes, I might not find it in myself to care.

This is the last moment I will be able to turn back. The cold air stings my cheeks and my hands as I hesitate. I can walk away now. Take refuge in the Dauntless compound. Hope and pray and wish that no one else dies because of my selfishness.

But I can't walk away, or the guilt, the weight of Will's life, and my parents' lives, and now Marlene's life, will break my bones, will make it impossible to breathe.

I slowly walk toward the building and push open the doors.

This is the only way to keep from suffocating.

+ + +

For a second after my feet touch the wood floors, and I stand before the giant portrait of Jeanine Matthews hung on the opposite wall, no one notices me, not even the two Dauntless traitor guards milling around near the entryway. I walk up to the front desk, where a middle-aged man with a bald patch on the crown of his head sits, sorting through a stack of paper. I set my hands on the desk.

"Excuse me," I say.

"Give me a moment," he says without looking up.

"No."

At *that* he looks up, his glasses askew, scowling like he's about to chastise me. Whatever words he was about to use seem to stick in his throat. He stares at me with an open mouth, his eyes skipping from my face to the black sweatshirt I wear.

In my terror, his expression seems amusing. I smile a little and conceal my hands, which are trembling.

"I believe Jeanine Matthews wanted to see me," I say. "So I would appreciate it if you would contact her."

He signals to the Dauntless traitors by the door, but

there is no need. The guards have finally caught on. Dauntless soldiers from the other parts of the room have also started forward, and they all surround me, but don't touch me, and don't speak to me. I scan their faces, trying to look as placid as possible.

"Divergent?" one of them finally asks as the man behind the desk picks up the receiver of the building's communication system.

If I close my hands into fists, I can stop them from shaking. I nod.

My eyes shift to the Dauntless coming out of the elevator on the left side of the room, and the muscles in my face go slack. Peter is coming toward us.

A thousand potential reactions, ranging from launching myself at Peter's throat to crying to making some kind of joke, rush through my mind at once. I can't decide on one. So I stand still and watch him. Jeanine must have known that I would come, she must have chosen Peter on purpose to collect me, she must have.

"We've been instructed to take you upstairs," says Peter.

I mean to say something sharp, or nonchalant, but the only sound that escapes me is an assenting noise, squeezed tight by my swollen throat. Peter starts toward the elevators, and I follow him.

We walk down a series of sleek corridors. Despite the

fact that we climb a few flights of stairs, I still feel like I am plunging into the earth.

I expect them to take me to Jeanine, but they don't. They stop walking in a short hallway with a series of metal doors on each side. Peter types in a code to open one of the doors, and the traitor Dauntless surround me, shoulder to shoulder, forming a narrow tunnel for me to pass through on my way into the room.

The room is small, maybe six feet long by six feet wide. The floor, the walls, and the ceiling are all made of the same light panels, dim now, that glowed in the aptitude test room. In each corner is a tiny black camera.

I finally let myself panic.

I look from corner to corner, at the cameras, and fight the scream building in my stomach, chest, and throat, the scream that fills every part of me. Again I feel guilt and grief clawing inside me, warring with each other for dominance, but terror is stronger than both. I breathe in, and don't breathe out. My father once told me it was a cure for hiccups. I asked him if I could die from holding my breath.

"No," he said. "Your body's instincts will take over, and force you to breathe."

A shame, really. I could use a way out. The thought makes me want to laugh. And then scream.

I curl up so I can press my face to my knees. I have to make a plan. If I can make a plan, I won't be so afraid.

But there is no plan. No escape from deep in Erudite headquarters, no escape from Jeanine, and no other escape from what I've done.

CHAPTER
TWENTY-NINE

I FORGOT MY watch.

Minutes or hours later, when the panic subsides, that is what I most regret. Not coming here in the first place—that seemed like an obvious choice—but my bare wrist, which makes it impossible for me to know how long I have been sitting in this room. My back aches, which is some indication, but it is not definite enough.

After a while I get up and pace, stretching my arms above my head. I hesitate to do anything while the cameras are there, but they can't learn anything by watching me touch my toes.

The thought makes my hands tremble, but I don't try to push it from my mind. Instead I tell myself that I am Dauntless and I am no stranger to fear. I will die in this place. Perhaps soon. Those are the facts.

But there are other ways to think of it. Soon I will honor my parents by dying as they died. And if all they believed about death was true, soon I will join them in whatever comes next.

I shake my hands as I pace. They're still trembling. I want to know what time it is. I arrived a little after midnight. It must be early in the morning by now, maybe 4:00, or 5:00. Or maybe it hasn't been that long, and only seems that way because I haven't been doing anything.

The door opens, and at last I stand face-to-face with my enemy and her Dauntless guards.

"Hello, Beatrice," Jeanine says. She wears Erudite blue and Erudite spectacles and an Erudite look of superiority that I was taught by my father to hate. "I thought you might be the one who came."

But I don't feel hate when I look at her. I don't feel anything at all, even though I know she's responsible for countless deaths, including Marlene's. The deaths exist in my mind as a string of meaningless equations, and I stand frozen, unable to solve them.

"Hello, Jeanine," I say, because it is the only thing that comes to mind.

I look from Jeanine's watery gray eyes to the Dauntless who flank her. Peter stands at her right shoulder, and a woman with lines on either side of her mouth stands at her left. Behind her is a bald man with sharp planes in his skull. I frown.

How does Peter find himself in such a prestigious position, as Jeanine Matthews's bodyguard? Where is the logic in that?

"I'd like to know what time it is," I say.

"Would you," she says. "That's interesting."

I should have known she wouldn't tell me. Every piece of information she receives factors into her strategy, and she won't tell me what time it is unless she decides that providing the information is more useful than withholding it.

"I'm sure my Dauntless companions are disappointed," she says, "that you have not tried to claw my eyes out yet."

"That would be stupid."

"True. But in keeping with your 'act first, think second' behavioral trend."

"I'm sixteen." I purse my lips. "I change."

"How refreshing." She has a way of flattening even those phrases that should have inflection built into them. "Let's go on a little tour, shall we?"

She steps back and gestures toward the doorway. The last thing I want to do is walk out of this room and toward an uncertain destination, but I don't hesitate. I walk out, the severe-looking Dauntless woman in front of me. Peter follows me soon afterward.

The hallway is long and pale. We turn a corner and walk down a second one exactly like the first.

Two more hallways follow. I am so disoriented I could never find my way back. But then my surroundings change—the white tunnel opens to a large room where Erudite men and women in long blue jackets stand behind tables, some holding tools, some mixing multicolored liquids, some staring at computer screens. If I had to guess, I would say they are mixing simulation serum, but I hesitate to confine Erudite's work to simulations alone.

Most of them stop to watch us as we walk down the center aisle. Or rather, they watch *me*. Some of them whisper, but most remain silent. It is so quiet here.

I follow the Dauntless traitor woman through a doorway, and stop so abruptly Peter runs into me.

This room is just as large as the last one, but there is only one thing in it: a large metal table with a machine next to it. A machine I vaguely recognize as a heart monitor. And dangling above it, a camera. I shudder without meaning to. Because I know what this is.

"I am very pleased that *you*, in particular, are here," says Jeanine. She walks past me and perches on the table, her fingers curled around the edge.

"I am pleased, of course, because of your aptitude test results." Her blond hair, pulled tight to her skull, reflects the light, catches my attention.

"Even among the Divergent, you are somewhat of an oddity, because you have aptitude for three factions. Abnegation, Dauntless, and Erudite."

"How . . ." My voice croaks. I push the question out. "How do you know that?"

"All in good time," she says. "From your results I have determined that you are one of the strongest Divergent, which I say not to compliment you but to explain my purpose. If I am to develop a simulation that cannot be thwarted by the Divergent mind, I must study the strongest Divergent mind in order to shore up all weaknesses in the technology. Understand?"

I don't respond. I am still staring at the heart monitor next to the table.

"Therefore, for as long as possible, my fellow scientists and I will be studying you." She smiles a little. "And then, at the conclusion of my study, you will be executed."

I knew that. I knew it, so why do my knees feel weak, why is my stomach writhing, why?

"That execution will take place here." She runs her fingertips over the table beneath her. "On this table. I thought it would be interesting to show it to you."

She wants to study my response. I barely breathe. I used to think that cruelty required malice, but that is not true. Jeanine has no reason to act out of malice. But she is cruel because she doesn't care what she does, as long as it fascinates her. I may as well be a puzzle or a broken machine she wants to fix. She will break open my skull just to see the inner workings of my brain; I will die here, and that will be the merciful thing.

"I knew what would happen when I came here," I say. "It's just a table. And I'd like to go back to my room now."

+ + +

I don't really comprehend time's passing, at least not in the way that I used to, when time was available to me. So when the door opens again and Peter walks into my cell, I don't know how much time has gone by, only that I am exhausted.

"Let's go, Stiff," he says.

"I'm not Abnegation." I stretch my arms above my head so they brush against the wall. "And now that you're an Erudite lackey, you can't call me 'Stiff.' It's inaccurate."

"I said, let's go."

"What, no snide comments?" I look up at him with mock surprise. "No 'You're an idiot for coming here; your brain must be deficient as well as Divergent'?"

"That really goes without saying, doesn't it?" he says. "You can either get up or I can drag you down the hallway. Your choice."

I feel calmer. Peter is always mean to me; this is familiar.

I stand and walk out of the room. I notice as I walk that Peter's arm, the one I shot, is no longer in a sling.

"Did they fix up your bullet wound?"

"Yeah," he says. "Now you'll need to find a different weakness to exploit. Too bad I'm fresh out of them." He grabs my good arm and walks faster, pulling me along beside him. "We're late."

Despite the length and emptiness of the hallway, our footsteps don't echo much. I feel like someone put their hands over my ears and I only just noticed it. I try to keep track of the hallways we walk down, but I lose count after a while. We reach the end of one and turn left, into a dim room that reminds me of an aquarium. One of the walls is made of one-way glass—reflective on my side, but I'm sure it's transparent on the other side.

A large machine stands on the other side, with a man-sized tray coming out of it. I recognize it from my Faction History textbook, the unit on Erudite and medicine. An MRI machine. It will take pictures of my brain.

Something sparks inside me. It's been so long since I

felt it that I barely recognize it at first. Curiosity.

A voice—Jeanine's voice—speaks over an intercom.

"Lie down, Beatrice."

I look at the man-sized tray that will slide me into the machine.

"No."

She sighs. "If you don't do it yourself, we have ways of making you."

Peter is standing behind me. Even with an injured arm, he was stronger than me. I imagine his hands on me, wrestling me toward the tray, shoving me against the metal, pulling the straps that dangle from the tray across my body, too tightly.

"Let's make a deal," I say. "If I cooperate, I get to see the scan."

"You will cooperate whether you want to or not."

I hold up a finger. "That's not true."

I look at the mirror. It's not so difficult to pretend that I'm speaking to Jeanine when I speak to my own reflection. My hair is blond like hers; we are both pale and stern-looking. The thought is so disturbing to me that I lose my train of thought for a few seconds, and instead stand with my finger in the air in silence.

I am pale-skinned, pale-haired, and cold. I am curious about the pictures of my brain. I am like Jeanine. And I can either despise it, attack it, eradicate it . . . or I can use it.

"That's not true," I repeat. "No matter how many restraints you use, you can't keep me as still as I need to be for the pictures to be clear." I clear my throat. "I want to see the scans. You're going to kill me anyway, so does it really matter how much I know about my own brain before you do?"

Silence.

"Why do you want to see them so badly?" she says.

"Surely you, of all people, understand. I have equal aptitude for Erudite as I do for Dauntless and Abnegation, after all."

"All right. You can see them. Lie down."

I walk over to the tray and lie down. The metal feels like ice. The tray slides back, and I am inside the machine. I stare up at whiteness. When I was young, I thought that was what heaven would be like, all white light and nothing else. Now I know that can't be true, because white light is menacing.

I hear thumping, and I close my eyes as I remember one of the obstacles in my fear landscape, the fists pounding against my windows and the sightless men trying to kidnap me. I pretend the pounding is a heartbeat, a drumbeat. The river crashing against the walls of the chasm in the Dauntless compound. Feet stamping at the end-of-initiation ceremony. Feet pounding on the staircase after the Choosing Ceremony.

I don't know how much time has passed when the thumping stops and the tray slides back. I sit up and rub my neck with my fingertips.

The door opens, revealing Peter in the hallway. He beckons to me. "Come on. You can go see the scans now."

I hop down from the tray and walk toward him. When we're in the hallway, he shakes his head at me.

"What?"

"I don't know how you manage to always get what you want."

"Yeah, because I wanted to get myself into a cell in Erudite headquarters. I wanted to be executed."

I sound cavalier, like executions are something I face on a regular basis. But forming my lips around the word "executed" makes me shudder. I pretend I'm cold, squeezing my arms with my hands.

"Didn't you, though?" he says. "I mean, you did come here of your own free will. That's not what I call a good survival instinct."

He types in a series of numbers on a keypad outside the next door, and it opens. I enter the room on the other side of the mirror. It's full of screens and light, reflecting off the glass in the Erudites' spectacles. Across the room, another door clicks shut. There is an empty chair behind one of the screens, still turning. Someone just left.

Peter stands too close behind me—ready to grab me if I decide to attack anyone. But I won't attack anyone. How far could I get if I did? Down one hallway, or two? And then I would be lost. I couldn't get out of here even if there weren't guards stopping me from leaving.

"Put them up there," says Jeanine, pointing toward the large screen on the left wall. One of the Erudite scientists taps his own computer screen, and an image appears on the left wall. An image of my brain.

I don't know what I'm looking at, exactly. I know what a brain looks like, and generally what each region of it does, but I don't know how mine compares to others. Jeanine taps her chin and stares for what feels like a long time.

Finally she says, "Someone instruct Ms. Prior as to what the prefrontal cortex does."

"It's the region of the brain behind the forehead, so to speak," one of the scientists says. She doesn't look much older than I am, and wears large round glasses that make her eyes look bigger. "It's responsible for organizing your thoughts and actions to attain your goals."

"Correct," Jeanine says. "Now someone tell me what they observe about Ms. Prior's lateral prefrontal cortex."

"It's large," another scientist—this one a man with thinning hair—says.

"Specificity," says Jeanine. Like she's chastising him.

I am in a classroom, I realize, because every room with more than one Erudite in it is a classroom. And among them, Jeanine is their most valued teacher. They all stare at her with wide eyes and eager, open mouths, waiting to impress her.

"It's much larger than average," the man with thinning hair corrects himself.

"Better." Jeanine tilts her head. "In fact, it is one of the largest lateral prefrontal cortexes I've ever seen. Yet the orbitofrontal cortex is remarkably small. What do these two facts indicate?"

"The orbitofrontal cortex is the reward center of the brain. Those who exhibit reward-seeking behavior have a large orbitofrontal cortex," someone says. "That means that Ms. Prior engages in very little reward-seeking behavior."

"Not just that." Jeanine smiles a little. Blue light from the screens makes her cheekbones and forehead brighter but casts shadows in her eye sockets. "It does not merely indicate something about her behavior, but about her desires. She is not reward motivated. Yet she is extremely good at directing her thoughts and actions toward her goals. This explains both her tendency toward harmful-but-selfless behavior and, perhaps, her ability to wriggle out of simulations. How does this change our approach to the new simulation serum?"

"It should suppress some, but not all, of the activity in the prefrontal cortex," the scientist with the round glasses says.

"Precisely," says Jeanine. She finally looks at me, her eyes gleaming with delight. "Then that is how we will proceed. Did this satisfy my end of our agreement, Ms. Prior?"

My mouth is dry, so it's difficult to swallow.

And what happens if they suppress the activity in my prefrontal cortex—if they damage my ability to make decisions? What if this serum works, and I become a slave to the simulations like everyone else? What if I forget reality entirely?

I did not know that my entire personality, my entire being, could be discarded as the byproduct of my anatomy. What if I really am just someone with a large prefrontal cortex . . . and nothing more?

"Yes," I say. "It did."

+ + +

In silence Peter and I make our way back to my room. We turn left, and a group of people stands at the other end of the hallway. It is the longest of the corridors we will travel through, but that distance shrinks when I see him.

Held at either arm by a Dauntless traitor, a gun aimed at the back of his skull.

Tobias, blood trailing down the side of his face and marking his white shirt with red; Tobias, fellow Divergent, standing in the mouth of this furnace in which I will burn.

Peter's hands clamp around my shoulders, holding me in place.

"Tobias," I say, and it sounds like a gasp.

The Dauntless traitor with the gun presses Tobias toward me. Peter tries to push me forward too, but my feet remain planted. I came here so that no one else would die. I came here to protect as many people as I could. And I care more about Tobias's safety than anyone else's. So why am I here, if he's here? What's the point?

"What did you do?" I mumble. He is just a few feet away from me now, but not close enough to hear me. As he passes me he stretches out his hand. He wraps it around my palm and squeezes. Squeezes, then lets go. His eyes are bloodshot; he is pale.

"What did you do?" This time the question tears from my throat like a growl.

I throw myself toward him, struggling against Peter's grip, though his hands chafe.

"What did you do?" I scream.

"You die, I die too." Tobias looks over his shoulder at me. "I asked you not to do this. You made your decision. These are the repercussions."

He disappears around the corner. The last I see of him and the Dauntless traitors leading him is the gleam of the gun barrel and blood on the back of his earlobe from an injury I didn't see before.

All the life goes out of me as soon as he's gone. I stop struggling and let Peter's hands push me toward my cell. I slump to the ground as soon as I walk in, waiting for the door to slide shut to signify Peter's departure, but it doesn't.

"Why did he come here?" Peter says.

I glance at him.

"Because he's an idiot."

"Well, yeah."

I rest my head against the wall.

"Did he think he could rescue you?" Peter snorts a little. "Sounds like a Stiff-born thing to do."

"I don't think so," I say. If Tobias intended to rescue me, he would have thought it through; he would have brought others. He would not have burst into Erudite headquarters alone.

Tears well up in my eyes, and I don't try to blink them away. Instead I stare through them and watch my surroundings smear together. A few days ago I would never have cried in front of Peter, but I don't care anymore. He is the least of all my enemies.

"I think he came to die with me," I say. I clamp my hand over my mouth to stifle a sob. If I can keep breathing, I can stop crying. I didn't need or want him to die with me. I wanted to keep him safe. *What an idiot,* I think, but my heart isn't in it.

"That's ridiculous," he says. "That doesn't make any sense. He's eighteen; he'll find another girlfriend once you're dead. And he's stupid if he doesn't know that."

Tears run down my cheeks, hot at first and then cold. I close my eyes. "If you think that's what it's about . . ." I swallow another sob. ". . . you're the stupid one."

"Yeah. Whatever."

His shoes squeak as he turns away. About to leave.

"Wait!" I look up at his blurry silhouette, unable to make out his face. "What will they do to him? The same thing they're doing to me?"

"I don't know."

"Can you find out?" I wipe my cheeks with the heels of my hands, frustrated. "Can you at least find out if he's all right?"

He says, "Why would I do that? Why would I do anything for you?"

A moment later I hear the door slide shut.

CHAPTER
THIRTY

I READ SOMEWHERE, once, that crying defies scientific explanation. Tears are only meant to lubricate the eyes. There is no real reason for tear glands to overproduce tears at the behest of emotion.

I think we cry to release the animal parts of us without losing our humanity. Because inside me is a beast that snarls, and growls, and strains toward freedom, toward Tobias, and, above all, toward life. And as hard as I try, I cannot kill it.

So I sob into my hands instead.

+++

Left, right, right. Left, right, left. Right, right. Our turns, in order, from our point of origin—my cell—to our destination.

It is a new room. In it is a partially reclined chair, like a dentist's chair. In one corner is a screen and a desk. Jeanine sits at the desk.

"Where is he?" I say.

I have been waiting for hours to ask that question. I fell asleep and dreamed that I was chasing Tobias through Dauntless headquarters. No matter how fast I ran he was always just far enough ahead of me that I watched him disappear around corners, catching sight of a sleeve or the heel of a shoe.

Jeanine gives me a puzzled look. But she is not puzzled. She is playing with me.

"Tobias," I say anyway. My hands shake, but not from fear this time—from anger. "Where is he? What are you doing to him?"

"I see no reason to provide that information," says Jeanine. "And since you are all out of leverage, I see no way for you to give me a reason, unless you would like to change the terms of our agreement."

I want to scream at her that of course, of *course* I would rather know about Tobias than about my Divergence, but I don't. I can't make hasty decisions. She will do what she intends to do to Tobias whether I know about it or not. It is more important that I fully understand what is happening to me.

I breathe in through my nose, and out through my nose. I shake my hands. I sit down in the chair.

"Interesting," she says.

"Aren't you supposed to be running a faction and planning a war?" I say. "What are you doing here, running tests on a sixteen-year-old girl?"

"You choose different ways of referring to yourself depending on what is convenient," she says, leaning back in her chair. "Sometimes you insist that you are not a little girl, and sometimes you insist that you are. What I am curious to know is: How do you really view yourself? As one or the other? As both? As neither?"

I make my voice flat and factual, like hers. "I see no reason to provide that information."

I hear a faint snort. Peter is covering his mouth. Jeanine glares at him, and his laughter effortlessly transforms into a coughing fit.

"Mockery is childish, Beatrice," she says. "It does not become you."

"Mockery is childish, Beatrice," I repeat in my best imitation of her voice. *"It does not become you."*

"The serum," Jeanine says, eyeing Peter. He steps forward and fumbles with a black box on the desk, taking out a syringe with a needle already attached to it.

Peter starts toward me, and I hold out my hand.

"Allow me," I say.

He looks at Jeanine for permission, and she says, "All right, then." He hands me the syringe and I shove the needle into the side of my neck, pressing down on the plunger. Jeanine jabs one of the buttons with her finger, and everything goes dark.

+ + +

My mother stands in the aisle with her arm stretched above her head so she can hold the bar. Her face is turned, not toward the people sitting around me, but toward the city we pass as the bus lurches forward. I see wrinkles in her forehead and around her mouth when she frowns.

"What is it?" I ask her.

"There is so much to be done," she says with a small gesture toward the bus windows. "And so few of us left to do it."

It is clear what she's referring to. Beyond the bus is rubble as far as I can see. Across the street, a building lies in ruins. Fragments of glass litter the alleyways. I wonder what caused so much destruction.

"Where are we going?" I say.

She smiles at me, and I see different wrinkles than before, at the corners of her eyes. "We're going to Erudite headquarters."

I frown. Most of my life has been spent avoiding Erudite headquarters. My father used to say that he didn't even like to breathe the air in there. "Why are we going there?"

"They're going to help us."

Why do I feel a pang in my stomach when I think of my father? I picture his face, weathered by a lifetime of frustration with the world around him, and his hair, kept short by Abnegation standard practice, and feel the same kind of pain in my stomach that I get when I have not eaten in too long—a hollow pain.

"Did something happen to Dad?" I say.

She shakes her head. "Why would you ask that?"

"I don't know."

I don't feel the pain when I look at my mother. But I do feel like every second we spend standing these inches apart is one that I must impress upon my mind until my entire memory conforms to its shape. But if she is not permanent, what is she?

The bus stops, and the doors creak open. My mother starts down the aisle, and I follow her. She is taller than I am, so I stare between her shoulders, at the top of her spine. She looks fragile, but she is not.

I step down onto the pavement. Pieces of glass crinkle beneath my feet. They are blue and, judging by the holes in the building to my right, used to be windows.

"What happened?"

"War," my mother says. "This is what we've been trying so hard to avoid."

"And the Erudite will help us . . . by doing what?"

"I worry that all your father's blustering about Erudite has been to your detriment," she says gently. "They've made mistakes, of course, but they, like everyone else, are a blend of good and bad, not one or the other. What would we do without our doctors, our scientists, our teachers?"

She smooths down my hair.

"Take care to remember that, Beatrice."

"I will," I promise.

We keep walking. But something about what she said bothers me. Is it what she said about my father? No—my father is always complaining about Erudite. Is it what she said about Erudite? I hop over a large shard of glass. No, that can't be it. She was right about Erudite. All my teachers were Erudite, and so was the doctor who set my mother's arm when she broke it several years ago.

It's the last part. "Take care to remember." As if she won't have the opportunity to remind me later.

I feel something shift in my mind, like something that was closed has just opened.

"Mom?" I say.

She looks back at me. A lock of blond hair falls from

its knot and touches her cheek.

"I love you."

I point at a window to my left, and it explodes. Particles of glass rain over us.

I don't want to wake up in a room in Erudite headquarters, so I don't open my eyes right away, not even when the simulation fades. I try to preserve the image of my mother and the hair sticking to her cheekbone for as long as I can. But when all I see is the redness of my own eyelids, I open them.

"You'll have to do better than that," I say to Jeanine.

She says, "That was only the beginning."

CHAPTER
THIRTY-ONE

THAT NIGHT I dream, not of Tobias, and not of Will, but of my mother. We stand in the Amity orchards, where the apples are ripe and dangle just inches above our heads. Leaf shadows pattern her face, and she wears black, though I never saw her in black when she was alive. She is teaching me to braid hair, demonstrating on a lock of her own, laughing when my fingers fumble.

I wake wondering how I did not notice, every day I sat across from her at the breakfast table, that she was full to bursting with Dauntless energy. Was it because she hid it well? Or was it because I wasn't looking?

I bury my face in the thin mattress I slept on. I will never know her. But at least she will never know what I did to Will, either. At this point I don't think I could bear it if she did.

I am still blinking the haze of sleep from my eyes when I follow Peter down the corridor, seconds or minutes later, I can't tell.

"Peter." My throat aches; I must have screamed while I slept. "What time is it?"

He wears a watch, but the face is covered, so I can't see it. He doesn't even bother to look at it.

"Why are you constantly escorting me places?" I say. "Isn't there a depraved activity you're supposed to be taking part in? Kicking puppies or spying on girls while they change, or something?"

"I know what you did to Will, you know. Don't pretend that you're better than I am, because you and I, we're exactly the same."

The only thing that distinguishes one hallway from another, here, is their length. I decide to label them according to how many steps I take before I turn. Ten. Forty-seven. Twenty-nine.

"You're wrong," I say. "We may both be bad, but there's a huge difference between us—I'm not content with being this way."

Peter snorts a little, and we walk between the Erudite lab tables. That's when I realize where I am, and where we're going: back to the room Jeanine showed me. The room where I will be executed. I shudder so hard my teeth chatter, and it's difficult to keep walking, hard to keep my thoughts straight. *It's just a room,* I tell myself. *Just a room like any other room.*

I am such a liar.

This time the execution chamber is not empty. Four Dauntless traitors mill around in one corner, and two of the Erudite, one a dark-skinned woman, one an older man, both wearing lab coats, stand with Jeanine near the metal table in the center. Several machines are set up around it, and there are wires everywhere.

I don't know what most of those machines do, but among them is a heart monitor. What does Jeanine plan to do that requires a heart monitor?

"Get her on the table," says Jeanine, sounding bored. I stare for a second at the sheet of steel that awaits me. What if she changed her mind about waiting to execute me? What if this is when I die? Peter's hands clamp around my arms and I writhe, throwing all my strength into the struggle.

But he just lifts me up, dodging my kicking feet, and slams me down on the metal slab, knocking the wind out of me. I gasp, and fling a fist out at whatever I can hit, which just happens to be Peter's wrist. He winces, but by now the other Dauntless traitors have come forward to help.

One of them holds down my ankles, and the other holds down my shoulders as Peter pulls black straps across my body to keep me pinned. I flinch at the pain in my wounded shoulder and stop struggling.

"What the hell is going on?" I demand, craning my neck to look at Jeanine. "We agreed—cooperation in exchange for results! We *agreed*—"

"This is entirely separate from our agreement," says Jeanine, glancing at her watch. "This is not about you, Beatrice."

The door opens again.

Tobias walks in—*limps* in—flanked by Dauntless traitors. His face is bruised and there's a cut above his eyebrow. He does not move with his usual care; he's holding himself perfectly straight. He must be injured. I try not to think about how he got that way.

"What is this?" he says, his voice rough and creaky.

From screaming, probably.

My throat feels swollen.

"Tris," he says, and he lurches toward me, but the Dauntless traitors are too quick. They grab him before he can move more than a few steps. "Tris, are you okay?"

"Yeah," I say. "Are you?"

He nods. I don't believe him.

"Rather than waste any more time, Mr. Eaton, I thought

I would take the most logical approach. Truth serum would be preferable, of course, but it would take days to coerce Jack Kang into handing some over, as it is jealously guarded by the Candor, and I'd rather not waste a few days." She steps forward, a syringe in hand. This serum is tinted gray. It could be a new version of the simulation serum, but I doubt it.

I wonder what it does. It can't be good, if she looks this pleased with herself.

"In a few seconds, I will inject Tris with this liquid. At that point, I trust, your selfless instincts will take over and you will tell me exactly what I need to know."

"What does she need to know?" I say, interrupting her.

"Information about the factionless safe houses," he replies without looking at me.

My eyes widen. The factionless are the last hope any of us has, now that half the loyal Dauntless and all the Candor are simulation-ready, and half the Abnegation are dead.

"Don't give it to her. I'm going to die anyway. Don't give her anything."

"Remind me, Mr. Eaton," says Jeanine. "What do Dauntless simulations do?"

"This isn't a classroom," he replies through gritted teeth. "Tell me what you're going to do."

"I will if you answer my very simple question."

"Fine." Tobias's eyes shift to me. "The simulations stimulate the amygdala, which is responsible for processing fear, induce a hallucination based on that fear, and then transmit the data to a computer to be processed and observed."

It sounds like he's had that memorized for a long time. Maybe he has—he did spend a lot of time running simulations.

"Very good," she says. "When I was developing the Dauntless simulations, years ago, we discovered that certain levels of potency overwhelmed the brain and made it too insensible with terror to invent new surroundings, which was when we diluted the solution so that the simulations would be more instructive. But I still remember how to make it."

She taps the syringe with her fingernail.

"Fear," she says, "is more powerful than pain. So is there anything you'd like to say, before I inject Ms. Prior?"

Tobias presses his lips together.

And Jeanine inserts the needle.

+ + +

It begins quietly, with the pounding of a heart. I am not sure, at first, whose heartbeat I'm hearing, because it's far too loud to be my own. But then I realize that it is my own, and it's getting faster and faster.

Sweat collects in my palms and behind my knees.

And then I have to gasp in order to breathe.

That's when the screaming starts

And I

Can't

Think.

+ + +

Tobias is fighting the Dauntless traitors by the door.

I hear what sounds like a child's scream beside me, and wrench my head around to see where it's coming from, but there is only a heart monitor. Above me the lines between the ceiling tiles warp and twist into monstrous creatures. The scent of rotting flesh fills the air and I gag. The monstrous creatures take on a more definite shape— they are birds, crows, with beaks as long as my forearm and wings so dark they seem to swallow all the light.

"Tris," says Tobias. I look away from the crows.

He stands by the door, where he was before I was injected, but now he has a knife. He holds it out from his body and turns it so the blade points in, at his stomach. Then he brings it toward himself, touching the tip of the blade to his stomach.

"What are you doing? Stop!"

He smiles a little and says, "I'm doing this for you."

He pushes the knife in farther, slow, and blood stains the hem of his shirt. I gag, and throw myself against the bonds holding me to the table. "No, stop!" I thrash and in a simulation I would have pulled free by now so this must mean that this is real, it's real. I scream and he sticks the knife in to the handle. He collapses to the floor and his blood spills fast and surrounds him. The shadow-birds turn their beady eyes on him and swarm in a tornado of wings and talons, pecking at his skin. I see his eyes through the whirling feathers and he is still awake.

A bird lands on the fingers that hold the knife. He draws it out again and it clatters to the ground and I should hope that he is dead but I'm selfish so I can't. My back lifts from the table and all my muscles clench and my throat aches from this scream that no longer shapes itself into words and will not stop.

+++

"Sedative," a stern voice commands.

Another needle in my neck, and my heart begins to slow down. I sob with relief. For seconds all I can do is sob with relief.

That was not fear. That was something else; an emotion that should not exist.

"Let me go," Tobias says, and he sounds scratchier than before. I blink fast so I can see him through my tears. There are red marks on his arms from where the Dauntless traitors held him back, but he is not dying; he is all right. "That's the only way I'll tell you, is if you let me go."

Jeanine nods, and he runs to me. He wraps one hand around mine and touches my hair with the other. His fingertips come away wet with tears. He doesn't wipe them off. He leans over and presses his forehead to mine.

"The factionless safe houses," he says dully, right against my cheek. "Get me a map and I'll mark them for you."

His forehead feels cool and dry against mine. My muscles ache, probably from being clenched for however long Jeanine left me with that serum pulsing through me.

He pulls back, his fingers wrapped around my fingers for as long as they can be until the Dauntless traitors pull him from my grasp to escort him elsewhere. My hand falls heavy on the table. I don't want to struggle against the restraints anymore. All I want to do is sleep.

"While you're here . . ." Jeanine says once Tobias and his escorts are gone. She looks up and focuses her watery eyes on one of the Erudite. "Get him and bring him in here. It's time."

She looks back down at me.

"While you sleep, we will be performing a short procedure to observe a few things about your brain. It will not be invasive. But before that . . . I promised you full transparency with these procedures. So I feel it's only fair that you know exactly who has been assisting me in my endeavors." She smiles a little. "Who told me what three factions you had an aptitude for, and what our best chance was to get you to come here, and to put your mother in the last simulation to make it more effective."

She looks toward the doorway as the sedative sets in, making everything blur at the edges. I look over my shoulder, and through the haze of drugs I see him.

Caleb.

CHAPTER
THIRTY-TWO

I WAKE TO a headache. I try to go back to sleep—at least when I'm asleep, I'm calm—but the image of Caleb standing in the doorway runs through my mind over and over again, accompanied by the sound of squawking crows.

Why did I never wonder how Eric and Jeanine knew that I had aptitude for three factions?

Why did it never occur to me that only three people in the world knew that particular fact: Tori, Caleb, and Tobias?

My head pounds. I can't make sense of it. I don't know why Caleb would betray me. I wonder when it happened—after the attack simulation? After the escape from Amity? Or was it earlier than that—was it back when my father was still alive? Caleb told us he left Erudite when he found out what they were planning—was he lying?

He must have been. I press the heel of my hand to my forehead. My brother chose faction over blood. There has to be a reason. She must have threatened him. Or coerced him in some way.

The door opens. I don't lift my head or open my eyes.

"Stiff." It's Peter. Of course.

"Yes." When I let my hand fall from my face, a lock of hair falls with it. I look at it from the corner of my eye. My hair has never been this greasy before.

Peter sets a bottle of water next to the bed, and a sandwich. The thought of eating it nauseates me.

"You brain-dead?" he asks.

"Don't think so."

"Don't be so sure."

"Ha-ha," I say. "How long have I been asleep?"

"About a day. I'm supposed to escort you to the showers."

"If you say something about how badly I need one," I say tiredly, "I *will* poke you in the eye."

The room spins when I lift my head, but I manage to put my legs over the edge of the bed and stand. Peter and I start down the hallway. When we turn the corner to get to the bathroom, though, there are people at the end of the hallway.

One of them is Tobias. I can see where our paths will

intersect, between where I stand now and my cell door. I stare, not at him but at where he will be when he reaches for my hand, as he did the last time we passed each other. My skin tingles with anticipation. For just a moment, I will touch him again.

Six steps until we pass each other. Five steps.

At four steps, though, Tobias stops. His entire body goes limp, catching his Dauntless traitor escort off guard. The guard loses his grip on him for just a second, and Tobias crumples to the floor.

Then he twists around. Lurches forward. And grabs a gun from the shorter Dauntless traitor's holster.

The gun goes off. Peter dives to the right, dragging me with him. My head skims the wall. The Dauntless guard's mouth is open—he must be screaming. I can't hear him.

Tobias kicks him hard in the stomach. The Dauntless in me admires his form—perfect—and his speed—incredible. Then he turns, training the gun on Peter. But Peter has already released me.

Tobias reaches for my left arm, helps me to my feet, and starts running. I stumble after him. Each time my foot hits the ground, pain slices into my head, but I can't stop. I blink tears from my eyes. *Run*, I tell myself, as if that will make it easier. Tobias's hand is rough and strong. I let it guide me around a corner.

"Tobias," I wheeze.

He stops, and looks back at me. "Oh no," he says, brushing my cheek with his fingers. "Come on. On my back."

He bends, and I put my arms around his neck, burying my face between his shoulder blades. He lifts me without difficulty and holds on to my leg with his left hand. His right hand still holds the gun.

He runs, and even with my weight, he is fast. Idly I think, *How could he ever have been Abnegation?* He seems designed specifically for speed and deadly accuracy. But not strength, not particularly—he is smart, but not strong. Only strong enough to carry me.

The hallways are empty now, but not for long. Soon every Dauntless in the building will rush toward us from every angle, and we will be trapped in this pale maze. I wonder how Tobias plans to get past them.

I lift my head long enough to see that he just ran past an exit.

"Tobias, you missed it."

"Missed . . . what?" he says between breaths.

"An exit."

"Not trying to escape. We'd get shot if we did," he says. "Trying to . . . find something."

I would suspect that I'm dreaming if the pain in my head wasn't so intense. Usually only my dreams make this little sense. Why, if he was not trying to escape, did he take me with him? And what is he doing, if not escaping?

He stops abruptly, almost dropping me, as he reaches a wide hallway with panes of glass on either side, revealing offices. The Erudite sit frozen at their desks, staring at us. Tobias pays no attention to them; his eyes, as far as I can tell, are fixed on the door at the end of the corridor. A sign outside the door says CONTROL-A.

Tobias searches every corner of the room, and then shoots at the camera attached to the ceiling on our right. The camera drops. He shoots at the camera attached to the ceiling on our left. Its lens shatters.

"Time to get down," he says. "No more running, I promise."

I slide off his back and take his hand instead. He walks toward a closed door that we passed already, and into a supply closet. He shuts the door and wedges a busted chair under the doorknob. I face him, a shelf stacked with paper at my back. Above us, the blue light flickers. His eyes roam over my face almost hungrily.

"I don't have much time, so I'm going to be direct," he says.

I nod.

"I didn't come here on some suicide mission," he says. "I came for two reasons. The first was to find Erudite's two central control rooms so that when we invade, we'll know what to destroy first to get rid of all the simulation data, so she can't activate the Dauntless's transmitters."

That explains the running without escaping. And we found a control room, at the end of that hallway.

I stare at him, still dazed from the past few minutes.

"The second," he says, clearing his throat, "is to make sure you hold on, because we have a plan."

"What plan?"

"According to one of our insiders, your execution is tentatively scheduled for two weeks from today," he says. "At least, that's Jeanine's target date for the new, Divergent-proof simulation. So fourteen days from now, the factionless, the loyal Dauntless, and the Abnegation who are willing to fight will storm the Erudite compound and take out their best weapon—their computer system. That means we'll outnumber the traitor Dauntless, and therefore the Erudite."

"But you told Jeanine where the factionless safe houses were."

"Yeah." He frowns a little. "That is problematic. But as you and I know, a lot of the factionless are Divergent, and many of them were already moving toward the Abnegation sector when I left, so only some of the safe houses will be affected. So they will still have a huge population to contribute to the invasion."

Two weeks. Will I be able to make it through two weeks of this? I am already so tired I'm finding it difficult to stand on my own. Even the rescue that Tobias is proposing barely appeals to me. I don't want freedom. I want sleep. I want this to end.

"I don't . . ." I choke on the words and start to cry. "I can't . . . make it . . . that long."

"Tris," he says sternly. He never coddles me. I wish that, just this once, he would coddle me. "You have to. You have to survive this."

"Why?" The question forms in my stomach and launches from my throat like a moan. I feel like thumping my fists against his chest, like a child throwing a tantrum. Tears cover my cheeks, and I know I'm acting ridiculous but I can't stop. "Why do I have to? Why can't someone else do something for once? What if I don't want to do this anymore?"

And what *this* is, I realize, is life. I don't want it. I want my parents and I have for weeks. I've been trying to claw my way back to them, and now I am so close and he is telling me not to.

"I know." I have never heard his voice sound so soft. "I know it's hard. The hardest thing you've had to do."

I shake my head.

"I can't force you. I can't make you want to survive this." He pulls me against him and runs his hand over my hair, tucking it behind my ear. His fingers trail down my neck and over my shoulder, and he says, "But you will do it. It doesn't matter if you believe you can or not. You will, because that's who you are."

I pull back and fit my mouth to his, not gently, not hesitantly. I kiss him like I used to, when I felt sure of us, and run my hands over his back, down his arms, like I used to.

I don't want to tell him the truth: that he is wrong, and I do not want to survive this.

The door opens. Dauntless traitors crowd into the supply closet. Tobias steps back, turns the gun in his hand, and offers it, handle first, to the nearest Dauntless traitor.

CHAPTER
THIRTY-THREE

"BEATRICE."

I jerk awake. The room I am in now—for whatever experiment they want to run on me—is large, with screens along the back wall and blue lights glowing just above the floor and rows of padded benches across the middle. I'm sitting on the farthest bench back with Peter at my left shoulder, my head leaning against the wall. I still can't seem to get enough sleep.

Now I wish I hadn't woken up. Caleb stands a few feet away, his weight on one foot, an uncertain posture.

"Did you *ever* leave Erudite?" I say.

"It's not that simple," he starts. "I—"

"It is that simple." I want to yell, but instead my voice comes out flat. "At what point did you betray our family?

Before our parents died, or after?"

"I did what I had to do. You think you understand this, Beatrice, but you don't. This whole situation . . . it's much bigger than you think it is." His eyes plead with me to understand, but I recognize his tone—it's the one he employed when we were younger, to scold me. It is condescending.

Arrogance is one of the flaws in the Erudite heart—I know. It is often in mine.

But greed is the other. And I do not have that. So I am halfway in and halfway out, as always.

I push myself to my feet. "You still haven't answered my question."

Caleb steps back.

"This isn't about Erudite; it's about everyone. All the factions," he says, "and the city. And what's outside the fence."

"I don't care," I say, but that isn't true. The phrase "outside the fence" prickles in my brain. Outside? How could any of this have to do with what's outside?

Something itches at the back of my mind. Marcus said that information the Abnegation possessed motivated Jeanine's attack on Abnegation. Does that information have to do with what's outside, too?

I push the thought away for the time being.

"I thought you were all about facts. About freedom of information? Well, how about *this* fact, Caleb? When—" My voice quakes. "*When* did you betray our parents?"

"I have always been Erudite," he says softly. "Even when I was supposed to be Abnegation."

"If you're with Jeanine, then I hate you. Just like our father would have."

"Our father." Caleb snorts a little. "Our father *was* Erudite, Beatrice. Jeanine told me—he was in her year at school."

"He wasn't Erudite," I say after a few seconds. "He chose to leave them. He chose a different identity, just like you, and became something else. Only you chose this . . . this *evil*."

"Spoken like a true Dauntless," says Caleb sharply. "It's either one way or the other way. No nuances. The world doesn't *work* like that, Beatrice. Evil depends on where you're standing."

"No matter where I stand, I'll still think mind controlling an entire city of people is evil." I feel my lip wobble. "I'll still think delivering your sister to be prodded and executed is evil!"

He is my brother, but I want to tear him to pieces.

Instead of trying to, though, I find myself sitting down again. I could never hurt him enough to make his betrayal stop hurting. And it *hurts*, in every part of my body. I press my fingers to my chest to massage some of the smarting tension away.

Jeanine and her army of Erudite scientists and Dauntless traitors walk in just as I wipe tears from my cheeks. I blink rapidly so she won't see. She barely even gives me a glance.

"Let us view the results, shall we?" she announces. Caleb, now standing by the screens, presses something at the front of the room, and the screens turn on. Words and numbers I don't understand fill them.

"We discovered something extremcly intcresting, Ms. Prior." I have never seen her so cheerful before. She almost smiles—but not quite. "You have an abundance of a particular kind of neuron, called, quite simply, a mirror neuron. Would someone like to explain to Ms. Prior exactly what mirror neurons do?"

The Erudite scientists raise their hands in unison. She points to an older woman in the front.

"Mirror neurons fire both when one performs an action and when one sees another person performing that action. They allow us to imitate behavior."

"What else are they responsible for?" Jeanine scans her "class" the same way my teachers did in Upper Levels. Another Erudite raises his hand.

"Learning language, understanding other people's intentions based on their behavior, um . . ." He frowns. "And empathy."

"More specifically," Jeanine says, and this time she does smile at me, broadly, forcing creases into her cheeks, "someone with many, strong mirror neurons could have a flexible personality—capable of mimicking others as the situation calls for it rather than remaining constant."

I understand why she smiles. I feel like my mind is cracked open, its secrets spilling over the floor for me to finally see.

"A flexible personality," she says, "would probably have aptitude for more than one faction, don't you agree, Ms. Prior?"

"Probably," I say. "Now if only you could get a simulation to suppress that particular ability, we could be done with this."

"One thing at a time." She pauses. "I must admit, it confuses me that you are so eager for your own execution."

"No, it doesn't." I close my eyes. "It doesn't confuse you at all." I sigh. "Can I go back to my cell now?"

I must seem nonchalant, but I'm not. I want to go back to my room so that I can cry in peace. But I don't want her to know that.

"Don't get too comfortable," she chirps. "We'll have

a simulation serum to try out soon."

"Yeah," I say. "Whatever."

+ + +

Someone shakes my shoulder. I jerk awake, my eyes wide and searching, and I see Tobias kneeling over me. He wears a Dauntless traitor jacket, and one side of his head is coated with blood. The blood streams from a wound on his ear—the top of his ear is gone. I wince.

"What happened?" I say.

"Get up. We have to run."

"It's too soon. It hasn't been two weeks."

"I don't have time to explain. Come on."

"Oh God. Tobias."

I sit up and wrap my arms around him, pressing my face into his neck. His arms tighten around me and squeeze. Warmth courses through me, and comfort. If he is here, that means I'm safe. My tears make his skin slippery.

He stands and pulls me to my feet, which makes my wounded shoulder throb.

"Reinforcements will be here soon. Come on."

I let him lead me out of the room. We make it down the first hallway without difficulty, but in the second hallway, we encounter two Dauntless guards, one a young man and one a middle-aged woman. Tobias fires twice in a matter of seconds, both hits, one in the head and one in the chest. The woman, who was hit in the chest, slumps against the wall but doesn't die.

We keep moving. One hallway, then another, all of them look the same. Tobias's grip on my hand never falters. I know that if he can throw a knife so that it hits just the tip of my ear, he can fire accurately at the Dauntless soldiers who ambush us. We step over fallen bodies—the people Tobias killed on the way in, probably—and finally reach a fire exit.

Tobias lets go of my hand to open the door, and the fire alarm screeches in my ears, but we keep running. I am gasping for air but I don't care, not when I'm finally escaping, not when this nightmare is finally over. My vision starts to go black at the edges, so I grab Tobias's arm and hold on tight, trusting him to lead me safely to the bottom of the stairs.

I run out of steps to run down, and I open my eyes. Tobias is about to open the exit door, but I hold him back. "Got to . . . catch my breath. . . ."

He pauses, and I put my hands on my knees, leaning over. My shoulder still throbs. I frown, and look up at him.

"Come on, let's get out of here," he says insistently.

My stomach sinks. I stare into his eyes. They are dark blue, with a patch of light blue on his right iris.

I take his chin in hand and pull his lips down to mine, kissing him slowly, sighing as I pull back.

"We can't get out of here," I say. "Because this is a simulation."

He pulled me to my feet with my right hand. The real Tobias would have remembered the wound in my shoulder.

"What?" He scowls at me. "Don't you think I would know if I was under a simulation?"

"You aren't under a simulation. You *are* the simulation." I look up and say in a loud voice, "You'll have to do better than that, Jeanine."

All I have to do now is wake up, and I know how—I have done it before, in my fear landscape, when I broke a glass tank just by touching my palm to it, or when I made a gun appear in the grass to shoot descending birds. I take a knife from my pocket—a knife that wasn't there a moment ago—and will my leg to be hard as diamond.

I thrust the knife toward my thigh, and the blade bends.

+ + +

I wake with tears in my eyes. I wake to Jeanine's scream of frustration.

"What is it?" She grabs Peter's gun out of his hand and stalks across the room, pressing the barrel to my forehead. My body stiffens, goes cold. She won't shoot me. I am a problem she can't solve. She won't shoot me.

"What is it that clues you in? Tell me. Tell me or I will kill you."

I slowly push myself up from the chair, coming to my feet, pushing my skin harder into the cold barrel.

"You think I'm going to tell you?" I say. "You think I believe that you would kill me without figuring out the answer to this question?"

"You stupid girl," she says. "You think this is about you, and your abnormal brain? This is not about you. It is not about me. It is about keeping this city safe from the people who intend to plunge it into hell!"

I summon the last of my strength and launch myself at her, clawing at whatever skin my fingernails find, digging in as hard as I can. She screams at the top of her lungs, a sound that turns my blood into fire. I punch her hard in the face.

A pair of arms wrap around me, pulling me off her, and a fist meets my side. I groan, and lunge toward her, held at bay by Peter.

"Pain can't make me tell you. Truth serum can't make me tell you. Simulations can't make me tell you. I'm immune to all three."

Her nose is bleeding, and I see lines of fingernail scrapes in her cheeks, on the side of her throat, turning red with blossoming blood. She glares at me, pinching her nose closed, her hair disheveled, her free hand trembling.

"You have *failed*. You can't control me!" I scream, so loud it hurts my throat. I stop struggling and sag against Peter's chest. "You will *never* be able to control me."

I laugh, mirthless, a mad laugh. I savor the scowl on her face, the hate in her eyes. She was like a machine; she was cold and emotionless, bound by logic alone. And I broke her.

I broke her.

CHAPTER
THIRTY-FOUR

ONCE I'M IN the hallway, I stop struggling toward Jeanine. My side throbs from where Peter punched me, but it's nothing compared to the pulse of triumph in my cheeks.

Peter walks me back to my cell without a word. I stand in the middle of the room for a long time, staring at the camera in the back-left corner. Who is watching me all the time? Is it Dauntless traitors, guarding me, or the Erudite, observing me?

Once the heat leaves my face and my side stops hurting, I lie down.

A picture of my parents floats into my head the moment I close my eyes. Once, when I was about eleven, I stopped at the doorway to my parents' bedroom to watch them make the bed together. My father smiled at my mother as they pulled the sheets back and smoothed them down in perfect synchronicity. I knew by the way he looked at her that he held her in a higher regard than he held even himself.

No selfishness or insecurity kept him from seeing the full extent of her goodness, as it so often does with the rest of us. That kind of love may only be possible in Abnegation. I do not know.

My father: Erudite-born, Abnegation-grown. He often found it difficult to live up to the demands of his chosen faction, just as I did. But he tried, and he knew true self-lessness when he saw it.

I clutch my pillow to my chest and bury my face in it. I don't cry. I just ache.

Grief is not as heavy as guilt, but it takes more away from you.

+ + +

"Stiff."

I wake with a start, my hands still clutching the pillow. There is a wet patch on the mattress under my face. I sit up, wiping my eyes with my fingertips.

Peter's eyebrows, which usually turn up in the middle, are furrowed.

"What happened?" Whatever it is, it can't be good.

"Your execution has been scheduled for tomorrow morning at eight o'clock."

"My execution? But she . . . she hasn't developed the right simulation yet; she couldn't *possibly* . . ."

"She said that she will continue the experiments on Tobias instead of you," he says.

All I can say is: "Oh."

I clutch the mattress and rock forward and back, forward and back. Tomorrow my life will be over. Tobias may survive long enough to escape in the factionless invasion. The Dauntless will elect a new leader. All the loose ends I will leave will be easily tied up.

I nod. No family left, no loose ends, no great loss.

"I could have forgiven you, you know," I say. "For trying to kill me during initiation. I probably could have."

We are both quiet for a while. I don't know why I told him that. Maybe just because it's true, and tonight, of all nights, is the time for honesty. Tonight I will be honest, and selfless, and brave. Divergent.

"I never asked you to," he says, and turns to leave. But then he stops at the door frame and says, "It's 9:24."

Telling me the time is a small act of betrayal—and therefore an ordinary act of bravery. It is maybe the first time I've seen Peter be truly Dauntless.

+ + +

I'm going to die tomorrow. It has been a long time since I felt certainty about anything, so this feels like a gift. Tonight, nothing. Tomorrow, whatever comes after life. And Jeanine still doesn't know how to control the Divergent.

When I start to cry, I clutch the pillow to my chest and let it happen. I cry hard, like a child cries, until my face is hot and I feel like I might be sick. I can pretend to be brave, but I'm not.

I suppose that now would be the time to ask for forgiveness for all the things I've done, but I'm sure my list would never be complete. I also don't believe that whatever comes after life depends on my correctly reciting a list of my transgressions—that sounds too much like an Erudite afterlife to me, all accuracy and no feeling. I don't believe that what comes after depends on anything I do at all.

I am better off doing as Abnegation taught me: turning away from myself, projecting always outward, and hoping that in whatever is next, I will be better than I am now.

I smile a little. I wish I could tell my parents that I will die like the Abnegation. They would be proud, I think.

CHAPTER
THIRTY-FIVE

THIS MORNING I put on the clean clothes I am given: black pants—too loose, but who cares?—and a long-sleeved black shirt. No shoes.

It is not time yet. I find myself lacing my fingers together and bowing my head. Sometimes my father did this in the morning before sitting down at the breakfast table, but I never asked him what he was doing. Still, I would like to feel like I belong to my father again before I . . . well, before it's over.

A few silent moments later, Peter tells me it's time to go. He barely looks at me, scowls at the back wall instead. I suppose it would have been too much to ask, to see a friendly face this morning. I stand, and together we walk down the hallway.

My toes are cold. My feet stick to the tiles. We turn a corner, and I hear muffled shouts. At first I can't tell what the voice is saying, but as we draw closer, it takes shape.

"I want to . . . her!" Tobias. "I . . . *see* her!"

I glance at Peter. "I can't speak to him one last time, can I?"

Peter shakes his head. "There's a window, though. Maybe if he sees you he'll finally shut up."

He takes me down a dead-end corridor that's only six feet long. At the end is a door, and Peter is right, there's a small window near the top, about a foot above my head.

"Tris!" Tobias's voice is even clearer here. "I want to see her!"

I reach up and press my palm to the glass. The shouts stop, and his face appears behind the glass. His eyes are red; his face, blotchy. Handsome. He stares down at me for a few seconds and then presses his hand to the glass so it lines up with mine. I pretend I can feel the warmth of it through the window.

He leans his forehead against the door and squeezes his eyes shut.

I take my hand down and turn away before he can open his eyes. I feel pain in my chest, worse than when I got shot in the shoulder. I clutch the front of my shirt, blink away tears, and rejoin Peter in the main hallway.

"Thank you," I say quietly. I meant to say it louder.

"Whatever." Peter scowls again. "Let's just go."

I hear rumbling somewhere ahead of us—the sound of a crowd. The next hallway is packed with Dauntless traitors, tall and short, young and old, armed and unarmed. They all wear the blue armband of betrayal.

"Hey!" Peter shouts. "Clear a path!"

The Dauntless traitors closest to us hear him, and press against the walls to make way for us. The other Dauntless traitors follow suit soon after, and everyone is quiet. Peter steps back to let me go ahead of him. I know the way from here.

I don't know where the pounding starts, but someone drums their fists against the wall, and someone else joins in, and I walk down the aisle between solemn-but-raucous Dauntless traitors, their hands in motion at their sides. The pounding is so fast my heart races to keep up with it.

Some of the Dauntless traitors incline their heads to me—I'm not sure why. It doesn't matter.

I reach the end of the hallway and open the door to my execution chamber.

I open it.

Dauntless traitors crowded the hallway; the Erudite crowd the execution room, but there, they have made a path for me already. Silently they study me as I walk to the metal table in the center of the room. Jeanine stands a few steps away. The scratches on her face show through hastily applied makeup. She doesn't look at me.

Four cameras dangle from the ceiling, one at each corner of the table. I sit down first, wipe my hands off on my pants, and then lie down.

The table is cold. Frigid, seeping into my skin, into my bones. Appropriate, perhaps, because that is what will happen to my body when all the life leaves it; it will become cold and heavy, heavier than I have ever been. As for the rest of me, I am not sure. Some people believe that I will go nowhere, and maybe they're right, but maybe they're not. Such speculations are no longer useful to me anyway.

Peter slips an electrode beneath the collar of my shirt and presses it to my chest, right over my heart. He then attaches a wire to the electrode and switches on the heart monitor. I hear my heartbeat, fast and strong. Soon, where that steady rhythm was, there will be nothing.

And then rising from within me is a single thought:

I don't want to die.

All those times Tobias scolded me for risking my life, I never took him seriously. I believed that I wanted to be with my parents and for all of this to be over. I was sure I wanted to emulate their self-sacrifice. But no. No, no.

Burning and boiling inside me is the desire to live.

I don't want to die I don't want to die I don't want to!

Jeanine steps forward with a syringe full of purple serum. Her glasses reflect the fluorescent light above us, so I can barely see her eyes.

Every part of my body chants it in unison. *Live, live, live.* I thought that in order to give my life in exchange for Will's, in exchange for my parents', that I needed to die, but I was wrong; I need to live my life in the light of their deaths. I need to live.

Jeanine holds my head steady with one hand and inserts the needle into my neck with the other.

I'm not done! I shout in my head, and not at Jeanine. *I am not done here!*

She presses the plunger down. Peter leans forward and looks into my eyes.

"The serum will go into effect in one minute," he says. "Be brave, Tris."

The words startle me, because that is exactly what Tobias said when he put me under my first simulation.

My heart begins to race.

Why would Peter tell me to be brave? Why would he offer any kind words at all?

All the muscles in my body relax at once. A heavy, liquid

feeling fills my limbs. If this is death, it isn't so bad. My eyes stay open, but my head drops to the side. I try to close my eyes, but I can't—I can't move.

Then the heart monitor stops beeping.

CHAPTER
THIRTY-SIX

BUT I'M STILL breathing. Not deeply; not enough to satisfy, but *breathing*. Peter pushes my eyelids over my eyes. Does he know I'm not dead? Does Jeanine? Can she see me breathing?

"Take the body to the lab," Jeanine says. "The autopsy is scheduled for this afternoon."

"All right," Peter replies.

Peter pushes the table forward. I hear mutters all around me as we pass the group of Erudite bystanders. My hand falls off the edge of the table as we turn a corner, and smacks into the wall. I feel a prickle of pain in my finger-tips, but I can't move my hand, as hard as I try.

This time, when we go down the hallway of Dauntless traitors, it is silent. Peter walks slowly at first, then turns another corner and picks up the pace. He almost sprints down the next corridor, and stops abruptly. Where am I? I can't be in the lab already. Why did he stop?

Peter's arms slide under my knees and shoulders, and he lifts me. My head falls against his shoulder.

"For someone so small, you're *heavy*, Stiff," he mutters.

He knows I'm awake. He *knows*.

I hear a series of beeps, and a slide—a locked door, opening.

"What do—" Tobias's voice. *Tobias!* "Oh my God. Oh—"

"Spare me your blubbering, okay?" Peter says. "She's not dead; she's just paralyzed. It'll only last for about a minute. Now get ready to run."

I don't understand.

How does Peter know?

"Let me carry her," Tobias says.

"No. You're a better shot than I am. Take my gun. I'll carry her."

I hear the gun slide out of its holster. Tobias brushes a hand over my forehead. They both start running.

At first all I hear is the pounding of their feet, and my head snaps back painfully. I feel tingling in my hands and feet. Peter shouts, "Left!" at Tobias.

Then a shout from down the hallway. "Hey, what—!"

A bang. And nothing.

More running. Peter shouts, "Right!" I hear another bang, and another. "Whoa," he mumbles. "Wait, stop here!"

Tingling down my spine. I open my eyes as Peter opens another door. He charges through it, and just before I smack my head against the door frame, I stick my arm out and stop us.

"Careful!" I say, my voice strained. My throat still feels as tight as it did when he first injected me and I found it difficult to breathe. Peter turns sideways to bring me through the door, then nudges it shut with his heel and drops me on the floor.

The room is almost empty, except for a row of empty trash cans along one wall and a square metal door large enough for one of the cans to fit through it along the other wall.

"Tris," Tobias says, crouching next to me. His face is pale, almost yellow.

There is too much I want to say. The first thing that comes out is, "Beatrice."

He laughs weakly.

"Beatrice," he amends, and touches his lips to mine. I curl my fingers into his shirt.

"Unless you want me to throw up all over you guys, you might want to save it for later."

"Where are we?" I ask.

"This is the trash incinerator," says Peter, slapping the square door. "I turned it off. It'll take us to the alley. And then your aim had better be perfect, Four, if you want to get out of the Erudite sector alive."

"Don't concern yourself with my aim," Tobias retorts. He, like me, is barefoot.

Peter opens the door to the incinerator. "Tris, you first."

The trash chute is about three feet wide and four feet high. I slide one leg down the chute and, with Tobias's help, swing the other leg in. My stomach drops as I slide down a short metal tube. Then a series of rollers pound against my back as I slip over them.

I smell fire and ash, but I am not burned. Then I drop, and my arm smacks into a metal wall, making me groan. I land on a cement floor, hard, and pain from the impact prickles up my shins.

"Ow." I limp away from the opening and shout, "Go ahead!"

My legs have recovered by the time Peter lands, on his side instead of his feet. He groans, and drags himself away from the opening to recover.

I look around. We are inside the incinerator, which would be completely dark if not for the lines of light glowing in the shape of a small door on the other side.

The floor is solid metal in some places and metal grating in others. Everything smells like rotting garbage and fire.

"Don't say I never took you anywhere nice," Peter says.

"Wouldn't dream of it," I say.

Tobias drops to the floor, landing first on his feet and then tilting forward to his knees, wincing. I pull him to his feet and then draw close to his side. All the smells and sights and feelings of the world feel magnified. I was almost dead, but instead I am alive. Because of Peter.

Of all people.

Peter walks across the grate and opens the small door. Light streams into the incinerator. Tobias walks with me away from the fire smell, away from the metal furnace, into the cement-walled room that contains it.

"Got that gun?" Peter says to Tobias.

"No," says Tobias, "I figured I would shoot the bullets out of my nostrils, so I left it upstairs."

"Oh, shut up."

Peter holds another gun in front of him and leaves the incinerator room. A dank hallway with exposed pipes in the ceiling greets us, but it's only ten feet long. The sign next to the door at the end says EXIT. I am alive, and I am leaving.

+++

The stretch of land between Dauntless headquarters and Erudite headquarters does not look the same in reverse. I suppose everything is bound to look different when you aren't on your way to die.

When we reach the end of the alley, Tobias presses his shoulder to one wall and leans forward just enough to see around the corner. His face blank, he puts one arm around the corner, steadying it with the building wall, and fires twice. I shove my fingers in my ears and try not to pay attention to the gunshots and what they make me remember.

"Hurry," Tobias says.

We sprint, Peter first, me second, and Tobias last, down Wabash Avenue. I look over my shoulder to see what Tobias shot at, and see two men on the ground behind Erudite headquarters. One isn't moving, and the other is clutching his arm and running toward the door. They will send others after us.

My head feels muddled, probably from exhaustion, but the adrenaline keeps me running.

"Take the least logical route!" shouts Tobias.

"What?" Peter says.

"The least logical route," Tobias says. "So they won't find us!"

Peter swerves to the left, down another alley, this one

full of cardboard boxes that contain frayed blankets and stained pillows—old factionless dwellings, I assume. He jumps over a box that I go crashing through, kicking it behind me.

At the end of the alley he turns left, toward the marsh. We are back on Michigan Avenue. In plain sight of Erudite headquarters, if anyone cares to glance down the street.

"Bad idea!" I shout.

Peter takes the next right. At least all the streets here are clear—no fallen street signs to dodge or holes to jump over. My lungs burn like I inhaled poison. My legs, which ached at first, are now numb, which is better. Somewhere far away, I hear shouts.

Then it occurs to me: The least logical thing to do is stop running.

I grab Peter's sleeve and drag him toward the nearest building. It is six stories high, with wide windows arranged into a grid, divided by pillars of brick. The first door I try is locked, but Tobias fires at the window next to it until it breaks, and unlocks the door from the inside.

The building is completely empty. Not a single chair or table. And there are too many windows. We walk toward the emergency stairwell, and I crawl beneath the first flight so that we are hidden by the staircase. Tobias sits next to me, and Peter across from us both, his knees drawn to his chest.

I try to catch my breath and calm myself down, but it isn't easy. I was dead. I was *dead*, and then I wasn't, and why? Because of Peter? *Peter?*

I stare at him. He still looks so innocent, despite all that he has done to prove that he is not. His hair lies smooth against his head, shiny and dark, like we didn't just run for a mile at full speed. His round eyes scan the stairwell and then rest on my face.

"What?" he says. "Why are you looking at me like that?"

"How did you do it?" I say.

"It wasn't that hard," he says. "I dyed a paralytic serum purple and switched it out with the death serum. Replaced the wire that was supposed to read your heartbeat with a dead one. The bit with the heart monitor was harder; I had to get some Erudite help with a remote and stuff—you wouldn't understand it if I explained it to you."

"*Why* did you do it?" I say. "You *want* me dead. You were willing to do it yourself! What changed?"

He presses his lips together and doesn't look away, not for a long time. Then he opens his mouth, hesitates, and finally says, "I can't be in anyone's debt. Okay? The idea that I owed you something made me sick. I would wake up in the middle of the night feeling like I was going to vomit.

Indebted to a Stiff? It's ridiculous. Absolutely ridiculous. And I couldn't have it."

"What are you talking about? You owed me something?"

He rolls his eyes. "The Amity compound. Someone shot me—the bullet was at head level; it would have hit me right between the eyes. And you shoved me out of the way. We were even before that—I almost killed you during initiation, you almost killed me during the attack simulation; we're square, right? But after that . . ."

"You're insane," says Tobias. "That's not the way the world works . . . with everyone keeping score."

"It's not?" Peter raises his eyebrows. "I don't know what world *you* live in, but in mine, people only do things for you for one of two reasons. The first is if they want something in return. And the second is if they feel like they owe you something."

"Those aren't the only reasons people do things for you," I say. "Sometimes they do them because they love you. Well, maybe not *you*, but . . ."

Peter snorts. "That's exactly the kind of garbage I expect a delusional Stiff to say."

"I guess we just have to make sure you owe us," says Tobias. "Or you'll go running to whoever offers you the best deal."

"Yeah," Peter says. "That's pretty much how it is."

I shake my head. I can't imagine living the way he does—always keeping track of who gave me what and what I should give them in return, incapable of love or loyalty or forgiveness, a one-eyed man with a knife in hand, looking for someone else's eye to poke out. That isn't life. It's some paler version of life. I wonder where he learned it from.

"So when can we get out of here, you think?" Peter says.

"Couple hours," says Tobias. "We should go to the Abnegation sector. That's where the factionless and the Dauntless who aren't wired for simulations will be by now."

"Fantastic," says Peter.

Tobias puts his arm around me. I press my cheek into his shoulder, and close my eyes so I don't have to look at Peter. I know there is a lot to say, though I'm not sure exactly what it is, but we can't say it here, or now.

+ + +

As we walk the streets I once called home, conversations sputter and die, and eyes cling to my face and body. As far as they knew—and I'm sure they knew, because Jeanine knows how to spread news—I died less than six hours ago. I notice that some of the factionless I pass are marked with patches of blue dye. They are simulation-ready.

Now that we're here, and safe, I realize that there are cuts all over the bottoms of my feet from running over rough pavement and bits of glass from broken windows. Every step stings. I focus on that instead of all the stares.

"Tris?" someone calls out ahead of us. I lift my head, and see Uriah and Christina on the sidewalk, comparing revolvers. Uriah drops his gun in the grass and sprints toward me. Christina follows him, but at a slower pace.

Uriah reaches for me, but Tobias sets a hand on his shoulder to stop him. I feel a surge of gratitude. I don't think I can handle Uriah's embrace, or his questions, or his surprise, right now.

"She's been through a lot," Tobias says. "She just needs to sleep. She'll be down the street—number thirty-seven. Come visit tomorrow."

Uriah frowns at me. The Dauntless don't usually understand restraint, and Uriah has only ever known the Dauntless. But he must respect Tobias's assessment of me, because he nods and says, "Okay. Tomorrow."

Christina reaches out as I pass her and squeezes my shoulder lightly. I try to stand up straighter, but my muscles feel like a cage, holding my shoulders hunched. The eyes follow me down the street, pinching the back of my neck. I am relieved when Tobias leads us up the front walk of the gray house that belonged to Marcus Eaton.

I don't know by what strength Tobias marches through the doorway. For him this house must contain echoes of screaming parents and belt snaps and hours spent in small, dark closets, yet he doesn't look troubled as he leads Peter and me into the kitchen. If anything he stands taller. But maybe that is Tobias—when he's supposed to be weak, he's strong.

Tori, Harrison, and Evelyn stand in the kitchen. The sight overwhelms me. I lean my shoulder into the wall and squeeze my eyes shut. The outline of the execution table is printed on my eyelids. I open my eyes. I try to breathe. They are talking but I can't hear what they're saying. Why is Evelyn here, in Marcus's house? Where is Marcus?

Evelyn puts one arm around Tobias and touches his face with the other, pressing her cheek to his. She says something to him. He smiles at her when he pulls away. Mother and son, reconciled. I am not sure it's wise.

Tobias turns me around and, keeping one hand on my arm and one on my waist, to avoid my shoulder wound, presses me toward the staircase. We climb the steps together.

Upstairs are his parents' old bedroom and his old bedroom, with a bathroom between them, and that's it. He takes me into his bedroom, and I stand for a moment, looking around at the room where he spent most of his life.

He keeps his hand on my arm. He has been touching me in some way since we left the stairwell of that building, like he thinks I might break apart if he doesn't hold me together.

"Marcus didn't go into this room after I left, I'm pretty sure," says Tobias. "Because nothing was moved when I came back here."

Members of Abnegation don't own many decorations, since they are viewed as self-indulgent, but what few things we were allowed, he has. A stack of school papers. A small bookshelf. And, strangely, a sculpture made of blue glass on his dresser.

"My mother smuggled that to me when I was young. Told me to hide it," he says. "The day of the ceremony, I put it on my dresser before I left. So he would see it. A small act of defiance."

I nod. It is strange to be in a place that carries one single memory so completely. This room is sixteen-year-old Tobias, about to choose Dauntless to escape his father.

"Let's take care of your feet," he says. But he doesn't move, just shifts his fingers to the inside of my elbow.

"Okay," I say.

We walk into the adjoined bathroom, and I sit on the edge of the tub. He sits next to me, a hand on my knee as he turns on the faucet and plugs the drain. Water spills into the tub, covering my toenails. My blood turns the water pink.

He crouches in the tub and puts my foot in his lap, dabbing at the deeper cuts with a washcloth. I don't feel it. Even when he smears soap lather over them, I don't feel anything. The bathwater turns gray.

I pick up the bar of soap and turn it in my hands until my skin is coated with white lather. I reach for him and run my fingers over his hands, careful to get the lines in his palms and the spaces between his fingers. It feels good to do something, to clean something, and to have my hands on him again.

We get water all over the bathroom floor as we both splash it on ourselves to get the soap off. The water makes me cold, but I shiver and I don't care. He gets a towel and starts to dry my hands.

"I don't . . ." I sound like I am being strangled. "My family is all *dead*, or traitors; how can I . . ."

I am not making any sense. The sobs take over my body, my mind, everything. He gathers me to him, and bathwater soaks my legs. His hold is tight. I listen to his heartbeat and, after a while, find a way to let the rhythm calm me.

"I'll be your family now," he says.

"I love you," I say.

I said that once, before I went to Erudite headquarters, but he was asleep then. I don't know why I didn't say it when he could hear it. Maybe I was afraid to trust him with something so personal as my devotion. Or afraid that I did not know what it was to love someone. But now I think the scary thing was not saying it before it was almost too late. Not saying it before it was almost too late for me.

I am his, and he is mine, and it has been that way all along.

He stares at me. I wait with my hands clutching his arms for stability as he considers his response.

He frowns at me. "Say it again."

"Tobias," I say, "I love you."

His skin is slippery with water and he smells like sweat and my shirt sticks to his arms when he slides them around me. He presses his face to my neck and kisses me right above the collarbone, kisses my cheek, kisses my lips.

"I love you, too," he says.

CHAPTER
THIRTY-SEVEN

HE LIES NEXT to me as I fall sleep. I expect to have nightmares, but I must be too tired, because my mind stays
empty. When I open my eyes next, he's gone, but there's a
stack of clothes on the bed beside me.

I get up and walk into the bathroom and I feel raw,
like my skin was scraped clean and every breath of air
stings it a little, but stable. I don't turn on the lights
in the bathroom because I know they will be pale and
bright, just like the lights in the Erudite compound. I
shower in the dark, barely able to tell soap from condi-
tioner, and tell myself that I will emerge new and strong,
that the water will heal me.

Before I leave the bathroom, I pinch my cheeks hard to
bring blood to the surface of my skin. It's stupid, but I don't

want to look weak and exhausted in front of everyone.

When I walk back into Tobias's room, Uriah is sprawled across the bed facedown; Christina is holding the blue sculpture above Tobias's desk, examining it; and Lynn is poised above Uriah with a pillow, a wicked grin creeping across her face.

Lynn smacks Uriah hard in the back of the head, Christina says, "Hey Tris!" and Uriah cries, "Ow! How on earth do you make a *pillow* hurt, Lynn?"

"My exceptional strength," she says. "Did you get smacked, Tris? One of your cheeks is bright red."

I must not have pinched the other one hard enough. "No, it's just . . . my morning glow."

I try the joke out on my tongue like it's a new language. Christina laughs, maybe a little harder than my comment warrants, but I appreciate the effort. Uriah bounces on the bed a few times when he moves to the edge.

"So, the thing we're all not talking about," he says. He gestures to me. "You almost died, a sadistic pansycake saved you, and now we're all waging some serious war with the factionless as allies."

"Pansycake?" says Christina.

"Dauntless slang." Lynn smirks. "Supposed to be a huge insult, only no one uses it anymore."

"Because it's so offensive," says Uriah, nodding.

"No. Because it's so stupid no Dauntless w̶

would speak it, let alone think it. Pansycal

you, twelve?"

"And a half," he says.

I get the feeling their banter is for my _____, so

that I don't have to say anything; I can just laugh. And

I do, enough to warm the stone that has formed in my

stomach.

"There's food downstairs," says Christina. "Tobias

made scrambled eggs, which, as it turns out, is a disgust-

ing food."

"Hey," I say. "I *like* scrambled eggs."

"Must be a Stiff breakfast, then." She grabs my arm.

"C'mon."

Together we go down the stairs, our footsteps thun-

dering as they never would have been allowed to in my

parents' house. My father used to scold me for running

down the stairs. "Do not call attention to yourself," he

said. "It is not courteous to the people around you."

I hear voices in the living room—a chorus of them, in

fact, joined by occasional bursts of laughter and a faint

melody plucked on an instrument, a banjo or a guitar.

It is not what I expect in an Abnegation house, where

everything is always quiet, no matter how many people

are gathered within. The voices and the laughter and

...usic breathe life into the sullen walls. I feel even ..armer.

I stand in the doorway to the living room. Five people are crowded onto the three-person couch, playing a card game I recognize from Candor headquarters. A man sits in the armchair with a woman balanced on his lap, and someone else perches on the arm, a can of soup in hand. Tobias sits on the floor, his back against the coffee table. Every part of his posture suggests ease—one leg bent, the other straight, an arm slung across his knee, his head tilted to listen. I have never seen him look so comfortable without a gun. I didn't think it was possible.

I get the same sinking feeling in my stomach that I always get when I know I've been lied to, but I don't know who it was that lied to me this time, or about what, exactly. But this is not what I was taught to expect of factionlessness. I was taught that it was worse than death.

I stand there for just a few seconds before people realize that I'm there. Their conversation peters out. I wipe my palms off on the hem of my shirt. Too many eyes, and too much silence.

Evelyn clears her throat. "Everyone, this is Tris Prior. I believe you may have heard a lot about her yesterday."

"And Christina, Uriah, and Lynn," supplies Tobias. I'm grateful for his attempt to divert everyone's attention from me, but it doesn't work.

I stand glued to the door frame for a few seconds, and then one of the factionless men—older, his wrinkled skin patterned with tattoos—speaks up.

"Aren't you supposed to be dead?"

Some of the others laugh, and I try a smile. It emerges crooked and small.

"Supposed to be," I say.

"We don't like to give Jeanine Matthews what she wants, though," Tobias says. He gets up and hands me a can of peas—but it isn't full of peas; it's full of scrambled eggs. The aluminum warms my fingers.

He sits, so I sit next to him, and scoop some of the eggs into my mouth. I am not hungry, but I know I need to eat, so I chew and swallow anyway. I am familiar with the way the factionless eat, so I pass the eggs to Christina, and take a can of peaches from Tobias.

"Why is everyone camped out in Marcus's house?" I ask him.

"Evelyn kicked him out. Said it was her house, too, and he'd gotten to use it for years, and it was her turn." Tobias grins. "It caused a huge blowup on the front lawn, but eventually Evelyn won."

I glance at Tobias's mother. She is in the far corner of the room, talking to Peter and eating more eggs from another can. My stomach churns. Tobias talks about her almost reverently. But I still remember what she said to me about my transience in Tobias's life.

"There's bread somewhere." He picks up a basket from the coffee table and hands it to me. "Take two pieces. You need it."

As I chew on the bread crust, I look at Peter and Evelyn again.

"I think she's trying to recruit him," Tobias says. "She has a way of making the factionless life sound extraordinarily appealing."

"Anything to get him out of Dauntless. I don't care if he saved my life, I still don't like him."

"Hopefully we won't have to worry about faction distinctions anymore by the time this is over. It'll be nice, I think."

I don't say anything. I don't feel like picking a fight with him here. Or reminding him that it won't be so easy to persuade Dauntless and Candor to join the factionless in their crusade against the faction system. It may take another war.

The front door opens, and Edward enters. Today he wears a patch with a blue eye painted on it, complete with a half-lowered eyelid. The effect of the overlarge eye against his otherwise handsome face is both grotesque and amusing.

"Eddie!" someone calls out in greeting. But Edward's good eye has already fallen on Peter. He starts across the room, nearly kicking a can of food out of someone's hand. Peter presses into the shadow of the door frame like he is trying to disappear into it.

Edward stops inches from Peter's feet, and then jerks toward him like he is about to throw a punch. Peter jolts back so hard he slams his head into the wall. Edward grins, and all around us, the factionless laugh.

"Not so brave in broad daylight," Edward says. And then, to Evelyn, "Make sure you don't give him any utensils. Never know what he might do with them."

As he speaks, he plucks the fork from Peter's hand.

"Give that back," says Peter.

Edward slams his free hand into Peter's throat, and presses the tines of the fork between his fingers, right against Peter's Adam's apple. Peter stiffens, blood rushing into his face.

"Keep your mouth shut around me," he says, his voice low, "or I will do this again, only next time, I'll shove it right through your esophagus."

"That's enough," Evelyn says. Edward drops the fork

and releases Peter. Then he walks across the room and sits next to the person who called him "Eddie" a moment before.

"I don't know if you know this," Tobias says, "but Edward is a little unstable."

"I'm getting that," I say.

"That Drew guy, who helped Peter perform that butter-knife maneuver," Tobias says. "Apparently when he got kicked out of Dauntless, he tried to join the same group of factionless Edward was a part of. Notice that you haven't seen Drew anywhere."

"Did Edward kill him?" I say.

"Nearly," Tobias says. "Evidently that's why that other transfer—Myra, I think her name was?—left Edward. Too gentle to bear it."

I feel hollow at the thought of Drew, almost dead at the hands of Edward. Drew attacked me, too.

"I don't want to talk about this," I say.

"Okay," Tobias says. He touches my shoulder. "Is it hard for you to be in an Abnegation house again? I meant to ask before. We can go somewhere else, if it is."

I finish my second piece of bread. All Abnegation houses are the same, so this living room is exactly the same as my own, and it does bring back memories, if I look at it carefully. Light glowing through the blinds every morning, enough for my father to read by. The click of my mother's knitting needles every evening. But I don't feel like I'm choking. It's a start.

"Yes," I say. "But not as hard as you might think."

He raises an eyebrow.

"Really. The simulations in Erudite headquarters . . . helped me, somehow. To hold on, maybe." I frown. "Or maybe not. Maybe they helped me to stop holding on so tightly." That sounds right. "Someday I'll tell you about it." My voice sounds far away.

He touches my cheek and, even though we're in a room full of people, crowded by laughter and conversation, slowly kisses me.

"Whoa there, Tobias," says the man to my left. "Weren't you raised a Stiff? I thought the most you people did was . . . graze hands or something."

"Then how do you explain all the Abnegation children?" Tobias raises his eyebrows.

"They're brought into being by sheer force of will," the woman on the arm of the chair interjects. "Didn't you know that, Tobias?"

"No, I wasn't aware." He grins. "My apologies."

They all laugh. *We* all laugh. And it occurs to me that I might be meeting Tobias's true faction. They are not characterized by a particular virtue. They claim all colors, all activities, all virtues, and all flaws as their own.

I don't know what binds them together. The only common ground they have, as far as I know, is failure. Whatever it is, it seems to be enough.

I feel, as I look at him, that I am finally seeing him as he is, instead of how he is in relation to me. So how well do I really know him, if I have not seen this before?

+ + +

The sun is beginning to set. The Abnegation sector is far from quiet. The Dauntless and factionless wander the streets, some with bottles in their hands, some with guns in their other hands.

Ahead of me, Zeke pushes Shauna in her wheelchair past the house of Alice Brewster, former Abnegation leader. They don't see me.

"Do it again!" she says.

"Are you sure?"

"Yes!"

"Okay . . ." Zeke starts to jog behind the wheelchair. Then, when he's almost too far away for me to see, he pushes himself up with the handles so that his feet aren't touching the ground, and together they fly down the middle of the street, Shauna shrieking, Zeke laughing.

I turn left at the next intersection and start down the

cracked sidewalk toward the building where Abnegation had its monthly faction-wide meetings. Though it feels like it has been a long time since I last went there, I still remember where it is. One block south, two blocks west.

The sun inches toward the horizon as I walk. The color drains from the surrounding buildings in the evening light, so that they all appear to be gray.

The face of Abnegation headquarters is just a cement rectangle, like all the other buildings in the Abnegation sector. But when I shove the front door open, familiar wood floors and rows of wooden benches arranged in a square greet me. In the center of the room is a skylight that lets in a square of orange sunlight. It is the room's only adornment.

I sit on my family's old bench. I used to sit next to my father, and Caleb, next to my mother. Now I feel like the only one left. The last Prior.

"It's nice, isn't it?" Marcus walks in and sits down across from me, his hands folded in his lap. The sunlight is between us.

He has a large bruise on his jaw from where Tobias hit him, and his hair is freshly buzzed.

"It's fine," I say, straightening. "What are you doing here?"

"I saw you come in." He examines his fingernails

carefully. "And I want to have a word with you about the information Jeanine Matthews stole."

"What if you're too late? What if I already know what it is?"

Marcus looks up from his fingernails, and his dark eyes narrow. The look is far more poisonous than any Tobias could muster, though he has his father's eyes. "You can't possibly."

"You don't know that."

"I do, actually. Because I have seen what happens to people when they hear the truth. They look like they have forgotten what they were searching for, and are just wandering around trying to remember."

A chill makes its way up my spine and spreads down my arms, giving me goose bumps.

"I know that Jeanine decided to murder half a faction to steal it, so it must be incredibly important," I say. I pause. I know something else, too, but I only just realized it.

Right before I attacked Jeanine, she said, "This is not about you! It's not about me!"

And *this* meant what she was doing to me—trying to find a simulation that worked on me. On the Divergent.

"I know it has something to do with the Divergent," I blurt out. "I know the information is about what's outside the fence."

"That is not the same thing as knowing what's outside the fence."

"Well, are you going to tell me or are you going to dangle it over my head and make me jump for it?"

"I did not come here for self-indulgent arguing. And no, I am not going to tell you, but not because I don't want to. It's because I have no idea how to describe it to you. You have to see it for yourself."

As he speaks, I notice the sunlight turning more orange than yellow, and casting darker shadows over his face.

"I think Tobias might be right," I say. "You *like* to be the only one who knows. You like that I don't know. It makes you feel important. That's why you won't tell me, not because it's indescribable."

"That's not true."

"How am I supposed to know that?"

Marcus stares, and I stare back.

"A week before the simulation attack, the Abnegation leaders decided it was time to reveal the information in the file to everyone. *Everyone*, in the entire city. The day we intended to reveal it was approximately seven days after the simulation attack. Obviously we were unable to do so."

"She didn't want you to reveal what was outside the fence? Why not? How did she even know about it in the first place? I thought you said only the Abnegation leaders knew."

"We are not *from* here, Beatrice. We were all placed here, for a specific purpose. A while ago, the Abnegation were forced to enlist the help of Erudite in order to achieve that purpose, but eventually everything went awry because of Jeanine. Because she doesn't want to do what we are supposed to do. She would rather resort to murder."

Placed here.

My brain feels like it is buzzing with information. I clutch the edge of the bench beneath me.

"What are we supposed to do?" I say, my voice barely more than a whisper.

"I have told you enough to convince you that I am not a liar. As for the rest, I truly find myself unequal to the task of explaining it to you. I only told you as much as I did because the situation has become dire."

Dire. Suddenly I understand the problem. The factionless plan to destroy, not only the important figures in Erudite, but all the data they have. They will level everything.

I have never thought that plan was a good idea, but I knew that we could come back from it, because the Erudite still *know* the relevant information, even if they don't have their data. But this is something even the most intelligent Erudite do not know; something that, if every-thing is destroyed, we cannot replicate.

"If I help you, I betray Tobias. I will lose him." I swallow hard. "So you have to give me a good reason."

"Aside from the good of everyone in our society?" Marcus wrinkles his nose in disgust. "That isn't enough for you?"

"Our society is in pieces. So no, it's not."

Marcus sighs.

"Your parents died for *you*, it's true. But the reason your mother was in Abnegation headquarters the night you were almost executed was not to save you. She didn't know you were there. She was trying to rescue the file from Jeanine. And when she heard that you were about to die, she rushed to save you, and left the file in Jeanine's hands."

"That's not what she told me," I say hotly.

"She was lying. Because she had to. But Beatrice, the point is . . . the point is, your mother knew she probably would not get out of Abnegation headquarters alive, but she had to try. This file, it was something she was willing to die for. Understand?"

The Abnegation are willing to die for any person, friend or enemy, if the situation calls for it. That is, perhaps, why they find it difficult to survive in life-threatening situations. But there are few *things* they are willing to die for. They don't value many things in the physical world.

So if he's telling me the truth, and my mother really was willing to die for this information to become public . . . I would do just about anything to accomplish the goal she failed to achieve.

"You're trying to manipulate me. Aren't you."

"I suppose," he says as shadows slip into his eye sockets like dark water, "that is something you must decide for yourself."

CHAPTER
THIRTY-EIGHT

I TAKE MY time on my walk back to the Eaton house, and try to remember what my mother told me when she saved me from the tank during the simulation attack. Something about having watched the trains since the attack started. *I didn't know what I would do when I found you. But it was always my intention to save you.*

But when I go over the memory of her voice in my mind, it sounds different. *I didn't know what I would do, when I found you.* Meaning: I didn't know how to save both you and the file. *But it was always my intention to save you.*

I shake my head. Is that how she said it, or am I manipulating my own memory because of what Marcus told me? There is no way to know. All I can do is decide if I trust Marcus or not.

And while he has done cruel, evil things, our society is not divided into "good" and "bad." Cruelty does not make a person dishonest, the same way bravery does not make a person kind. Marcus is not good or bad, but both.

Well, he is probably more bad than good.

But that doesn't mean he's lying.

On the street ahead of me, I see the orange glow of fire. Alarmed, I walk faster, and see that the fire rises from large, man-sized metal bowls set up on the sidewalks. The Dauntless and the factionless have gathered between them, a narrow divide separating one group from the other. And before them stand Evelyn, Harrison, Tori, and Tobias.

I spot Christina, Uriah, Lynn, Zeke, and Shauna on the right side of the cluster of Dauntless, and stand with them.

"Where've you been?" Christina says. "We looked all over for you."

"I went for a walk. What's going on?"

"They're finally going to tell us the attack plan," says Uriah, looking eager.

"Oh," I say.

Evelyn lifts her hands, palms out, and the factionless fall silent. They are better trained than the Dauntless, whose voices take thirty seconds to peter out.

"The past few weeks, we have been developing a plan to fight the Erudite," Evelyn says, her low voice carrying easily. "And now that we have finished, we would like to share it with you."

Evelyn nods at Tori, who takes over. "Our strategy is not pointed, but broad. There is no way to know who among the Erudite supports Jeanine and who does not. It is therefore safer to assume that all those who do not support her have already vacated Erudite headquarters."

"We all know that Erudite's power lies not in its people but in its information," says Evelyn. "As long as they still possess that information, we will never be free of them, especially while large numbers of us are wired for simulations. They have used information to control us and keep us under their thumb for far too long."

A shout, beginning among the factionless and spreading to the Dauntless, rises up from the crowd like we are all parts of one organism, following the commands of a single brain. But I am not sure what I think, or how I feel. There is a part of me that is shouting, too—clamoring for the destruction of every single Erudite and all that they hold dear.

I look at Tobias. His expression is neutral, and he stands behind the glow of firelight, where he is difficult to see. I wonder what he thinks of this.

"I am sorry to tell you that those of you who were shot with simulation transmitters will have to remain here," says Tori, "or you can be activated as a weapon of Erudite at any time."

There are a few cries of protest, but no one seems all that surprised. They know too well what Jeanine can do with simulations, maybe.

Lynn groans and looks at Uriah. "We have to *stay*?"

"*You* have to stay," he says.

"You got shot too," she says. "I saw it."

"Divergent, remember?" he says. Lynn rolls her eyes, and he hurries on, probably to avoid hearing Lynn's Divergent conspiracy theory again. "Anyway, I bet you no one checks, and what are the odds she'll activate you, specifically, if she knows everyone else with simulation transmitters is staying behind?"

Lynn frowns, considering this. But she looks more cheerful—as cheerful as Lynn gets, anyway—as Tori begins speaking again.

"The rest of us will divide into groups of mixed factionless and Dauntless," says Tori. "A single, large group will attempt to penetrate Erudite headquarters and work its way up through the building, cleansing it of Erudite's influence. Several other, smaller groups will proceed immediately to the higher levels of the building to dispense with certain key Erudite officials. You will receive your group assignments later this evening."

"The attack will occur in three days' time," says Evelyn. "Prepare yourselves. This will be dangerous and difficult. But the factionless are familiar with difficulty—"

At this the factionless cheer, and I am reminded that we, the Dauntless, are the same people who, just a few weeks ago, were criticizing Abnegation for giving the factionless food and other necessary items. How was that so easy to forget?

"And the Dauntless are familiar with danger—"

Everyone around me punches the air with their fists and screams. I feel their voices inside my head, and the burn of triumph in my chest that makes me want to join them.

Evelyn's expression is too empty for someone giving an impassioned speech. Her face looks like a mask.

"Down with Erudite!" Tori yells, and everyone repeats her, all voices joining together, regardless of faction. We share a common enemy, but does that make us friends?

I notice that Tobias does not join in the chant, and neither does Christina.

"This doesn't feel right," she says.

"What do you mean?" Lynn says as the voices rise around us. "Don't you remember what they did to us? Put our minds under a simulation and forced us to shoot people without even knowing it? Murdered every single Abnegation leader?"

"Yeah," says Christina. "It's just . . . Invading a faction's headquarters and killing everyone, isn't that what the Erudite just did to Abnegation?"

"This is different. *This* is not an attack out of nowhere, unprovoked," says Lynn, scowling at her.

"Yeah," Christina says. "Yeah, I know."

She looks at me. I don't say anything. She has a point—it doesn't feel right.

I walk toward the Eaton house in search of silence.

I open the front door and climb the stairs. When I reach Tobias's old room, I sit on the bed and look out the window, where factionless and Dauntless are gathered around the fires, laughing and talking. But they aren't mixed together; there is still an uneasy divide between them, factionless on one side and Dauntless on the other.

I watch Lynn, Uriah, and Christina by one of the fires. Uriah snatches at the flames, too quickly to be burned. His smile looks more like a grimace, twisted as it is by grief.

After a few minutes I hear footsteps on the stairs, and Tobias comes into the room, slipping off his shoes by the doorway.

"What's wrong?" he says.

"Nothing, really," I say. "I was just thinking, I'm surprised the factionless agreed to work with Dauntless so easily. It's not like the Dauntless were ever kind to them."

He stands beside me at the window and leans into the frame.

"It's not a natural alliance, is it," he says. "But we have the same goal."

"Right now. But what happens when the goals change? The factionless want to get rid of factions, and the Dauntless don't."

Tobias presses his mouth into a line. I suddenly remember Marcus and Johanna, walking together through the orchard—Marcus wore the same expression when he was keeping something from her.

Did Tobias get that expression from his father? Or does it mean something different?

"You're in my group," he says. "During the attack. I hope you don't mind. We're supposed to lead the way to the control rooms."

The attack. If I participate in the attack, I can't go after the information Jeanine stole from Abnegation. I have to choose one or the other.

Tobias said that dealing with Erudite was more important than finding out the truth. And if he had not promised the factionless control over all of Erudite's data, he might have been right. But he left me no choice. I have to help Marcus, if there is even a chance that he is telling the truth. I have to work against the people I love best.

And right now, I have to lie.

I twist my fingers together.

"What is it?" he says.

"I still can't fire a gun." I look up at him. "And after what happened in Erudite headquarters . . ." I clear my throat. "Risking my life doesn't seem so appealing anymore."

"Tris." He brushes my cheek with his fingertips. "You don't have to go."

"I don't want to seem like a coward."

"Hey." His fingers fit beneath my jaw. They are cool against my skin. He looks sternly at me. "You have done more for this faction than any other person. You . . ."

He sighs, and touches his forehead to mine.

"You're the bravest person I've ever met. Stay here. Let yourself mend."

He kisses me, and I feel like I am crumbling again,

beginning with the deepest parts of me. He thinks I will be here, but I will be working against him, working with the father he despises. This lie—this lie is the worst I have ever told. I will never be able to take it back.

When we part, I am afraid he will hear my breaths shake, so I turn toward the window.

CHAPTER
THIRTY-NINE

"OH YEAH. YOU totally look like a banjo-strumming softie," says Christina.

"Really?"

"No. Not at all, actually. Just . . . let me fix it, okay?"

She rummages in her bag for a few seconds and pulls out a small box. In it are different-sized tubes and containers that I recognize as makeup, but wouldn't know what to do with.

We are in my parents' house. It was the only place I could think of to go to get ready. Christina has no reservations about poking around—she already discovered two textbooks wedged between the dresser and the wall, evidence of Caleb's Erudite leanings.

"Let me get this straight. So you left the Dauntless

compound to get ready for war . . . and took your makeup bag with you?"

"Yep. Figured it would be harder for anyone to shoot me if they saw how devastatingly attractive I was," she says, arching an eyebrow. "Hold still."

She takes the cap off a black tube about the size of one of my fingers, revealing a red stick. Lipstick, obviously. She touches it to my mouth and dabs it until my lips are covered in color. I can see it when I purse them.

"Has anyone ever talked to you about the miracle of eyebrow tweezing?" she says, holding up a pair of tweezers.

"Get those away from me."

"Fine." She sighs. "I would take out the blush, but I'm pretty sure it's not the right color for you."

"Shocking, considering we're so similar in skin tone."

"Ha-ha," she says.

By the time we leave, I have red lips and curled eyelashes, and I'm wearing a bright red dress. And there's a knife strapped to the inside of my knee. This all makes perfect sense.

"Where's Marcus, Destroyer of Lives, going to meet us?" Christina says. She wears Amity yellow instead of red, and it glows against her skin.

I laugh. "Behind Abnegation headquarters."

We walk down the sidewalk in the dark. All the others

should be eating dinner now—I made sure of that—but in case we run into someone, we wear black jackets to conceal most of our Amity clothing. I hop over a crack in the cement out of habit.

"Where are you two going?" Peter's voice says. I look over my shoulder. He's standing on the sidewalk behind us. I wonder how long he's been there.

"Why aren't you with your attack group, eating dinner?" I say.

"I don't have one." He taps the arm I shot. "I'm injured."

"Yeah right, you are!" says Christina.

"Well, I don't want to go to battle with a bunch of factionless," he says, his green eyes glinting. "So I'm going to stay here."

"Like a coward," says Christina, her lip curled in disgust. "Let everyone else clean up the mess for you."

"Yep!" he says with a kind of malicious cheer. He claps his hands. "Have fun dying."

He crosses the street, whistling, and walks in the other direction.

"Well, we distracted him," she says. "He didn't ask where we were going again."

"Yeah. Good." I clear my throat. "So, this plan. It's kind of stupid, right?"

"It's not . . . *stupid*."

"Oh, come on. Trusting Marcus is stupid. Trying to get past the Dauntless at the fence is stupid. Going against the Dauntless and factionless is stupid. All three combined is . . . a different kind of stupid formerly unheard of by humankind."

"Unfortunately it's also the best plan we have," she points out. "If we want everyone to know the truth."

I trusted Christina to take up this mission when I thought I would die, so it seemed stupid not to trust her now. I was worried she wouldn't want to come with me, but I forgot where Christina came from: Candor, where the pursuit of truth is more important than anything else. She may be Dauntless now, but if there's one thing I've learned through all this, it's that we never leave our old factions behind.

"So this is where you grew up. Did you like it here?" She frowns. "I guess you couldn't have, if you wanted to leave."

The sun inches toward the horizon as we walk. I never used to like evening light because it made everything in the Abnegation sector look more monochromatic than it already is, but now I find the unchanging gray comforting.

"I liked some things and hated some things," I say. "And there were some things I didn't know I had until I lost them."

We reach Abnegation headquarters, and its face is just a cement square like everything else in the Abnegation sector. I would love to walk into the meeting room and breathe the smell of old wood, but we don't have time. We slip into the alley next to the building and walk to the back, where Marcus told me he would be waiting.

A powder-blue pickup truck waits there, its engine running. Marcus is behind the wheel. I let Christina walk ahead of me so that she can be the one to slide into the middle. I don't want to sit close to him if I can help it. I feel like hating him while I work with him lessens my betrayal of Tobias somehow.

You have no other choice, I tell myself. *There is no other way.*

With that in mind, I pull the door shut and look for a seat belt to buckle. I find only the frayed end of a seat belt and a broken buckle.

"Where did you find this piece of junk?" says Christina.

"I stole it from the factionless. They fix them up. It wasn't easy to get it to start. Better ditch those jackets, girls."

I ball up our jackets and toss them out the half-open window. Marcus shifts the truck into drive, and it groans.

I half expect it to stay still when he presses the gas pedal, but it moves.

From what I remember, it takes about an hour to drive from the Abnegation sector to Amity headquarters, and the trip requires a skilled driver. Marcus pulls onto one of the main thoroughfares and pushes his foot into the gas pedal. We lurch forward, narrowly avoiding a gaping hole in the road. I grab the dashboard to steady myself.

"Relax, Beatrice," says Marcus. "I've driven a car before."

"I've done a lot of things before, but that doesn't mean I'm any good at them!"

Marcus smiles and jerks the truck to the left so that we don't hit a fallen stoplight. Christina whoops as we bump over another piece of debris, like she's having the time of her life.

"A different kind of stupid, right?" she says, her voice loud enough to be heard over the rush of wind through the cab.

I clutch the seat beneath me and try not to think of what I ate for dinner.

+ + +

When we reach the fence, we see the Dauntless standing in our headlight beams, blocking the gate. Their blue armbands stand out against the rest of their clothing. I try to keep my expression pleasant. I will not be able to fool them into thinking I'm Amity with a scowl on my face.

A dark-skinned man with a gun in hand approaches Marcus's window. He shines a flashlight at Marcus first, then Christina, then me. I squint into the beam, and force a smile at the man like I don't mind bright lights in the eyes and guns pointed at my head in the slightest.

The Amity must be deranged if this is how they really think. Or they've been eating too much of that bread.

"So tell me," the man says. "What's an Abnegation member doing in a truck with two Amity?"

"These two girls volunteered to bring provisions to the city," Marcus says, "and I volunteered to escort them so that they would be safe."

"Also, we don't know how to drive," says Christina, grinning. "My dad tried to teach me years ago but I kept confusing the gas pedal for the brake pedal, and you can imagine what a disaster that was! Anyway, it was *really* nice of Joshua to volunteer to take us, because it would have taken us forever otherwise, and the boxes were *so* heavy—"

The Dauntless man holds up his hand. "Okay, I get it."

"Oh, of course. Sorry." Christina giggles. "I just thought I would explain, because you seemed so confused, and no wonder, because how many times do you encounter this—"

"Right," the man says. "And do you intend to return to the city?"

"Not anytime soon," Marcus says.

"All right. Go ahead, then." He nods to the other Dauntless by the gate. One of them types a series of numbers on the keypad, and the gate slides open to admit us. Marcus nods to the guard who let us through and drives over the worn path to Amity headquarters. The truck's headlights catch tire tracks and prairie grass and insects weaving back and forth. In the darkness to my right I see fireflies lighting up to a rhythm that is like a heartbeat.

After a few seconds, Marcus glances at Christina. "What on earth was *that*?"

"There's nothing the Dauntless hate more than cheerful Amity babble," says Christina, lifting a shoulder. "I figured if he got annoyed it would distract him and he would let us through."

I smile with all my teeth. "You are a *genius*."

"I know." She tosses her head like she's throwing her hair over one shoulder, only she doesn't have enough to throw.

"Except," says Marcus, "Joshua is not an Abnegation name."

"Whatever. As if anyone knows the difference."

I see the glow of Amity headquarters ahead, the familiar cluster of wooden buildings with the greenhouse in their center. We drive through the apple orchard. The air smells like warm earth.

Again I remember my mother stretching to pick an apple in this orchard, years ago when we came to help the Amity with the harvest. A pang hurts my chest, but the memory doesn't overwhelm me as it did a few weeks ago. Maybe it's because I am on a mission to honor her. Or maybe I am too apprehensive about what's coming to grieve properly. But something has changed.

Marcus parks the truck behind one of the sleeping cabins. For the first time I notice that there are no keys in the ignition.

"How did you get it to start?" I ask him.

"My father taught me a lot about mechanics and computers," he says. "Knowledge that I passed to my own son. You didn't think he figured it all out on his own, did you?"

"Actually yes, I did." I push the door open and climb out of the truck. Grass brushes my toes and the back of my calves. Christina stands at my right shoulder and tilts her head back.

"It's so different out here," she says. "You could almost forget what's going on in *there*." She points her thumb toward the city.

"And they often do," I say.

"They know what's beyond the city, though, right?" she asks.

"They know about as much as the Dauntless patrols," says Marcus. "Which is that the outside world is unknown and potentially dangerous."

"How do you know what they know?" I say.

"Because that's what we told them," he says, and he walks toward the greenhouse.

I exchange a look with Christina. Then we jog to catch up to him.

"What does *that* mean?"

"When you are entrusted with all the information, you have to decide how much other people should know," says Marcus. "The Abnegation leaders told them what we had to tell them. Now, let's hope Johanna is keeping up her normal habits. She is usually in the greenhouse this early in the evening."

He opens the greenhouse door. The air is just as dense as the last time I was in here, but now it is misty, too. The moisture cools my cheeks.

"Wow," Christina says.

The room is lit by moonlight, so it is hard to distinguish plant from tree from man-made structure. Leaves brush my face as I make my way around the outer edge of the room. And then I see Johanna, crouched beside a bush with a bowl in her hands, picking what appear to be raspberries. Her hair is pulled back, so I can see her scar.

"I didn't think I would see you here again, Ms. Prior," she says.

"Is that because I'm supposed to be dead?" I say.

"I always expect those who live by the gun to die by it. I am often pleasantly surprised." She balances the bowl on her knees and looks up at me. "Although I also know better than to think you came back because you like it here."

"No," I say. "We came for something else."

"All right," she says, standing. "Let's go talk about it, then."

She carries the bowl toward the middle of the room, where the Amity meetings are held. We follow her onto the tree roots, where she sits and offers me the bowl of raspberries. I take a small handful of berries and pass the bowl to Christina.

"Johanna, this is Christina," Marcus says. "Candor-born Dauntless."

"Welcome to Amity headquarters, Christina." Johanna smiles knowingly. It seems so strange, that two people born in Candor could end up in such different places: Dauntless, and Amity.

"Tell me, Marcus," says Johanna. "Why have you come to visit?"

"I think Beatrice should handle that," he says. "I am merely the transportation."

She shifts her focus to me without question, but I can tell by the wary look in her eyes that she would rather talk to Marcus. She would deny it if I asked her, but I am almost certain Johanna Reyes hates me.

"Um . . ." I say. Not my most brilliant opening. I wipe my palms on my skirt. "Things have gotten bad."

The words start to spill out, without finesse or sophistication. I explain that the Dauntless have allied with the factionless, and they plan to destroy all of Erudite, leaving us without one of the two essential factions. I tell her that there is important information in the Erudite compound, in addition to all the knowledge they possess, that especially needs to be recovered. When I finish, I realize I haven't told her why that has anything to do with her or her faction, but I don't know how to say it.

"I'm confused, Beatrice," she says. "What exactly do you want us to do?"

"I didn't come here to ask you for help," I say. "I thought you should know that a lot of people are going to die, very soon. And I know you don't want to stay here doing nothing while that happens, even if some of your faction does."

She looks down, her crooked mouth betraying just how right I am.

"I also wanted to ask you if we can talk to the Erudite you're keeping safe here," I say. "I know they're hidden, but I need access to them."

"And what do you intend to do?" she says.

"Shoot them," I say, rolling my eyes.

"That isn't funny."

I sigh. "Sorry. I need information. That's all."

"Well, you'll have to wait until tomorrow," Johanna says. "You can sleep here."

+++

I sleep as soon as my head touches the pillow, but wake earlier than I planned. I can tell by the glow near the horizon that the sun is about to rise.

Across the narrow aisle between two beds is Christina, her face pressed to the mattress with her pillow over her head. A dresser with a lamp on top of it stands between us. The wooden floorboards creak no matter where you step on them. And on the left wall is a mirror, casually placed. Everyone but the Abnegation takes mirrors for granted. I still feel a prickle of shock whenever I see one in the open.

I get dressed, not bothering to be quiet—five hundred stomping Dauntless can't wake Christina when she's deeply asleep, though an Erudite whisper might be able to. She is odd that way.

I walk outside as the sun peeks through the tree branches, and see a small group of Amity gathered near the orchard. I move closer to see what they are doing.

They stand in a circle, hands clasped. Half of them are in their early teens, and the other half are adults. The oldest one, a woman with braided gray hair, speaks.

"We believe in a God who gives peace and cherishes it," she says. "So we give peace to each other, and cherish it."

I would not hear that as a cue, but the Amity seem to. They all begin to move at once, finding someone across the circle and clasping hands with them. When everyone is paired off, they stand for several seconds, looking at each other. Some of them mutter a phrase, some smile, some remain silent and still. Then they break apart and move to someone else, performing the same series of actions again.

I have never seen an Amity religious ceremony before.

I am only familiar with the religion of my parents' faction, which part of me still holds to and the other rejects as foolishness—the prayers before dinner, the weekly meetings, the acts of service, the poems about a selfless God. This is something different, something mysterious.

"Come and join us," the gray-haired woman says. It takes me a few seconds to realize she's talking to me. She beckons to me, smiling.

"Oh no," I say. "I'm just—"

"Come," she says again, and I feel like I have no choice but to walk forward and stand among them.

She approaches me first, clasping my hand. Her fingers are dry and rough and her eyes seek mine, persistent, though I feel strange meeting her gaze.

Once I do, the effect is immediate and peculiar. I stand still, and every part of me is still, like it weighs more than it used to, only the weight is not unpleasant. Her eyes are brown, the same shade throughout, and unmoving.

"May the peace of God be with you," she says, her voice low, "even in the midst of trouble."

"Why would it?" I say softly, so no one else can hear. "After all I've done . . ."

"It isn't about you," she says. "It is a gift. You cannot earn it, or it ceases to be a gift."

She releases me and moves to someone else, but I stand

with my hand outstretched, alone. Someone moves to take my hand, but I withdraw from the group, first at a walk, and then at a run.

I sprint into the trees as fast as I can, and only when my lungs feel like they are on fire do I stop.

I press my forehead to the nearest tree trunk, though it scrapes my skin, and fight off tears.

+ + +

Later that morning I walk through light rain to the main greenhouse. Johanna has called an emergency meeting.

I stay as hidden as possible at the edge of the room, between two large plants that are suspended in mineral solution. It takes me a few minutes to find Christina, dressed in Amity yellow on the right side of the room, but it is easy to spot Marcus, who stands on the roots of the giant tree with Johanna.

Johanna has her hands clasped in front of her and her hair pulled back. The injury that gave her the scar also damaged her eye—her pupil is so dilated it overwhelms her iris, and her left eye doesn't move with the right one as she scans the Amity in front of her.

But there are not just Amity. There are people with close-cropped hair and tightly twisted buns who must belong to Abnegation, and a few rows of people in glasses who must be Erudite. Cara is among them.

"I have received a message from the city," says Johanna when everyone quiets down. "And I would like to communicate it to you."

She tugs at the hem of her shirt, then clasps her hands in front of her. She seems nervous.

"The Dauntless have allied with the factionless," she says. "They intend to attack Erudite in two days' time. Their battle will be waged not against the Erudite-Dauntless army but against Erudite innocents and the knowledge they have worked so hard to acquire."

She looks down, breathes deeply, and continues: "I know that we recognize no leader, so I have no right to address you as if that is what I am," she says. "But I am hoping that you will forgive me, just this once, for asking if we can reconsider our previous decision to remain uninvolved."

There are murmurs. They are nothing like Dauntless murmurs—they are gentler, like birds launching from branches.

"Our relationship with Erudite notwithstanding, we know better than any faction how essential their role in this society is," she says. "They must be protected from needless slaughter, if not because they are human beings, then because we cannot survive without them. I propose that we enter the city as nonviolent, impartial peacekeepers in order to curb in whatever way possible the extreme violence that will undoubtedly occur. Please discuss this."

Rain dusts the glass panels above our heads. Johanna sits on a tree root to wait, but the Amity do not burst into conversation as they did the last time I was here. Whispers, almost indistinguishable from the rain, turn to normal speech, and I hear some voices lift above others, almost yelling, but not quite.

Every lifted voice sends a jolt through me. I've sat through plenty of arguments in my life, mostly in the last two months, but none of them ever scared me like this. The Amity aren't supposed to argue.

I decide not to wait any longer. I walk along the edge of the meeting area, squeezing past the Amity who are on their feet and hopping over hands and outstretched legs. Some of them stare at me—I may be wearing a red shirt, but the tattoos along my collarbone are clear as ever, even from a distance.

I pause near the row of Erudite. Cara stands when I get close, her arms folded.

"What are you doing here?" she says.

"I came to tell Johanna what was going on," I say. "And to ask you for help."

"Me?" she says. "Why—"

"Not *you*," I say. I try to forget what she said about my nose, but it's hard. "All of you. I have a plan to save some of your faction's data, but I need your help."

"Actually," Christina says, appearing at my left shoulder, "*we* have a plan."

Cara looks from me to Christina and back to me again.

"*You* want to help Erudite?" she says. "I'm confused."

"You wanted to help Dauntless," I say. "You think you're the only one who doesn't just blindly do what your faction tells you to?"

"It is in keeping with your pattern of behavior," says Cara. "Shooting people who get in your way is a Dauntless trait, after all."

I feel a pinch at the back of my throat. She looks so much like her brother, down to the crease between her eyebrows and the dark streaks in her otherwise blond hair.

"Cara," says Christina. "Will you help us, or not?"

Cara sighs. "Obviously I will. I'm sure the others will, too. Meet us in the Erudite dormitory at the end of the meeting, and tell us the plan."

+++

The meeting lasts for another hour. By then the rain has stopped, though water still sprinkles the wall and ceiling panels. Christina and I have been sitting against one of

444

the walls, playing a game in which each of us tries to pin down the other's thumb. She always wins.

Finally Johanna and the others who emerged as discussion leaders stand in a line on the tree roots. Johanna's hair now hangs over her lowered face. She is supposed to tell us the outcome of the conversation, but she just stands with her arms folded, her fingers tapping against her elbow.

"What's going on?" Christina says.

Finally Johanna looks up.

"Obviously it was difficult to find agreement," she says. "But the majority of you wish to uphold our policy of uninvolvement."

It does not matter to me whether the Amity decide to go into the city or not. But I had begun to hope they were not all cowards, and to me, this decision sounds very much like cowardice. I sink back against the window.

"It is not my wish to encourage division in this community, which has given so much to me," says Johanna. "But my conscience forces me to go against this decision. Anyone else whose conscience drives them toward the city is welcome to come with me."

At first I, like everyone else, am not sure what she's saying. Johanna tilts her head so that her scar is again visible, and adds, "I understand if this means I can't be a part of Amity anymore." She sniffs. "But please know that if I have to leave you, I leave you with love, rather than malice."

Johanna bows in the general direction of the crowd, tucks her hair behind her ears, and walks toward the exit. A few of the Amity scramble to their feet, then a few more, and soon the entire crowd is on their feet, and some of them—not many, but some—are walking out behind her.

"That," says Christina, "is not what I was expecting."

CHAPTER
FORTY

THE ERUDITE DORMITORY is one of the larger sleeping rooms in Amity headquarters. There are twelve beds total: a row of eight crammed together along the far wall, and two pressed together on each side, leaving a huge space in the middle of the room. A large table occupies that space, covered with tools and scraps of metal and gears and old computer parts and wires.

Christina and I just finished explaining our plan, which sounded a lot dumber with more than a dozen Erudite staring us down as we talked.

"Your plan is flawed," Cara says. She is the first to respond.

"That's why we came to you," I say. "So you could tell us how to fix it."

"Well, first of all, this important data you want to rescue," she says. "Putting it on a disc is a ridiculous idea. Discs just end up breaking or in the wrong person's hands, like all other physical objects. I suggest you make use of the data network."

"The . . . what?"

She glances at the other Erudite. One of the others—a brown-skinned young man in glasses—says, "Go on. Tell them. There's no reason to keep secrets anymore."

Cara looks back at me. "Many of the computers in the Erudite compound are set up to access data from the computers in other factions. That's how it was so easy for Jeanine to run the attack simulation from a Dauntless computer instead of an Erudite one."

"What?" says Christina. "You mean you can just take a stroll through every faction's data whenever you want?"

"You can't 'take a stroll' through data," the young man says. "That's illogical."

"It's a metaphor," says Christina. She frowns. "Right?"

"A metaphor, or simply a figure of speech?" he says, also frowning. "Or is a metaphor a definite category beneath the heading of 'figure of speech'?"

"Fernando," says Cara. "Focus."

He nods.

"The fact is," Cara continues, "the data network exists,

and that is ethically questionable, but I believe it can work to our advantage here. Just as the computers can access data from other factions, they can *send* data to other factions. If we sent the data you wished to rescue to every other faction, destroying it all would be impossible."

"When you say 'we,'" I say, "are you implying that—"

"That we would be going with you?" she says. "Obviously not all of us would go, but some of us must. How do you expect to navigate Erudite headquarters on your own?"

"You do realize that if you come with us, you might get shot," says Christina. She smiles. "And no hiding behind us because you don't want to break your glasses, or whatever."

Cara removes her glasses and snaps them in half at the bridge.

"We risked our lives by defecting from our faction," says Cara, "and we will risk them again to save our faction from itself."

"Also," pipes up a small voice behind Cara. A girl no older than ten or eleven peers around Cara's elbow. Her black hair is short, like mine, and a halo of frizz surrounds her head. "We have useful gadgets."

Christina and I exchange a look.

I say, "What kinds of gadgets?"

"They're just prototypes," Fernando says, "so there's no need to scrutinize them."

"Scrutiny's not really our thing," says Christina.

"Then how do you make things better?" the little girl asks.

"We don't, really," Christina says, sighing. "They kind of just keep getting worse."

The little girl nods. "Entropy."

"What?"

"Entropy," she chirps. "It's the theory that all matter in the universe is gradually moving toward the same temperature. Also known as 'heat death.'"

"Elia," Cara says, "that is a gross oversimplification."

Elia sticks out her tongue at Cara. I can't help but laugh. I have never seen one of the Erudite stick out her tongue before. But then again, I haven't interacted with many young Erudite. Only Jeanine and the people who work for her. Including my brother.

Fernando crouches next to one of the beds and takes out a box. He digs inside it for a few seconds, then picks up a small, round disc. It is made of a pale metal that I saw often in Erudite headquarters but have never seen anywhere else. He carries it toward me on his palm. When I reach for it, he jerks it away from me.

"Careful!" he says. "I brought this from headquarters. It's not something we invented here. Were you there when they attacked Candor?"

"Yes," I say. "*Right* there."

"Remember when the glass shattered?"

"Were *you* there?" I say, narrowing my eyes.

"No. They recorded it and showed the footage at Erudite headquarters," he says. "Well, it looked like the glass shattered because they shot at it, but that's not really true. One of the Dauntless soldiers tossed one of *these* near the windows. It emits a signal that you can't hear, but that will cause glass to shatter."

"Okay," I say. "And how will that be useful to us?"

"You may find that it's rather distracting for people when all their windows shatter at once," he says with a small smile. "Especially in Erudite headquarters, where there are a lot of windows."

"Right," I say.

"What else have you got?" says Christina.

"The Amity will like this," Cara says. "Where is it? Ah. Here."

She picks up a black box made of plastic, small enough for her to wrap her fingers around it. At the top of the box are two pieces of metal that look like teeth. She flips a switch at the bottom of the box, and a thread of blue light stretches across the gap between the teeth.

"Fernando," says Cara. "Want to demonstrate?"

"Are you joking?" he says, his eyes wide. "I'm never doing that again. You're dangerous with that thing."

Cara grins at him, and explains, "If I touched you with this stunner right now, it would be extremely painful, and then it would disable you. Fernando found that out the hard way yesterday. I made it so that the Amity would have a way of defending themselves without shooting anyone."

"That's . . ." I frown. "Understanding of you."

"Well, technology is supposed to make life better," she says. "No matter what you believe, there's a technology out there for you."

What did my mother say, in that simulation? "I worry that your father's blustering about Erudite has been to your detriment." What if she was right, even if she was just a part of a simulation? My father taught me to see Erudite a particular way. He never taught me that they made no judgments about what people believed, but designed things for them within the confines of those beliefs. He never told me that they could be funny, or that they could critique their own faction from the inside.

Cara lunges toward Fernando with the stunner,

laughing when he jumps back.

He never told me that an Erudite could offer to help me even after I killed her brother.

+ + +

The attack will begin in the afternoon, before it is too dark to see the blue armbands that mark some of the Dauntless as traitors. As soon as our plans are finalized, we walk through the orchard to the clearing where the trucks are kept. When I emerge from the trees, I see that Johanna Reyes is perched on the hood of one of the trucks, the keys dangling from her fingers.

Behind her waits a small convoy of vehicles packed with Amity—but not just Amity, because Abnegation, with their severe hairstyles and still mouths, are among them. Robert, Susan's older brother, is with them.

Johanna hops down from the hood. In the back of the truck she was just sitting on is a stack of crates marked APPLES and FLOUR and CORN. It's a good thing we only have to fit two people in the back.

"Hello, Johanna," says Marcus.

"Marcus," she says. "I hope you don't mind if we accompany you to the city."

"Of course not," he says. "Lead the way."

Johanna gives Marcus the keys and climbs into the

bed of one of the other trucks. Christina starts toward the truck cab, and I go for the truck bed, with Fernando behind me.

"You don't want to sit up front?" says Christina. "And you call yourself a Dauntless. . . ."

"I went for the part of the truck in which I was least likely to vomit," I say.

"Puking is a part of life."

I am about to ask her exactly how often she intends to throw up in the future when the truck surges forward. I grab the side with both hands so that I don't fall out, but after a few minutes, when I get used to the bumping and jostling, I let go. The other trucks trundle along in front of us, behind Johanna's, which leads the way.

I feel calm until we reach the fence. I expect to encounter the same guards who tried to stop us on the way in, but the gate is abandoned, left open. A tremor starts in my chest and spreads to my hands. In the midst of meeting new people and making plans, I forgot that my plan is to walk straight into a battle that could claim my life. Right after I realized that my life was worth living.

The convoy slows down as we pass through the fence, like they expect someone to jump out and stop us. Everything is silent apart from the cicadas in the distant trees and the truck engines.

"Do you think it's already started?" I say to Fernando.

"Perhaps. Perhaps not," he says. "Jeanine has many informants. Someone probably told her that something was going to happen, so she called all the Dauntless forces back to Erudite headquarters."

I nod, but I am really thinking of Caleb. He was one of those informants. I wonder why he believed so strongly that the outside world should be hidden from us that he would betray everyone he supposedly cared about for Jeanine, who cares about no one.

"Did you ever meet someone named Caleb?" I say.

"Caleb," Fernando says. "Yes, there was a Caleb in my initiate class. Brilliant, but he was . . . what's the colloquial term for it? A suck-up." He smirks. "There was a bit of a division between initiates. Those who embraced everything Jeanine said and those who didn't. Obviously I was a member of the latter group. Caleb was a member of the former. Why do you ask?"

"I met him while I was imprisoned," I say, and my voice sounds far away even to me. "I was just curious."

"I wouldn't judge him too harshly," says Fernando. "Jeanine can be extraordinarily persuasive to those who aren't naturally suspicious. I have always been naturally suspicious."

I stare over his left shoulder, at the skyline that gets

clearer the closer we get to the city. I search for the two prongs at the top of the Hub, and when I find them, I feel better and worse at the same time—better, because the building is so familiar, and worse, because seeing the prongs means that we are getting closer.

"Yeah," I say. "So have I."

CHAPTER
FORTY-ONE

BY THE TIME we reach the city, all conversation has halted in the truck, replaced by pressed lips and pale faces. Marcus steers around potholes the size of a person and parts from broken-down buses. The ride is smoother when we get out of factionless territory and into the clean parts of the city.

Then I hear gunshots. From this distance they sound like popping.

For a moment I am disoriented, and all I can see are the leaders of Abnegation on their knees on the pavement and the slack-faced Dauntless with guns in hand; all I can see is my mother turning to embrace the bullets, and Will dropping to the ground. I bite my fist to keep from crying out, and the pain brings me back to the present.

My mother told me to be brave. But if she had known

that her death would make me so afraid, would she have sacrificed herself so willingly?

Breaking away from the convoy of trucks, Marcus turns on Madison Avenue and, when we are just two blocks away from Michigan Avenue, where the fighting is, he pulls the truck into an alley and turns off the engine.

Fernando hops out of the truck bed and offers me his arm.

"Come on, Insurgent," he says with a wink.

"What?" I say. I take his arm and slide down the side of the truck.

He opens the bag he was sitting with. It is full of blue clothes. He sorts through them, tossing garments to Christina and me. I get a bright blue T-shirt and a pair of blue jeans.

"Insurgent," he says. "Noun. A person who acts in opposition to the established authority, who is not necessarily regarded as a belligerent."

"Do you need to give *everything* a name?" says Cara, running her hands over her dull blond hair to tuck the stray pieces back. "We're just doing something and it happens to be in a group. No need for a new title."

"I happen to enjoy categorization," Fernando replies, arching a dark eyebrow.

I look at Fernando. The last time I broke into a faction's

headquarters, I did it with a gun in my hand, and I left bodies behind me. I want this time to be different. I *need* this time to be different. "I like it," I say. "Insurgent. It's perfect."

"See?" Fernando says to Cara. "I'm not the only one."

"Congratulations," she says wryly.

I stare at my Erudite clothes while the others strip off their outer layers of clothing.

"No time for modesty, Stiff!" Christina says, giving me a pointed look.

I know she's right, so I pull off the red shirt I was wearing and put on the blue one instead. I glance at Fernando and Marcus to make sure they aren't watching, and change out of my pants too. I have to roll up the jeans four times, and when I belt them, they bunch at the top like the neck of a crushed paper bag.

"Did she just call you 'Stiff'?" Fernando says.

"Yeah," I say. "I transferred into Dauntless from Abnegation."

"Huh." He frowns. "That's quite a shift. That kind of leap in personality between generations is almost genetically impossible these days."

"Sometimes personality has nothing to do with a person's choice of faction," I say, thinking of my mother. She left Dauntless not because she was ill-suited for it but because it was safer to be Divergent in Abnegation. And then there's Tobias, who switched to Dauntless to escape his father. "There are many factors to consider."

To escape the man I have made my ally. I feel a twinge of guilt.

"Keep talking like that and they'll never discover you're not really Erudite," Fernando says.

I run a comb through my hair to smooth it down and then tuck it behind my ears.

"Here," says Cara. She lifts a piece of hair from my face and pins it back with a silver hair clip, the way Erudite girls do.

Christina takes out the guns we brought with us and looks at me.

"Do you want one?" she says. "Or would you rather carry the stunner?"

I stare at the gun in her hand. If I don't take the stunner, I leave myself completely undefended against people who will gladly shoot me. If I do, I admit to weakness in front of Fernando, Cara, and Marcus.

"You know what Will would say?" says Christina.

"What?" I say, my voice breaking.

"He would tell you to get over it," she says. "To stop being so irrational and take the stupid gun."

Will had little patience for the irrational. Christina

must be right; she knew him better than I did.

And she—who lost someone dear to her that day, just as I did—was able to forgive me, an act that must have been nearly impossible. It would have been impossible for me, if the situation were reversed. So why is it so difficult for me to forgive myself?

I close my hand around the gun Christina offered me. The metal is warm from where she touched it. I feel the memory of shooting him poking at the back of my mind, and try to stifle it. But it won't be stifled. I let go of the gun.

"The stunner is a perfectly good option," Cara says as she plucks a hair from her shirtsleeve. "If you ask me, the Dauntless are too gun-happy anyway."

Fernando offers me the stunner. I wish I could communicate my gratitude to Cara, but she isn't looking at me.

"How am I going to conceal this thing?" I say.

"Don't bother," Fernando says.

"Right."

"We'd better go," says Marcus, glancing at his watch.

My heart beats so hard it marks each second for me, but the rest of me is numb. I can barely feel the ground. I have never been this afraid before, and considering all that I have seen in simulations, and all that I did during the attack simulation, that doesn't make any sense.

Or maybe it does. Whatever the Abnegation were about to show everyone before the attack, it was enough to make Jeanine take drastic and terrible measures to stop them. And now I am about to finish their work, the work my old faction died for. So much more than my life is at stake now.

Christina and I lead the way. We run down the clean, even sidewalks on Madison Avenue, passing State Street, toward Michigan Avenue.

Half a block from Erudite headquarters, I come to a sudden stop.

Standing in four rows in front of us are a group of people, mostly dressed in black and white, spaced two feet apart, guns held up and ready. I blink and they become simulation-controlled Dauntless in the Abnegation sector, during the simulation attack. *Get a grip! Get a grip get a grip get a grip. . . .* I blink again and they are the Candor again—though some of them, dressed all in black, do look like Dauntless. If I'm not careful I'll lose touch with where, and when, I am.

"Oh my God," Christina says. "My sister, my *parents* . . . what if they . . ."

She looks at me, and I think I know her thoughts, because I have experienced them before. *Where are my parents? I have to find them.* But if her parents are like these Candor, simulation controlled and armed, there is nothing she can do for them.

I wonder if Lynn stands in one of these rows, somewhere else.

"What do we do?" Fernando asks.

I step toward the Candor. Maybe they aren't programmed to shoot. I stare into the glazed eyes of a woman in a white blouse and black slacks. She looks like she just came from work. I take another step.

Bang. By instinct I drop to the ground, covering my head with my arms, and scramble backward, toward Fernando's shoes. He helps me to my feet.

"How about let's not do *that*?" he says.

I lean forward—not too far—and peer into the alley between the building next to us and Erudite headquarters. The Candor are in the alley too. I wouldn't be surprised if there was a dense layer of Candor surrounding the entire complex of Erudite buildings.

"Is there any other way to Erudite headquarters?" I say.

"Not that I know of," says Cara. "Unless you want to jump from one roof to another."

She laughs a little as she says it, like it's a joke. I raise my eyebrows at her.

"Wait," she says. "You aren't considering—"

"The roof?" I say. "No. Windows."

I walk to the left, careful not to advance even an inch

toward the Candor. The building on my left overlaps with Erudite headquarters on its far left side. There have to be a few windows that face each other.

Cara mutters something about crazy Dauntless stunts, but runs after me, and Fernando, Marcus, and Christina follow. I try to open the back door of the building, but it's locked.

Christina steps forward and says, "Stand back." She points her gun at the lock. I shield my face with an arm as she fires. We hear a loud bang, and then a high ringing, the aftereffects of firing a gun in such a close space. The lock is broken.

I pull the door open and walk inside. A long hallway with a tile floor greets me, doors on either side, some open, some closed. When I look into the open rooms, I see rows of old desks, and chalkboards on the walls like the ones in Dauntless headquarters. The air smells musty, like the pages of a library book mixed with cleaning solution.

"This used to be a commercial building," says Fernando, "but Erudite converted it into a school, for post-Choosing education. After the major renovations in Erudite headquarters about a decade ago—you know, when all the buildings across from Millennium were connected?—they stopped teaching there. Too old, hard to update."

"Thanks for the history lesson," says Christina.

When I reach the end of the hallway, I walk into one of the classrooms to see where I am. I see the back of Erudite headquarters, but there are no windows across the alley at street level.

Right outside the window, so close I could touch her if I stretched my hand through the window, is a Candor child, a girl, holding a gun that is as long as her forearm. She stands so still I wonder if she is even breathing.

I crane my neck to see the windows above street level. Over my head in the school building there are plenty of windows. At the back of Erudite headquarters, there is only one that lines up. And it's on the third story.

"Good news," I say. "I found a way across."

CHAPTER
FORTY-TWO

EVERYONE SPREADS THROUGHOUT the building in search of
janitor's closets, per my instruction to find a ladder. I hear
sneakers squeaking on the tile and shouts of "I found
one—no, wait, it's just got buckets in it, never mind" and
"How long does the ladder have to be? A stepladder won't
work, right?"

While they search, I find the third-floor classroom
that looks into the Erudite window. It takes me three tries
to open the right window.

I lean out, over the alley, and shout, "Hey!" Then I duck
as fast as I can. But I don't hear gunshots—*Good,* I think.
They don't respond to noise.

Christina marches into the classroom with a ladder
under her arm, the others behind her. "Got one! I think

it'll be long enough once we stretch it out."

She tries to turn too soon, and the ladder smacks into Fernando's shoulder.

"Oh! Sorry, Nando."

The jolt knocked his glasses askew. He smiles at Christina and takes the glasses off, shoving them into his pocket.

"Nando?" I say to him. "I thought the Erudite didn't like nicknames?"

"When a pretty girl calls you by a nickname," he says, "it is only logical to respond to it."

Christina looks away, and at first I think she is bashful, but then I see her face contort like he slapped her instead of complimented her. It is too soon after Will's death for her to be flirted with.

I help her guide the end of the ladder through the classroom window and across the gap between buildings. Marcus helps us steady it. Fernando whoops when the ladder hits the Erudite window across the alley.

"Time to break the glass," I say.

Fernando takes the glass-breaking device from his pocket and offers it to me. "You probably have the best aim."

"I wouldn't count on it," I say. "My right arm is out of commission. I'd have to throw with my left."

"I'll do it," says Christina.

She presses the button on the side of the device and tosses it across the alley, underhand. I clench my hands as I wait for it to land. It bounces onto the windowsill and rolls into the glass. An orange light flashes, and all at once the window—and the windows above, below, and next to it—shatters into hundreds of tiny pebbles that shower over the Candor below.

At the same time, the Candor twist and fire up into the sky. Everyone else drops to the ground, but I stay on my feet, part of me marveling at the perfect synchronicity of it, and the other part disgusted at how Jeanine Matthews has turned yet another faction from human beings into parts of a machine. None of the bullets even hit the classroom windows, let alone penetrate the room.

When the Candor do not fire another round, I peer down at them. They have returned to their original position, half facing Madison Avenue and half facing Washington Street.

"They respond to movement only, so . . . don't fall off the ladder," I say. "Whoever goes first will secure the ladder on the other side."

I notice that Marcus, who is supposed to selflessly offer himself up for every task, does not volunteer.

"Not feeling very Stiff today, Marcus?" says Christina.

"If I were you, I would be careful who you insult," he says. "I am still the only person here who can find what we're looking for."

"Is that a *threat*?"

"I'll go," I say, before Marcus can answer. "I'm part Stiff too, right?"

I shove the stunner under the waistband of my jeans and climb onto a desk to get a better angle on the window. Christina holds the ladder from the side as I clamber on top of it and start forward.

Once I'm through the window, I position my feet on the narrow edges of the ladder and my hands on the rungs. The ladder feels about as solid and stable as an aluminum can. It creaks and sags beneath my weight. I try not to look down at the Candor; try not to think about their guns lifting and firing at me.

Taking quick breaths, I stare at my destination, the Erudite window. Just a few rungs left.

A breeze blows through the alley, pushing me to one side, and I think of scaling the Ferris wheel with Tobias. He kept me steady then. There is no one left to keep me steady now.

I catch a glimpse of the ground, three stories down, the bricks smaller than they should be, the lines of Candor Jeanine enslaved. My arms—especially my right arm—ache as I inch my way across the gap.

The ladder shifts, moving closer to the edge of the window frame on the other side. Christina is holding one side steady, but she can't keep the ladder from slipping off the other windowsill. I grit my teeth and try not to move it too much, but I can't move both legs at the same time. I have to let the ladder sway a little. Just four more rungs to go.

The ladder jerks to the left, and then, as I move my right foot forward, I miss the edge of the rung.

I yell as my body shifts to the side, my arms wrapping around the ladder and my leg dangling in space.

"Are you okay?" Christina calls from behind me.

I don't answer. I bring my leg up and wedge it beneath my body. My fall made the ladder slip even farther off the windowsill. It is now supported by just a millimeter of concrete.

I decide to move fast. I lurch toward the opposite windowsill just as the ladder slips off. My hands catch the sill and concrete scrapes my fingertips as they bear my body weight. Several voices behind me scream.

I grit my teeth as I pull myself up, my right shoulder shrieking with pain. I kick at the brick building, hoping it will give me traction, but it doesn't help. I scream into my teeth as I pull myself up and over the windowsill, half my body in the building and the other half still dangling. Thankfully Christina didn't let the ladder drop too far. None of the Candor shoot me.

I pull myself into the Erudite room across the alley. It is a bathroom. I collapse to the floor on my left shoulder, and try to breathe through the pain. Sweat trickles down my forehead.

An Erudite woman comes out of a stall, and I scramble to my feet, draw the stunner, and point it at her, all without thinking.

She freezes, her arms up, toilet paper stuck to her shoe.

"Don't shoot!" Her eyes bulge from her head.

I remember, then, that I am dressed like the Erudite. I set the stunner on the edge of a sink.

"My apologies," I say. I try to adopt the formal speech common to the Erudite. "I am slightly edgy, with everything that's occurring. We are reentering in order to retrieve some of our test results from . . . Laboratory 4-A."

"Oh," the woman says. "That seems rather unwise."

"The data is of the utmost importance," I say, trying to sound as arrogant as some of the Erudite I've met. "I would rather not leave it to get riddled with bullets."

"It's hardly my place to prevent you from trying to recover it," she says. "Now if you'll excuse me, I'm going to wash my hands and take cover."

"Sounds good," I say. I decide not to tell her she has toilet paper on her shoe.

I turn back to the window. Across the alley, Christina and Fernando are trying to lift the ladder back onto the windowsill. Though my arms and hands ache, I lean out the window and grab the other end of the ladder, lifting it back onto the windowsill. Then I hold it in place as Christina crawls across.

This time the ladder is more stable, and Christina makes it across the gap without trouble. She takes my place holding it as I shove the trash can in front of the door so no one else can come in. I then run my fingers under cool water to soothe them.

"This is pretty smart, Tris," she says.

"You don't have to sound so surprised."

"It's just . . ." She pauses. "You had aptitude for Erudite, didn't you?"

"Does it matter?" I say too sharply. "The factions are destroyed, and it was all stupid to begin with."

I have never said anything like that before. I have never even thought it. But I'm surprised to find that I believe it—surprised to find that I agree with Tobias.

"I wasn't trying to insult you," says Christina. "Having aptitude for Erudite isn't a bad thing. Especially right now."

"Sorry. I'm just . . . tense. That's all."

Marcus comes through the window and drops to the tile floor. Cara is surprisingly nimble—she moves over the rungs like she's plucking banjo strings, touching each one only briefly before she moves to the next one.

Fernando will be last, and he will be in the same position I was in, with the ladder secured from only one side. I move closer to the window so I can tell him to stop if I see the ladder slip.

Fernando, who I didn't think would have trouble, moves more awkwardly than anyone else. He has probably spent his entire life behind a computer or a book. He shuffles forward, his face bright red, and holds the rungs so tightly that his hands turn blotchy and purple.

Halfway across the alley, I see something slip out of his pocket. It is his spectacles.

I scream, "Fernan—"

But I am too late.

The spectacles fall, hit the edge of the ladder, and topple to the pavement.

In a wave, the Candor below twist and fire upward. Fernando yells, and collapses against the ladder. One bullet hit his leg. I didn't see where the others went, but I know when I see blood drip between the rungs of the ladder that it was not a good place.

Fernando stares at Christina, his face ashen. Christina surges forward, through the window, about to reach for him.

"Don't be an idiot!" he says, his voice weak. "Leave me."

It is the last thing he says.

CHAPTER
FORTY-THREE

CHRISTINA STEPS BACK into the room. We are all still.

"I don't mean to be insensitive," says Marcus, "but we have to go before the Dauntless and factionless enter this building. If they haven't already."

I hear tapping against the window and jerk my head to the side, for a split second believing that it is Fernando, trying to get in. But it's just rain.

We follow Cara out of the bathroom. She is our leader now. She knows Erudite headquarters best. Christina follows, then Marcus, then me. We leave the bathroom, and we are in an Erudite hallway like every other Erudite hallway: pale, bright, sterile.

But this hallway is more active than I have ever seen it. People in Erudite blue sprint back and forth, in groups and alone, shouting things at each other like, "They're at the front doors! Go as high as you can!" and "They've disabled the elevators! Run for the stairs!" It's only there, in the midst of chaos, that I realize I forgot the stunner in the bathroom. I am unarmed again.

Dauntless traitors also run past us, though they are less frantic than the Erudite. I wonder what Johanna, the Amity, and the Abnegation are doing in this chaos. Are they tending to the wounded? Or are they standing between Dauntless guns and Erudite innocents, taking bullets for the sake of peace?

I shudder. Cara leads us to a back staircase, and we join a group of terrified Erudite as we run up one, two, three flights of stairs. Then Cara shoves her shoulder into a door next to the landing, holding her gun close to her chest.

I recognize this floor.

It is my floor.

My thoughts become sluggish. I almost died here. I craved death here.

I slow down and fall behind. I can't break out of the daze, though people keep rushing past me, and Marcus shouts something at me, but his voice is muffled. Christina doubles back and grabs me, dragging me toward Control-A.

Inside the control room, I see rows of computers but I don't really see them; there is a film covering my eyes. I try to blink it away. Marcus sits at one of the computers, and Cara sits at another. They will send all the data from the Erudite computers to the other faction computers.

Behind me, the door opens.

And I hear Caleb say, "What are you doing here?"

+ + +

His voice wakes me. I turn and stare right at his gun.

His eyes are my mother's eyes—a dull green, almost gray, though his blue shirt makes their color appear more potent.

"Caleb," I say. "What do you think you're doing?"

"I'm here to stop whatever you're doing!" His voice trembles. The gun wavers in his hands.

"We're here to save the Erudite data that the faction-less want to destroy," I say. "I don't think you want to stop us."

"That's not true," he says. He jerks his head toward Marcus. "Why would you bring him if you weren't trying to find something else? Something more important to him than all the Erudite data combined?"

"She told *you* about it?" Marcus says. "*You*, a child?"

"She didn't tell me at first," Caleb says. "But she didn't want me to choose a side without knowing the facts!"

"The facts," says Marcus, "are that she is terrified of

reality, and the Abnegation were not. Are not. And neither is your sister. To her credit."

I scowl. Even when he is complimenting me, I want to smack him.

"My sister," says Caleb gently, looking at me again, "doesn't know what she's getting into. Doesn't know what it is that you want to show everyone . . . doesn't know it will ruin *everything*!"

"We are here to serve a purpose!" Marcus is almost yelling now. "We have completed our mission, and it is time for us to do what we were sent here to do!"

I don't know the purpose or the mission that Marcus is referring to, but Caleb doesn't look confused.

"*We* were not sent here," Caleb says. "We have no responsibility to anyone but ourselves."

"That kind of self-interested thinking is what I have come to expect from those who have spent too much time with Jeanine Matthews. You are so unwilling to relinquish your comfort that your selfishness drains you of humanity!"

I don't care to hear more. While Caleb stares down Marcus, I turn and kick hard at Caleb's wrist. The impact shocks him, and his gun topples from his hands. I slide it across the floor with my toes.

"You need to trust me, Beatrice," he says, chin wobbling.

"After you helped her torture me? After you let her almost *kill* me?"

"I didn't help her tort—"

"You certainly didn't stop her! You were right there, and you just *watched*—"

"What could I have done? What—"

"You could have *tried*, you coward!" I scream so loud my face gets hot and tears jump into my eyes. "Tried, and failed, because you love me!"

I gasp, just to take in enough air. All I hear is the click of keys as Cara works on the task at hand. Caleb doesn't seem to have a response. His pleading look slowly disappears, replaced by a blank stare.

"You won't find what you're looking for here," he says. "She wouldn't keep such important files on public computers. That would be illogical."

"So she hasn't destroyed it?" Marcus says.

Caleb shakes his head. "She does not believe in the destruction of information. Only its containment."

"Well, thank God for that," says Marcus. "Where is she keeping it?"

"I'm not going to tell you," Caleb says.

"I think I know," I say. Caleb said she wouldn't keep

the information on a public computer. So he must mean she is keeping it on a private one: either the one in her office or the one in the laboratory Tori told me about.

Caleb doesn't look at me.

Marcus picks up Caleb's revolver and turns it in his hand so the butt of the gun protrudes from his fist. Then he swings, striking Caleb under the jaw. Caleb's eyes roll back, and he falls to the floor.

I don't want to know how Marcus perfected that maneuver.

"We can't have him running off to tell someone what we're doing," says Marcus. "Let's go. Cara can take care of the rest, right?"

Cara nods without looking up from her computer. A sick feeling in my stomach, I follow Marcus and Christina out of the control room and toward the stairs.

+ + +

The hallway outside is now empty. There are scraps of paper and footprints on the tile. Marcus, Christina, and I jog in a line to the stairwell. I stare at the back of his head, where the shape of his skull shows through his buzzed hair.

All I can see when I look at him is a belt swinging toward Tobias, and the butt of a gun slamming into

Caleb's jaw. I don't care that he hurt Caleb—I would have done it, too—but that he is simultaneously a man who knows how to hurt people and a man who parades around as the self-effacing leader of Abnegation, suddenly makes me so angry I can't see straight.

Especially because I chose him. I chose *him* over Tobias.

"Your brother is a traitor," says Marcus as we turn a corner. "He deserved worse. There's no need to look at me that way."

"Shut up!" I shout, shoving him hard into the wall. He is too surprised to push back. "I hate you, you know that! I hate you for what you did to him, and I am *not* talking about Caleb." I lean close to his face and whisper, "And while I may not shoot you myself, I will definitely not help you if someone tries to kill you, so you'd better hope to God we don't get into that situation."

He stares at me, apparently indifferent. I release him and start toward the stairs again, Christina on my heels, Marcus a few steps behind.

"Where are we going?" she says.

"Caleb said what we're looking for won't be on a public computer, so it has to be on a private one. As far as I know, Jeanine only has two private computers, one in her office, and one in her laboratory," I say.

"So which one do we go to?"

"Tori told me there were insane security measures protecting Jeanine's laboratory," I say. "And I've been to her office; it's just another room."

"So . . . laboratory, then."

"Top floor."

We reach the door to the stairwell, and when I throw it open, a group of Erudite, including children, are sprinting down the stairs. I cling to the railing and force my way through them with my elbow, not looking at their faces, like they are not human, just a wall of mass to push aside.

I expect the stream to stop, but more come from the next landing, a steady flow of blue-clad people in dim blue light, the whites of their eyes bright as lamps by contrast to everything else. Their terrified sobs echo in the cement chamber a hundred times, the shrieks of the demons with glowing eyes.

When we reach the seventh-floor landing, the crowd thins, and then disappears. I run my hands along my arms to get rid of the ghosts of hair, sleeves, and skin that brushed against me on the way up. I can see the top of the stairs from where we stand.

I also see the body of a guard, his arm dangling over the edge of a stair, and standing over him, a factionless man with an eye patch.

Edward.

+ + +

"Look who it is," Edward says. He stands at the top of a short flight, only seven steps long, and I stand at the bottom. The Dauntless traitor guard lies between us, his eyes glazed, a dark patch on his chest from where someone—Edward, probably—shot him.

"That's a strange outfit for someone who is supposed to despise Erudite," he says. "I thought you were supposed to be at home, waiting for your boyfriend to come back a hero?"

"As you may have gathered," I say, walking up a step, "that was never going to happen."

The blue light casts shadows into the faint hollows beneath Edward's cheekbones. He reaches behind him.

If he is here, that means Tori is already up here. Which means that Jeanine might already be dead.

I feel Christina close behind me; I hear her breaths.

"We are going to get past you," I say, walking up another step.

"I doubt that," he replies. He grabs his gun. I launch myself forward, over the fallen guard. He fires, but my hands are wrapped around his wrist, so he doesn't fire straight.

My ears ring, and my feet scramble for stability on the dead guard's back.

Christina punches over my head. Her knuckles connect with Edward's nose. I can't balance on top of the body; I fall to my knees, digging my fingernails into his wrist. He wrenches me to the side and fires again, hitting Christina in the leg.

Gasping, Christina draws her gun and shoots. The bullet hits him in the side. Edward screams and drops the gun, pitching forward. He falls on top of me, and I smack my head against one of the cement steps. The dead guard's arm is jammed into my spine.

Marcus picks up Edward's gun and trains it on both of us.

"Get up, Tris," he says. And to Edward: "You. Don't move."

My hand searches for the corner of a step, and I squeeze from between Edward and the dead guard. Edward pushes himself to a sitting position on top of the guard—like he's some kind of *cushion*—clutching his side with both hands.

"You okay?" I ask Christina.

Her face contorts. "*Ahh.* Yeah. It hit the side, not the bone."

I reach for her, to help her up.

"Beatrice," Marcus says. "We have to leave her."

"What do you mean *leave*?" I demand. "We can't leave! Something terrible could happen!"

Marcus presses his index finger to my sternum, in the gap between my collarbones, and leans over me.

"Listen to me," he says. "Jeanine Matthews will have retreated to her laboratory at the first sign of attack, because it is the safest room in this building. And at any moment, she will decide that Erudite is lost and it is better to delete the data than risk anyone else finding it, and this mission of ours will be useless."

And I will have lost everyone: my parents, Caleb, and finally, Tobias, who will never forgive me for working with his father, especially if I have no way to prove that it was worthwhile.

"We are going to leave your friend here." His breath smells stale. "And move on, unless you would rather me go on alone."

"He's right," says Christina. "There's no time. I'll stay here and keep Ed from coming after you."

I nod. Marcus removes his finger, leaving an aching circle behind. I rub the pain away and open the door at the top of the landing. I look back before I walk through it, and Christina gives me a pained smile, her hand pressed to her thigh.

CHAPTER
FORTY-FOUR

THE NEXT ROOM is more like a hallway: it is wide, but not deep, with blue tile, blue walls, and a blue ceiling, all the same shade. Everything glows, but I can't tell where the light is coming from.

At first I don't see any doors, but once my eyes adjust to the shock of color, I see a rectangle in the wall to my left, and another one in the wall to my right. Just two doors.

"We have to split up," I say. "We don't have time to try each one together."

"Which one do you want?" Marcus says.

"Right," I say. "Wait, no. Left."

"Fine. I will go right."

"If I'm the one who finds the computer," I say, "what should I look for?"

"If you find the computer, you will find Jeanine. I assume you know a few ways to coerce her into doing what you want. She is not, after all, accustomed to pain," he says.

I nod. We walk at the same pace toward our respective doors. A moment ago I would have said that separating from Marcus would be a relief. But going on alone is its own burden. What if I can't get through the security measures Jeanine undoubtedly has in place to keep out intruders? What if, if I somehow manage to get through them, I can't find the right file?

I put my hand on the door handle. There doesn't seem to be a lock. When Tori said there were insane security measures, I thought she meant eye scanners and passwords and locks, but so far, everything has been open.

Why does that worry me?

I open my door, and Marcus opens his. We share a look. I walk into the next room.

+++

The room, like the hallway outside, is blue, though here it is clear where the light is coming from. It glows from the center of every panel, ceiling, floor, and walls.

Once the door closes behind me, I hear a thud like a dead bolt shifting into place. I grab the door handle again and push down as hard as I can, but it doesn't budge. I am trapped.

Small, piercing lights come at me from all angles. My eyelids aren't enough to block them, so I have to press my palms over my eye sockets.

I hear a calm, feminine voice:

"Beatrice Prior, second generation. Faction of origin: Abnegation. Selected faction: Dauntless. Confirmed Divergent."

How does this room know who I am?

And what does "second generation" mean?

"Status: Intruder."

I hear a click, and pull my fingers apart just enough to see if the lights are gone. They aren't, but fixtures in the ceiling spray tinted vapor. Instinctively I clap my hand over my mouth. In seconds I stare through a blue fog. And then I stare at nothing.

I now stand in darkness so complete that when I hold my hand in front of my nose, I can't even see its silhouette. I should walk forward and search for a door on the other side of the room, but I am afraid to move—who knows what would happen to me here if I did?

Then the lights lift, and I stand in the Dauntless training room, in the circle in which we used to spar. I have so many mixed memories of this circle, some triumphant, like beating Molly, and some haunting—Peter punching me until I fell unconscious. I sniff, and the air smells the same, like sweat and dust.

Across the circle is a blue door that doesn't belong there. I frown at it.

"Intruder," the voice says, and now it sounds like Jeanine, but that could be my imagination. "You have five minutes to reach the blue door before the poison will kick in."

"*What?*"

But I know what she said. Poison. Five minutes. I shouldn't be surprised; this is Jeanine's work, just as empty of conscience as she is. My body shudders, and I wonder if that is the poison, if the poison is already shutting down my brain.

Focus. I can't get out; I have to move forward, or . . .

Or nothing. I have to move forward.

I start toward the door, and someone appears in my path. She is short, thin, and blond, with dark circles under her eyes. She is me.

A reflection? I wave at her to see if she will mirror me. She doesn't.

"Hello," I say. She doesn't answer. I didn't really think she would.

What is this? I swallow hard to pop my ears, which feel

like they are stuffed with cotton. If Jeanine designed this, it is probably a test of intelligence or logic, which means I will have to think clearly, which means I will have to calm down. I clasp my hands over my chest and press down, hoping the pressure will make me feel safe, like an embrace.

It doesn't.

I step to the right to get a better angle on the door, and my double hops to the side, her shoes scraping the dirt, to block my way again.

I think I know what will happen if I start toward the door, but I have to try. I break into a run, intending to swerve around her, but she is ready for me: she grabs my wounded shoulder and wrenches me to the side. I scream so loud it scrapes my throat; I feel like knives are stabbing deeper and deeper into my right side. As I begin to sink to my knees, she kicks me in the stomach and I sprawl across the floor, inhaling dust.

That, I realize as I clutch my stomach, is exactly what I would have done if I had been in her position. Which means that in order to defeat her, I have to think of a way to defeat myself. And how can I be a better fighter than myself, if she knows the same strategies I know, and is exactly as resourceful and clever as I am?

She starts toward me again, so I scramble to my feet

and try to put aside the pain in my shoulder. My heart beats faster. I want to punch her, but she gets there first. I duck at the last second, and her fist hits my ear, knocking me off balance.

I back up a few steps, hoping that she won't pursue me, but she does. She comes at me again, this time seizing my shoulders and pulling me down, toward her bent knee.

I put my hands up, between my stomach and her knee, and push as hard as I can. She was not expecting that; she stumbles back, but doesn't fall.

I run at her, and as the desire to kick her slips into my mind, I realize that it is also *her* desire. I twist away from her foot.

The second I want something, she also wants it. She and I can only be, at best, at a standstill—but I need to *beat* her to get through the door. To survive.

I try to think it through, but she is coming at me again, her forehead tightened into a scowl of concentration. She grabs my arm, and I grab hers, so that we are clutched forearm to forearm.

At the same time, we yank our elbows back and thrust them forward. I lean in at the last second, and my elbow smashes into her teeth.

Both of us cry out. Blood spills over her lip, and runs down my forearm. She grits her teeth and yells, diving at me, stronger than I anticipated.

Her weight knocks me down. She pins me to the floor with her knees and tries to punch my face, but I cross my arms in front of me. Her fists hit my arms instead, each one like a stone striking my skin.

With a heavy exhale, I grab at one of her wrists, and I notice that spots are dancing at the corners of my eyes. *Poison.*

Focus.

As she struggles to free herself, I bring my knee up to my chest. Then I push her back, grunting with effort, until I can press my foot to her stomach. I kick her, my face boiling hot.

The logical puzzle: In a fight between two perfect equals, how can one win?

The answer: One can't.

She pushes herself to her feet and wipes the blood from her lip.

Therefore: we must not be perfectly equal. So what is different about us?

She walks toward me again, but I need more time to think, so for every step she takes forward, I take back. The room sways, and then twists, and I lurch to the side, brushing my fingertips on the ground to steady myself.

What is different about us? We have the same mass,

skill level, patterns of thinking . . .

I see the door over her shoulder, and I realize: We have different goals. I *have* to get through that door. She has to protect it. But even in a simulation, there is no way she is as desperate as I am.

I sprint toward the edge of the circle, where there is a table. A moment ago, it was empty, but I know the rules of simulations and how to control them. A gun appears on it as soon as I think it.

I slam into the table, the spots crowding my view of it. I don't even feel pain when I collide with it. I feel my heartbeat in my face, like my heart has detached from its moorings in my chest and begun to migrate to my brain.

Across the room, a gun appears on the ground before my double. We both reach for our weapons.

I feel the weight of the gun, and its smoothness, and I forget about her; I forget about the poison; I forget about everything.

My throat constricts, and I feel like there is a hand around it, tightening. My head throbs from the sudden loss of air, and I feel my heartbeat everywhere, everywhere.

Across the room, it's no longer my double who stands between me and my goal; it's Will. *No, no.* It can't be Will. I force myself to breathe in. The poison is cutting off oxygen to my brain. He is just a hallucination within a simulation. I exhale in a sob.

For a moment I see my double again, holding the gun but visibly shuddering, the weapon as far out from her body as she can possibly hold it. She is as weak as I am. No, not as weak, because she is not going blind and losing air, but almost as weak, almost.

Then Will is back, his eyes simulation-dead, his hair a yellow halo around his head. Brick buildings loom from each side, but behind him is the door, the door that separates me from my father and brother.

No, no, it is the door that separates me from Jeanine and my goal.

I have to get through that door. I *have to.*

I lift the gun, though it hurts my shoulder to do it, and wrap one hand around the other to steady it.

"I . . ." I choke, and tears smear my cheeks, run into my mouth. I taste salt. "I'm sorry."

And I do the one thing my double is unable to do, because she is not desperate enough:

I fire.

CHAPTER
FORTY-FIVE

I DON'T SEE him die again.

I close my eyes at the moment the trigger presses back, and when I open them, it is the other Tris who lies on the ground between the dark patches in my vision; it is me.

I drop the gun and sprint toward the door, almost tripping over her. I throw my body against the door, twist the handle, and fall through. My hands numb, I press it closed behind me, and shake them to regain feeling.

The next room is twice as big as the first one, and it, too, is blue-lit, but paler. A large table stands in the middle, and taped to the walls are photographs, diagrams, and lists.

I take deep breaths, and my vision begins to clear, my heart rate returning to normal. Among the photographs on the walls, I recognize my own face, and Tobias's, and Marcus's, and Uriah's. A long list of what appear to be chemicals is posted on the wall beside our pictures. Each one is crossed out with red marker. This must be where Jeanine develops the simulation serums.

I hear voices somewhere ahead of me, and scold myself. *What are you doing? Hurry!*

"My brother's name," I hear. "I want to hear you say it." Tori's voice.

How did she get through that simulation? Is she Divergent too?

"I didn't kill him." Jeanine's voice.

"Do you think that exonerates you? Do you think that means you don't deserve to die?"

Tori is not screaming, but wailing, the whole of her grief escaping through her mouth. I start toward the door. Too quickly, though, because my hip slams into the corner of the table in the middle of the room, and I have to stop, wincing.

"The reasons for my actions are beyond your understanding," Jeanine says. "I was willing to make a sacrifice for the greater good, something you have never understood, not even when we were classmates!"

I limp toward the door, which is a pane of frosted glass. It slides back to admit me, and I see Jeanine, pressed against a wall, with Tori standing a few feet away, her gun high.

Behind them is a glass table with a silver box on it—a computer—and a keyboard. The entire far wall is covered with a computer screen.

Jeanine stares at me, but Tori doesn't move an inch; doesn't seem to hear me. Her face is red and tear-streaked, her hand shaking.

I have no confidence that I can find the video file on my own. If Jeanine is here, I can get her to find it for me, but if she's dead . . .

"No!" I scream. "Tori, don't!"

But her finger is already over the trigger. I launch myself at her as hard as I can, my arms slamming into her side. The gun goes off, and I hear a scream.

My head hits the tile. I ignore the stars in my eyes and throw myself across Tori. I shove the gun forward and it slides away from us.

Why didn't you grab it, you idiot?!

Tori's fist connects with the side of my throat. I choke, and she uses the opportunity to throw me off, to crawl toward the gun.

Jeanine is slumped against the wall, blood soaking her leg. *Leg!* I remember, and punch Tori hard near the bullet wound in her thigh. She yells, and I find my feet.

I step toward the fallen weapon, but Tori is too quick. She wraps her arms around my legs and pulls them out from under me. My knees slam into the ground, but I am still above her; I punch down, at her rib cage.

She groans, but it doesn't stop her; as I drag myself toward the gun, she sinks her teeth into my hand. It is a different pain than any blow I've ever received, different even from a bullet wound. I scream louder than I thought possible, tears blurring my vision.

I have not come this far to let Tori shoot Jeanine before I've gotten what I need.

I yank my hand from between her teeth, my vision going black at the edges, and with a lurch, smack my hand around the handle of the gun. I twist, and point it at Tori.

My hand. My hand is covered in blood, and so is Tori's chin. I hide my hand from view so that it's easier to ignore the pain and get up, still pointing the gun at her.

"I didn't take you for a traitor, Tris," she says, and it sounds like a snarl, not a sound any human can make.

"I'm not," I say. I blink the tears down my cheeks so that I can see her better. "I can't explain it right now, but . . . all I'm asking is for you to trust me, please. There's something important, something only she knows the location of—"

"That's right!" says Jeanine. "It is on *that* computer,

Beatrice, and only I can locate it. If you don't help me survive this, it will die with me."

"She is a liar," says Tori. "A *liar*, and if you believe her, you are both an idiot and a traitor, Tris!"

"I do believe her," I say. "I believe her because it makes perfect sense! The most sensitive information that exists and it's hidden on *that computer*, Tori!" I take a deep breath, and lower my voice. "Please listen to me. I hate her as much as you do. I have no reason to defend her. I'm telling you the truth. This is important."

Tori is silent. I think, for a moment, that I've won, that I've persuaded her. But then she says, "Nothing is more important than her death."

"If that's what you insist upon believing," I say, "I can't help you. But I'm also not going to let you kill her."

Tori pushes herself to her knees, and wipes my blood from her chin. She looks up into my eyes.

"I am a Dauntless leader," she says. "You don't get to decide what I do."

And before I can think—

Before I can even think about firing the gun I'm holding—

She draws a long knife from the side of her boot, lunges, and stabs Jeanine in the stomach.

I yell. Jeanine releases a horrible sound—a gurgling,

screaming, dying sound. I see Tori's gritted teeth, I hear her murmur her brother's name—"Jonathan Wu"—and then I watch the knife go in again.

And Jeanine's eyes turn into glass.

CHAPTER
FORTY-SIX

TORI STANDS, A wild look in her eyes, and turns toward me.

I feel numb.

All the risks I took to get here—conspiring with Marcus, asking the Erudite for help, crawling across a ladder three stories up, shooting myself in a simulation—and all the sacrifices I made—my relationship with Tobias, Fernando's life, my standing among the Dauntless—were for nothing.

Nothing.

A moment later, the glass door opens again. Tobias and Uriah storm in as if to fight a battle—Uriah coughing, probably from the poison—but the battle is done. Jeanine is dead, Tori is triumphant, and I am a Dauntless traitor.

Tobias stops in the middle of a step, almost stumbling

over his feet, when he sees me. His eyes open wider.

"She is a traitor," says Tori. "She just almost shot me to defend Jeanine."

"What?" says Uriah. "Tris, what's going on? Is she right? Why are you even here?"

But I look only at Tobias. A sliver of hope pierces me, strangely painful, when combined with the guilt I feel for how I deceived him. Tobias is stubborn and proud, but he is mine—maybe he will listen, maybe there's a chance that all I did was not in vain—

"You know why I'm here," I say quietly. "Don't you?"

I hold out Tori's gun. He walks forward, a little unsteady on his feet, and takes it.

"We found Marcus in the next room, caught in a simulation," Tobias says. "You came up here with him."

"Yes, I did," I say, blood from Tori's bite trickling down my arm.

"I trusted you," he says, his body shaking with rage. "I *trusted* you and you abandoned me to work with *him*?"

"No." I shake my head. "He told me something, and everything my brother said, everything Jeanine said while I was in Erudite headquarters, fit perfectly with what he told me. And I wanted—I *needed* to know the truth."

"The truth." He snorts. "You think you learned the

truth from a liar, a traitor, and a sociopath?"

"The truth?" says Tori. "What are you talking about?"

Tobias and I stare at each other. His blue eyes, usually so thoughtful, are now hard and critical, like they are peeling back layer after layer of me and searching each one.

"I think," I say. I have to pause and take a breath, because I have not convinced him; I have failed, and this is probably the last thing they will let me say before they arrest me.

"I think that *you* are the liar!" I say, my voice quaking. "You tell me you love me, you trust me, you think I'm more perceptive than the average person. And the first second that belief in my perceptiveness, that trust, that *love* is put to the test, it all falls apart." I am crying now, but I am not ashamed of the tears shining on my cheeks or the thickness of my voice. "So you must have lied when you told me all those things . . . you must have, because I can't believe your love is really that feeble."

I step closer to him, so that there are only inches between us, and none of the others can hear me.

"I am still the person who would have died rather than kill you," I say, remembering the attack simulation and the feel of his heartbeat under my hand. "I am exactly who you think I am. And right now, I'm telling you that I know . . . I *know* this information will change everything. Everything we have done, and everything we are about to do."

I stare at him like I can communicate the truth with my eyes, but that is impossible. He looks away, and I'm not sure he even heard what I said.

"Enough of this," says Tori. "Take her downstairs. She will be tried along with all the other war criminals."

Tobias doesn't move. Uriah takes my arm and leads me away from him, through the laboratory, through the room of light, through the blue hallway. Therese of the faction-less joins us there, eyeing me curiously.

Once we're in the stairwell, I feel something nudge my side. When I look back, I see a wad of gauze in Uriah's hand. I take it, trying to give him a grateful smile and failing.

As we descend the stairs, I wrap the gauze tightly around my hand, sidestepping bodies without looking at their faces. Uriah takes my elbow to keep me from falling. The gauze wrapping doesn't help with the pain of the bite, but it makes me feel a little better, and so does the fact that Uriah, at least, doesn't seem to hate me.

For the first time the Dauntless's disregard for age does not seem like an opportunity. It seems like the thing that will condemn me. They will not say, *But she's young; she must have been confused.* They will say, *She is an adult, and she made her choice.*

Of course, I agree with them. I did make my choice. I chose my mother and father, and what they fought for.

+ + +

Walking down the stairs is easier than going up. We reach the fifth level before I realize that we're going down to the lobby.

"Give me your gun, Uriah," says Therese. "Someone needs to be able to shoot potential belligerents, and you can't do it if you're keeping her from falling down the stairs."

Uriah surrenders his gun without question. I frown—Therese already *has* a gun, so why did it matter for him to give his? But I don't ask. I am in enough trouble as it is.

We reach the bottom floor and walk past a large meeting room full of people dressed in black and white. I pause for a moment to watch them. Some of them are huddled in small groups, leaning on one another, tears streaking their faces. Others are alone, leaning against walls or sitting in corners, their eyes hollow or staring at something that is far away.

"We had to shoot so many," Uriah mutters, squeezing my arm. "Just to get into the building, we had to."

"I know," I say.

I see Christina's sister and mother clutched together on the right side of the room. And on the left side, a young man with dark hair that gleams in the fluorescent light—Peter. His hand is on the shoulder of a middle-aged woman I recognize as his mother.

"What is he doing here?" I say.

"Little coward came in the aftermath, after all the work was done," Uriah says. "I heard his dad's dead. Looks like his mother's okay, though."

Peter looks over his shoulder, and his gaze meets mine, just for a second. In that second I try to summon some pity for the person who saved my life. But while the hatred I once had for him is gone, I still feel nothing.

"What's the holdup?" demands Therese. "Let's get going."

We walk past the meeting room to the main lobby, where I once embraced Caleb. The giant portrait of Jeanine is in pieces on the floor. The smoke that hovers in the air is condensed around the bookshelves, which are burned to cinders. All the computers are in pieces, strewn across the floor.

Sitting in rows in the center of the room are some of the Erudite who didn't get away, and the Dauntless traitors who survived. I search the faces for anything familiar. I find Caleb near the back, looking dazed. I look away.

"Tris!" I hear. Christina sits near the front, next to Cara, her leg wrapped tightly with fabric. She beckons to me, and I sit down next to her.

"No success?" she says quietly.

I shake my head.

She sighs, and puts her arm around me. The gesture is so comforting I almost start to cry. But Christina and I are not people who cry together; we're people who fight together. So I hold my tears in.

"I saw your mom and your sister in the next room," I say.

"Yeah, me too," she says. "My family is okay."

"Good," I say. "How's your leg?"

"Fine. Cara said it'll be fine; it's not bleeding too much. One of the Erudite nurses stuffed some pain meds and antiseptic and gauze into her pockets before they took her down here, so it doesn't hurt too bad either," she says. Beside her, Cara is examining another Erudite's arm. "Where's Marcus?"

"Dunno," I say. "We had to split up. He should be down here. Unless they killed him or something."

"I wouldn't be that surprised, honestly," she says.

The room is chaotic for a while—people rushing in and rushing out again, our factionless guards trading places, new people in Erudite blue brought to sit among us—but gradually everything gets quieter, and then I see him: Tobias, walking through the stairwell door.

I bite my lip, hard, and try not to think, try not to dwell on the cold feeling that surrounds my chest and the weight that hangs over my head. He hates me. He does not believe me.

Christina clutches me tighter as he walks past us, without even looking at me. I watch him over my shoulder. He stops next to Caleb, grabs his arm, and wrenches him to his feet. Caleb wriggles for a second, but he is not half as strong as Tobias and can't break away.

"What?" Caleb says, panicking. "What do you want?"

"I want you to disarm the security system for Jeanine's laboratory," says Tobias without looking back. "So that the factionless can access her computer."

And destroy it, I think, and if possible, my heart becomes even heavier. Tobias and Caleb disappear into the stairwell again.

Christina slumps against me, and I slump against her, so we hold each other up.

"Jeanine activated all the Dauntless transmitters, you know," Christina says. "One of the factionless groups got ambushed by simulation-controlled Dauntless, coming late from the Abnegation sector about ten minutes ago. I guess the factionless won, though I don't know how you call shooting a bunch of brain-dead people winning."

"Yeah." There isn't much more to say. She seems to realize that.

"What happened after I got shot?" she says.

I describe the blue hallway with two doors, and the simulation that followed, from the moment I recognized the Dauntless training room to the moment I shot myself. I do not tell her about hallucinating Will.

"Wait," she says. "It was a simulation? Without a transmitter?"

I frown. I hadn't bothered to wonder about that. Especially not at the time. "If the laboratory recognizes people, maybe it also knows data about everyone, and can present a corresponding simulated environment depending on your faction."

It doesn't matter, now, to figure out how Jeanine set up the security on her laboratory, of all things. But it feels good to put myself to some use, to think of a new problem to solve now that I have failed to solve the most important one.

Christina sits up straighter. Maybe she feels the same way.

"Or the poison somehow contains a transmitter."

I hadn't thought of that.

"But how did Tori get past it? She's not Divergent."

I tilt my head. "I don't know."

Maybe she is, I think. Her brother was, and after what happened to him, she might never admit it, no matter how accepted it becomes.

People, I have discovered, are layers and layers of secrets. You believe you know them, that you understand them, but their motives are always hidden from you, buried in their own hearts. You will never know them, but sometimes you decide to trust them.

"What do you think they're going to do to us when they find us guilty?" she says after a few minutes of silence have passed.

"Honestly?"

"Does now seem like the time for honesty?"

I look at her from the corner of my eye. "I think they're going to force us to eat lots of cake and then take an unreasonably long nap."

She laughs. I try not to—if I let myself laugh, I'll start to cry, too.

+ + +

I hear a yell, and peer around the crowd to see where it came from.

"Lynn!" The yell came from Uriah. He runs toward

the door, where two Dauntless are carrying Lynn in on a makeshift stretcher, made of what looks like a shelf from a bookcase. She is pale—too pale—and her hands are folded over her stomach.

I jump to my feet and start toward her, but a few factionless guns stop me from going much farther. I put up my hands and stand still, watching.

Uriah walks around the crowd of war criminals and points to a severe-looking Erudite woman with gray hair. "You. Come here."

The woman gets to her feet and brushes off her pants. She walks, light-footed, to the edge of the seated crowd and looks expectantly at Uriah.

"You're a doctor, right?" he says.

"I am, yes," she says.

"Then fix her!" He scowls. "She's hurt."

The doctor approaches Lynn and asks the two Dauntless to set her down. They do, and she crouches over the stretcher.

"My dear," she says. "Please remove your hands from your wound."

"I can't," moans Lynn. "It hurts."

"I am aware that it hurts," the doctor says. "But I won't be able to assess your wound if you do not reveal it to me."

Uriah kneels across from the doctor and helps her shift Lynn's hands away from her stomach. The doctor peels Lynn's shirt back from her stomach. The bullet wound itself is just a round, red circle in Lynn's skin, but surrounding it is what looks like a bruise. I have never seen a bruise that dark.

The doctor purses her lips, and I know that Lynn is as good as dead.

"Fix her!" says Uriah. "You can fix her, so do it!"

"On the contrary," the doctor says, looking up at him. "Because you set the hospital floors of this building on fire, I cannot fix her."

"There are other hospitals!" he says, almost shouting. "You can get stuff from there and heal her!"

"Her condition is far too advanced," the doctor says, her voice quiet. "If you had not insisted upon burning everything that came into your path, I could have tried, but as the situation stands, trying would be worthless."

"You shut up!" he says, pointing his gun at the doctor's chest. "I'm not the one who burned your hospital! She's my friend, and I . . . I just . . ."

"Uri," says Lynn. "Shut up. It's too late."

Uriah lets his gun clatter to the ground and grabs Lynn's hand, his lip quivering.

"I'm her friend too," I say to the factionless pointing guns at me. "Can you at least point guns at me from over there?"

They let me pass, and I run to Lynn's side, holding her free hand, which is sticky with blood. I ignore the gun barrels pointed at my head and focus on Lynn's face, which is now yellowish instead of white.

She doesn't seem to notice me. She focuses on Uriah.

"I'm just glad I didn't die while under the simulation," she says weakly.

"You're not gonna die now," he says.

"Don't be stupid," she says. "Uri, listen. I loved her too. I did."

"You loved who?" he says, his voice breaking.

"Marlene," says Lynn.

"Yeah, we all loved Marlene," he says.

"No, that's not what I mean." She shakes her head. She closes her eyes.

Still, it takes a few minutes before her hand goes limp in mine. I guide it across her stomach, and then take her other hand from Uriah and do the same to it. He wipes his eyes before his tears can fall. Our eyes meet across her body.

"You should tell Shauna," I say. "And Hector."

"Right." He sniffs and presses his palm to Lynn's face. I wonder if her cheek is still warm. I don't want to touch her and find that it's not.

I rise and walk back to Christina.

CHAPTER
FORTY-SEVEN

MY MIND KEEPS tugging me toward my memories of Lynn, in an attempt to persuade me that she is actually gone, but I push away the short flashes as they come. Someday I will stop doing that, if I'm not executed as a traitor, or whatever our new leaders have planned. But right now I fight to keep my mind blank, to pretend that this room is all that has ever existed and all that will ever exist. It should not be easy, but it is. I have learned how to fend off grief.

Tori and Harrison come to the lobby after a while, Tori limping toward a chair—I almost forgot about her bullet wound again; she was so nimble when she killed Jeanine—and Harrison following her.

Behind both of them is one of the Dauntless with Jeanine's body slung over his shoulder. He heaves it like a stone on a table in front of the rows of Erudite and Dauntless traitors.

Behind me I hear gasps and mutters, but no sobs. Jeanine was not the kind of leader people cry for.

I stare up at her body, which seems so much smaller in death than it did in life. She is only a few inches taller than I am, her hair only a few shades darker. She looks calm now, almost peaceful. I have trouble connecting this body with the woman I knew, the woman without a conscience.

And even she was more complicated than I thought, keeping a secret that she thought was too terrible to reveal, out of a heinously twisted protective instinct.

Johanna Reyes steps into the lobby, soaked to the bone from all the rain, her red clothes smeared with a darker red. The factionless flank her, but she doesn't appear to notice them or the guns they carry.

"Hello," she says to Harrison and Tori. "What is it that you want?"

"I didn't know the leader of Amity would be so curt," says Tori with a wry smile. "Isn't that against your manifesto?"

"If you were actually familiar with Amity's customs, you would know that they don't have a formal leader," says Johanna, her voice simultaneously gentle and firm. "But I'm not the representative of Amity anymore. I stepped down in order to come here."

"Yeah, I saw you and your little band of peacekeepers, getting in everyone's way," says Tori.

"Yes, that was intentional," Johanna replies. "Since getting in the way meant standing between guns and innocents, and saved a great number of lives."

Color fills her cheeks, and I think it again: that Johanna Reyes might still be beautiful. Except now I think that she isn't just beautiful in spite of the scar, she's somehow beautiful *with* it, like Lynn with her buzzed hair, like Tobias with the memories of his father's cruelty that he wears like armor, like my mother in her plain gray clothing.

"Since you are still so very generous," says Tori, "I wonder if you might carry a message back to the Amity."

"I don't feel comfortable leaving you and your army to dole out justice as you see fit," says Johanna, "but I will certainly send someone else to Amity with a message."

"Fine," says Tori. "Tell them that a new political system will soon be formed that will exclude them from representation. This, we believe, is their just punishment for failing to choose a side in this conflict. They will, of course, be obligated to continue to produce and deliver food to the city, but they will be under supervision by one of the leading factions."

For a second, I think that Johanna might launch herself

at Tori and strangle her. But she draws herself up taller and says, "Is that all?"

"Yes."

"Fine," she says. "I'm going to go do something useful. I don't suppose you would allow some of us to come in here and tend to *these* wounded?"

Tori gives her a look.

"I didn't think so," says Johanna. "Do remember, though, that sometimes the people you oppress become mightier than you would like."

She turns and walks out of the lobby.

Something about her words hits me. I am sure she meant them as a threat, and a feeble one, but it rings in my head like it was something more—like she could easily have been talking not about the Amity, but about another oppressed group. The factionless.

And as I look around the room, at every Dauntless soldier and every factionless soldier, I begin to see a pattern.

"Christina," I say. "The factionless have all the guns."

She looks around, and then back at me, frowning.

In my mind I see Therese, taking Uriah's gun when she already had one herself. I see Tobias's mouth pressed into a line when I asked him about the uneasy Dauntless-factionless alliance, holding something back.

Then Evelyn emerges into the lobby, her posture regal,

like a queen returning to her kingdom. Tobias does not follow her. *Where is he?*

Evelyn stands behind the table where Jeanine Matthews's body lies. Edward limps into the lobby behind her. Evelyn takes out a gun, points it at the fallen portrait of Jeanine, and fires.

A hush falls over the room. Evelyn drops the gun on the table, next to Jeanine's head.

"Thank you," she says. "I know that you are all wondering what will happen next, so I am here to tell you."

Tori sits up straighter in her chair and leans toward Evelyn, like she wants to say something. But Evelyn pays no attention.

"The faction system that has long supported itself on the backs of discarded human beings will be disbanded at once," says Evelyn. "We know this transition will be difficult for you, but—"

"We?" Tori breaks in, looking scandalized. "What are you talking about, disbanded?"

"What I am talking about," says Evelyn, looking at Tori for the first time, "is that your faction, which up until a few weeks ago was clamoring along with the Erudite for the restriction of food and goods to the factionless, a clamor that resulted in the destruction of the Abnegation, will no longer exist."

Evelyn smiles a little.

"And if you decide to take up arms against us," she says, "you will be hard pressed to find any arms to take up."

I watch, then, as each factionless soldier holds up a gun. Factionless are evenly spaced around the edge of the room, and they disappear into one of the stairwells. They have us all surrounded.

It is so elegant, so clever, that I almost laugh.

"I instructed my half of the army to relieve your half of the army of their weapons as soon as their missions were completed," says Evelyn. "I see now that they were successful. I regret the duplicity, but we knew that you have been conditioned to cling to the faction system like it is your own mother, and that we would have to help ease you into this new era."

"*Ease us?*" Tori demands. She pushes herself to her feet and limps toward Evelyn, who calmly takes her gun in hand and points it at Tori.

"I have not been starving for more than a decade just to give in to a Dauntless woman with a leg injury," Evelyn says. "So unless you want me to shoot you, take a seat with your fellow ex-faction members."

I see all the muscles in Evelyn's arm standing at attention, her eyes not cold, not quite like Jeanine's, but calculating, assessing, planning. I don't know how this woman could have ever bent to Marcus's will. She must not have been this woman then, all steel, tested in fire.

Tori stands before Evelyn for a few seconds. She then limps backward, away from the gun and toward the edge of the room.

"Those of you who assisted us in the effort to take down Erudite will be rewarded," says Evelyn. "Those of you who resisted us will be tried and punished according to your crimes." She raises her voice for the last sentence, and I am surprised by how well it carries over the space.

Behind her, the door to the stairwell opens, and Tobias steps out with Marcus and Caleb behind him, almost unnoticed. Almost, except I notice him, because I have trained myself to notice him. I watch his shoes as he comes closer. They are black sneakers with chrome eyelets for the laces. They stop right next to me, and he crouches by my shoulder.

I look at him, expecting to find his eyes cold and unyielding.

But I don't.

Evelyn is still talking, but her voice fades for me.

"You were right," Tobias says quietly, balancing on the balls of his feet. He smiles a little. "I do know who you are. I just needed to be reminded."

I open my mouth, but I don't have anything to say.

Then all the screens in the Erudite lobby—at least those that weren't destroyed in the attack—flicker on, including a projector positioned over the wall where Jeanine's portrait used to be.

Evelyn stops in the middle of whatever sentence she was speaking. Tobias takes my hand and helps me to my feet.

"What is this?" Evelyn demands.

"This," he says, only to me, "is the information that will change everything."

My legs shake with relief and apprehension.

"You did it?" I say.

"*You* did it," he says. "All I did was force Caleb to cooperate."

I throw my arm around his neck, and press my lips to his. He holds my face in both hands and kisses me back. I press into the distance between us until it is gone, crushing the secrets we have kept and the suspicions we have harbored—for good, I hope.

And then I hear a voice.

We pull apart and turn toward the wall, where a woman with short brown hair is projected. She sits at a metal desk with her hands folded, in a location I don't recognize. The background is too dim.

"Hello," she says. "My name is Amanda Ritter. In this

file I will tell you only what you need to know. I am the leader of an organization fighting for justice and peace. This fight has become increasingly more important—and consequently, nearly impossible—in the past few decades. That is because of this."

Images flash across the wall, almost too fast for me to see. A man on his knees with a gun pressed to his forehead. The woman pointing it at him, her face emotionless.

From a distance, a small person hanging by the neck from a telephone pole.

A hole in the ground the size of a house, full of bodies.

And there are other images too, but they move faster, so I get only impressions of blood and bone and death and cruelty, empty faces, soulless eyes, terrified eyes.

Just when I have had enough, when I feel like I am going to scream if I see any more, the woman reappears on the screen, behind her desk.

"You do not remember any of that," she says. "But if you are thinking these are the actions of a terrorist group or a tyrannical government regime, you are only partially correct. Half of the people in those pictures, committing those terrible acts, were your neighbors. Your relatives. Your coworkers. The battle we are fighting is not against a particular group. It is against human nature itself—or at least what it has become."

This is what Jeanine was willing to enslave minds and murder people for—to keep us all from knowing. To keep us all ignorant and safe and *inside the fence*.

There is a part of me that understands.

"That is why you are so important," Amanda says. "Our struggle against violence and cruelty is only treating the symptoms of a disease, not curing it. *You* are the cure.

"In order to keep you safe, we devised a way for you to be separated from us. From our water supply. From our technology. From our societal structure. We have formed your society in a particular way in the hope that you will rediscover the moral sense most of us have lost. Over time, we hope that you will begin to change as most of us cannot.

"The reason I am leaving this footage for you is so that you will know when it's time to help us. You will know that it is time when there are many among you whose minds appear to be more flexible than the others. The name you should give those people is Divergent. Once they become abundant among you, your leaders should give the command for Amity to unlock the gate forever, so that you may emerge from your isolation."

And that is what my parents wanted to do: to take what we had learned and use it to help others. Abnegation to the end.

"The information in this video is to be restricted to

those in government only," Amanda says. "You are to be a clean slate. But do not forget us."

She smiles a little.

"I am about to join your number," she says. "Like the rest of you, I will voluntarily forget my name, my family, and my home. I will take on a new identity, with false memories and a false history. But so that you know the information I have provided you with is accurate, I will tell you the name I am about to take as my own."

Her smile broadens, and for a moment, I feel that I recognize her.

"My name will be Edith Prior," she says. "And there is much I am happy to forget."

Prior.

The video stops. The projector glows blue against the wall. I clutch Tobias's hand, and there is a moment of silence like a withheld breath.

Then the shouting begins.

ACKNOWLEDGMENTS

Thank you, God, for keeping your promises.

Thank you:

Nelson, beta reader, tireless supporter, photographer, best friend, and most importantly, husband. . . . I think the Beach Boys said it best: God only knows what I'd be without you.

Joanna Volpe, I could not ask for a better agent or friend. Molly O'Neill, my editor of wonder, for your tireless work on this book in all arenas. Katherine Tegen, for being kind and discerning, and the whole KT Books crew, for your support.

Susan Jeffers, Andrea Curley, and the illustrious Brenna Franzitta, for watching my words; Joel Tippie and Amy Ryan, for making this book so beautiful; and Jean McGinley and Alpha Wong, for extending the reach of these books farther than I ever expected. Jessica Berg, Suzanne Daghlian, Barb Fitzsimmons, Lauren Flower, Kate Jackson, Susan Katz, Alison Lisnow, Casey McIntyre, Diane Naughton, Colleen O'Connell, Aubrey Parks-Fried, Andrea Pappenheimer, Shayna Ramos, Patty Rosati, Sandee Roston, Jenny Sheridan, Megan Sugrue, Molly Thomas, and Allison Verost, as well as everyone in audio, design, finance, international sales, inventory, legal, managing editorial, marketing, online marketing, publicity, production, sales, school and library marketing, special sales, and subrights at HarperCollins, for doing such fantastic work in the world of books as well as *my* world of books.

All the teachers, librarians, and booksellers who have supported my books with so much enthusiasm. Book bloggers, reviewers, and readers of all ages and varieties and countries of origin. I'm probably biased, but I think I have the best readers ever.

Lara Ehrlich, for much writing wisdom. My writer friends—listing all of the people in the writer community who have been kind to me would take multiple pages, but I could not ask for better peers. Alice, Mary Katherine, Mallory, and Danielle—what fantastic friends I have.

Nancy Coffey, for your eyes and your wisdom. Pouya Shahbazian and Steve Younger, my fantastic film team; and Summit Entertainment, Red Wagon, and Evan Daugherty, for wanting to live in this world I made.

My family: My incredible mother-slash-psychologist-slash-cheerleader, Frank Sr., Karl, Ingrid, Frank Jr., Candice, McCall, and Dave. You are incredible people and I am so glad I have you.

Beth and Darby, who have won me more readers than I can possibly count through charm and sheer determination; and Chase-baci and Sha-neni, who took such good care of us in Romania. Also Roger, Trevor, Tyler, Rachel, Fred, Billie, and Granny, for so effortlessly embracing me as one of you.

Mulțumesc/Köszönöm to Cluj-Napoca/Kolozsvár, for all the inspiration and the dear friends I left there—but not forever.

"What's your name?"

"Um…" I don't know why I hesitate. But "Beatrice" just doesn't sound right anymore. A new place, a new name. I can be remade here.

"Tris," I say firmly.

Table of Contents

Acknowledgments

This book became a reality due to the tremendous foresight of Michael and Patricia Snell. Literary agents par excellence, they were able to see the intrinsic value in the seed of an idea and make it grow into a full-fledged book. We are grateful for their wisdom and guidance and hope that they are proud of and enjoying the finished product.

We thank all of our family members and friends, who not only encouraged us to write this book but supported us every step of the way. The stories they told us that showed how words can hurt or heal gave us more than enough material for this book—and probably a couple more!

Special thanks to Aileen and Heather Bloom, June's sister and niece, for their enthusiastic support that spurred us on to complete the project.

Thank you to our publisher, New Harbinger, and to our editor, Melissa Kirk, for seeking and publishing self-help books on communication to help people improve their relationships.

Thank you to all of the people at New Harbinger who helped us with the book, especially Jasmine Star, who did outstanding work helping us make it a well-written, polished, and finished book.

Most importantly, our biggest debt of gratitude is to the One Above, Who gave us the laws of ethical speech in order to bring people closer to each other. He has guided us and inspired us in a multitude of ways to write this book so that we could bring thoughtful communication to everyone.

Introduction: The Power of Positive Communication

The three biggest problems in the world today
are communications, communications,
communications. —Kenny Blanchard

How many times each day do you say things you regret, sometimes immediately, sometimes later? Perhaps you blurted out comments on your friend's new dress that you meant to be helpful but turned out to be hurtful. Or maybe you jumped to hasty conclusions about your spouse's behavior and, filled with suspicion, accused him or her of some thoughtless act, only to find out later that it was done for your benefit. Or perhaps you've said things in frustration to visiting family, forgetting that they are your guests and deserve the patience and consideration you would give to anyone invited to your house for the holidays. In these situations, the problem is that you've already said it and can't un-say it, no matter how much you'd like to.

Now the solution is here in a series of "Questions for Positive Thinking and Speaking" (Q-pts, or Q-points) you can use whenever the temptation to grouse, complain, whine, accuse, belittle, or be mean raises its destructive head. Instead of blundering your way into making life miserable for others and yourself by shooting off your mouth, you can learn to avoid misunderstandings and hurt feelings by considering these questions: Who am I speaking to? What am I not seeing? Where will my words lead me? How will the other person react to my words? Why must I say it at all? And if I must say something, when do I say it?

Asking and answering these questions may save days and even years of grief and hard feelings. It can save marriages, friendships, and other relationships. It can make you a better parent, spouse, friend, boss, or colleague, because when you take the time to consider the Q-pts, you'll show others that you care about them and that you don't need to build yourself up by tearing others down.

Using the Q-pts is simple. It doesn't require a Ph.D. in rocket science to remember them during everyday conversations. This approach is just common sense. But maybe that's a problem. Many commonsense ways of doing things are appallingly uncommon in our everyday lives. It's common sense to drive carefully and use one's turn signal for the safety of all concerned. But surely you've noticed that many drivers simply don't do so. It's common sense to eat well and get lots of exercise. But do you and all of your friends and family do that? It's common sense to pay off your credit card bill each month, even if you have to borrow the money from a bank to do it. Yet untold numbers of people choose to pay 18 to 21 percent interest on their outstanding balance instead.

Likewise, it's common sense to think carefully and to weigh the consequences of what you're about to say before you burst forth with unsolicited advice (or even solicited advice), before you react with anger or frustration to some perceived slight to you or your loved ones, or before you spread a dark rumor or some silly gossip about a friend or neighbor. Yet how many of us habitually give enough consideration to what we're about to say and what the results of saying it might be? We certainly don't. But working on this book has helped us do so much more than ever before. And now each of us often chooses to not say anything at all in situations where we previously might have shot off our mouth. These days, not saying anything seems a very reasonable course of action more often than not. And nobody seems to miss what we haven't said—not even ourselves!

Although this book takes an entertaining and accessible approach, it's grounded in the science of how what we say makes sense to others. Research into conversation shows that people often misunderstand each other. That happens because words can mean many different things to different people— even to ourselves when we use them at different times in different contexts. Words always mean more than we can ever say because each of us attaches meaning to them that comes from our own experiences. Both speakers and listeners actively make sense of what's being spoken, each in their own way. Although they may understand the words in the same way, that doesn't happen automatically. "I love your dress" may mean "I truly do think it looks great and is the right choice for you," or the speaker may be saying "It would look wonderful on a model, but you're no model." Or the speaker may mean "I understand that you're playing a joke on me, and I know that you yourself think the dress is awful." There's lots of room for misunderstanding here.

The ambiguity of words makes clear communication difficult. It means we have no trouble meaning what we say, but lots of trouble saying what we mean. Because our words, once spoken, belong to our listeners, we depend on others to make sense of what we say in the way we intended. But because that often doesn't happen, we end up with misunderstandings that can be hurtful and destructive and have a quite different effect from what was intended.

This book can't completely eliminate the problem of ambiguity in conversation. Unfortunately, nothing can do that! But it can certainly make you a better, more considerate, more ethical, more sensitive communicator by helping you learn to think before you speak. Giving the Q-pts more than a passing glance will help stifle your urge to "shoot from the lip." These questions, and all the other helpful ideas in our book, can and will make you a better spouse, mother, sister, father, brother, friend, board member, colleague, or boss. You need only get into the habit of using them. We promise you that most of the things you decide not to say, or that you say in a much different way, will never come back to haunt you.

As you read through the many real-life situations in this book, consider how they relate to your own experience. When you begin using these approaches and techniques in your own life, you'll see how most situations—whether simple or difficult—can be handled more thoughtfully. With an intelligent sensitivity to the people, the situation, the purpose, the timing, and the knowable facts, you'll know what to say and how to say it or when it's best to say nothing at all, at least for the moment.

1

Making Thoughtful Communication Work for You

Words Can Wound: Amy's Story

"There's talk all over town that I beat my son!" Amy cried. "Even my neighbors believe it. They won't let their kids come over to our house anymore."

In between Amy's sobs, Rachel, one of the authors of this book, listened in shock to her friend's story. Not long after they moved to town, Amy's son, Mike, who was a bit of a daredevil, decided to ride his bike down the basement stairs. Amy confided that Mike's fall had been an ordeal, but his stitches and bruises would heal. What people were saying about her had become the bigger problem. People had looked at Mike's bruises and made the assumption that they weren't due to an accident but were inflicted by his mother. No one had stopped to question the truth of that assumption before talking.

Until the talk about Amy died down, Rachel was one of her few supporters. Having known Amy and her family for years, she knew there was no basis to the rumor and was horrified that someone as sweet natured and caring as her friend Amy could be accused of hurting her own child. Although Rachel's support was comforting, Amy was still devastated by the unfounded gossip. And while Rachel understood that most people, even good people, like to gossip, she wondered whether they realized how much power their words had to hurt others. Having long been guided by the principles of ethical speech, Rachel knew that there were ways to talk without causing others pain, but it was only after Amy's situation brought the issue to the forefront that Rachel decided she had to do something to help others be more thoughtful before speaking.

Ethical Speech Eliminates the Pain

Having been raised in an ethical and devout home, Rachel was trained not to talk for the sake of talking but to consider the purpose of her every word. She grew up with the understanding that every situation can be viewed in more than one way and that rumors start from not seeing the whole picture.

If the people in Amy's town had been more aware of the principles of ethical speech, she would have been spared a great deal of pain. People would have checked the facts before condemning Amy as an abusive mother. Instead of gossiping behind Amy's back, they would have put their mouths to good use with words of compassion and advice about how to deal with the antics of an overactive child.

Bringing Ethical Speech to Everyone

With Amy's story weighing on Rachel's mind, an idea for a book that would teach the principles of ethical speech took hold of her imagination. She envisioned a book of stories, like Amy's, that would illustrate how much better our lives could be if we consistently followed these principles. Everyone Rachel spoke to encouraged her to write the book, but it was only when she met June that her idea became a reality. June, a writer, shared her unbridled enthusiasm for ethical speech, and she sat Rachel down the very next day to write their first story.

Having discovered and studied the principles of ethical speech on her own, June knew firsthand how dramatically they improve one's life. "I used to be known as a motormouth," June says. "I'd get into all kinds of trouble by saying whatever popped into my head. Ethical speech taught me how to evaluate when to speak and when to keep quiet. I'm grateful to have learned how to control my mouth, and I'm much happier because of it."

Working together, Rachel and June condensed and distilled the laws of ethical speech into six simple questions to ask yourself before speaking—six questions that will help anyone develop more skill in what we term "thoughtful communication." These six questions help you think before you speak, and as you start to ask yourself any of them before you speak, you'll soon notice a change in the way you see people, talk to people, and deal with people.

Rachel and June shared these concepts with Dr. Richard Heyman, an internationally recognized professor of communication and education at the University of Calgary. Dr. Heyman has taught courses, written books and articles, and presented numerous scholarly papers and lectures on different aspects of everyday communications. He found this idea of thoughtful communication to be both simple and useful, and he readily agreed to be part of this project as coauthor of the book.

Thoughtful Communication Works

With plans for the project underway, we decided to offer our program to a few friends and acquaintances for feedback. We introduced the six questions of thoughtful communication to Marty, a personal trainer who admitted that his wife was about ready to walk out on him if he didn't learn to control his angry outbursts. "Thank you for letting me try your program," he said. "It took a little effort, but after a few times it got easier, and my relationship with Laura has never been better."

Nancy, a dental assistant, said the six questions helped her learn how to get along with a difficult coworker. To her amazement, using this approach transformed their relationship. The woman, who had been an adversary, became her greatest ally.

And Fran, who had always spoken her mind, managed not to tell the owner of her favorite beauty salon what she thought about the new girl who had washed her hair. "I kept my mouth closed," Fran says with a grin, "and I'm glad I did. The girl turned out to be the owner's daughter. I would never have been able to go back to that beauty salon. I would have been a loser in every way."

Thoughtful communication can be a winning skill for you, helping your words work positively for you in any situation and in any relationship. Whether you use all six questions or just one, you're guaranteed to find that you'll no longer have to defend yourself by saying "But I didn't mean that!"

How to Get the Most out of This Book

Chapter 2 provides an in-depth study of the six questions of thoughtful communication and illustrates their practical application. Read this chapter carefully and refer back to it often. Keep it handy to guide you throughout your day.

The remainder of the book consists of stories—stories about families, friends, neighbors, coworkers, and even strangers. These stories reinforce the program by illustrating how much better your life could be if you consistently follow the principles of thoughtful communication.

In some of these stories you'll meet people who didn't think before they spoke. You'll laugh as you recognize and relate to the sticky situations they create. To show you how people in each of these stories could have saved themselves needless aggravation and stress, we answer the six questions of thoughtful communication for them. Use these people's experiences to learn what you can do in similar situations to give your own stories happy endings.

In other stories, you'll meet people who faced their challenges using the skills of thoughtful communication. We explore how they might have answered the six questions to create a more positive outcome. Through their stories, you'll start to see how you too can use your words to get similar results.

The stories are divided into chapters, each chapter concentrating on a particular situation in which people often talk without taking the time to assess the damage their words can cause. Be honest with yourself and consider when you're most likely to lose control over what you say. Is it when you're in emotional turmoil, or is it when you deal with difficult people? Focus on the chapters that cover situations in which you feel you need the most help until you master the skills.

For practical tips on what you can say or shouldn't say in various situations, read the sections "How to Say It" and "What Not to Say" after each story. The suggestions in "How to Say It" are safe bets to help you to say the right thing, but we encourage you to be yourself and use your own words. The comments in the "What Not to Say" sections are to be avoided no matter what!

To give you some experience in using each of the six questions, we've provided exercises at the end of chapters 3 through 8. Use the examples in these exercises to test your reactions to common encounters and to see how, as a thoughtful communicator, you would respond differently. Remember, though, that the best practice of all occurs when you come face-to-face with the people in your life. View every encounter as an opportunity to practice being a thoughtful communicator and enjoy the pleasant results it brings!

2
Taking Control of Your Words

But I Didn't Mean That! offers a simple program to put *you* in control of your words. Our program provides you with six basic questions to ask yourself before you unwittingly put your foot in your mouth. These questions will prevent you from "shooting from the lip" by keeping your emotions from dictating what comes out of your mouth. They'll help you zero in on who you're talking to while enabling you to step back and see the situation in a new light.

These questions, which we've named "the six Questions for Positive Thinking and Speaking" (Q-pts), will neutralize your negative thoughts by helping you see a broader picture. And when your thoughts become more positive, so will your words.

By taking a moment to focus on the answer to at least one of the six questions, you'll automatically minimize your chances of putting your foot in your mouth. The more you use the Q-pts, the better you'll become at making your words work for you and the more control you'll have in every situation.

The Blurt That Hurt: Liz's Story

Liz was losing patience. Having the family over for the holiday was turning out to be too much for her. "Where is that sister of mine?" she wondered as she rescued a big bottle of apple juice from the clutches of her four-year-old nephew, Johnny. "Don't you go into Auntie Lizzie's refrigerator," she scolded as she poured him a drink.

With one eye on Johnny, she scanned the kitchen for signs of his little brother. With only seconds to spare, she grabbed him off of the counter just as he was about to open one of her china cabinets. "If you want something, ask me," she chided. Giving each boy a cookie, she shooed them out of the kitchen.

"Beth's got to do something about those wild kids of hers," she sighed.

Glancing irritably at the clock, Liz decided it was about time for her to set the table for dinner. With a tray of Waterford goblets balanced carefully in her hands, Liz made her way to the dining room. No sooner had she stepped foot out of the kitchen than Johnny raced past her, rattling the goblets and nearly knocking the entire tray to the floor. Shaking, Liz set the tray on the table.

Beth approached her sister with a big smile on her face. "Need any help?" she asked.

Liz eyed her sister and blurted, "Help? Do you really want to know how you can help? Start by being a mother and disciplining your children."

The second the words were out of her mouth, Liz knew that they weren't what she meant to say. But it was too late. She watched Beth's face turn to stone. "I knew that coming here for the holiday was a mistake," her sister said.

THE SIX QUESTIONS OF POSITIVE THINKING AND SPEAKING

To avoid verbal blunders, before you utter a sound take a moment to think. It only takes a moment to ask yourself at least one of these questions:

- **Who** am I speaking to?

- **What** am I not seeing?

- **Where** will my words lead me?

- **How** will the other person react to my words?

- **Why** must I say it at all?

- **When** do I say it?

If Liz had taken a moment to consider the Q-pts, she would have communicated more effectively and avoided a very unpleasant situation with her sister. Let's take a look at how this would have worked.

Q-pts

Who am I speaking to? I'm speaking to my sister, who has come to my home as a guest to celebrate the holidays.

What am I not seeing? I invited Beth to be a guest in my home. I still expect her to be on top of her children at my house, but she probably thinks she can relax and let her guard down. That doesn't make her a bad mother.

Where will my words lead me? All I want is for Beth to keep a better eye on her kids so I can serve dinner without them being underfoot. I feel like telling her to start acting like a mother because that will definitely get my point across. But those words will ruin the holiday spirit and damage our relationship.

How will she react to my words? Beth will most likely react to a nasty remark (like "Start acting like a mother") by feeling hurt. But I do need her help. I'm sure that if I ask her nicely to keep an eye on her children, she'll do so.

Why must I say it at all? If I don't say something to correct the situation, I'm going to end up resenting my sister and regretting ever having invited her. It will discourage me from inviting the family again.

When do I say it? I can only ask her when I've calmed down and can say what I want to say nicely.

Think about it: If Liz had answered these six questions before saying the first thing that came into her mind, it would have saved the dinner, saved the family endless grief and recriminations, and saved her relationship with her sister. Taking the time to consider any of the questions would have allowed her to bring fresh insights into dealing with the situation. Instead of blurting out hurtful words, Liz would have been able to say something like "I'm setting the table now, so maybe you could settle the kids down and get them ready for dinner."

Read ahead to learn in detail how to use each of the six Q-pts. With a little practice, you'll never again have to say "But I didn't mean that!"

Who Am I Speaking To?

Toby gently ran her fingers over the freshly polished floor to see if it was dry. It was still a bit damp, and she smiled at her reflection in the glistening tiles and stretched her aching back.

"There!" she thought. "That's the way a floor should look. Before Dan and Ron come home from the soccer game, I'll put new mats by the front door for them to wipe their feet."

Humming happily to herself, Toby rinsed out the mop and put it on the back porch to dry. She paused for a few moments to pluck a few dead leaves from her hanging plants.

Turning back to the house, she could hear the front door slam and the sound of playful laughter. Helplessly, Toby gasped as the trampling of dirty sneakers echoed through the house.

Tears filled her eyes for all the work that her husband and son had ruined in a matter of seconds.

As she walked back into the kitchen, she came face-to-face with her husband and son, who were grinning from ear to ear.

What can Toby possibly do to stop herself from yelling at her husband and son for tracking mud across her freshly polished floor? How can she avoid spoiling their happy mood or making them feel that the floor means more to her than they do?

Before saying any hurtful words that she'll later regret, Toby needs to stop and think "Who am I speaking to?" This question will help her focus her attention on what is most important to her. Though the dirty floor may seem crucial at the moment, the relationship she has with her husband and son matters more. If she doesn't stop to focus on her priorities, her relationship with her family could be damaged just as quickly as her clean floor was ruined.

Before you utter one word to someone you care about, stop to focus on that person. As you think about who you're talking to, keep these considerations in mind:

- Do I care about this person?

- Do I want this relationship to thrive?

- Will my words help support the relationship?

- Is this person considerate in other ways?

- How do I feel about this person when I picture a considerate thing he did?

- Have my feelings about him really changed?

If Toby stops a moment to consider the "who" question, she won't yell at her husband and son about the floor. Instead, she'll have thoughts along these lines: I'm speaking to my husband and son. I love them, and I know they love me. Even though they messed up my floor today, they're generally considerate about keeping the house neat and clean. In fact, when I was laid up sick a while back, they took turns cleaning the floors. I still remember how each one looked with the mop in his hands. They're still the same thoughtful guys they were then. Because of all the thoughtful things they do, I can't yell at them. I care enough about their feelings that when I see their smiling faces I can say, "Well, it looks like you two had quite an exciting day!"

What Am I Not Seeing?

"Why so blue?" Bill stopped to ask his son, who was sitting alone on the front steps of the house. "That's no way to look the first week of vacation."

Jimmy gave his baseball mitt a punch. "Sammy's father said he's not allowed to play with me," he said bitterly.

Bill looked at his son in surprise. "What did Mr. Brown say to you?" he asked.

"Every time I knocked on the door to play with Sammy, Mr. Brown told me that Sammy was busy and couldn't play with me. But I know that Sammy isn't busy. We made plans to play together this week."

Bill thought about the Browns. He had a warm friendship with them that went back as many years as they had lived on the block. "Did he say anything more than that?" he asked.

"He was so mean!" Jimmy cried. "He wouldn't even let me speak to Sammy."

Bill decided to get to the bottom of things. He called the Browns and minutes later slammed down the phone. "What a brush-off!" he exclaimed. "After years of being neighbors, he won't even explain himself."

Bill thought he had every right to be irritated about his neighbor's behavior. Yet learning one important fact about what was going on with the Brown family would change his entire perspective in an instant. Before judging them negatively and breaking up the friendship with sharp words, Bill decided to think about what he was not seeing with considerations such as these:

- Am I only seeing a part of the picture?

- I can't know everything that goes on in his life, so how can I possibly judge him?

- I'm sure that he has a very good reason for what he's doing, even if I don't get it.

The question "What am I not seeing?" helped Bill realize that he didn't have enough information to get angry at the Browns. Though he was fairly close to them, he didn't know everything that went on in their lives. Bill calmed down and decided to reserve judgment.

"I know you feel bad about Jimmy," he told Sammy. "But we can't be angry with the Browns because we don't know the whole story."

Later that week, Bill got a call from a broken Mr. Brown. "My wife died today," he said his voice choking. "It was all so sudden. We didn't tell anybody. I didn't let Sammy out of the house all week so that my wife could spend her last days with her family."

By acknowledging that you don't always see the whole picture, you can avoid harsh and hasty judgments. Your opinions and reactions will be softened, and your words will be, too.

Where Will My Words Lead Me?

Donald jiggled his keys in the old lock and to his dismay found that the door was already open. "Oh, no," he thought, "the old man must have opened up again. I've told him more than once he doesn't have to come in to the office anymore."

Tensing, Donald entered the ancient elevator. He had tried to arrive early, before his father-in-law, so that he could start making some changes, but even at 7:30 the old man was already there. Donald pressed the button to the second floor, where he had set up his new office, thinking "He sold me the business fair and square but doesn't trust me enough to let go."

Only the dim hallway lights were on as Donald stepped out onto the second floor. "Sits in the dark to save an extra dime," Donald thought, "but I know he must be around somewhere." He opened the door to his new office.

"Hey!" Donald cried out in surprise. There, sitting at his desk, was his father-in-law, hunched intently over an old ledger. Donald could have let his father-in-law know once and for all that he didn't want him around. But something held him back—a measure of self-control that came from being able to stop and to think, "Where will my words lead me?" This question made him consider the long-term effect of his words.

He probably had thoughts along these lines: "My father-in-law is well-respected in the industry. If I kick him out, everyone will hear about it. All I'll succeed in doing is getting some negative public attention for myself. And not only that, what will my wife say?"

Even though Donald felt that his father-in-law was clearly overstepping his bounds, he anticipated the damage harsh words could do to his professional life, and to his personal life. He kept the "where" question in mind by considering questions like these:

- What do I hope to accomplish with this remark?

- Will these words encourage people to like and respect me?

- If all I hope to gain from my words is self-satisfaction, is it worth the risk of ruining my relationship?

- If I tried speaking this way before and it didn't get me where I wanted, do I need to try another approach?

Donald concluded that he needed to try a different approach than telling off his father-in-law. Trying to be respectful while also making it clear exactly who was in charge, Donald said, "Since we both came in so early, let's go over some things together so that you can show me how I should do them."

With these words, Donald showed his father-in-law that he was willing to learn and recognized that he had much to gain from his many years of experience. Over time, this approach built a relationship where the older man was eventually comfortable enough to trust Donald to run the business alone.

How Will the Other Person React to My Words?

Travis stared intently at the man across from him on the train. He looked vaguely familiar. But where was he familiar from? Travis usually rode this same train every morning, and he was certain he hadn't seen the man on the train before.

The man put down his paper, and Travis buried his head behind his *Wall Street Journal*. Peering over his paper, Travis got a good look at the man as he sipped his coffee. "Could be our old next-door neighbor Freddy," he mused. "I haven't seen him since he got divorced and sold the house. He used to neglect his appearance and was quite overweight. Looks about fifty pounds lighter and years younger."

When the man rose to put on his jacket, Travis was convinced. "That's got to be Freddy," he decided. "It'll be nice to hear how he's doing after all this time."

He tapped Freddy on the shoulder. "Freddy?" he asked. "It's Travis, your old next-door neighbor."

Freddy's eyes lit up in recognition.

"I wasn't sure it was you," Travis continued, "I didn't think you could ever look so good!"

Travis didn't stop to think how Freddy might react to his words. When Freddy turned his back on him and walked away, Travis was dumbfounded.

To ensure a better outcome, Travis should have taken the time to think, "How will he react? Will he take my words as the compliment I intended, or will he think I'm being rude? If you want your words to build and improve your relationships, you have to ask yourself these sorts of questions:

- Are these the best words to use to get my message across?

- Is my tone of voice or body language giving the person a different message than my words?

- How would I prefer to be spoken to if the tables were turned?

Travis would have approached Freddy much differently if he had thought about how he'd feel if the tables were turned. He would have said something that sounded more like a compliment, such as "It's so nice to see you again. You really look great." With a comment like this, Travis probably would have gotten the positive response from Freddy that he was hoping for. By considering how the other person might react, you're less likely to blunder and have others turn their backs on you.

Why Must I Say It At All?

"It certainly is a funny development," Mary thought, covering her mouth to stifle a laugh.

Although she tried to get back to work, Mary found herself mulling over what she'd just heard. Sal had sworn he'd never get married, but she just found out that he'd gotten engaged after knowing the woman only two weeks! Giggling, she burst into Carol's office

"Sal's engaged!" Mary blurted. "She's from L.A. They met over the Internet, then talked on the phone. He flew to L.A. to meet her, and now she's got a huge rock on her finger!"

Enjoying the snickers she elicited from Carol, Mary scurried back to her office to think of who else she could tell.

"I would love to tell Kayla," she thought, grabbing the phone. Suddenly Mary froze. "What am I doing?"

Even though she was dying to tell this juicy gossip to someone else, Mary stopped herself from calling Kayla. She contemplated "Why must I say it at all?" with questions like these:

- Will any good come from my words?

- Will my words embarrass or hurt anyone?

- Will my words come back later to haunt me?

After considering these questions, Mary decided to keep quiet. She realized that Kayla could still be hurt about Sal. Sal and Kayla had dated seriously for a year before Sal had a sudden change of heart. Mary decided that as much as she relished sharing the news, no good could come from sharing it with Kayla.

By asking yourself "Why must I say it at all?" you can avoid inflicting needless pain on the people in your life. Even if what you see or hear is absolutely true, unless you're certain that only good will come from your words, you're best advised not to say anything. Mary knew that Kayla would probably eventually hear the news from someone else, but she didn't want her words to be the ones that caused Kayla pain. Mary never regretted keeping her mouth shut.

When Do I Say It?

Jill plunked the heavy bags of groceries on the kitchen counter. "Kim, I'm home," she called.

Spotting dirty plates in the sink and crumbs on the table, signs that her daughter was definitely in the house, Jill called out again, "Kim, I'm home! Can you please come help me unpack the groceries?"

"Hi, Mom," a muffled voice came from upstairs. "Erica and I are in my room doing our hair."

Jill shook her head in annoyance. "I wish Kim would clean up after herself and help me more around the house," she thought. As Jill put away the groceries and cleaned up the kitchen, her annoyance with her daughter's thoughtlessness grew. "I work all day and then I have to come home to this mess," she grumbled. Exhausted, Jill put her feet up on the couch for a few minutes before starting supper.

No sooner did she get comfortable than Kim and Erica came bounding down the stairs. "Mom, we're totally starved. Call us when supper's ready."

Jill was just about ready to explode at her daughter. When would Kim ever learn that life isn't a one-way street? But before she gave her a piece of her mind about her thoughtlessness and sent Kim flying into her room for refuge, Jill had the presence of mind to stop and think "When do I say it?"

The "when" question asks you to take into account your state of mind so that you don't speak unless you can do so calmly. To know whether you're calm enough to speak, ask yourself these sorts of questions:

- Am I free of anger, resentment, or a desire for revenge?

- Can I stick to the issue at hand and not attack the person?

- Can I assure the other person privacy, so that no one will overhear our conversation?

- Will the person feel my concern for her and know that I only have her best interests in mind?

- Is the other person in the proper frame of mind to accept what I have to say?

When Jill paused to answer these questions, she realized that she was too angry with Kim to deal with her calmly. Knowing this, Jill was able to honestly and calmly say to

Kim, "I'm exhausted now. You and Erica can heat up a pizza." Shutting her eyes so as not to let the conversation go any further, Jill vowed to have a discussion with Kim about her lack of responsibility at a better time.

The question "When do I say it?" helped Jill choose a good time to say what she had to say. To increase the chances of a positive outcome, Jill waited until Kim was alone and in a better state of mind to listen. When she and Kim were both calm, Jill was able to sit down with her daughter and explain what she expected of her.

MAKE THESE VALUABLE TOOLS YOURS

The next time someone close to you is thoughtless or inconsiderate, remember how the question "When do I say it?" helped Jill to restrain herself from blowing up at Kim; instead, she waited until they could have a constructive discussion. Or remember how Toby defused her initial outrage over her muddied floor by focusing on what was most important to her and asking herself "Who am I speaking to?"

When you can't understand why someone is brushing you off, keep in mind what happened to Travis on the train when he didn't stop to think "How will Freddy react to my words?" And if someone is acting in a way that makes no sense to you, think of Bill, who asked himself "What am I not seeing?" Doing so allowed him to reserve judgment until he found out the sad news about Mrs. Brown.

Before you say something that could get you unwanted public attention, remember how Donald thought "Where will my words lead me?" This helped him take a respectful approach with his father-in-law, which was ultimately more beneficial for everyone involved. And if you're bursting with news about someone else's personal affairs, stop and think about how Mary used the Q-pts to ask herself "Why must I say it at all?" This simple question helped her avoid causing her friend unnecessary pain.

With practice, you too can have no regrets over your words. By applying the Q-pts to all aspects of your life, you'll discover how you can avoid verbal blunders, solve personal problems, build healthy relationships, and make sincere amends.

When Emotions Run High

The greatest challenges to being a thoughtful communicator occur when things go wrong. Anger, resentment, and disappointment can cause words to pour out of your mouth so fast that you don't even know what you're saying.

In this chapter, you'll read about real-life situations and what happened when people let their emotions take over. You'll witness the pain and hurt their words caused to those closest to them and learn from their experiences how to avoid making the same mistakes.

BLAME

Eric stormed into the house, throwing his car keys on the kitchen counter in front of his wife. "Why did you park the car in the driveway like that?" he demanded. "What a stupid thing to do!"

Not waiting for an answer, Eric proceeded to pull out kitchen drawers rifling through them in search of something. "Where's our car insurance policy?" he finally yelled, too engrossed to even look at her. "I need to find their phone number. Both our cars are dented, thanks to you."

Emily felt an all-too-familiar feeling of air being sucked out of her body. "What do mean, thanks to me?" she questioned. "You were the one driving. You didn't look where you were going when you pulled out of the driveway."

Eric stopped his rummaging and faced her. "Haven't I told you at least a thousand times where I want you to park the car? If you had listened to me, this would never have happened. I don't need this aggravation."

"Well neither do I," Emily shot back, grabbing her car keys and her purse. "I'm tired of taking the blame for every mistake you make. From now on you can deal with your own mistakes." Without looking back, she marched out of the house, slamming the door in Eric's gaping face.

Eric would have been in better control of himself and would have spoken much differently to Emily if he had used the Q-pts.

Who am I speaking to? Emily is my wife, who shouldn't have to put up with my tendency to blame.

What am I not seeing? Because I'm upset with myself and my own stupidity, my reaction is to rant and to find someone else to blame.

Where will my words lead me? I think that by blaming Emily I'll feel better, but in the long run I'll only be hurting myself and my relationship with her.

How will she react to my words? Emily usually gets upset when I blame her, and I may be fooling myself if I think that she gets over it completely.

Why must I say it at all? I feel that the way Emily parks the car causes problems for me and contributed to the accident. I need to convince her that it's important that she park where I want her to park.

When do I say it? While I'm upset is definitely not the time to say anything about Emily's parking. I must first accept my share of the blame and wait until I'm calm enough to patiently explain to Emily why I'd like her to park the car differently.

How to Say It

"I made a mistake." There's nothing wrong with admitting that you made a mistake. Everyone makes mistakes.

Consider: If you accept responsibility for your actions, one collision need not lead to another.

"I just dented the cars." State the facts and be sure to put the responsibility where it belongs.

"Could you help me find the insurance papers?" Keep your voice soft and your words polite, and you'll get cooperation instead of antagonism.

What Not to Say

"What a stupid thing to do!" Try to avoid using words like "stupid." Even though this word is used freely, it still makes a person feel bad.

"Both our cars are dented, *thanks to you*." Sarcastic remarks are belittling and cause additional pain and bad feelings.

"I don't need this aggravation." Nobody needs aggravation. Take the time to think about someone else and the aggravation you may be causing her.

"Why did *you* park like that?" Focus on your own actions. Only after taking responsibilities for your mistakes can you expect others to take responsibility for theirs.

MISTAKES

Maxine stood in front of the mirror in the fitting room. "Oh, no," she gasped. "This gown is white."

She tore out of the room to the salesman. "There's been a terrible mistake," she said. "This gown is white and I ordered it in champagne."

The salesman looked at the gown. "It's just this halogen lighting," he said. "Go out in the sunlight and see for yourself."

Maxine ran outside, followed by the salesman. They stood on the sidewalk and stared at the gown. There was no mistake. The gown was white.

"The swatch didn't look like this," Maxine croaked, her face paler than the gown, as she followed the salesman back into the store.

He pulled out the color chart, and Maxine pointed out the color she had ordered. "You ordered white," he said, "The swatch had yellowed. Not a problem; I can have it remade for you in champagne. We can have it for you in two weeks."

"That's not going to help me now," Maxine said. "The wedding is Sunday night and today is already Thursday."

The salesman offered her a reduced price on the gown, but Maxine wasn't mollified. All the other bridesmaids would be wearing champagne. She would still have to walk down the aisle as a bridesmaid wearing white, the same color as the bride.

"Donna will never forgive me," she thought as she left the store with the gown. "She wants everything at her wedding to be perfect. I don't know how many times she told me exactly what color to get. She'll never understand how such a mistake happened."

Maxine sat by the phone a long time before she got up enough nerve to make the call.

After explaining the situation to Donna, she apologized. "I'm sorry," she said. "It was a mistake. Please forgive me."

"A mistake?" Donna asked incredulously. "I've been working so hard to make sure that my wedding is perfect, then you go and ruin it."

Maxine choked back her tears. "Don't worry, Donna," she managed to say. "I won't ruin your wedding. I just won't come." Then she hung up the phone.

When Maxine came home from work that day, she was astonished to find Donna waiting for her in the lobby of her building. "I'm sorry I upset you. You must feel awful," Donna said. "I've been so stressed-out about this wedding that I just can't think straight. What would ruin my wedding more than anything would be if you didn't come. Please come, and definitely wear the dress."

When Sunday night arrived and the music began for the procession down the aisle, Maxine slipped into place. Later that night when Donna threw her bouquet, Maxine caught it with a squeal of delight.

Donna grinned. "Looks like white is your color after all," she said.

Donna almost made a bigger mistake than Maxine did. Fortunately, Donna was able to make up for her thoughtless communication by using the Q-pts.

Q-pts

Who am I speaking to? Maxine is one of my friends, and I chose her to be a bridesmaid at my wedding.

What am I not seeing? Mistakes happen. Though I would have liked Maxine's gown to match the other bridesmaids' dresses, the color of her gown won't significantly mar the beauty of the wedding, and it won't take away from my happiness over my upcoming marriage.

Where will my words lead me? At this point, there's nothing I can do to change the color of the gown. If I don't show Maxine that I'm ready to overlook her mistake, I could spoil our friendship, and friendships are much more lasting than a six-hour wedding party.

How will she react to my words? Maxine reacted to my initial outburst by saying she wouldn't attend my wedding. I have to go see her in person and use my words to pacify her so that she'll attend the wedding with a smile.

Why must I say it at all? Maxine's friendship is too important to me to lose over an innocent mistake.

When do I say it? The sooner I tell her that I can overlook her mistake, the better it will be for both of us.

How to Say It

"You must feel awful." Try to understand and then put into words how the other person must feel about the mistake.

Consider: It's better to laugh over the mistakes you overlooked than to cry over the ones you didn't.

"Please come, and wear the dress." Convince your friend that having her at your wedding, in any way, shape, or form, is the most important thing to you.

"Looks like white is your color." This sort of statement shows that you've turned the situation around. Instead of the friendship ending in tears, you and your friend can laugh about what happened for many years to come.

What Not to Say

"You're ruining my wedding." Don't make someone feel worse about her mistake than she already does. Remember, it's your wedding and what you make of it is up to you.

"A mistake?" Don't make it sound as if you think the mistake was due to negligence. Remember that honest mistakes can happen to anyone.

"I've been working so hard to make sure that everything is perfect." You'll never be able to overlook others' mistakes if all you focus on is your own needs. Be sure to consider others' needs as well.

UNDERMINING

Denise stepped back to survey her handiwork. The small shrubs she'd planted were lined up neatly along the walk with pink begonias interspersed between them. In front of the house she'd planted a row of red azaleas to hide the foundation wall. She smiled at the sight as she wiped the sweat from her forehead.

"I think that I used my time well," she thought as she put down the hoe to take a peek at her baby in the stroller. "Won't Gary be happy that I saved him all this work." At that moment, the baby cried. Denise nestled her in one arm and picked up the hose with the other.

"Today was a perfect day for planting," she thought as she watered. Even though Gary had said he'd do it, a friend had called and offered him a ticket to the big playoff game. Denise was glad he'd gone to the game and had some fun.

Denise turned off the hose and carried the baby inside. As she entered the house, she felt elated. Having to see the bare foundation wall every time she and Gary walked up the front steps had irritated both of them. Now the outside of their home was just as attractive as the inside.

"Mommy bought plants and planted them herself," Denise told the baby as she changed her. "It's a good lesson for you. There's nothing a woman can't do if she sets her mind to it. Won't your Daddy be proud?"

Just then Denise heard the front door slam. She recognized Gary's footsteps. "Why'd you go and do that for?" he snapped at her. "You messed up the landscaping. Can't you see that the shrubs aren't even in a straight line? Why didn't you wait for me to do it?"

Too shocked to speak, Denise turned away from her husband so that he wouldn't see her tears. The baby in her arms began to cry, too. Gary approached her softly from behind, clearly regretting his words.

"I'm sorry, Honey," he said. "I didn't mean it. You did a great job. I'll just fix it up a little, and then it will be fine."

Denise swung around and faced her husband.

"'Sorry' means nothing," she retorted, her eyes blazing. "The damage has been done. I worked hard all day just to make things easier for you, and that's the thanks I get!"

Gary could have avoided hurting his wife by asking himself the six basic questions of positive thinking and speaking.

Who am I speaking to? Denise is my life's partner. She's always tries to be considerate of me and even encouraged me to go to the game instead of working around the house.

What am I not seeing? I'm not seeing the thought and care for me that she put into the planting. She did it to make things easier for me. It must have been hard for her do it with the baby around. She's probably expecting that I'll appreciate her efforts.

Where will my words lead me? By complaining about the job she did, I'm not going to make the plants straight, and even worse, Denise will get bent out of shape, making us both unhappy.

How will Denise react to my words? If I'd worked all day to surprise someone, I'd certainly resent that person attacking my efforts. In fact, I'd want the person to say something nice about what I'd done.

Why must I say anything at all? It isn't enough for me to control my temper and not say anything. I need to say something nice about what Denise did or she's going to be hurt.

When do I say it? Denise worked hard on this project, and she did it, in part, to help me. I need to compliment her on what she did right away.

How to Say It

"I like the shrubs you bought." Find something positive to say about what the person did. The shrubs might not be in as straight a line as Gary would have liked, but he could still say that he liked them.

Consider: When a person puts effort into a task, find the positive in what she's done and don't say anything to undermine her work.

"I see that you worked hard on this." By acknowledging her efforts, Gary could show Denise that he sees value in what she did. He can avoid criticizing her or her work, and she'll be gratified to hear that he realizes she worked hard all day.

"I see that you really wanted to help me." No matter how well the job was done, Gary should acknowledge that Denise's intent was to help him. When someone does something to help you, it can only improve your relationship if you recognize her efforts and communicate your appreciation.

"The house looks more like a home with the shrubs planted in front of it." Looking at the big picture and not the details of the job Denise had done, Gary could focus on the benefits of her work and not its shortcomings.

What Not to Say

"Why didn't you wait for me to do it?" This question incites confrontation. More a complaint than a question, it puts the other person immediately on the defensive.

"Why did you do it that way?" or as Gary said, "You messed up the landscaping." This implies that the job should have been done better. By being critical and condescending, you strip a person of her sense of accomplishment and self-worth. Even if she didn't do exactly what you would have done, there's more than one way to do a job.

"Can't you see . . .?" Don't turn your anger into personal criticism. Comments such as "Are you blind?" or "You must be deaf" are personal attacks. If you have a problem with someone's work, look for a constructive way to communicate that; don't make it personal.

DISAPPOINTMENT

William sat hunched in his cramped little home office, staring numbly at the big file opened on his desk. When the phone rang, he automatically reached for it.

"Hi, Dad," William said, barely able to get the words out.

"What's the matter, Will?" Mr. Adams asked in alarm.

William hesitated. He licked his dry lips and sighed.

"What happened now?" his father asked. "It's the business, isn't it?"

William didn't want to answer, but his dad was persistent. "What did you do this time?"

"I sold the business, and I just found out that the guy who bought it went bankrupt," William answered lifelessly. "He says that he'll pay me as soon as he can."

There was silence on the other end of the phone. Mr. Adams was crushed. His son had fallen flat on his face again. William had finally disentangled himself from his struggling business only to lose everything he'd put into it.

"No matter what he tries to do, he fails," Mr. Adams thought bitterly. Will had started out as an engineer, but not long after he started working with oil technology, oil went bust. So he learned all about mainframe computers just in time for micros to become the trend. And now this.

"What's going to become of you, William?" his father finally blurted. "I guess you just don't have what it takes. And to think I had such high hopes for you."

William tightened his grip on the phone, his face turning a ghastly white. This was the last thing he needed now. He already felt so defeated, and he didn't need his father's disappointment on top of it.

William's father was so caught up in his own disappointment that he didn't realize what his words would do to his son. He should have taken the time to use the Q-pts.

Q-pts

Who am I speaking to? William is my son, and as his father I should be there to support him.

What am I not seeing? I'm only thinking of my own disappointment. What I'm not seeing is that this latest financial setback is a greater disappointment for William than it is for me.

Where will my words lead me? Since William is already down, anything I say that shows disappointment or disapproval will cause him even more pain. This will damage our relationship.

How will he react to my words? If I show my disappointment, William will feel like a total failure.

Why must I say it at all? William needs someone to support him without being judgmental. If I can only think of my own disappointment, then I'm best off not saying anything.

When do I say it? If I can say something that will encourage William, I should do it right away.

How to Say It

"I'm so sorry to hear that." A little empathy can do a lot for the person you're speaking to.

"What a tough break." Your words should show disappointment in the situation, not in the person.

Consider: Verbalizing disappointment in others only compounds the disappointment they already feel in themselves.

What Not to Say

"What did you do this time?" This type of statement places blame on the person before you know the facts about the whole situation.

"What's going to become of you, William?" Don't make the person feel that past failures mean he's doomed to always fail.

"You just don't have what it takes." You aren't taking into consideration any of the person's strengths, essentially making him feel that you've given up on him. This reduces the person's incentive to try again.

"And to think I had such high hopes for you." When someone is in emotional turmoil, it isn't the time to talk about your feelings. Think about the other person's feelings instead.

Focusing on the "Who"

Those who are closest to you are usually the first to suffer when your emotions run high. That's because you feel so comfortable with them that you forget it's important to be considerate and thoughtful with them. It's likely that you let your emotions and impulses do the talking by saying the first thing that pops into your head. Instead, allow your mind to take control. Before you say anything, stop and think "Who am I speaking to?" This question will remind you that there's someone at the receiving end of your words. It will give you time and help you focus on the whole person: who he is to you and the many good qualities that endear him to you. If you're upset at the moment, it will cool your jets so you won't say anything you'll later regret.

Think of an important person in your life. It would be helpful to choose someone you really care about but with whom your emotions tend to run high.

- Write down at least two of the person's positive qualities that you like, admire, or appreciate.

- Picture that person when he or she is doing something that you like, admire, or appreciate.

- Write down as many incidents as you can think of when that person was kind and understanding toward you.

The next time you see this person, remind yourself of the positive qualities and incidents you listed. Let these positive thoughts wash over you until you realize how fortunate you are to have this person in your life.

As soon as you find your emotions beginning to run high with this important person in your life, don't say anything until you've stopped to think "Who am I speaking to?" Use the positive qualities and incidents you've listed to help you see that person in a more balanced way. Take a moment to visualize that person doing something kind and understanding for you. Don't say anything until you can feel yourself calming down. See the encounter as a test to determine how well you're mastering the skill of focusing on the "who."

4

When Telling It Like It Is

This chapter is an eye-opener that will help you see what can happen when people say it as they see it. It will help you understand the downside of reporting anything you've seen or heard or saying whatever's on your mind. In the stories in this chapter, you'll see that these sorts of comments, no matter how true or how innocently spoken, can affect other people in ways you never intended or dreamed possible. Although the people in these stories were just speaking the truth as they saw it, the outcome of these conversations makes it clear that even in the most casual of conversations, a thoughtful communicator must think before speaking.

IN ALL HONESTY

The girls giggled uncontrollably. Ginny had swept Renee's long brown hair up in an exotic knot mimicking a style they had seen in one of their fashion magazines.

"Renee," Kim exclaimed, "I never realized before, but you have the same mouth as Julia Roberts!" The girls studied Renee's mouth and oohed and aahed.

"What about me?" Ginny asked. "Who do I look like?" Ginny felt their gaze on her and she waited expectantly.

"Why of course!" Renee proclaimed. "Why didn't I ever notice it before? It's your nose! In all honesty, you have the same nose as Sylvester Stallone."

The other girls nodded and laughed in appreciation of Renee's astute observation. No one seemed to notice that Ginny was very quiet.

That night Ginny cried into her pillow. "I never realized that I had a man's nose," she thought. "But it must be true, because all my friends agreed about it. Somehow, someway, I'm going to fix it."

The next day, Ginny asked her parents if she could have a nose job for her birthday. "Where did you get such a ridiculous idea?" her mother asked. "You have a beautiful nose!"

Convinced that her mother just didn't want to hurt her feelings and that her friends knew better, she drove her parents crazy until they agreed to take her to a plastic surgeon.

When Ginny finally saw the doctor, he kindly asked how he could help her. "Isn't it obvious? It's this awful nose!"

The doctor stared at her incredulously. "What's wrong with your nose?" he asked.

"Look at it," she cried. "I have the same nose as Sylvester Stallone."

"Yes, you do," the doctor replied. "And I must say that it looks a lot better on you than on him. I hate to disappoint you, but I won't touch your nose."

Although Renee's comment about Ginny's nose had been truthful, Renee didn't expect Ginny to take it so seriously, and she certainly didn't intend to upset her. Before Renee pronounced her judgment, she should have used the Q-pts.

Q-pts

Who am I speaking to? Ginny is my friend, and she wants me to think of someone she looks like. As her friend, I should give her an example of someone she'd be happy to resemble.

What am I not seeing? Ginny doesn't really want the truth. She wants an answer that will make her feel good about herself.

Where will my words lead me? There's no benefit to Ginny if I tell her what I honestly think. She might get really upset. I'd hate to feel responsible for hurting her, and it might damage our friendship, too. I just have to think a little harder to give her a truthful answer that she'll be happy with.

How will she react to my words? If I say the first thing that pops into my head, even if it's true, Ginny might get insulted. If I were in her shoes, I wouldn't want to hear that my nose looked like a man's nose, no matter how good-looking he is.

Why must I say it at all? I should only give my opinion about her appearance if I think she'll be happy to hear what I say.

When do I say it? An opinion that will hurt my friend's feelings is better left unsaid.

How to Say It

Saying "I can't think of who you look like" is better than saying something hurtful, even though it may not be the complete truth.

"Who do *you* think you look like?" Your friend's answer will give you an idea of what she wants to hear and will get you off the hook at the same time.

Consider: When someone asks you for your honest opinion, consider if the truth is what she really wants to hear.

What Not to Say

"You have the same nose as Sylvester Stallone." Your assessment may be "on the nose," but it's better to keep potentially hurtful comments to yourself and spare your friend's feelings.

"In all honesty." When other people's feelings are at stake, honesty isn't always the best policy.

CHATTING

When Diane opened the door to the teachers' lounge, the silence jarred her. She drew a deep breath, relaxed her face, and entered. The usual assortment of teachers was there, but when Diane's gaze swept the room, no one's eyes met hers. She grabbed her lunch and made a beeline for the secretary's office.

"The other teachers are talking about me," she whispered to her friend Jen. "I just left the teachers' lounge, and the silence was deafening. They're not that quiet unless they're hiding something. Tell me what you know," she demanded.

Jen gestured for Diane to sit down. "Talk is that you're thinking of quitting," she whispered.

"What? Where did they get that idea?" Diane asked in amazement.

"Lynn says that you're upset with the class you were given this year and that if you don't get an assistant, you're quitting."

"Thanks, Jen," Diane said. "Now I get it. You can't say anything around here without the whole school knowing. When I was having a rough day, I made the mistake of complaining to Lynn."

Diane ran down the hall to find Lynn, but the assistant principal stopped her. "What's this I hear, that you're thinking of leaving?" she asked, clearly perturbed. "If you're having difficulties with your class, why don't you just discuss it with me?"

Mortified, Diane told her that everything was fine, despite the gossip that was going around.

Then Diane cornered Lynn in the ladies' room.

"But you told me yourself that you're upset," Lynn said in her defense.

"I was having a hard day," Diane said. "I just wanted to talk to someone about it, and I didn't expect you to go blab it to everyone."

Lynn's eyes opened wide with innocence. "But I didn't mean anything by it. I was just chatting with the other teachers."

Lynn's chatting in the teachers' lounge was in actuality much more than just small talk. Although she didn't think any harm could come from repeating a conversation she'd shared with Diane, stopping to consider the six Q-pts would have convinced her otherwise.

Q-pts

Who am I speaking to? I'm speaking to the other teachers, and from experience I know they consider everything they're told to be public knowledge.

What I am not seeing? Maybe Diane doesn't want her struggles with her class to become public knowledge. It could be that she just told me her troubles in a moment of frustration and expects me to keep it to myself.

Where will my words lead me? Telling the other teachers about Diane's problem is not going to help Diane, and in fact, it may hurt her position in the school. If I tell the other teachers and it causes Diane trouble, I'll feel bad that I was the cause.

How will others react to my words? Whoever I tell will most likely find it interesting and tell someone else. If I were in Diane's shoes, I wouldn't want everyone talking about me.

Why must I say it at all? Though Diane didn't specifically tell me to keep our conversation between the two of us, I can't think of any reason why I should repeat it to anyone.

When do I say it? Never.

How to Say It

"Would you like me to keep this confidential?" If you know that you work in a chatty environment, you should find out whether it's okay to repeat what someone's told you.

If someone asks what's going on with a friend who's shared her troubles with you, you can truthfully answer "Nothing she can't handle."

Consider: Schools and offices are places where people tend to gossip. Don't let your environment determine your behavior; let your behavior affect your environment.

What Not to Say

"Diane told me that she...." If someone tells you something about herself that not everyone knows, assume she doesn't want you to repeat it.

"I'm telling you this, but don't tell anyone else." Don't expect others to hold a trust that you couldn't hold. If the information was told to you, you're the one who has to protect it.

CURIOSITY

It was the most trying time for the Morris family. The week before his daughter Judy was to announce her engagement, Joe Morris was diagnosed with lung cancer. With heavy hearts, Joe and his wife, Eileen, decided not to tell Judy about her father's condition until after the engagement party. Despite this devastating news, they were determined not to cast a shadow over her happiness.

At the engagement party, the mood was jubilant. As Judy and her fiancé showed off the diamond ring he had bought her, people said what a cute couple they made. They glowed with happiness, and Eileen and Joe were glowing too. Looking at Joe, no one could tell he'd just received such a grim diagnosis. They were grateful to be pulling it off with no one the wiser.

While Eileen and Joe were standing around the dessert table with their children, their neighbor Paul came over to them. "I heard you two were at the oncologist's office last week," he said, loud enough for everyone to hear. "Is everything all right?"

Eileen was horrified and couldn't control her face. Judy took one look at her mother's pained expression and ran from the room.

Realizing that he'd said something wrong, Paul tried to recover from his mistake. "I didn't know it was a secret," he defended himself. "I'm sorry if I upset anyone. I was just curious."

Paul's curiosity drove him to ask an inappropriate question at the worst possible time for the Morris family. Before blurting what was on his mind, Paul should have used the Q-pts.

Q-pts

Who am I speaking to? I'm speaking to my neighbors, who are in the midst of celebrating a happy occasion with their family.

What am I not seeing? I'm quite certain that either Eileen or Joe is very sick. But if the word isn't out, maybe they have a reason for wanting to keep it quiet.

Where will my words lead me? Though I want to know what's going on in their lives, by openly asking them at their party, I might be putting them in an awkward spot in front of everybody. I'll just come across as a prying neighbor—and the person who ruined the party.

How will they react to my words? Joe and Eileen both seem to be in a cheerful mood. Even if I were to ask when I just meet them casually on the street, my question would be likely to bring them down. On this special occasion, my question will put a damper on things for sure.

Why must I say it at all? Aside from my own morbid curiosity, there's no reason for me to ask Joe and Eileen about their health.

When do I say it? Since I'm just asking out of curiosity, I can hold my question. The news will eventually come out.

How to Say It (to Yourself)

"This is not my business." Thoughts such as these help you rein in your curiosity and hold your tongue.

Consider: Curiosity is just another word for nosiness.

"This may be something they want to keep to themselves." Try to empathize with others and understand that they may have reasons for not sharing certain information. Reminding yourself of this can save both them and you from embarrassment.

What Not to Say

"I heard you were at.... Is everything okay?" Be careful not to ask personal questions out of idle curiosity. What you consider an innocent question might be a very sensitive subject to someone else.

"I was just curious." Your desire to know is not a reasonable excuse to ask whatever's on your mind.

BREACHES OF CONFIDENCE

When Jack heard of an opening in his office for an administrative assistant, his friend Todd immediately came to mind. Todd's company had downsized and Jack knew he was looking for work, yet he hesitated. He knew that the job required someone who could juggle many tasks at once. And though he knew Todd to be conscientious and reliable, he was worried he might be too rigid. In the end, Jack decided to suggest Todd to his boss, Ken, praising his strengths.

"He sounds like the type of person I'm looking for," Ken said. "But you know how busy it can get around here. Everyone has to pitch in and do whatever needs to get done, even if it means doing something that's not in their job description."

Jack didn't want to ruin Todd's chances of getting the job, but he also felt a responsibility to tell Ken the truth: that Todd might be a little rigid. Ken listened to what Jack had to say and decided to interview Todd for the job anyway.

The interview must have gone very well, because Ken hired Todd right away. Jack was happy on all counts: His friend had a job, and his boss had filled the position.

On Todd's first day on the job, Jack stopped by his cubicle to welcome him aboard. Todd's greeting was stiff and a bit frosty. Although Jack was taken aback, he attributed it to first-day jitters.

But as the days went by, Jack sensed that something besides nerves was bothering Todd. "I got him the job," Jack thought as he tried to concentrate on his work. "Is this the way he shows his gratitude?"

Jack decided to confront Todd. During their coffee break, Jack asked him point-blank what was wrong.

"It's what you told Ken about me," Todd said with a pained look. "When Ken interviewed me, he told me that he had only one concern. He said that you told him I'm rigid. Why did you say that to him about me?"

Jack stood dumbfounded, the blood draining from his face. "I—I can't believe Ken told you that," he stammered.

Trying to learn if Jack was right for job, Ken repeated to Todd what Jack had told him in confidence. Ken not only compromised his own business ethics, he compromised his employee's trust in him and that employee's relationship with his friend. Ken should have stopped to consider the principles of ethical communication.

Q-pts

Who am I speaking to? I'm speaking to Todd, a prospective employee, about a job that requires him to be versatile.

What am I not seeing? Jack gave me a piece of information about Todd that he felt I needed to know. It's true that I can probably get the information I need by repeating Jack's comment to Todd, but I can get the same information without mentioning anything about what Jack told me.

Where will my words lead me? If Jack finds out that I told Todd, he'd probably feel I've betrayed him. And if Todd's feelings are hurt, he and Jack won't get along, which could be bad for employee morale.

How will he react to my words? If I were Todd, I would consider Jack's comment backstabbing, especially when told to a prospective employer, and I would never forgive him.

Why must I say it at all? There's no point in telling Todd what Jack has told me, especially when I can find out what I need to know without it.

When do I say it? Never.

How to Say It

"How would you respond if I handed you someone else's work and asked you to type it up?" Ask a specific question that will get you the answer you're looking for.

Consider: Not everything you know needs to be said.

"How would you rate your flexibility on a scale from one to ten?" By asking the person to rate himself, you can get a better idea of who you're dealing with.

What Not to Say

"Jack tells me that you might be a little rigid." Proper business ethics requires you to keep this information confidential.

Working on the "What"

You can give your honest opinion and share information with others. But as a thoughtful communicator, you want your opinion to be valuable and not hurtful. Before you speak what's on your mind, be sure that the information you want to relate won't be detrimental to anyone.

The question "What am I not seeing?" opens your mind to consider aspects of a person and her situation that you probably hadn't taken into account. It gives you a chance to try to understand where she's coming from before you make any comments to her—or to anyone about her. Once you have this bigger picture, then it's more likely that your comments and inquiries will make you and those around you feel good.

Imagine you're faced with the following scenarios, then write down your initial reaction to each. Next, consider the question "What am I not seeing?" Try to come up with possible reasons for the person's behavior that will help you see them in a more positive light. Don't always assume the worst, and don't assume their behavior is about you. Here's an example:

Your friend canceled your date to go to the mall claiming an excruciating headache, but later you find out she went with someone else.

Initial reaction: She really didn't want to go with me.

What am I not seeing? When she felt better, she tried calling me, but I wasn't home.

Now give it a try yourself:

- You've left countless messages on your friend's answering machine, but she hasn't called you back. What is your initial reaction? What might you not be seeing?

- You neighbor is putting an expensive addition onto his house even though he's always complaining about financial woes. What is your initial reaction? What might you not be seeing?

- Everyone you know was invited to a friend's wedding, but you didn't receive an invitation. What is your initial reaction? What might you not be seeing?

- When you were in the hospital, someone you thought of as a good friend didn't call. What is your initial reaction? What might you not be seeing?

- Now come up with a scenario of your own, preferably taken from your own life, and analyze it in the same way. What was your initial reaction? What might you not be seeing?

5

When You Are Your Worst Enemy

Surely the one person you would never purposely hurt with your words is yourself. Yet, when said without thought, your own words can often come back to haunt you. As you read the stories in this chapter, you'll come to see just how much harm people can bring on themselves when they don't stop to think past the moment.

JUDGING

Linda stood on the step stool to reach her grandmother's china. She carefully placed the quilted plastic bags that cradled the china on the counter and then removed the cream-colored dishes one by one.

"You're really going all out for this dinner," her husband, Jerry, commented as he came into the kitchen.

"The new neighbors are coming," Linda answered as she carried the china into the dining room.

Jerry followed her. "But why are you putting out your grandmother's china?" he asked, watching her arrange the plates on the gold tablecloth. "I thought that you only use it for holidays."

Linda opened her box of silver and neatly arranged the cutlery beside each place setting. "Our new neighbors are wealthy and refined," she said. "I just want them to feel comfortable."

Jerry stared at his wife. Then he broke into a huge grin. "So why would they want to come to our house for dinner?"

Linda was too preoccupied to respond to his playful needling.

"Here's the perfect final touch—this special reserve wine I bought," she said, placing the bottle of red wine in the center of the table. Just then, the doorbell rang. "Please answer it, Jerry," she said.

Jerry opened the door and welcomed the most dignified and impeccably dressed couple he had ever seen. The man wore a tailored navy blazer with an embroidered coat of arms on the pocket, and his wife was dressed in a crisp white suit with an identical emblem on her pocket.

Jerry was taken aback but kept his composure as he welcomed his new neighbors into his home. He showed them to the table and offered them a glass of wine.

Politely refusing the wine, the man complimented Jerry and Linda on their beautiful home and elegant dining room. He expressed his delight with the china, and then to Jerry's amazement he picked up a saucer and turned it over to see who had made it.

Excusing himself, Jerry gestured for Linda to join him in the kitchen. "Linda," he whispered, "this guy puts on a good act, but he's obviously not what he appears to be. Anyone with any manners or breeding would never check out our china. Even I know that."

Linda looked at her husband, eyebrows raised. "Maybe you're wrong about him."

"I'm not wrong," Jerry retorted. "You know what a good judge of people I am. I'm going to find out who he really is."

When they returned to the dining room, their guest greeted them with excitement. "Just as I thought!" he exclaimed. "Your china is very rare. I haven't seen this pattern in such fine condition anywhere."

Jerry gasped. "Is that why you were examining our china?" he asked, turning beet red.

"I was hoping to do you a favor," his neighbor explained. "You see, china is my business and my passion. Whenever I see a special set of china, I try to do my host and hostess a favor by checking the manufacturer. I once turned up quite a fortune at a friend's house, and he was eternally grateful."

Jerry turned to his wife. "You didn't tell me our guest was in the china business," he managed to say.

"I had no idea," she answered.

Like Jerry, we all make quick judgments about people we meet—sometimes based on only the slimmest bit of evidence—and this can lead to some embarrassing moments. Jerry could have avoided feeling foolish because of his snap judgment if he had just stopped to consider the six questions for positive thinking and speaking.

Q-pts

Who am I speaking to? I'm speaking to my wife Linda, who has gone out of her way to prepare an elegant dinner for our new neighbors.

What am I not seeing? Our new neighbor may have acted inappropriately at our dinner table, but that doesn't mean he isn't who he claims to be. After all, I really don't know very much about this man. And different people have different standards; maybe what he did isn't universally considered to be impolite.

Where will my words lead me? If I act on my assumption before knowing all the facts and try to expose this man as a phony, I'll ruin the dinner party that Linda worked so hard on. And if it turns out I'm wrong, I'll feel like a fool.

How will my wife react to my words? Linda will be more impressed with my judgments if I take the time to verify the facts.

Why must I say it at all? I should tell Linda if the man is a phony because I wouldn't want to socialize with him in the future. But I really don't have much evidence, so it's probably best to say nothing. Besides, as an invited guest in my home he deserves to be treated with dignity.

How to Say It

"I see that you have an interest in china." Steer the conversation gently to give the other person an opening to explain his unusual behavior. People generally have good reasons for what they do.

Consider: The quicker you are to make judgments, the more likely you are to make mistakes.

What Not to Say

"He's obviously not what he appears to be." If you assert that something is obvious before you know all of the facts, you're more likely to be humbled if you're proven wrong.

"I'm going to find out who he really is." As a host, your job is to make your guests feel comfortable, not put them on the spot with snap judgments.

"I'm not wrong" or "I'm a very good judge of people." No matter how astute you are, your assessments can be way off target if you don't get all the facts.

BADGERING

Dori put down her book for a moment to take in the scene around her. It was Memorial Day weekend, the kickoff of the summer season at the beach. The spot she and her friend had chosen to put their chairs and umbrellas gave them a perfect view of the ocean, and she noted with satisfaction that it wasn't too crowded around them.

She turned to her friend Holly to tell her how pleased she was, but Holly was already fast asleep with a magazine over her belly. Smiling, Dori strolled to the water to take a dip.

The water was refreshing, and Dori lingered a while. By the time she returned to her lounge chair, Holly was awake. As Dori dried herself off, she caught Holly laughing.

"What's so funny?" Dori asked.

"It's nothing," Holly said, trying to control her face.

"Try me," she said. "You know I like a good laugh."

"Forget it," Holly said, burying her head in her magazine.

Dori pushed the magazine away from her friend's face. "What is it that you're holding back from me?" she demanded. "You have to tell me."

"Nothing you'd think was funny," Holly replied.

"Let me be the judge of that," Dori said indignantly, swiping her sunglasses off her face and looking Holly straight in the eye.

Holly sighed, realizing that she would have no peace until she satisfied Dori's demands.

"The girls over there on that blanket stopped by to say hello," she said. "They wanted to know if the woman who had been sitting next to me was my mother."

Dori gasped. "Your mother? You've got to be kidding! They thought I was your mother?" She plopped down on her chair, put on her sunglasses, covered herself with her robe, and put up her umbrella.

"They really didn't get a good look at you," Holly tried to mollify her.

"Really?" Dori simmered beneath the umbrella. "And they never will. I'm staying as far away from them as I can before they ruin the rest of my summer."

Dori ruined her own summer. Before she badgered her friend into telling her what was so funny, she should have used the Q-pts.

Who am I speaking to? Holly is my friend, but that doesn't mean that she has to share everything with me.

What am I not seeing? I'm assuming that if Holly found something amusing, then I would too. But that isn't always the case. Holly may have a good reason for not wanting to tell me what she found so funny.

Where will my words lead me? Holly will be irritated that I didn't respect her right to keep her thoughts to herself. She might think that a good friend shouldn't be so pushy. She could even be clamming up to protect me, in which case badgering her may lead to my feelings being hurt.

How will she react to my words? If I badger Holly enough, I know that she'll eventually tell me what I want to know—even if she'd really rather not.

Why must I say it at all? If I see that Holly is reluctant to tell me something, I should drop it and not put pressure on her. I should trust her judgment and remember that a truly good friend may have a reason for not divulging all.

When do I say it? Never.

How to Say It

"If you think I won't appreciate the joke, I respect your opinion." Letting go of having to know others' every thought and comment will make you a happier person.

Consider: If you're told that you probably don't want to know something, chances are you really don't.

"How was your nap?" or "How's your magazine?" You'll probably have an easier time letting go of your desire to know if you change the subject. This lets your friend know she's off the hook, too.

What Not to Say

"You have to tell me." Dori is making her friend choose between what she thinks she wants to hear and what her friend knows she doesn't want to hear.

"Let me be the judge of that." Dori should have trusted her friend to be the judge. A good friend would try to protect her from hearing something hurtful, offensive, or troubling.

"Tell me. I promise I won't get upset." How often do we badger others with this line but still get upset when they tell us?

SEEKING ATTENTION

Taking a deep breath, Kathy approached the group of girls gathered at the lockers. "Did you hear the latest?" she asked.

Like magic, all the girls turned to hear what Kathy had to say. She paused for effect, reveling in having captured their interest. "I heard that Mr. Roth called Stephanie's parents in for a conference."

The news brought a barrage of comments and questions, and to Kathy's delight she found herself the center of attention. While most of the girls assumed the conference with the principal was about Stephanie's grades, others were convinced that it was something more serious.

"I have a feeling it's pretty bad," Kathy insinuated.

That set off another round of speculation, and by the time the talk finally died down, the girls had decided that Stephanie was in deep trouble. What Kathy didn't tell the girls, however, was that she didn't even know for sure that the principal had actually called Stephanie's parents in. She had only heard about it from a not-so-reliable source. But at the moment, the accuracy of her information wasn't her main concern.

"Everyone looks up to these girls," she thought. "Now I'm one of them."

Kathy was so elated to be part of the in crowd that she managed to convince herself that Stephanie would never find out about her betrayal. But as Kathy walked down the hall surrounded by the group of popular girls, a livid Stephanie stepped out from the shadows of a doorway across the hall from the girls' lockers.

"How can she talk about me like that?" Stephanie fumed. "I thought she was my friend. Boy, was I wrong."

That night Stephanie wouldn't answer the phone when Kathy called, nor would she respond to Kathy's e-mails. And when Kathy greeted that popular group of girls the next day, they didn't even look at her.

Kathy was willing to gossip about her friend to get attention from the popular group, but the attention she gained was short-lived, and worse, she lost one of the few true friends she had. Before saying a word, she should have given some thought to the Q-pts.

Q-pts

Who am I speaking to? They're a group of popular girls that I want very much to be part of, but they seem to have no interest in me.

What am I not seeing? I haven't been able to break into their group until now. If I tell them what I heard about my friend Stephanie, they may be interested, but there's no guarantee that they'll accept me. I may get some temporary satisfaction from their interest in what I have to say, but that won't mean that they like me.

Where will my words lead me? I'm risking my friendship with Stephanie by talking to these girls behind her back. If Stephanie ever finds out, she wouldn't understand that I meant her no harm.

How will these girls react to my words? They'll be interested in what I have to say, but they won't be any more interested in *me* than they were before.

Why must I say it at all? It's not worth gossiping about a friend just to gain some temporary approval or popularity.

When do I say it? Never. I'm not going to say anything at all.

How to Say It (to Yourself)

"Stephanie is my friend." Focus on who your genuine friends are so you won't be tempted to sacrifice them for social opportunities (which may not even pan out).

"Gossiping is wrong." Don't let a need to be popular or interesting make you do something you know is wrong.

Consider: If you want to be popular, start by not speaking negatively about other people.

"If they don't accept me, then I'll have lost everything, even my self-respect." If you compromise your principles in order to fit in, you'll stand to lose more than just a friendship.

What Not to Say (to Yourself)

"Everyone looks up to these girls." Don't generalize. Not everyone looks up to these girls.

"Stephanie will never find out." Even if Stephanie doesn't find out, it's still wrong and disloyal to talk about her behind her back.

What Not to Say

"Have you heard the latest?" Knowing the latest will only make you popular until it's no longer the latest.

"I have a feeling it's pretty bad." Insinuation leaves too much to the imagination and usually leads to more talk and worse rumors.

VENTING

When Danny received his college diploma, his dad, Larry, felt as if he had received his, too. Danny had given him a tough time in his teenage years, and it was a huge relief that Danny had finally settled down. Now here he was graduating in the top 10 percent of his class.

Danny had already started interviewing for jobs, but Larry was confident that he could secure him a position at the hottest firm in his field because the CEO was none other than his closest friend, John. He and John had been friends since college, and they had stayed in touch ever since. John was someone Larry could talk to about anything—including about Danny.

In his desire to vent about his frustration with his son, Larry spared none of the details. He told John how Danny had been suspended from school for fighting with a teacher. And it was John that Larry turned to when Danny was arrested for drunk driving. "I'm afraid he's not going to amount to much of anything," Larry had admitted.

Larry liked having a listening ear in his friend, who always responded sympathetically to his troubles with Danny. However, Larry focused on what was going wrong; John never heard about any of Danny's successes or finer moments. Then, once Danny got serious and pulled himself together in college,

Larry didn't need John as his sounding board anymore. Besides, John became a busy CEO, and in the past few years they had hardly spoken at all. When Larry called to share the triumph of Danny's graduation, John was happy for him. But when Larry asked about a job for Danny, there was a slight pause before John said, "I'll see what I can do."

"I just know John will come through," Larry thought. "He's always been there for me."

Larry didn't hear from John for two weeks, and he began to get a little uneasy. "Something's not right," he thought. "It isn't like John to not follow through."

Larry finally picked up the phone and called his friend again. After a few minutes of small talk, he finally brought up the subject of a job for Danny again.

"Larry," John said, "when you asked me about giving Danny a job, I did give it a lot of thought. But because of everything you've told me about him over the years, I just couldn't do it."

"But he's changed," Larry insisted. "He's matured."

"I'm sorry, Larry," John said. "This is business, and I can't take a chance on him."

Larry didn't realize that all of his venting about Danny had given John an extremely negative opinion of him. Larry could have avoided becoming his own worst enemy if he had considered the Q-pts before venting.

Q-pts

Who am I speaking to? John is a very close friend, and that's why I vent about all of my frustrations to him.

What am I not seeing? John isn't an expert on child rearing, and he may not be the right person to talk to about Danny. What I'm failing to see is that I'm only using him as a sounding board and that he's not offering me any constructive advice.

Where will my words lead me? By only discussing Danny's failures and never sharing his accomplishments, it's inevitable that John will think poorly of my son. For that matter, he may form a negative opinion of me, since I probably seem less than effective as a parent.

How will he react to my words? John is a good listener, but he's only human and everything I tell him could leave him with a negative impression of Danny.

Why must I say it at all? There are times when I need advice about raising my son, but there's no good reason to discuss this issue with John. It's important that I talk to the right person so that I can get some help with Danny, not just vent.

When do I say it? I must speak when my words will benefit my child—and that means when I'm speaking to the right person, too.

How to Say It

"I'm having a hard time with Danny. Can you recommend a child psychologist?" Ask your friend for help that he's qualified to give.

"Danny sometimes gets into trouble, but he's also bright and capable." We all need to talk about our troubles with a friend from time to time. But try to temper your negative statements with positive ones so that the person you're speaking to can see the whole picture.

"Danny just won a science award at school." If you inform others of your child's failings, you should also notify them of his successes.

> **Consider:** Venting helps us forget our problems, but it makes others remember them.

What Not to Say

"I have to talk to *you* about Danny." You may have a need to discuss your difficulties in regard to a family member or friend, but be conscious of who you choose to speak to.

"Danny was suspended from school for fighting with a teacher." When relaying information in order to get advice, it usually isn't necessary to reveal all the details.

"He'll never make anything of himself" or "He can never change." If you speak like this, don't be surprised if people don't go along with you when you change your assessment.

Developing the "Where"

In this chapter, you read about Jerry, Dori, Kathy, and Larry, who created their own problems with careless words. Had they given some thought to where their words would lead them, they need not have become their own worst enemies. If you consider the long-term effects of your words, you can expect what you say to work for you, not against you.

This exercise will help you develop more awareness and foresight about where your words might lead you. When you're caught up in the moment, it can be difficult to remember to balance your urge to speak with the possible consequences of your words. Becoming more aware of the potential pitfalls will help you remember to be more thoughtful.

- Have you ever misjudged anyone? Think of at least one time when you obviously missed the mark—when, like Jerry, you were too quick in your judgments—and you shared your mistaken opinion with others. What did you gain with your words? Thinking as a thoughtful communicator, would you handle that same situation differently now?

- Have you ever badgered someone into telling you something she didn't want to tell? When she finally told you, did you, like Dori, find out something you would have been happier not knowing? If you could do it over, would you still badger that person to find out what she was keeping from you?

- Have you ever been in a social setting where you found yourself saying things better left unsaid just to have something interesting to say so you'd feel like part of the group? Did you later regret those words? Did they ever come back to haunt you?

- Have you ever let off steam by venting? Think back on at least one occasion when you fell into the same bad habit as Larry and vented about someone you care about to a family member, friend, or coworker. What did you hope to accomplish by venting? Where did your words lead you instead? As a thoughtful communicator, what would you say in the same situation now? Why or how might that change the outcome?

6
Making Your
Words Count

Words that count are constructive. They build people up rather than knocking them down. They bring people closer together, enhancing relationships rather than tearing them apart. To demonstrate these simple truths, this chapter focuses on stories about people who had golden opportunities to make their words count. You'll see that only those who thought carefully before they spoke created outcomes that were best for all involved.

GIVING ADVICE

Jennifer snuggled close to Grandma Ruth to get the best view of the wedding album. "Isn't Aunt Vicki beautiful?" she sighed.

Ruth shared her granddaughter's admiration. Her entire family—four generations—had arranged themselves around the bride in front of the camera. It was a moment to cherish.

"Look, Grandma, there I am and there you are. But Grandma, why aren't you smiling? You don't seem happy like everyone else."

"I guess the camera caught me thinking," she said lightly. "Come, let's go get some cookies."

Ruth pulled her granddaughter up from the couch, and they made their way to the kitchen. "Smiling still doesn't come naturally to me," Ruth thought sadly.

As she watched her granddaughter nibbling on her cookie, she reflected on that fateful day that had left her so self-conscious. Although she had long forgotten what occasion had brought the family together, she knew she had been about seventeen-years-old. She had struck up a conversation with Uncle Harry, who always had a way of amusing his listeners with an interesting yarn about one of the family members. That time was no exception, and Ruth remembered laughing about something he had said.

As she laughed, Uncle Harry leaned in to whisper something in her ear. She could still remember the smell of cigar smoke on his breath. "Ruthie," Uncle Harry had said, "you are so pretty, but listen to my advice: Don't open your mouth when you smile. Your teeth are too big, and men don't like women with big teeth."

After that day it became impossible for Ruth to smile naturally. She became so self-conscious about her teeth that soon she didn't smile at all. She had married and had children and grandchildren, but she couldn't even smile at her grandchild's wedding.

"Grandma, were you thinking again?" Jennifer's voice brought her out of that unpleasant reverie.

"Yes, I was," she answered. "Thinking how fortunate I am to have a beautiful granddaughter like you."

We all have an "Uncle Harry" in us who tends to give others advice. But we need to learn from Uncle Harry's mistake and temper our "helpful" advice with thoughtful compassion. Before advising Ruth about her smile, Uncle Harry should have used the six Q-pts to make sure that what he said was helpful, not hurtful.

Who am I speaking to? Ruth is my niece, and I care about her. She's a very pretty young woman, and in my eyes, her only physical imperfection is her toothy smile.

What am I not seeing? Instead of seeing her one flaw, I should see that even with a toothy smile, Ruth is still very pretty. And even though I don't like women with big teeth, I can't speak for all men.

Where will my words lead me? Recommending that Ruth keep her mouth closed when she smiles isn't practical. She might look stiff and unnatural, which certainly isn't attractive. And if she takes offense, from this day forward, she may always associate me with a hurtful comment.

How will she react to my words? The next time Ruth looks in the mirror, she'll only see her big teeth. I remember the first time someone pointed out my receding hairline. I was obsessed about it until all of my hair finally fell out. I certainly don't want Ruth to be self-conscious until the day all of her teeth have fallen out!

Why must I say it at all? Since I care about Ruth, I want to give her advice that will improve her appearance. But now that I'm thinking about it, I realize that my advice could hurt her more than help.

When do I say it? Never.

How to Say It

"You are so pretty." Look at the whole person rather than focusing on her flaws, and you'll have nothing more to add.

"You have such an infectious laugh." Even a "flaw" can have a redeeming quality. Always try to focus on the positive.

Consider: A positive self-image is more beautiful than a perfect smile.

What Not to Say

"Listen to my advice." Before you offer your advice, consider if your advice will help or hurt.

"Your teeth are too big." It isn't constructive to give advice about physical attributes that can't be changed.

"Don't open your mouth when you smile." This type of advice is unrealistic and will only make a person self-conscious.

"Men don't like big teeth." Don't make generalizations. Remember not everyone has the same preferences you do.

TAKING SIDES

Adele was enjoying the relaxed atmosphere of her sister Joan's kitchen when suddenly the side door flew open and her niece Naomi burst in.

"Oh, Ma!" Naomi cried out to her mother. "Matt's done it again. He took one look at the credit card bill and went crazy. It's not as if I don't work. Aren't I allowed to spend money without asking his permission?"

"Matt sounds worse than Lauren's ex-husband," Adele thought, shaking her head in disgust. "I wouldn't let him get away with treating my daughter like that."

But as Adele watched in amazement, her sister turned a calm face to Naomi. "You just disagree on how to spend money," Joan said. "Matt's way of being a good husband is by saving money to buy a house. That's because he loves you."

"How could you say he loves me?" Naomi cried. "He doesn't spend any time with me. When he comes home from work, he sits in front of the computer buying and selling stocks. When I want to talk, he's always too busy. Is that any way to treat a wife?"

"You're right," Joan said, putting a piece of cake in front of Naomi. "A wife needs attention from her husband. If you ask him to spend more time with you, I'm sure he will. Maybe he doesn't realize that you'd like more togetherness."

Adele was ready to explode. She opened her mouth to side with Naomi but was struck dumb as Naomi sighed and smiled through her tears.

"Thanks, Ma," Naomi said. "I feel better. You're right; Matt really is a good husband. Most couples our age can't even begin to think about buying a house yet, but we can."

Later, after Naomi had left, Adele confronted her sister. "How can you defend Matt?" she demanded. "If he was my son-in-law...."

"But you don't have a son-in-law anymore," Joan reminded her. "Even if Matt isn't perfect, he's my daughter's husband. I'm just helping Naomi see him in a positive light. After all, she loved him enough to marry him."

Adele's mouth turned dry, and she felt a lump form in her throat. Her thoughts turned to her daughter, Lauren. "Lauren's marriage could have been better," she thought, "if I had been more like Joan."

Joan's responses to Naomi's disagreement with her husband helped Naomi see Matt's behavior from a different perspective. Instead of rushing to Naomi's defense or joining her in criticizing Matt, Joan made sure that what she said reflected her love for her daughter and support for her marriage. She assuredly reflected on one or more of the questions for positive thinking and speaking before responding.

Q-pts

Who am I speaking to? I'm speaking to my daughter, who I love. Since she's married to Matt and wants her marriage to work, I want to help her make it work.

What am I not seeing? This is just a simple disagreement. Usually Naomi is happy with her husband and her marriage. If I don't turn this into a problem, it won't become a problem.

Where will my words lead me? Naomi might feel vindicated if I agree with her now, but it's more important that I consider her long-term happiness.

How will she react to my words? I want my words to calm Naomi down and give her a chance to understand her husband's motives.

Why must I say it at all? I want Matt and Naomi to get along, because experience has shown that Naomi values her marriage. I also want to help her see that she has a right to ask for what she wants, and that there's a chance Matt doesn't realize that his behavior is bothering her.

When do I say it? Immediately.

How to Say It

"You disagree on how to spend money." Help the person zero in on what the issue really is.

"Matt's way of being a good husband is...." Try to put the "problematic" person's behavior in a positive light by explaining how he might be thinking. This can help those you love resolve conflicts by seeing the bigger picture.

Consider:

Disagreement is often just a matter of different perspectives, not different values or goals.

"You're right. A wife needs attention." By validating the other person's feelings and needs, you're showing that you understand her point of view.

"Ask him to spend more time with you." This is sound advice. If something about the behavior of someone close to you is bothering you, discuss it with him—keeping the Q-pts in mind, of course!

What Not to Say

"You're right" or "I never did like him" or "He's a real tightwad" are all statements that would make Naomi feel justified in being angry with her husband. These statements will only fuel any problems the couple might be having.

"How could you speak about your husband that way?" If you want to try to smooth over a disagreement, avoid asking this type of question. Instead, try to understand and have compassion about whatever is bothering the person about her relationship.

ACCEPTING GIFTS

"Please be careful where you put the apple pie," Margo told her husband as he loaded the car. "I worked so hard. I don't want anything to crush it." Margo checked the trunk to see if her apple pie was in a safe place and then got in the car.

"I sure hope your mother appreciates that pie," Ben said as they headed west on the expressway. "If I remember correctly, she returned the last gift you brought her."

"You're right," Margo said. "That's why I decided to make something I'm sure she likes. Clothes, jewelry, knickknacks—nothing has worked. But I know for a fact that she loves apple pie."

Hours later, Margo and Ben arrived at her mother's building. With Margo cradling the pie protectively, they rode the creaky elevator up to the fifth floor.

"Happy Mother's Day!" Margo announced with fanfare as she presented her mother with her beautiful homemade apple pie. Her mother unwrapped the package and frowned.

"Why did you fuss?" she asked. "Why did you waste your time? Please take it home. I just started a diet yesterday."

Margo's insides churned with disappointment and hurt. Her mother noticed the change of expression on her face.

"Okay, okay, I'll taste it," she said as she carried the pie into the kitchen.

"She did it again, didn't she?" Ben whispered.

"All I wanted was for her to say 'thank you,'" Margo sighed. "That's all I wanted."

Like many people, Margo's mother finds it hard to accept gifts graciously. But she should have taken a moment to consider her daughter's feelings and the bigger picture by reflecting on one or more of the Q-pts.

Who am I speaking to? Margo is my daughter, who cares enough about me to have taken the time to prepare a gift she thought I'd like.

What am I not seeing? I don't like accepting gifts from others, especially from my children, but I have to take note of other people's feelings, not just my own, when accepting gifts.

Where will my words lead me? If I tell Margo that I don't want the pie, that will start our visit off on the wrong foot. Since she doesn't visit that often, I want us to have a pleasant time.

How will she react to my words? I know it isn't easy to choose a gift for me. If I tell her I don't like the pie, she's only going to be hurt. I'd be hurt if I made something for her and she refused it.

Why must I say it at all? I'd better just say "thank you" and eat a slice while she's here. I want her to know that I appreciate her thoughtfulness. I'll have months between now and her next visit to compensate for the extra calories.

When do I say it? I should thank her right away, and I don't ever need to tell her that I don't want the pie, or any other gift, for that matter.

How to Say It

"How thoughtful that you remembered how much I like apple pie." Acknowledge the thought behind the gift.

"You don't have to bring me anything. Your visit is a wonderful gift." This is a gentler way of letting the other person know that you'd rather not receive gifts.

Consider: If you like to give rather than receive, remember: Accepting a gift graciously is really a form of giving, since it gives pleasure to the giver.

"This is delicious. I'd love to get your recipe." Imitation is the highest form of flattery. By asking for the recipe, you're reinforcing how much you enjoy the gift.

"I'm going to save it for the weekend." If you truly are on a diet, you can still accept the gift graciously without eating it.

What Not to Say

"Why did you fuss?" People get pleasure from doing things for others and giving gifts. Don't take it away from them.

"Why did you waste your time?" If Margo's mother had accepted the gift graciously, it wouldn't have been a waste of Margo's time.

"I just started a diet yesterday." Even if this is true, you don't have to say it. It's going to take the pleasure out of her gift.

NOT STANDING ON PRINCIPLE

"You're not really going to see him, are you?" Betty asked her husband again. "How could you after everything he did to you?"

Lou didn't seem to hear his wife as he hunched intently over the map, squinting and finally removing his glasses to get a better look at the streets.

When Lou was satisfied that he knew the way to his brother's house, he got up and made his way out to the garage, wincing in pain with every step. His knees were hurting him more these days, and he didn't know how much longer he would be able to walk, but he could still drive and he was determined to see his brother again.

"We say and do a lot of stupid things when we're young," Lou told himself as he watched for signs on the highway. "I don't want our old feud to come between us anymore. We're not getting any younger; we're both grandfathers now. It's time to let bygones be bygones."

Years ago, when the brothers had dissolved the family business, Lou's brother Arthur was convinced that Lou withheld assets from him. He made an ugly scene, bringing in his own accountant and lawyer to investigate the situation. Lou was devastated to think his brother didn't trust him, and even though Lou was eventually vindicated, the brothers hadn't been able to talk to each other after that—until Lou called to tell Arthur he'd like to come visit.

When Lou pulled up in front of the house, Arthur instantly came out to greet him. Lou was shocked to see how much his brother had aged. As he shook hands with the gray, fragile man his brother had become, he could hardly see through his tears. How could he still be angry with this man? The arrogant youth who had maligned him years ago was gone. As the two hobbled toward the house, Arthur took Lou's arm and helped him up the stairs.

Although his visit with his brother was brief, Lou felt like a great burden had been lifted off of him.

"You look pleased with yourself," Betty commented, noting the smile on her husband's face.

"Yes," he replied, "Arthur and I may not be the closest of brothers, but at least we're not enemies anymore."

Although it had been hard for Lou to pick up the phone and make the initial phone call, he realized that he was getting on in years and wanted to make amends with his brother. He put his resentment and "the principle of the matter" aside and kept in mind that the relationship was what mattered. This helped him summon up his courage to make the call. By using the Q-pts to make sure he communicated thoughtfully, he ensured that his brother would be more receptive to meeting him halfway.

Q-pts

Who am I speaking to? Arthur is my brother, and although he's my flesh and blood, I believe he severely wronged me.

What am I not seeing? Even though I had every right to feel insulted and hurt with Arthur for accusing me of trying to cheat him, I have no way of knowing that Arthur doesn't regret what he did. Who knows, maybe the reason he's never contacted me is because he feels so guilty. Or maybe he thinks I could never forgive him.

Where will my words lead me? My words of reconciliation might be met with indifference, in which case I will have lost nothing. And if Arthur is willing to make amends, I have so much to gain.

How will he react to my words? All these years, I've been standing on principle, hoping that Arthur would call and apologize. Had he called me, I would have jumped at the chance to make amends. Even though I finally had to break down and make the first move, I hope Arthur will be as willing to make amends as I am.

Why must I say anything at all? I don't think I can live with myself any longer if I don't do something to mend the rift between us.

How to Say It (to Yourself)

"We say and do a lot of stupid things when we're young." People grow and change with time. You need not hold on to a mistake that was made long ago. It's never too late to try and fix it.

"I don't want our old feud to come between us anymore." Remind yourself that you want the relationship more than you want to stand on principle.

Consider: You can stand on your principles, but you may find yourself standing alone.

"It's time to let bygones be bygones." Show that you're willing to let go of the past in order to make way for the future.

What Not to Say (to Yourself)

"It's a matter of principle." Principles are a poor substitute for a relationship with someone you care about.

"I just can't forget it." Even if you can't forget it, you can change how you think and feel about something that happened in the past. Also, make sure you also remember all of the good things about the person; it isn't fair to equate a person with a single mistake they've made.

Mastering the "How"

This chapter helped you see how you can make your words count. You can do this by making sure you communicate constructively, with a focus on what will support your relationships with others. To help you decide whether your words will help or hurt, ask yourself "How will the other person react to my words?"

Learn from Uncle Harry. Before you make comments about another person's appearance, consider how your words might affect her. Remember how Margo's mother unthinkingly hurt her daughter, and next time someone gives you a gift, put yourself in the other person's shoes so that you can accept the gift graciously.

Developing an awareness of the other person's feelings will help you when you try to make amends or help people who are embroiled in conflicts. When you take a moment to imagine what it might be like to be in the other person's shoes, you'll become much more understanding of where that person's coming from. Let this be your guide in finding the right thing to say to make your words count.

This exercise gives you practice in putting yourself in another person's shoes. You'll know that you've succeeded if you can find a way to forgive the person's behavior.

- Your neighbor finally returned an item that he borrowed weeks ago. Although he kept promising to return it, he kept forgetting. What's your initial response? Now put yourself in his shoes. If you were the one who forgot to return an item you borrowed from your neighbor, how would you want him to react to you?

- Your friend is wearing a new jacket, and she's very pleased with herself that she found it for a good price. However, you know for a fact she overpaid. Put yourself in her shoes. What kind of reaction would you hope for?

- You were counting on someone to help you with an upcoming event, but he backed out on his commitment, leaving you with all the work. You see him at the event, and he apologizes sincerely for not being able to come through for you. Put yourself in his shoes. What kind of reaction would you hope to receive?

- Your daughter comes home from school and shows you her grade on her math test. You spent hours helping her study for the test, and you're disappointed with her grade. Now she's waiting to hear what you think. Put yourself in her shoes. What kind of reaction would you want to receive from your parent?

7

When Dealing with Difficult People

Difficult people can get to you. Because they're so frustrating, they get under your skin and cause you to say things you normally wouldn't—or that you don't even really mean. This chapter gives you a sampling of some tough personalities and how people dealt with them. You're bound to find someone you recognize in these stories. Hopefully the insight you'll gain here will help you deal with the difficult people in your life. Remember, you can't control what other people say or how they behave—only what you say and do. In the end, you'll feel better if you speak and treat others with integrity. And you may benefit in other ways. When you follow the principles of ethical speech, you create a ripple effect that often leads others to communicate more thoughtfully, too.

THOSE WHO ARE RUDE

Rita is a shopper. She's especially savvy in department stores and knows when and how to get the best merchandise at the best price. When she discovered exactly the style of pants she was looking for on the sale rack in the men's department, she grabbed them all.

Thrilled with her bargain, she darted to the cashier and placed the heap of pants on the counter. The salesman narrowed his eyes at Rita. "You've got to be kidding me," he said barely moving his lips. "Are you really going to keep all this stuff?"

Rita steadied the pile to keep it from falling and tried to explain. "They're for my husband and three sons," she said in her nicest voice. "I'm not sure what's going to fit, so I need to buy a few different sizes. Whatever doesn't fit, I'll return."

"You mean that you're expecting to return half of this?" He shook his head with disgust as he carelessly pulled the top pair of pants off the pile, causing some of the others to tumble to the floor. "You're making me do all this work for nothing, and when you return them you'll make me work again for nothing."

Rita's heart started to pound, but as she picked up the pants that had fallen on the floor, she told herself, "This guy has a problem, but I'm not going to let it get to me."

When she stood up again, she was composed. "If it's a problem for you," she said calmly, "I'll go to someone else when I do the return."

"You're missing the point," the man hissed as he grabbed one pair of pants after another, flinging them into one huge mass, then shoving them into a bag.

Rita kept her eyes on the pants and refused to look at the salesman. "This store has a return policy," she assured herself. "I know I'm not doing anything wrong."

When he completed the transaction, the salesman shoved the bag toward her and turned away.

As Rita left the store, a huge grin slowly spread across her face. "Not only did I get a great deal on these pants," she thought, "I kept my cool in the bargain."

Instead of allowing rude people to raise your blood pressure and put a damper on your day, follow Rita's example and use the six Q-pts to deal with them.

Q-pts

Who am I speaking to? This is someone I'll never have to deal with again, and right now I only have to deal with him for five minutes.

What am I not seeing? If I let this person get to me, it could sour my entire day.

Where will my words lead me? I can call a manager and cause a scene, but the satisfaction I'd get would be fleeting and not worth the stress it would cause me.

How will this person react to my words? I'll try to speak to him nicely. That's the only way he might change how he's treating me. If I argue or make a fuss, he'll just get more confrontational.

Why must I say it at all? I've tried speaking nicely to this man without results. Nothing I say is going to make him treat me with courtesy, so it's probably best to just say the minimum to conclude the transaction.

When do I say it? When I feel my heart pounding, it's *not* the time to say something. I need to remind myself that he isn't worth the stress and only speak to him when I feel composed.

How to Say It

"I'm shopping for several people." Try explaining your actions or even apologizing to the person, but if this doesn't work, drop it.

How to Say It (to Yourself)

Consider: **You can choose whether you let rude people get to you or not. Not every encounter is worth turning into a battle.**

"This guy has a problem." Remind yourself you're not responsible for the other person's rudeness. Behaving that way is a choice the other person made.

"I'm not going to let his problem get to me." Saying this to yourself reminds you that you need not let the other person's rudeness get to you. Even if his behavior still troubles you, this reminder will stop you from being rude in return.

"This store has a return policy." Assure yourself of your rights; don't let the other person's rudeness obscure the facts.

"I got a great deal on these pants and I kept my cool in the bargain." Make sure you give yourself a pat on the back when you stay in control. This is a prize more valuable and lasting than any clever comeback.

What Not to Say (to Yourself)

"He has no business talking to me like that" or "How dare he treat me that way!" Don't take it personally. Getting yourself riled up over an inconsiderate person isn't worth it. In fact, doing so gives them more power over you—the last thing you want!

"He ruined my whole day." Put it in perspective. An isolated incident need not spoil the rest of your day.

"I should never have told him I was going to return the pants." Don't beat up on yourself if someone is rude to you. Remember, he owns the problem.

THOSE WHO ARE GRUMPS

"Give me my blanket already," the old man growled at his companion. "You're so slow. Do you want me to freeze to death?"

"Oh no, Mr. Stern, I wouldn't want that," the woman said with concern, patiently tucking the blanket around the old man's thin legs.

Caren had been observing the scene as she followed her toddler around the small park. "I can't get over how much patience Norma has," she thought. "Mr. Stern is such a sourpuss. I don't think I've ever heard him say a kind word."

"Hi, Norma," she greeted the woman. "And how are you today, Mr. Stern?" she asked.

Mr. Stern grunted and Norma chuckled.

"He's not himself today," she said.

Caren was puzzled. To her, Mr. Stern didn't seem any different than he was on any other day.

"The sun is in my eyes," Mr. Stern complained. "Why'd you go and put me in the sun?"

Norma pulled out Mr. Stern's sunglasses from her bag. "Here," she offered. "These should help."

Mr. Stern put on his sunglasses and was soon fast asleep.

"How do you keep your cool, Norma?" Caren whispered.

Norma laughed softly. "I try to imagine what it would be like to have someone do everything for me," she said. "It would bring out the bad side of me, too."

Caren picked up her toddler and held him close. "It's just like a baby," Norma continued. "If there's something bothering him, he cries. You have to try to figure out what's wrong and fix it."

The toddler in Caren's arms wailed and squirmed, demanding to be set back on the ground. Caren let him go and began to chase after him.

"You have to love him," Norma called after her. "But you don't have to like his ways."

To be able to do her job with the utmost patience and care, Norma needed to have the right attitude. She needed to look past Mr. Stern's grumpiness and think like a thoughtful communicator.

Q-pts

Who am I speaking to? Mr. Stern is someone who's dependent on me, and he usually feels a great deal of pain and discomfort.

What am I not seeing? It must be hard on him to depend on me to fulfill his needs. His grumpiness is a result of everything that he's feeling, and though he may direct it at me, it isn't about me, and it isn't about how I'm treating him.

Where will my words lead me? Arguing with Mr. Stern when he's grumpy will only aggravate him. As a caregiver, my job is to make him more comfortable and do what I can to improve his mood, not to escalate the situation even if I know he isn't treating me fairly.

How will he react to my words? If I use my words to show him that I'm compassionate and understand his situation, I can smooth things over. He may not thank me for what I say or what I do for him, but I can take his silence as his way of expressing that he's grateful.

Why must I say it at all? When I speak to Mr. Stern in a friendly and caring manner, I not only improve his mood, I also improve my own. Speaking kindly keeps me from getting caught up in his negativity.

When do I say it? When he barks at me about something, I must say and do whatever I can to help him.

How to Say It

"Oh no, Mr. Stern, I wouldn't want that." This shows the other person that you have his needs and not your own in mind.

"These should help." Try to remedy the situation and only say what's necessary. Until the person's mood has improved, there's a good chance that anything you say will be the wrong thing.

"I try to imagine what it would be like...." To deal successfully with difficult people, you need to try to understand how they see things. This will increase your understanding and therefore your patience.

"You have to love him, but you don't have to like his ways." This way of thinking will help you improve your relationship with anyone you care about.

Consider: There's a grump in each of us who just wants to be understood.

What Not to Say

"I'm not slow." When someone is grumpy, don't try to defend yourself even if you're right. The person isn't in a state of mind to admit that he's wrong.

"You don't need a blanket." Unless it's harmful to him, give the person what he thinks he needs.

THOSE WHO CRITICIZE

Valerie unwrapped her canvas and hung it carefully on the wall of the exhibit hall. After years of working in watercolors, she had finally completed her first oil painting. "I put my heart and soul into this painting," she thought as she straightened the canvas, "and I'm really pleased with it."

Other students filtered in to set up their work for the art show. "You finally tried oils!" one of her classmates exclaimed, peering at it closely and then stepping back to admire Valerie's work. "You really have a talent for it."

Valerie grinned. "Thanks for the encouragement," she said. "But let's see what our professor has to say. He hasn't seen it yet."

"Don't expect any compliments from him," the girl warned. "You know what he always says, 'If you want to be an artist, you have to be able to take criticism.'"

As the girl walked away, Valerie took a deep breath and told herself, "What I have to remember is that even if my professor criticizes my work, that doesn't mean it has no merit."

As Valerie was filling out the identification card with her name and the name of her painting, a cool voice rose from behind her. "What exactly were you trying to do here?"

Valerie turned and found herself face-to-face with her art professor.

"Your work lacks dimension," he stated, careful to enunciate each syllable. "It's flat and lifeless. Oils are not watercolors. Leave oil painting to those who know what they are doing."

His words stung, but Valerie said nothing. The professor stared at her painting a few seconds longer and then moved away.

Another classmate stopped by. "It looks like you just had a meeting with our professor," he said.

Valerie forced herself to look at him, fighting back tears. "Our professor's critiques are hard to take," she managed to say. "They've caused too many of us to switch majors. But I won't let him do that to me."

Valerie's first oil painting didn't win any prizes at that exhibit, but she didn't let that stop her from exhibiting it elsewhere, and eventually she sold it at a very respectable price. Fortunately for Valerie, she didn't allow her professor to deter her from pursuing her talents. Critical people are certain to crop up in your life from time to time. To deal with them, be strong like Valerie and use the Q-pts.

Q-pts

Who am I speaking to? This man is a talented but highly critical professor. It's virtually impossible for students to get his approval.

What am I not seeing? Just because he criticizes my work doesn't mean that I'm untalented. I must remember that, in the big picture, he's just one person and his opinion is only one opinion

Where will my words lead me? I can try to defend my work, but he's said his piece. Being the professor and a supposed authority, he expects me to listen. I have nothing to gain by challenging him.

How will he react to my words? If I argue with him, he'll probably only become more critical of me and my work. He's likely to view me as defensive and misguided.

Why must I say it all? There's nothing I can say to him. If I remain silent, he'll be satisfied that he's done his job by critiquing his student. But it doesn't mean I have to give up painting in oil.

When do I say it? I don't need to defend myself to him now, or ever. When I become an established artist, my reputation will speak for itself.

How to Say It (to Yourself)

"I'm really pleased with it." If you feel that you've done a good job, trust your own opinion.

"Even if my professor criticizes my work, that doesn't mean it has no merit." If you feel crushed by someone's criticism, remember that it's just one opinion. Bolster yourself with other positive opinions, including your own.

Consider: When faced with criticism, take it for what it's worth but don't let it take you for what you're worth.

"The professor's criticism is hard to take." Know who your critic is and put his criticism in perspective. If the person has a pattern of being critical, this should help you see that his criticism is more about him than about you.

What Not to Say (to Yourself)

"He's right. My work lacks substance." Remember that (constructive) criticism is meant to make you better. Look for any truth in what the other person has said. If there is any, make what use of it you can; if there isn't, discard it.

THOSE WHO BRAG

Sharon hadn't seen her friend Tracy since Tracy and her husband moved to the coast three years ago. She was finally back in town for a visit, and Sharon was looking forward to having lunch with her.

When Tracy sat down at the table, Sharon was stunned. Around Tracy's neck hung a heavy, ornate diamond and gold necklace. It sparkled and glittered against Tracy's black cashmere sweater with her every move. "What's with this gorgeous jewelry?" Sharon wondered. "I've never known Tracy to wear anything like it."

"That's a pretty necklace," Sharon finally commented.

Tracy tossed her long blond hair proudly and said, "My husband had it designed for me. He loves to buy me things, and with his business going so well he can certainly afford to. In fact, he just ordered me matching earrings."

Sharon couldn't answer. She buried her head in the menu, pretending to study it, but she was so swept up in trying to remember the last time her husband bought her a gift that she didn't take in a word she was reading.

"Do you know what else my husband just did for me?" Tracy went on. "He surprised me with a four-week vacation to Europe and the Mediterranean."

Listening to Tracy describe her extensive itinerary, Sharon crunched the ice from her drink and impatiently thought, "I don't remember Tracy being so talkative. Now all she does is go on about her wonderful husband."

"And where have you and your husband traveled?" Tracy finally thought to ask.

"Well, um, my husband can't really take time off from work," Sharon stammered. But maybe this summer...." As her voice trailed off, Tracy picked up without missing a beat.

"We're also planning a trip this summer. We're thinking of Hawaii."

By this time, Sharon had had enough. She looked at her watch and said that she had to go.

"So soon?" Tracy asked in surprise. "We've only just had our appetizers."

"I've lost my appetite," Sharon said.

That night when her husband came home, Sharon snapped at him for every little thing he did. "What's wrong with you tonight?" he demanded.

"My lunch didn't agree with me today." Sharon answered.

Sharon could have saved herself and her husband a lot of pain if she had dealt with Tracy's bragging more effectively. She could have used the Q-pts to handle the situation better.

Q-pts

Who am I speaking to? Tracy is a close friend, and she wants to share her success with me.

What am I not seeing? All I can see now are sparkling diamonds, but I have to look past the glitter to find the Tracy I used to know. Tracy was never a show-off. It must be that she really thinks I'd be interested in what she's telling me.

Where will my words lead me? If I have to keep listening to Tracy talk about her husband and his money, it's going to ruin our time together. I have to say something to change the subject.

How will she react to my words? Tracy may be disappointed at having to stop talking about what's apparently her favorite subject, but if she's the friend I think she is, she'll agree to talk about something else.

Why must I say it at all? If I let her go on and on and don't say something to change the subject, I'll probably be miserable all day. Beyond that, if we don't change the subject, I'm afraid I'll be so resentful that it will wreck our friendship.

When do I say it? As soon as I can get a word in.

How to Say It

"Did you hear that they're tearing down our old high school building?" Pick a neutral topic on which you share common ground. Change the subject and get off whatever issue is rubbing you the wrong way.

"Wow! The last necklace I got was made out of macaroni." Use a joke to lighten the mood. This will also take some of the wind out of the other person's sails.

Consider: Don't let someone else's bragging about what they have rob you of your pleasure in the things you have.

"I'm so happy for you." Acknowledge your friend's good fortune. That's probably what she's waiting for.

"Can we talk about something else?" Be direct and ask your friend to change the subject.

What Not to Say

"Well, um, my husband...." Don't allow yourself to be drawn into a competition with someone who's bragging. She's probably going to top you anyway.

What Not to Say (to Yourself)

"What I wouldn't give for...." Don't let your thoughts settle on what she has and you don't.

Making the Most of the "Why"

When dealing with difficult people, your initial reaction may be to put them in their place by giving back in kind. Though it's tempting, this almost never works, and in fact, the only outcome you're guaranteed is frayed nerves. When Rita was faced with a rude salesman, she realized that she had nothing to gain by confronting him and chose to swallow her words instead. When Valerie, knowing her professor's reputation, was faced with his negative critique, she knew her best option was to say nothing.

The question "Why must I say it at all?" asks you to consider whether you have a good reason for saying something. As a thoughtful communicator, you must keep in mind that communication is almost never neutral. Anything you say will probably have either a positive or negative effect. When dealing with a difficult or inconsiderate person, ask yourself whether your words are diffusing or escalating the tension.

If you don't think your words will have a positive effect, your best bet is to say nothing or to say as little as possible without appearing brusque. When dealing with a difficult person, saying nothing can put you in a position of strength and prevent you from getting caught up in his negativity.

Imagine yourself in each of the following scenarios and ask yourself "Why must I say it at all?" Consider whether your words will help and encourage or hurt and discourage. Decide if you have a good reason to say something or if you're better off saying nothing at all.

- Your friend insists on keeping all the blinds in her house shut. Every time you visit, she's sitting in the dark. You've repeatedly told her to open the blinds and let some sun in, but she stubbornly refuses to listen to you. Consider whether you need to bring it up again. Is there anything you can say that you haven't said already to convince her to open the blinds? Will she get upset or insulted? What good reason do you have for saying anything to her again?

- Your neighbor just called you, again, to complain about your children's behavior. This time she's upset because your children walked on her lawn. You're really getting annoyed with her constant complaints. Do you give her a piece of your mind? Will doing so make things better? Will anyone be hurt or embarrassed by what you want to say? Might your words come back to haunt you?

- A man in your carpool who loves to talk is always pumping you for information about yourself and your family. Is there any reason you have to tell him these things? What might you say to put an end to his prying and blabbering? What good can come from your words? Do you think that what you tell him might come back to haunt you?

- You're dressed to go a wedding. You've spent hours getting ready and you know you look great. Your mother, who is always critical, can't possibly find anything wrong since she helped you choose the outfit. But when she sees you she says, "The outfit is nice, but your makeup is all wrong." Do you say something to her, or do you just chalk it up to her nature? Is there anything you can say that will make her change without hurting her feelings? Is there anything you can say to yourself to take away the sting?

8

When an Extra Dose of Sensitivity Helps

People need a kind word. They need to hear that they're doing a good job, that they're valued, or that others care for them. The stories gathered in this chapter will inspire you with the wonders a kind word can do. The people you'll read about made an extra effort to tune into the needs of others, and then they used their words to help the other person feel better. You'll see that a kind word does as much for the giver as the receiver.

COMPLIMENTS

"A cup of cappuccino, please," Shelly called to the woman behind the counter. "I'm celebrating."

Three in the afternoon and Shelly was free: no meetings, no deadlines. She had finally mustered up the courage to quit her job.

"I doubt if anyone will even notice I'm not in the office today," she thought bitterly. "In that company they treat you like a machine, easily replaceable."

Shelly pulled some money out of her wallet to pay for the coffee and distractedly handed it to the woman. She took the steaming mug and strolled to her favorite table in the outdoor garden. "What a relaxing sensation," she thought as she took her first sip of the aromatic brew, "to enjoy this warm afternoon with nothing pressing to do."

Shelly had been under pressure in her job for the last three years. She had given it her all, and from her clients' feedback, she knew she'd done an excellent job. Unfortunately, nobody in the company had thought it was necessary to compliment her work. She had finally worked up the nerve to ask her boss for some recognition, but he'd just said, "If there's something wrong with your work, I'll let you know. The compliment is that you're still working here."

"That's just not good enough for me anymore," Shelly thought, "I want to work someplace where my efforts will be appreciated."

She finished the coffee and reflected on how much she had enjoyed it. Then she tossed the cup in the trash and resolutely walked up to the counter.

"Can I help you?" the woman behind the counter asked.

"Yes," Shelly said. "I was wondering if you could tell me who makes the cappuccino."

"I do," the woman answered hesitantly. "Why? Is there a problem?"

"Oh, no! Not at all," Shelly said. "I just want you to know that you make the most delicious cup of cappuccino in this city. I really enjoyed it."

The woman's eyes opened wide. "Thank you for the compliment," she said, and as Shelly watched with satisfaction, a big smile spread across the woman's face. "You just made my day," the woman said.

Because she had just quit a job where she felt unappreciated, Shelly realized how valuable a compliment could be. She used this insight to approach the woman behind the counter with an extra dose of sensitivity.

Who am I speaking to? The woman behind the counter has been serving me for years, and I've never considered her feelings before.

What am I not seeing? I know what it feels like to work without recognition. What I've never seen before is that this woman might feel the same way.

Where will my words lead me? I'll feel good about myself if I can offer a sincere compliment that will lift her spirits. I'll also be putting into action the principles that I wish others would use in regard to me and my work.

How will this woman react to my words? If I were in her shoes, I would love to receive compliments from my customers.

Why must I say it at all? By complimenting this woman's cappuccino, I'll have a positive effect on her entire day. She'll be happier and friendlier to all her customers.

When do I say it? The best time for me to compliment this woman is when the taste of the cappuccino still lingers in my mouth.

How to Say It

Consider: Receiving a compliment can make even a tedious task worth the effort.

"Who makes the cappuccino?" Be sure to direct your compliment to the person who should receive it.

"You make the most delicious cup of cappuccino in this city." When giving a compliment, be as specific as possible.

"I really enjoyed it." Let the person know that you personally noticed and appreciated whatever she did.

What Not to Say

"If there's something wrong with your work, I'll let you know." Compliments go much further than criticism in improving a person's outlook about her work. And though occasional criticism is inevitable in almost any relationship, it will be much better received if you've offered a healthy dose of praise to balance it out.

"The compliment is that you're still working here." While you might believe that you're paying someone the biggest compliment by not firing her, remember, it is you who needs her work. Take the time to compliment her on her work so maybe she'll be around when you need her.

What Not to Say (to Yourself)

"This is her job." When a person does her job well, even if that's what is expected, she deserves a compliment.

"I'll leave a nice tip." It isn't enough to leave a tip. Let the person know what it was for. Your actions should complement your words, not replace them.

ENCOURAGEMENT

Glancing at the clock every few minutes, Emily could hardly concentrate on her work. Her son David was competing in a countywide scholastic competition. This was the first time the teacher had seen something special in her son and given him a chance to shine.

When Mr. Brody, David's economics teacher had called to encourage David to enter the competition, Emily was thrilled. "David didn't sign up for the upcoming scholastic competition," Mr. Brody told her. "I'm calling because I know he could do well. It's a great experience for the kids, and if they win they go on to meet other kids from all over the state."

Emily handed David the phone and held her breath. Her heart fell as she heard him politely tell Mr. Brody that he couldn't do it. But Mr. Brody didn't give up. David continued to listen to what he had to say, and to Emily's amazement, he finally agreed to sign up.

"What did Mr. Brody say?" she asked as soon as he hung up the phone.

"He said I should try."

"That's all?" Emily asked, curious to know what magic words the teacher had used to motivate her son, a chronic underachiever.

"He said he knows I can do it. He said that I may not realize it yet, but because he's been a teacher of economics for so long, he knows a natural when he sees one. If I work hard and study, I have a strong chance of winning."

That afternoon, David picked up the thick economics textbook Mr. Brody gave him and tackled it from page one. Thinking back on it, Emily reflected that she had never seen him study so hard for anything before.

The slam of the front door jolted Emily from her thoughts, then David burst into the room, his face aglow and a gleaming trophy in his hand. "I won! I won!" He yelled. "This is the first time I ever won anything! And I get to compete in the state finals!"

Emily beamed and said a silent prayer of thanks to Mr. Brody.

David experienced those sweet moments of triumph because his teacher made an extra effort to encourage him. As a thoughtful communicator, Mr. Brody must have used one or more of the Q-pts to remind himself why it was important to speak up and how best to encourage David.

Q-pts

Who am I speaking to? David is someone who has the ability and potential to succeed but doesn't realize it yet.

What am I not seeing? If he hasn't come forward to sign up for the competition, it must be that he needs a push. He may not realize that he's got a gift—and a real chance of winning.

Where will my words lead me? Since I think he can compete successfully, I need to convince him that I believe in him. I like being a teacher for a lot of reasons, but the most rewarding thing is when my students succeed beyond their wildest dreams. That's when I know I've really touched their lives.

How will he react to my words? I'm likely to encounter some resistance, so if he turns me down I'm going to persist. I need to convince him of my unwavering conviction that he can do it.

Why must I say it at all? David's success is important to me—and important to his future. If I want David to compete, I have to encourage him.

When do I say it? Now.

How to Say It

Consider:
Encouragement
works when you
recognize someone's
strengths and help
him believe in them.

"You have a strong chance of winning." If someone doesn't recognize his own potential, point it out to him.

"I know you can do it." If you believe in someone, let him know it. You'll give him the impetus he needs to try.

"After so many years, I can recognize a natural." To give the other person confidence in your assessment and encouragement, explain why your belief has a solid base.

"If you work hard and study...." This clarifies that success doesn't come easily and helps the person understand what he'll need to do to succeed.

What Not to Say

"Well, if you won't do it, I can't force you." Don't give up too soon. Sometimes an extra push does the trick.

"Do it for me." Telling someone to do something for you isn't as effective as encouraging him to do it for himself.

"Just read the book. It will be a cinch." By being unrealistic about what's involved, you may set the person up for failure and disappointment.

EMPATHY

Jane stood in the long checkout line debating whether to give up and go back to work.

"I've been waiting half an hour," the woman in front of her grumbled.

"That woman is as slow as molasses," the man behind her added.

"I shouldn't have come in," Jane thought, ruefully glancing at her watch. "I've wasted my entire lunch hour."

She took another look at the silk outfit in her hand and held it up to see if it was worth it. "It is beautiful," she thought. "And it's only on sale today."

"This store stinks," another customer said—loud enough for the woman behind the counter to hear. "Why don't they hire someone who knows what she's doing?"

Jane took a closer look at the lone woman behind the counter. The woman stared straight ahead, her lips pursed as she waited for a manager to verify a price.

"I feel sorry for her," Jane thought. "I wouldn't want to have to deal with these unpleasant customers. I'm certainly not going to give her a hard time." She glanced at her watch and the silk outfit one more time and decided to hold her ground and use her time constructively. Pulling out her calendar and ignoring the fuss around her, Jane began planning out the dates for her vacation.

Finally her turn came. "I can't understand what all these people want from you," she said. "You're only one person,"

The woman behind the counter looked at her gratefully. "I'm so glad that someone understands," she said. She took a bonus coupon out of her own pocketbook and deducted another 20 percent off of the sale price. "That's for being so understanding."

"Thank you," Jane said, surprised.

"No, thank you," the woman said. "You're the nicest person I've served all day."

Because Jane used the Q-pts, she was able to empathize with the saleswoman. Rather than getting frustrated, she used her time productively—and reaped an unexpected reward because of the saleswoman's gratitude.

Q-pts

Who am I speaking to? This woman is just a sales-person. She has very little control over how the store is run.

What I am not seeing? There's a sale today, so the store is much busier than usual. This isn't the saleswoman's fault. In fact, she probably really wishes she had some help!

Where will my words lead me? I truly feel for this woman, especially because of the abuse she's getting from the other customers. My words will help her see that some of us do appreciate her service and realize that her situation is difficult.

How will she react to my words? She'll probably be grateful that I'm not complaining.

Why must I say it at all? I don't have to say something nice, but it would be the kind thing to do.

When do I say it? I'll take the first opportunity to show sensitivity to her predicament.

How to Say It (to Yourself)

"I wouldn't want to have to deal with these customers." The first thing you must do is put yourself in the other person's shoes.

Consider: Empathy opens the door to the heart—yours and the other person's.

"I'm certainly not going to give her a hard time." Think of how you'd want others to treat you if you were in that situation.

How to Say It

"You're only one person." Often a kind word accompanied by a sincere smile can make all the difference in the world.

What Not to Say

"I've been waiting half an hour." You've only had to deal with the line for half an hour, but the saleswoman has been dealing with it all day. Imagine *her* frustration. If you announce how long you've been waiting, that will only put you and everyone else more on edge.

"That woman is as slow as molasses" or "Why don't they hire someone who knows what she's doing?" Not only are these sorts of remarks hurtful and insulting, they're inaccurate, too. There's a limit to what one person can do, and sometimes the situation is beyond her control.

CONSOLATION

With a heavy heart, Nancy entered her friend's house, where a palpable stillness hung in the air. Reflecting on the many familiar faces around her, Nancy sadly thought, "So many of us are heartbroken that Mattie's gone."

She found Mattie's mother and embraced her. Through her tears, Mattie's mother said, "Everyone was praying for Mattie and the baby. At least she lived to see him born healthy."

Nancy didn't say a word. She simply held the weeping woman until her sobbing stopped. "Dean's still in shock," Mattie's mother whispered.

Nancy looked around and finally saw Dean, surrounded by people and with a dazed look on his face.

"You're still young," she heard one person say. "You have your whole life ahead of you."

"It would be good for you to consider remarrying right away," someone else said.

"That's a good idea," another voice chimed in. "The baby needs a mother."

"Oh no," Nancy gasped. "How can they do this to that poor man?"

Nancy made her way to Dean's side and said, "Dean, I'm so sorry. We all miss Mattie. She had a gift of knowing how to make people happy, and each of us felt like her best friend. I still remember when I first moved here. It was Mattie who knocked on my door and apologized for the half-burnt cookies she brought over as a welcome gift."

Dean latched on to every word, his eyes locked on Nancy.

"Give yourself time to grieve. Everyone in this room knows what a profound loss this is for you, Dean," she said, "but we're not going to let you deal with this alone. We were all Mattie's friends, and she would have wanted us to do that for you."

"Yes," Dean whispered, "that's what Mattie would have wanted. Thank you."

In times of loss, most words are inadequate, yet we all feel in our hearts the need to say something to help those who are grieving. The Q-pts helped Nancy approach this difficult situation as sensitively as possible.

Who am I speaking to? I'm speaking to Dean, who's grieving and experiencing intense pain from his recent and sudden loss.

What am I not seeing? Since I can't comprehend exactly what he's going through, the best thing I can do is to empathize with him based on my own experiences with loss.

Where will my words lead me? I want my words to alleviate his pain as much as possible. Thinking of the future without his wife is too painful, especially now. I want to help him keep her spirit alive by reminding him of what a wonderful person she was. I'd like to choose words that reflect what Mattie would want for Dean.

How will he react to my words? It's so hard to find words to comfort those who are grieving. If I were in his shoes, I'd want to know that others appreciated Mattie and are also feeling her absence.

Why must I say it all? As I listen to how the other people are speaking to Dean and watch his expression, I know that somebody has to speak to him with more sensitivity and sympathy about his loss.

When do I say it? The sooner I can say something to alleviate Dean's pain, the better.

How to Say It

"We all miss Mattie." Let the mourner know that their loved one touched many people's lives and that she will be missed.

Consider: Sincere and empathic words can be a salve to even the most wounded heart.

"I still remember...." Bring up a specific story about the person. It can help bring a smile to the mourner's face.

"Everyone in this room knows what a profound loss this is for you." Let the person know that you—and others—feel for him.

"We were all Mattie's friends." Reminding the person of the friendship you had with his loved one will reassure him that you can understand his pain.

"Give yourself time to grieve." This gives the mourner permission to grieve. The time to deal with the future will come.

"We're all here for you." If you say this, make sure that you're truly willing to be there for the person. Your sincerity is the greatest condolence you can offer.

What Not to Say

"You're still young" or "You have your whole life ahead of you." These sorts of statements minimize the mourner's love for the person he's lost. Right now he can't imagine living the rest of his life without her.

"It would be good for you to consider remarrying right away." When a loss is fresh, it's too soon to talk about the future. The thought of remarrying and loving someone else is incomprehensible.

"The baby needs a mother." This statement is a painful reminder to the mourner that he has lost more than a wife—he's lost a mother for his child.

Tuning In to the "When"

Let's assume that you've decided that a situation calls for you to say something. Your answer to the question "Why must I say it at all?" has convinced you that it will be beneficial for the other person and for you. Even so, pause for a moment. Are you really ready to communicate thoughtfully? Have you considered whether this is the best time for what you have to say—not just for you, but for the other person, too?

The question "When do I say it?" helps you to be honest with yourself and say something only when you have the best interests of the other person in mind. It asks you to think about the best time for the person to hear what you have to say. If emotions are heated or the other person is vulnerable, it might be best to wait until another time.

Of course, when you're offering an extra dose of sensitivity, be that a compliment, encouragement, empathy, or consolation, the time is almost always now. In that case, seize the moment and make the most of your encounter. When the time is right to speak and you know that you can make someone's life a little brighter, go for it!

Use these scenarios to practice when you would say something.

- One of your children cooked supper for the whole family for the first time, and he's very proud of his accomplishment. You need to compliment him. When do you say it? The only problem is, he made a huge mess of the kitchen and you need to give some feedback about this. When do you say it?

- You're mingling with a group of acquaintances, and a friend of yours joins the group. You know that he recently suffered a financial setback, and you want to know what you can do to help him to recover. When do you make your offer?

- Your teenage daughter took the initiative to stop at the supermarket to pick up some groceries she thought you needed. You need to thank her. When do you say it? Unfortunately, she bought the wrong type of orange juice, but you still want to encourage her to shop for you again. When do you explain about the type of juice?

- You had a disagreement with a close friend and the two of you haven't spoken in a few months. You're sorry about the disagreement and you miss your friend. You hear that she's going into the hospital for heart surgery. When do you contact her?

Conclusion:
All You Have to Do Is Try

If you've read through this book from cover to cover, one journey is over. But hopefully another has begun as you've started using the Q-pts in your conversations. Blame, undermining, gossip, breaches of confidence, badgering, venting, giving and getting advice, dealing with difficult people—these and all the other types of scenarios you've read about in this book are all too frequent in our interactions with one another. Although it's next to impossible to control circumstances, let alone the behavior of others, you can try to do your best to be compassionate and ethical in your interactions with others.

It's a challenge each and every day, but with the help of the stories you've read here and the advice and techniques we've offered, you can rise to meet this challenge. You won't be 100 percent successful (who among us is?), but your communication skills and relationships will improve with every effort. Using thoughtful and positive communication in whatever situations you encounter will make those interactions more positive and rewarding, and make you feel better about yourself.

Beyond the words and scenarios you've read in this book lie many things that we never actually wrote but clearly hinted at—all that stuff between the lines. As you reflect on all the ideas, thoughts, and reactions this book has evoked in you, and on all those occasions in your own experience when the wrong (or right) words were spoken and how that impacted people, then you assuredly see that a deeper current runs beneath the entertaining veneer of the stories we've shared. Thoughtful communication is more than a nicety and more than a way to ease your interactions with others—it's the moral and conscientious way to deal with others.

In writing this book, we've drawn upon ancient and revered religious principles of ethical speech:

1. Know your audience.

2. Understand the full context in which you're speaking.

3. Know the purpose of your communication.

4. Use language appropriate for that purpose.

5. Only say what needs to be said.

6. Speak at the appropriate time and place.

7. Know yourself as well as you know the person you're talking to.

8. Think about everything you say in the context of your purposes.

This book has given you a firm foundation in these principles, which are embodied in the Q-pts. Using the questions for positive thinking and speaking will go a long way toward assuring that you communicate thoughtfully. But we'd like to leave you with an introduction to two other important aids to thoughtful communication.

The first technique is to really listen to others before speaking. When you listen to what others have to say, you'll gather important information that can help you answer the Q-pts. You'll also stand a much better chance of achieving communication that stays on track and is satisfying for all involved.

The second technique is to ask questions before arriving at conclusions. The best way to know what others are thinking and feeling is to ask them about it. You may not always get an honest answer, but if you guess instead of asking, there's a pretty good chance you'll come to the wrong conclusions. Careful listening and asking questions are two important aspects of ethical communication, and both will help you think through those all-important Q-pts before you speak.

Think before you speak. The idea is so simple and so useful, yet so often ignored. We hope that you've already found yourself putting the Q-pts to work and asking "Why must I say it at all?" If you're like most of us, you've probably already found a few occasions to communicate more thoughtfully by *not* sharing whatever thought was going through your head! By thinking about who you're talking to, how that person will react, and where your words will lead you, you can ensure that you communicate in ways that support both of you and your relationship. You can choose the right time to communicate what needs to be said so that your words will really count and have a positive effect. And when in doubt, keep in mind how much you might not be seeing.

Finally, we invite you to send us by e-mail (info@but Ididntmeanthat.com), stories about your experiences using our book and the Q-pts. We'd like to know how it's worked for you. Your feedback will help us give better advice in future editions of this book. And as thoughtful listeners, we'll use your feedback to continue working on our own communication skills, thoughts, and behavior.

We'd like to close with a lovely quotation by that font of all wisdom, anonymous, because it speaks directly to the underlying theme of what we've written: "It's better to swallow your words *now* than to have to eat them later."

In these wonderful and trying times, hopefully we can all learn to think more carefully about what we're about to say before we say it. This thoughtfulness can contribute to making our relationships with others the best they can possibly be—and to making the world a better place to live.

Rachel Small is a former special education teacher. She is currently the vice president of a flourishing family business.

A freelance writer and writing teacher, **June Paris** has devoted years of study and training to the elements of ethical speech and how to communicate positively.

Richard Heyman, Ed.D, is a specialist in the use of language in everyday life. He is professor of communication and education at the University of Calgary and president of Richard Heyman Associates, a business communications consulting company. He was the founder and director (until 1988) of the Discourse Analysis Research Group, a think tank devoted to researching language and communication, and he has published more than thirty book chapters and articles on his research. He has more than thirty-five years of experience in communications consulting and has presented his work to professionals, academics, and laypeople.